Back to Your Love

KIANNA ALEXANDER

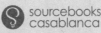

sourcebooks
casablanca

Copyright © 2017 by Kianna Alexander
Cover and internal design © 2017 by Sourcebooks, Inc.
Cover design by Michael Rehder
Cover images © XiXinXing/Getty Images, I2egulas/Getty Images

Sourcebooks and the colophon are registered trademarks of Sourcebooks, Inc.

All rights reserved. No part of this book may be reproduced in any form or by any electronic or mechanical means including information storage and retrieval systems—except in the case of brief quotations embodied in critical articles or reviews—without permission in writing from its publisher, Sourcebooks, Inc.

The characters and events portrayed in this book are fictitious or are used fictitiously. Any similarity to real persons, living or dead, is purely coincidental and not intended by the author.

All brand names and product names used in this book are trademarks, registered trademarks, or trade names of their holders. Sourcebooks, Inc., is not associated with any product or vendor in this book.

Published by Sourcebooks Casablanca, an imprint of Sourcebooks, Inc.
P.O. Box 4410, Naperville, Illinois 60567-4410
(630) 961-3900
Fax: (630) 961-2168
www.sourcebooks.com

Printed and bound in Canada.
MBP 10 9 8 7 6 5 4 3 2 1

Chapter 1

IMANI GRANT STOOD ON THE BALCONY OF HER HOTEL ROOM, taking in the marvelous view. The seventh-floor suite allowed her an unobstructed look at the wide, sandy band of beach below as well as the soft, rising waves of the Atlantic lapping at the shore. The late-afternoon sun steadily crept toward the horizon, and she shielded her eyes with a hand. Knowing her girlfriends would be expecting her for the rehearsal dinner, she drew in one last deep breath of the salt-tinged air, then withdrew into the room, closing the French doors behind her.

Since coming to Atlantic Beach earlier that morning, she'd been holed up in her room reading, relaxing, and girding her loins. This was the third time in fourteen months she'd been asked to serve as a bridesmaid for one of her friends. At this point, her nerves were beyond frazzled. If her mother inquired just once more about whether she was seeing anyone, she was pretty sure her head would explode.

She'd only reluctantly agreed to stay in this hotel with the wedding party. She had tired of all the pre-wedding madness, having done it twice in the last year, but she did want to be there for the bride, in case she needed anything. Georgia had been her college roommate and constant companion through four years of undergrad at Spelman. Imani was sick of weddings, but she would do anything for Georgia, so there she was. Luckily, neither the bride nor the coordinator had summoned her today, allowing her plenty of time to prepare herself to go through the motions once again.

She knew there would be questions from the well-intentioned older ladies present for the joyous event about why she was still single. She thought of Xavier, her first love, who'd crushed her heart like a bug beneath his shoe. She'd thought that was the pinnacle of pain until she'd lost her father to violence. Now, her focus was on her new business venture. She'd worked hard to reach her goal, and she didn't have time to deal with the inevitable drama relationships brought.

Adjusting the strapless, yellow maxi dress she'd chosen for the occasion, she put on a little makeup and a pair of gold, heart-shaped stud earrings. Standing in front of the full-length mirror on the wall, she pulled her hair up into a high ponytail and secured it. Satisfied with the results, she grabbed her purse, stuffed her keys inside, and left.

A brief walk through the hotel's paisley-carpeted interior took her to the private suite where the rehearsal dinner was being held. Georgia had opted to have all her events inside the hotel for the sake of convenience, which was easily accomplished due to the vast size of the property.

Waiting near the suite's open door was Georgia's mother, Diane. Seeing Imani approach, the older woman smiled, then stood to give her a big hug. "Hey, Imani. How are you doing, sweetheart?"

She returned the hug, giving the older woman a squeeze. It had been ages since she'd last seen her best friend's kindhearted mother. "I'm fine, Diane. And I'm so glad to be a part of Georgia's special day."

Diane nodded. "We're all so excited. I'll see you inside."

As Imani turned to go into the room, Diane gave her a gentle pat on the shoulder. "And don't you fret, sweetheart. We'll all be getting together for your wedding sometime soon. I just know it."

Imani stiffened a bit at the well-meaning remark but shook it off. A false smile stretched her lips as she turned back long enough to nod to Diane. Then, she strode into the large suite and looked around to get the lay of the land.

The enormous room had one long, rectangular table set up in its center. Above the table hung a beautiful crystal chandelier, the bulbs designed to look like the gas lamps of centuries past, casting a decidedly romantic glow on the whole room. Along the far wall, the buffet was so filled with silver-covered warmers and trays of food, it looked in danger of collapsing at any moment. Imani picked up one delicious scent after another, and her stomach rumbled in anticipation.

Most of Georgia's close relatives, as well as those of the groom, Tyrone Fields, were either already seated, or standing in various nooks and crannies around the room, carrying on lively conversations. She waved to the other two bridesmaids, as well as the matron of honor, Georgia's older sister, Gail. Seeing that they were all seated at the end of the table where Georgia was, Imani walked over to join them.

London and Julia, also classmates at Spelman, gestured to the empty chair between them.

"Squeeze in," London said as she slid her chair back to allow Imani room to sit down.

Georgia, sitting at the end of the table, was beaming

so much Imani couldn't help smiling in her direction. "I assume from that grin that everything is going as you planned, Georgia."

Georgia nodded, still smiling. "It sure is."

At first, it had seemed that Georgia was simply staring off into the distance. Now, Imani realized that she and the other women were all looking in the same direction. Confusion and curiosity knitting her brow, Imani turned to see what had captured everyone's attention.

That was when she saw Xavier Whitted striding across the room. There was no way she could have missed him—his six-foot-three-inch height made him tower over most of the people in attendance. Her heart began pounding so loud she was sure everyone in the room could hear it. *What in the hell is he doing here?*

She tore her eyes away from the handsome man from her past and looked at Georgia with a questioning gaze. At first, Georgia didn't seem to notice, but their gazes met after Imani loudly cleared her throat.

Georgia responded this time but still watched Xavier with appreciative eyes. "Isn't he fine? He's Tyrone's best man, one of his TDT brothers. His name is—"

Imani interrupted her. "I know his name. Xavier Whitted."

All the female eyes at that end of the table turned on her. The question hung in the air for a long second before Julia all but shouted, "Where do you know him from?"

"He was my high school boyfriend." Imani stood as she answered the question, because it now seemed Xavier had spotted her and was approaching fast.

"Small world." Gail winked.

Georgia made a sound of discovery. "Oh! So that

explains why he was so eager to take you out. He must still be carrying a torch for you."

Imani walked over and stood behind Georgia's chair and placed a hand on each of her shoulders. "Georgia, please tell me you didn't."

"What?" The bride-to-be feigned innocence.

"Georgia, did you set me up with him?" She uttered those words in a rushed whisper, because Xavier's long legs were bringing him closer at an alarming speed.

"I might have."

The noncommittal response was all Imani needed to know that her proverbial goose was cooked. She squeezed Georgia's shoulder. "I gave you a really nice wedding gift. I think I want it back."

It was all she had time to say before Xavier appeared next to her.

He smiled, showing off teeth so straight and white, they were almost too perfect. "Imani. It's so good to see you." He reached for her hand, capturing it in his much larger one.

It was the first touch she'd had from him in a decade, yet the shivers still danced across her skin. Aware of the four sets of nosy female eyes trained on them, she smiled, hoping to mask her nervousness. "It's good to see you again, too, Xavier."

He watched her for a few silent seconds, as if trying to read her. Then, he dipped his head and placed a soft kiss against her cheek. "I have to go sit with the boys at the other end of the table, but we'll chat later, okay?" He gave her hand a squeeze, then slipped away.

She'd been totally unprepared for the kiss, and while brief and chaste, it reminded her of other encounters they'd had, which were much the opposite. Tingles ran through her entire body, careening and colliding like a jar full of angry hornets. Recovering her senses as quickly as she could, she retook her seat and found everyone staring at her.

Glancing around at her friends, she fished around in her purse for her cell phone. "What? Why is everyone looking at me like that?"

Finally, Gail asked pointedly, "Did you bring a shawl or a jacket?"

Embarrassment heated her cheeks when she realized what Gail was referring to. She didn't have to look down to know that her nipples were standing like two pebbles inside the confines of her dress. Folding her arms over her chest, she cursed to herself. Apparently, even after a decade apart, Xavier Whitted still held the same magical power over her body.

During the rehearsal dinner, Xavier tried to appear interested in the conversation at his end of the table while stealing glances at Imani. Tyrone Fields was his closest friend, and Xavier didn't want to shirk his duties as best man. He'd spent the better part of the last week running errands all over the Tar Heel state, taking the burden off Ty's shoulders so Ty could concentrate on getting ready to marry his dream girl. It seemed pretty slack of Xavier now to ignore his buddy's words, but Xavier couldn't help it. Seeing Imani tonight had him so off-kilter, it was all he could do not to drag her out of the room to some dark corner of the hotel, where he could kiss her full lips the way he needed so badly to do.

Around their end of the table were all the boys from Central, who'd pledged to Theta Delta Theta fraternity ten years before. This was the first time they'd all been in the same place in nearly five years, when they'd come together for the funeral of their old TDT advisor, Dr. Mitcham. Among them, Xavier was the eldest by a matter of months and had been nicknamed "the Activist," based on his passionate pursuit of community and charity work. Over the years, they'd kept in contact and seen each other whenever possible, as each brother came into his own success as an adult. Each man had lived up to his nickname in one way or another.

Between mouthfuls of food, Tyrone was going on about his latest case in family court. "This York case is getting ugly, and there are children involved. It really makes me wonder why people don't spend more time getting to know each other before they fall into bed and make a baby."

Xavier half listened, picking up on key words and nodding occasionally in a show of interest. In reality, though, his attention was on Imani. There she sat, at the opposite end of the table, looking even more beautiful than he remembered her. When they'd dated in high school, she'd been a quiet, shy teenager, and she'd owned his whole heart. Nearly ten years had passed, and he hadn't seen more than a brief glimpse of her since they'd both gone away to college.

He'd wanted to contact her so many times over the years, but he knew she would never have taken his call. After the way he'd ended things between them after their senior year of high school, he understood why. He knew he'd hurt her and still lived with the regret.

His last relationship with a woman had left him with scars of his own. His ex had shown him just how conniving women could be. Imani was different, though. The Imani he knew would never do those things to him.

He could still see signs of the shy young girl he'd known all those years ago, but now she was all woman. It was hard to ignore the regal lines of her face, the glossy hair, and the yellow sundress that clung to her feminine frame in all the right places. There was nothing short of an act of God that would have made him miss his best friend's wedding, but having Imani there made this weekend even more important.

Orion MacMillan, dubbed "the Young'n" since he was the only freshman to pledge TDT that year, shook his head. "Damn, Ty. We all love you, but you are boring us to tears with all this legal talk. You don't hear me going on and on about Young-n-Wild." The popular preteen hip-hop duo was Orion's latest babysitting job as the head of A&R for Wilmington-based Fresh2Deff Records.

Bryan "the Legacy" James, grandson of one of TDT's founding members, snorted. "Actually, hearing about those little roughnecks would be way more interesting." Bryan, a marketing executive for Royal Textiles, made ass-loads of money while traveling the globe but rarely burdened his friends with the dull details of his work.

Devers Architectural Development's CEO, Maxwell Devers, "the Bad Boy," reclined in his seat, his arms folded and tucked behind his head. "We're all suffering through Ty's monologue here, but somebody at this table isn't even pretending to be interested." Max shifted his gaze pointedly.

Xavier became aware that all eyes at that end of the table were focused on him. Loosening the top button of his light-blue shirt, he groaned. "Come on, now. How you gonna call me out like that, Max?"

Maxwell shrugged, his default reaction to a direct question he had no interest in answering.

Tyrone slugged Xavier in the shoulder. "I knew you weren't listening. I was hoping if I kept talking, you might eventually give a damn about what I was saying."

"He's only got eyes for the honey in the yellow dress." Orion made the observation as he took a draw from his mug of beer.

Bryan chuckled as he swiped his finger across the screen of his smartphone. "Who could blame him? The sister is fine."

Xavier felt a bit of jealousy creep into his mind but pushed it aside. His Theta brothers were his closest friends, and he knew none of them would pursue a woman he was so obviously interested in. "We dated in high school. I'm just admiring the woman she's become."

"What time are we supposed to meet tomorrow and where?" Maxwell effectively changed the subject.

The groom looked to his best man, deferring to him.

Xavier cleared his throat. "Four o'clock sharp, in the lobby. We'll get dressed in one of the meeting rooms and then go to the shore for the ceremony."

"By the way, I saw the tuxes. Nice touch putting us in the green and silver, bro." Orion nodded his approval of their attire while taking in the scene around them.

Tyrone grinned. "Of course. The Theta colors were the natural choice for me. I'm just glad Georgia was willing to go along with it."

Their banter was interrupted by Misty, the high-strung, blond wedding coordinator. Her pointer finger extended, she pretty much stabbed Tyrone in the shoulder. "We're wrapping things up, Mr. Fields. It'd be a good time for you and Georgia to give a quick speech. You know, expressing your gratitude and whatnot." Her words were a bit disingenuous, but in Misty's thick Southern accent, everything sounded that way.

Tyrone stood. "All right, boys. Duty calls. I guess that's it until tomorrow."

Xavier watched his friend walk away and drape his arm around Georgia's waist. He listened while the two lovebirds expressed their thanks to everyone who'd traveled in to attend the wedding or contributed in some other way. Once the speech was over and the applause and cheering died down, the crowd began to disperse.

Saying a quick good-bye to his fraternity brothers, Xavier wove his way through the crowd, intent on getting to Imani before she disappeared for the evening. He knew he would see her tomorrow at the ceremony, but he really wanted to see her tonight.

Alone.

She floated around the room for a few moments, and he got the sense she was avoiding him. But as more people left, effectively emptying the room, she had fewer places to hide.

He strode up to where she stood by the crystal punch bowl, her glass in one hand and the ladle in the other. When she saw him, her eyes widened. To his mind, she had the look of a deer facing down a set of oncoming headlights.

He stuck his hand out and repositioned her glass just

in time to keep her from pouring a ladleful of bright-red punch onto the hotel's carpeted floor. "Hello again, Imani. Or should I say Dr. Grant? I heard about your new practice. Congratulations on that."

She blinked a few times, then seemed to recover her senses. Replacing the empty ladle in the bowl, she took a sip from the glass. "Thanks, but no need to be so formal. I'd prefer you call me Imani."

"Good. I prefer that as well." He felt an overwhelming urge to reach out and stroke her satin jaw but restrained himself since there were a few folks hanging around.

Still looking a little uncomfortable under his scrutiny, she asked, "So, what have you been up to since high school?"

"I'm a CPA, and I run my own little firm. It's probably not going to make me wealthy, but working for myself gives me the time I need to do community work."

The corners of her mouth turned up a bit. "I know. I've read about some of your work in the paper. I see you still have that good heart."

Honored by her acknowledgment, he gave a smile of his own. "I know this is kind of a crazy weekend, but if Georgia doesn't need you for anything else tonight, would you mind if we went somewhere to talk for a bit?"

The rapid blinking started again, her lids fluttering over those chocolate-brown eyes. She inhaled deeply, then answered, "Okay."

Pleased, he offered her the crook of his arm. She slid her delicate hand inside, and he led her out of the room.

Navigating the corridors of the hotel, Imani kept her arm looped loosely through Xavier's. Despite her attempts to avoid him tonight, he'd charmed her, and now here she was, heading off with him to "talk." She was partly annoyed at having to face the complicated array of emotions he evoked in her, but partly flattered. Apparently, in the years they'd been apart, he'd retained at least two of the qualities she'd known him for back then: persistence and handsomeness.

"Have you been here before?" She felt a need both to break the awkward silence that had fallen between them and to see if the long strides she struggled to keep up with were leading them somewhere in particular.

He nodded, not slowing his steps. "Yep. Came down here a few weeks ago with Georgia, Tyrone, and Gail to tour the hotel. Our bride and groom wanted us to be familiar with the property."

"Okay" was all she could think of to say.

"Don't worry. I know the perfect place to sit and talk. It's nice and quiet, too."

And secluded, I bet.

She let him lead her around a corner to the right, then down an interior hallway of the hotel. There were a few small meeting rooms on the left side of the hallway, but none of them seemed to be occupied. On the right side, however, she spied a section of the wall entirely made of glass. It looked out on a beautiful courtyard situated between two wings of the hotel.

Xavier stepped to the glass door and swung it open. "After you, Imani."

She stepped outside, and immediately lamented the loss of air-conditioning. Though the hour was late, the air was thick with the heat and humidity customary for early summer in North Carolina. The tart aroma of the salty waters lying just beyond the hotel property permeated the air. Lush tropical plants filled the small courtyard, some blooming with bright-colored flowers. In the center of it all, three stepping-stones led to a wrought-iron bench positioned among the leaves and vines.

By the time she finished gawking around, he had already taken a seat on the bench. He patted the empty space next to him. "Come sit with me. I won't bite unless you ask me to."

The sexy wink he threw her made her traitorous nipples pebble again beneath her dress. Ignoring her body's reaction as best she could, she eased into the spot.

Gently, he draped his arm around her bare shoulders.

The feel of his touch radiated through her, the growing warmth inside her far exceeding the temperature of the sultry June night. Being in his arms again didn't feel foreign, the way it should have after so many years. His touch felt as natural and familiar as her own heartbeat. She noticed the rapid pace of her breathing and wondered if he noticed it as well.

The low timbre of his voice broke the silence. "If I'm making you uncomfortable, just say so. That's the last thing I want to do, Imani."

So he had picked up on her nervousness. She shook her head. While her mind told her not to let him get behind her defenses, her heart didn't want him to withdraw his touch. Instead, she answered him but kept her eyes directed at her lap. "No. It's all right."

"If you say so. I brought you out here to talk, so let's

talk. What have you been up to these last ten years, other than growing more beautiful?"

She felt the smile creep over her face at the smoothly delivered compliment. "Let's see. I did undergrad in biology at Spelman, then med school at Meharry, then my dermatology certification—"

"Whoa. Are you telling me all you've been doing for the last decade is being a student?"

She shrugged. "I guess so. But I had a goal in mind, and hard work and lots of school were the only ways to reach it."

That drew a low, rumbling chuckle from him. "I can't say I'm surprised. You always were intelligent and determined. I'm glad to see you're accomplishing your goals."

She took a chance and raised her gaze to his. His rich, dark eyes held the same sincerity she'd detected in his words. "Thank you, Xavier. I appreciate that."

A silent moment passed between them, their gazes connecting.

When his scrutiny became too intense, she broke the silence. "So, uh, what have you been up to? I've read in the paper, and heard from Mama, that you're doing a lot of good work in the community."

A broad smile spread across his face. "I'm glad to know Ma Alma speaks of me so highly. When I'm not in the office handling the books for my clients, I volunteer at a youth center in the old neighborhood, and I do a little work at Second Harvest Food Bank from time to time. I'm no saint, but I do what I can for the community."

"I'm really impressed, Xavier."

"Thanks." His smile broadened, dazzling her. "Then

I hope I can count on your vote in the city council race. If I win, I can do even more."

Listening to him talk about his good works in such a modest way, she realized he still had a wonderful heart. In the few weeks she'd been home, her mother had gone on and on about Xavier's activism. As an all-star athlete and scholar in high school, he could have chosen any career path he'd wanted. But instead of taking some high-paying, high-profile position, he'd chosen to make a modest living so that he could give back to the community that had nurtured him as a child. Yes, Xavier Whitted was a rare bird, and if the look in his eyes was any indication, he was ready to build a nest.

There, beneath his searching gaze, she could feel her very soul opening up. Once upon a time, she'd been certain she'd marry this man. Now, she felt like an inexperienced adolescent. No matter how she tried, she couldn't look away from him.

The heartbreak she'd suffered at Xavier's hands had colored her perception of men. He'd been her first love and had shown her a first glimpse of real pain. Maybe she should thank him for that, because it had allowed her to focus on her goals, rather than be consumed by chasing after a suitable mate.

"Imani, I'm going to kiss you. Is that all right?"

She heard his soft words, and even as her brain yelled at her to back away before she lost her heart to him a second time, no words would come. All she could manage was to look into the endless pools of his eyes.

An instant later, his lips touched hers. The sweetness of his kiss and the buttery softness of his lips made her eyes shut. Her body overtook her brain once again, and she pressed herself closer to him. He pulled her close, surrounding her with his strong arms, and she loved it, God help her. The kiss deepened, and as his skilled tongue stroked against the interior of her mouth, she could feel her insides melting down into her shoes like hot wax.

When he finally broke the kiss, she sighed. It was a sound of pleasure, and by the time she covered her mouth to stop it, it was too late. Feeling the warm blood pooling in her cheeks, and in locations much farther south, she turned away from him.

His fingertips grazed her chin as he gently turned her back to face him. "It's chemistry, Imani. It can't be helped, and there's nothing to be ashamed of."

She nodded. "I wasn't ready for all of this. I just came to be here for Georgia."

"I know, and I won't interfere with that. I'm here as Ty's best man, so that's my priority now."

That made her feel somewhat relieved.

"Make no mistake, though. When this wedding is over, I intend to continue discovering the woman you've become, if you'll let me."

She drew a deep breath. "Xavier—"

He silenced her with a fleeting kiss on the cheek. "We don't have to talk about it now. It's late. Come on. I'll walk you to your room."

He got up and extended his hand to her, and she accepted it. Together, they reentered the hotel, navigating the corridors and elevators again until they stood before the door to her suite.

He squeezed her hand, then released it. "Get some rest, Imani. I'll see you tomorrow."

"Good night, Xavier."

He inclined his head, then began striding down the hall.

She slid her key card into the slot and opened the door.

But instead of going in, she stood in the doorway and watched him until he was out of sight.

Chapter 2

XAVIER RAISED HIS CHAMPAGNE FLUTE AND TOOK A SIP. Looking around the grand ballroom of the hotel, he watched the wedding guests mingling, dancing, and chatting. He caught sight of Tyrone and Georgia, occupying a quiet corner of the room behind the head table. Even from a distance, he could see the passionate gazes the newlyweds had fixed on each other. Seeing them cuddling and kissing made Xavier smile. A twinge of jealousy accompanied his happiness for his friend, not that he'd ever admit to it. His day would come around soon enough.

Throughout his early adulthood, he'd searched for a woman just like Imani. Of course, he'd never found anyone, because she was one of a kind. He wondered if he even deserved to have someone like that in his life after the way he'd hurt Imani back in the day. A frown turned down the corners of his mouth as he remembered Jessica, his ex. She'd been his last serious relationship, and her conniving ways had almost ruined his political career before he could even get it off the ground. Perhaps Jess was his karmic punishment, a penance he had to bear for his callous disregard for Imani's feelings.

Draining his drink, he placed the empty glass on the tray of a passing waiter. He made a quick visual sweep of the room, and he could easily spot his other fraternity brothers, decked out in their green and silver. Orion and Maxwell were on the dance floor, each having chosen a partner from the wedding party. Maxwell seemed particularly attracted to the silver-gowned bridesmaid he'd snagged. Bryan, on the other hand, was seated at one of the white-clothed tables near the dance floor, watching the revelry as he nursed a glass of dark liquor.

Everyone seemed to be having a great time, and Xavier felt relieved that he'd succeeded in completing his duties as Tyrone's best man. Having Imani around certainly didn't help his focus, but he'd managed to get things taken care of in spite of the distraction. Now that he'd gotten his best friend over the broom, he could place his full attention on Imani. He hoped she could forgive him for his past mistakes, so that they could explore what they might be now that they'd both evolved.

He loosened the Windsor knot of his green silk tie, letting his gaze travel the space until it landed on Imani. Her bridesmaid's dress was one-shouldered and made of some wonderful, figure-draping fabric in a shimmering silver. The bottom of the dress just grazed her knees, leaving the lean expanse of her golden-bronze legs visible. She eased around the room with an air of grace he would have thought impossible on those tall, green, peep-toe stilettos. Her shoulder-length brown curls were swept up and pinned at the crown with a small bunch of greenery and baby's breath. She was a vision, the picture of elegance and sophistication surrounding a molten core of sensuality.

He removed his tie and tucked it into an inner pocket of his sport coat, and opened the top button of his shirt to let some of the rising heat he was feeling escape.

Beneath the formal wear, he felt as if he were roasting. He knew some of it was from the sheer quantity of bodies in the room, but most of it came from watching Imani. Ever since he'd first laid eyes on her more than fifteen years ago, she'd had an uncanny ability to make his body temperature rise like a boiling kettle.

She was engrossed in conversation with one of the other bridesmaids, and she tossed her head back and laughed. Watching the humor light up her face brought a smile to his own lips.

Her laughter quieted, and she turned her head, as if she sensed him watching her.

Their eyes met. Her lashes fluttered, then dipped as she lowered her gaze. The gesture, both coy and alluring, tightened his groin.

Before he could draw another breath, his feet started moving in her direction.

She stayed where she was, waiting for him.

When he entered her personal space, he stopped. The last time he'd gotten this close to her, she'd seemed uncomfortable. As was always the case when he got close to her, his hands itched with the desire to touch her. But as much as he wanted her, he knew better than to press her. So, trying to remain considerate of her feelings, he kept his hands at his sides as he spoke to her. "Imani. You look lovely today."

A small smile tilted her glossy lips. "Thank you."

He took note of her body language, the way her torso tilted subtly in his direction, the relaxed curve of her shoulders. Wanting to keep the conversation going, he asked, "How did you sleep last night?"

The tip of her tongue darted out, passing over her

bottom lip briefly. Her gaze locking with his, she answered, "I slept fine, once I actually got to sleep."

He said nothing, but let his cocked eyebrow ask the question for him.

"You gave me a lot to think about, Xavier."

"Really?" He reached out, rested the open palm of his hand on her hip.

She didn't dodge him or try to move away from his touch. "Yes. And after the night I had, I think we need to have a long…chat."

He felt a bit taken aback by all this, even as he thanked the heavens for whatever had changed things in his favor. "Is that all you think we need to do, Imani?"

She hummed low in her throat. "There might be more to it. But it will have to wait until the festivities are over. It would be rude of us to sneak out before the bride and groom have left."

He agreed with her, but parts of him lamented her insistence on propriety. Still, there was another way he could get her into his arms, one that was perfectly proper for their current situation. "Would you like to dance?"

She grinned. "Sure." The idea of dancing with her filled him with a mixture of anxiety and anticipation, like a runner poised on the block, waiting for the starter pistol to fire.

He grasped both of her hands and led her out onto the polished dance floor. The DJ was spinning a great mix of classic soul and R & B from the eighties and nineties. Just as they eased into an empty spot on the floor, the beat dropped for the Somethin' for the People hit "My Love Is the Shhh!" He chuckled to himself, thinking of how serendipitous the song choice was for the moment, and looked to Imani. Her smile revealed her approval of the track. He pulled her body close to his, swaying his hips to the bass-heavy rhythm of the song.

She wasn't the kind of woman to twerk or grind; he knew her to be much too classy and reserved for that. Out of respect, he kept the dance tame, resisting the urge to palm the enticing curves of her body. She looped her arms loosely around his neck, leaving a bit of space between their bodies. Her movements were subtle, rhythmic, and incredibly seductive despite the distance between them. He had a great deal of respect for her and the way she carried herself. Honestly, the class she'd always exuded had been one of the main things that attracted him to her.

The music changed as the DJ played the LeVert classic "Casanova."

A broad grin crossed over her face. "This is my jam!"

He couldn't help mirroring her contagious joy. By the time the first chorus of the song played, they were both laughing and singing along. Something about sharing this moment with her, seeing her so carefree and happy, touched his heart. It reminded him of what they'd once had and what he hoped they could have again.

When the song ended, she chuckled. "I know I probably look silly, but I can't help myself when I hear a great song."

He gave her hand a squeeze. "Don't worry about it. We looked silly together."

She started to say something but then stopped when the familiar opening notes of "The Electric Slide" filled the ballroom. A squeal of delight escaped her lips. "Come on. We gotta do this." Grasping his hand, she pulled him farther out onto the floor, to join one of the lines forming up for the dance.

He dropped her hand once they were in position, her standing a few feet in front of him. His feet immediately fell into the steps as the crowd moved in unison, but his eyes stayed locked on Imani whenever he faced her. More than anything, he wanted to get some time alone with her. He just hoped he could hold on to his patience long enough for the newlyweds to make their exit. After all, his duties as best man weren't officially over until the happy couple dashed off to the honeymoon suite.

After the dance ended, fate kindly bent to his will. The sound of cheering drew his eyes to the head table, where a crowd had gathered. He took Imani's hand and led her through the onlookers to see what was going on.

In front of the table stood Tyrone, his arm draped around Georgia's waist. Not bothering to break eye contact with his new wife, Tyrone spoke loudly to be heard throughout the room. "Georgia and I want to thank you all for coming out. We love you and all that jazz, but it's time for me and my wife to get this honeymoon started."

More cheers met that declaration, followed by a round of hoots and whistles as Tyrone leaned down to kiss Georgia right on the lips.

The blushing bride tried to hide her smile behind her hand but didn't succeed.

Tyrone reached for Georgia, sweeping her off her feet and up into his arms. The sound of cheering and applause rose to epic levels as the groom carried the bride out of the ballroom.

As they disappeared through the door, Georgia tossed her pearl-encrusted brooch bouquet. A few women dashed in the direction of the sparkly, flying object.

Imani took a single step forward, stuck out her hand, and the bouquet fell right into it.

Grasping the bouquet to her chest, she turned to Xavier. "I think it's all right for us to leave now. Let's go somewhere and talk."

He agreed.

Holding her stilettos by the straps, Imani led Xavier out of the ballroom with her free hand. Across from the ballroom was a smaller room set aside for guests to use as a coat closet and storage area. She ducked into it, pulling him in behind her.

He followed her inside, confusion knitting his thick brow. "What are we doing in here?"

She tucked her heels into the large tote bag she'd brought in earlier, then stashed the brooch bouquet behind it. "I wanted to drop this stuff off without going back up to my room."

"So where are we going?"

She smiled. "The beach. Now get out of that penguin suit."

As if he finally got her meaning, he shrugged out of his sport coat. Hanging it and the green vest on a wooden hanger dangling from one of the three garment racks in the room, he sat for a moment to take off his wingtips and dress socks. When he stood again, he'd rolled up the legs of his slacks. "Let's go."

She smiled and grabbed his hand, and the two of

them strolled barefoot down the corridor to the double doors leading outside.

They traversed a stone patio, then a grassy knoll before arriving on the beach. The sandy strip stretched on for miles, surrounding the rear of the hotel.

As soon as her feet sank into the yielding sand, she felt a sense of peace wash over her. The half-moon hanging high overhead illuminated the dunes as well as the dark, crystalline surface of the Atlantic. The quiet was broken only by the sound of the waves and the muffled notes of the music still being played in the ballroom.

He squeezed her hand. "It's beautiful out here."

She sighed. "It is. I have a fantastic view of the water from my room."

"Lucky you. My balcony faces the parking lot of the hotel next door."

It was small talk. They both knew it; he was probably just matching her banter. He was the kind of man who was considerate and secure enough to follow her lead, and that was a quality she'd always found attractive.

She glanced up at him, taking in the sight of him. The moon glow revealed his features: the strong jaw, the full lips, and the dark, expressive pools of his eyes. "I'll show you the view from my balcony later."

His expression remained even. "No rush. You'll show me when you're ready."

She gave his hand a gentle tug, and they started to walk along the beach.

Mindful of their formal attire, she kept a good distance away from the water's edge. They took the first few steps in silence, and she enjoyed the feeling of his strong hand wrapped around hers. It had been a long time since she'd felt this relaxed, and she'd never really achieved this level of comfort with any other man. Xavier had been the only one to claim her heart, partly because he made her feel so protected, so cherished.

"Remember our senior trip to Atlantic Beach?" The deep timbre of his voice broke into her thoughts.

She smiled. "Sure, I remember." How could she have forgotten that trip? It was the first time she'd experienced the special magic that could exist between a man and a woman.

"It was right after your eighteenth birthday, wasn't it?" His gaze went past her, as if he were looking out over the surface of the water. "That last night still sticks in my mind, you know."

She watched his face, saw the wistful expression. Up until now, she'd had no idea men held on to memories like that; then again, Xavier wasn't like any other man she'd ever known. "Really? You still think about that night, all these years later?"

He nodded. "Why not? That night was special to me." He paused, shifted his gaze back to her. "You were special to me. You still are."

A shiver went down her spine. She stopped walking, and he stopped with her. There, in the circle of his arms, she let her feet sink into the warm sand as her mind drifted back to that night. Her eyes closed, and she could clearly recall the sensation of his warm mouth on her skin and the way she'd felt when he'd taken his kisses between her thighs.

He whispered in her ear, "We'd made love before that night. But that was the first time I took you…there."

A soft groan escaped her, because she knew just what

he was referring to. She'd given him her virginity on her birthday. But that night, the last night of their senior trip to celebrate their high school graduation, had been the first time he'd brought her to orgasm. That night, he'd effectively branded her, leaving an imprint on her body and soul that could never be taken away.

The feel of his lips pressing against her throat brought her back to the present. He placed a few fleeting kisses along her neck, trailing across the shoulder bared by her dress. "God, Imani. I can still hear you moaning, calling my name. It was like a song, like sweet music to my ears, baby."

Her knees went weak, buckled beneath her. The steadying strength of his embrace kept her upright. "Xavier…"

He smothered her words, placing his lips against hers. As the kiss deepened, she wound her arms around his neck and pressed her body close to his. Every nerve, every cell in her body cried out for this, for his touch, his kiss. Her tongue darted between his lips, and he suckled the tip of it. The action drew a groan from her.

His large hands slipped from her waist to move lower, where he gave her behind a series of gentle squeezes.

She groaned again, the sound muffled by his kiss. Having him touch her this way was sheer delight, sending her senses reeling.

He broke the kiss, straightened. "Baby, I think it's time we went upstairs. I would hate for these fancy clothes to be ruined in this wet sand."

She loved being on the beach, loved the feel of the breeze coming off the water as it played over her skin. She didn't know if it was his touch or the two glasses of champagne she'd had, or both, that was quelling her good judgment. At that moment, her desire for Xavier overrode all else. "Let's go."

They joined hands again and made their way back to the hotel.

Inside the building, they took the elevator to the eighth floor, stealing kisses as the car ascended. When the doors opened, they hurried down the hallway toward her room. A palpable sense of anticipation hung in the air between them.

When she extracted the key from inside her strapless bra, he chuckled. Unlocking the door, she opened it, and they entered the room.

The door closed behind them, and she fumbled around in the darkness until she snapped on a lamp. Dim light flooded the space.

He stood a few feet away from her. "I think you'd better show me the view now. Otherwise, we may not get around to it."

She slid the curtain open, then unlatched the sliding glass doors, gesturing for him to follow her.

Soon they were standing outside on the small balcony, overlooking the beach and the ocean beyond. A few thick clouds now encroached on the moonlight, but there was still enough light to see the beauty of the scenery.

He moved behind her, slid his arms around her waist. She leaned back into him, letting their bodies mold to each other. He was hard for her, and she took pleasure in feeling the hard length of him pushed up against her behind.

When his hand touched her bare leg and began to raise the hem of her dress, she was drawn out of the blissful, dreamlike state she'd been in. Suddenly things had gotten all too real. She used her hand to stay his.

His brow knit in confusion, but he stopped. "Are you okay, Imani?"

She turned around to face him. "I'm sorry, Xavier. I can't do this."

His eyes held concern. "Have I made you uncomfortable? If I have, I'm sorry."

She shook her head. "No, Xavier, you haven't. This is completely on me. I shouldn't have let things go this far in the first place."

Releasing his hold on her, he backed up a few inches. "I'm not going to lie and say I'm not disappointed. But I'm also not going to pressure you."

She released a soft sigh, feeling an odd mixture of relief and regret. "I'm sorry. I got a little carried away. You look so handsome today, and I know there's a connection between us, but it's been so long since we've seen each other."

"And you don't feel comfortable jumping into anything physical right now." He finished her statement.

"Right." She looked into his eyes, noting how they seemed both familiar and foreign. "It's almost as if we're starting over from scratch."

He offered a wry smile, brushed his knuckle over her cheek. "I won't stay and make this more awkward. But when all this is over, I'll get in contact with you."

"Okay." She didn't know what else to say.

They reentered her hotel room, and he crossed to the door. Opening it, he stopped long enough to glance back in her direction. "Good night, Imani."

"Good night, Xavier."

She watched as he slipped out, letting the door close behind him.

Then she lay back on the bed in the silent room, listening to the waves crashing against the shore.

Chapter 3

ARMS LOADED WITH THROW PILLOWS, IMANI TRIED HER BEST to kick open the door to the building she'd leased for her dermatology practice. After a few kicks, her cousin and soon-to-be office manager Maya took pity on her and opened the door.

"Thanks," Imani called from behind the mound of pillows.

"It was either open the door or let you kick it in," Maya replied in a humor-filled voice. "Why on earth would you need that many pillows anyway?"

Dropping the pile on the gray leather sofa in the waiting area, she flopped down next to them. "Come on, Maya. I'm trying to create an atmosphere for my patients." And she was. Everything, from the silvery paint on the walls to the gray-and-black marble floors and brushed-nickel knobs and fixtures, had been carefully chosen to create a professional but relaxing environment.

Maya rolled her eyes. "Girl, they're coming to get their skin problems fixed. They're not moving in." With a chuckle, she went back to hanging photos of exotic flowers and plants on the walls.

Imani placed the black-and-white pillows in the appointed spots on the sofa, overstuffed chairs, and love seat, then went back outside to bring in the last two chairs for the waiting area. Once the chairs, upholstered in the same black-and-white diamond pattern as the pillows, were slid into place near the small console table, she stood back and admired her work.

Maya called out over her hammering, "Do you think we'll really be ready to open in three days?"

"I hope so. I've got six patients on the schedule for the first day." She could feel herself perspiring from the day's labor. In a pair of gray sweatpants and a long-sleeved black T and sneakers, she wasn't feeling glamorous by any means but was properly dressed for arranging furniture. She snatched the bandana off her hair and used it to mop the sweat from her brow. "There's not much left to do."

Maya hung a photograph of a dew-dampened black orchid and stood back to admire it. "I'm quite the little photographer, aren't I?" She'd taken all the floral photographs on a vacation to South America with her husband last year.

Imani had to agree. "You are. It really does look nice." Looking around, she could see that the pictures were the perfect finishing touch for the waiting area.

A loud knock on the glass door caught the attention of both women.

"The cleaning crew isn't due for another hour," Maya remarked, glancing at her watch.

Shrugging her shoulders, Imani went to the door. Seeing the brown uniform of a deliveryman, she opened it. "Yes?"

"I've got a package for Imani Grant," he said, barely looking up from his plastic clipboard.

"That's me."

"Sign here, please." He thrust the clipboard and a

pen forward, and she signed in the place he indicated. With a murmured thanks, he handed her the package and departed.

Stepping back into the waiting area, she eyed the medium-sized package. It wasn't very heavy, so she carried it to the reception desk and set it down.

"What's that?" Maya stared, waiting for an answer.

"I don't know. Everything I ordered is already here." She sat in the chair behind the desk, turning the box this way and that. On the label, she saw the return address.

The package was from Xavier.

"Good grief," she groused. "It's from Xavier Whitted."

A wide grin spread across Maya's face. "When did y'all get back together?"

"We didn't," she replied, using a pair of scissors to break the seal of the clear packing tape. "He was in Georgia's wedding last weekend, and we ran into each other." Slicing through the tape, she added, "He still has feelings for me, or so he says." She left out their little encounter on the hotel room balcony. The last thing she needed was a lecture from Maya.

"That's my cousin, ever the skeptic." Maya sidled over to the desk, peering at the package with interest. "I wonder what it is."

"You're so nosy."

"And you're full of crap." Maya wagged a finger in her direction as she returned to hanging photos. "Something happened between you two at the wedding. I just know it."

Imani rolled her eyes. "Hush, Maya."

"Fine. Don't tell me." Maya began rocking side to side and sang the lyrics to the nineties hit by the R & B group the Rude Boys. "It's written all over your face. You don't have to say a word…"

Imani could feel her face getting warm, and she knew she was probably blushing. Maya was like a sister to her, and Imani sometimes hated that Maya could see right through her. As much as she loved her cousin, she didn't want to get into a debate with her about what happened with Xavier or about the crazy notion of them getting back together.

"Oh, so now you're getting quiet? I'm guessing he doesn't know about…Atlanta."

She cringed against the pain of that memory and the shame it brought. "No. No one knows about that except you. There's the little matter of the gag order, remember?"

Maya's smile held sympathy. "I know, girl. Still, they say love heals all."

Pursing her lips, Imani cut her cousin a look. "Chill, Maya. We're both very different from who we were in high school. I'm busy here with the practice, and Xavier's busy running his own business and mentoring kids. Neither of us has the time for involvement right now." She left out the fact that she felt a little strange about Xavier's mentoring of wayward youngsters. They were kids on the wrong path, just like the young men who'd murdered her father.

On a humid summer day in 2005, some young men decided to rob the hardware store Richard Grant had owned. He'd been killed during the robbery, and neither Imani nor her mother had been the same since. With no inclination to run it on her own, Imani's mother, Alma, had sold the store a couple of months later. The store had been renamed and remodeled after the sale—but

Imani still drove by there on occasion because it somehow made her feel close to her dad.

"Whatever, girl. You make time for what you really want." Maya stepped back from the last print she'd hung, narrowing her eyes. "Does this look straight to you?"

Imani looked at the photo. "I think so." She was relieved Maya seemed to be moving on from grilling her about Xavier. While she'd enjoyed their lovemaking when they were young, she just wasn't in a place where she could trust him.

Not now. Not yet.

Maya set the hammer down and came over to where Imani sat, still holding the package. "You gonna just sit there holding it, or are you gonna open it?"

Imani tugged the box's flaps. With the flaps finally free, Imani opened it. She pushed aside a layer of packing peanuts to get to the contents and lifted out an object.

It was a beautiful, intricately engraved eight-by-ten silver frame. Inside was an old photograph of her with Xavier, from back when they were in high school. He was a tall, grinning teen in a tracksuit, and she was the shorter, smiling girlfriend clinging to his arm.

Etched into the bottom of the silver frame were the words "Soul Mates."

She could hear her own heart pounding in her ears. She couldn't believe he'd kept the photo all these years. Her best guess was that she'd left her copy in a shoe box in her mother's house. Looking at his teenaged face, she could see something in his eyes that she'd missed back then: pure adoration. Maybe she'd been too busy with angst and college applications, but this was the first time she'd really noticed how he looked at her.

Maya's squeal of delight conveyed her feelings on the gift. "Oh, Imani. That's soooo sweet!" She clapped her hands together gleefully. "You've gotta take him back now."

Tearing her eyes away from the decade-old image, she placed the frame back into the box. Shaking her head, she stood. "Didn't you hear what I just said? There's too much work to be done around here. Plus Mom needs me."

Her older cousin waved her off. "Imani, please. I was on the career warpath too when I met Frederick." Her eyes softened wistfully as she spoke of her husband of five years. "I thought I didn't have time. But he showed me different."

Imani closed her eyes, feeling the headache coming on. "Maya, this isn't the same thing."

"No, it isn't, because this time, it's your happiness at stake." A small smile graced her face as she placed a gentle hand on Imani's shoulder. "Don't push him away just yet. He might be the one."

That said, Maya gathered the hammer and nails she'd used for the picture hanging and left the room.

In the silence, Imani blew out a pent-up breath. Xavier was playing hardball for her heart, she could see. His unexpected gift, while touching, did not guarantee him a place in her heart. He was a champion lover, that much she could admit. But he seemed determined to use their past together as a way back into her life. So many things had happened since the days they'd been a couple, the memories were fuzzy at best.

One particular memory, though, stood out clearly in her mind. The day she'd left for college, when he'd broken up with her. He'd come to her as she climbed into her car, declaring that it was best if they split up so they could "experience life." She'd known then, just as she knew now, what that really meant. It was code for "I want to date other people. I'm not in love with you anymore." Despite Xavier's efforts to rationalize what he'd done, she'd been devastated.

Her cousin's words echoed in her mind. She'd do her best not to hurt his feelings, but she had to look out for her own interests. Surrendering to him could mean losing focus on all the things she held dear, and she would not allow that to happen.

Within the hour, they finished placing everything where she wanted it. After a final sweep through each exam room, office, and restroom to make sure it all was in order, she smiled. "Well, Maya, looks like we can finally get out of here and enjoy the weekend."

Maya busted out with the cabbage patch, followed by the running man, chanting, "We finished, we finished."

All Imani could do was chuckle as she watched her cousin's celebratory dances. "Come on. Let's get out of here so the cleaning crew can do their thing."

As they edged out, the three-woman cleaning crew came inside. They would be responsible for scrubbing the floors and otherwise getting things sanitary for the opening of the practice. Leaving instructions with them to lock up on their way out, Imani and Maya stepped out into the chilly October evening.

"What are you doing this weekend?" Maya asked as she unlocked the door to her car.

Imani shrugged. "Just resting up and hanging out with Mom before the opening Monday."

"Well, I'll see you then. Later, Cuz." Maya slipped into the driver's seat.

"Later." She got into her own car and followed her cousin out of the parking lot.

On the way home, she let her Ledisi CD play and tried to relax. She realized she'd left the photo Xavier had sent on the reception desk but decided not to go back for it. It wasn't as if she'd planned to spend the weekend staring at it and pining for yesterday.

Still, she couldn't shake the feeling that Xavier wasn't going to let this thing go. When she arrived at the apartment she was renting near Cameron Village, she slipped inside and locked the door behind her. Everywhere she looked, thoughts of Xavier were waiting for her. After a steamy shower, she flopped down on the couch to watch some television. When she settled on a music video channel, a familiar tune filled the space.

It was an old Monica song, "For You I Will."

Hearing the opening notes of that song made her utter a very unladylike curse.

It made her recall a night many years ago when she'd given her virginity to Xavier. They'd both been fumbling teenagers, but he'd been so gentle and respectful. Her eyes slid closed, and as the song's lilting melody swirled around her, so did the memories. She remembered his warm, questing caress…the way he'd kissed her body…the way she'd wept when he took her fully.

When the video mercifully ended, she hastily changed the channel. Needing a distraction to regain her composure, she flipped to a cable news network. The talk about the upcoming elections was sure to bore her to sleep, so she settled in to let the talking heads work their magic.

As services ended Sunday afternoon, Imani accompanied her mother out of the sanctuary at Greenview Baptist Church. She always dressed conservatively for services and had chosen a simple eggplant sheath dress and a black overcoat. She'd fashioned her hair in a low bun, donned a pair of pearl studs, and deemed herself ready.

Her mother, however, believed church was an opportunity to "put on finery for the Lord." Moving slowly with the aid of her cane, Alma still carried herself like a true lady and mother of the church. She wore a carefully pressed, dove-gray suit and flats. Her matching hat, a confection of white silk flowers and feathers, was perched atop her close-cut hair at just the right angle.

After stopping in the vestibule to greet a few friends and Pastor Williams, they made their way out into the early-afternoon sunshine. Despite the brightness of the day, the air held the chill of October, and a few wind-swept leaves of gold and orange swept past them as they crossed the parking lot to Imani's car.

The ride to Alma's house in historic Oakwood took them through downtown, past the state capitol building. The Greek revival-style building, constructed in 1840, had been the site of many childhood field trips, and Imani knew most of the monuments like the back of her hand.

Pulling into Alma's driveway, she helped her mother out of the car and followed her up the three steps to the porch. As Alma unlocked the door, Imani turned at the sound of an engine. Seeing the person parking in the driveway, she sucked in a breath.

Alma simply smiled. "Looks like Xavier's a little early."

She could feel her nervousness rising, but she held the door as her mother went inside, then waited by the screen door. She'd known since she came home that Xavier would be there for Sunday dinner, but she'd hoped she would be more prepared when the time came. After last night's chance encounter with that old song and the memories it triggered, she needed a moment to get herself together. She didn't want their meal to be awkward.

He stepped up on the porch, and she drew a deep, calming breath. He'd probably been to service with his parents at the Methodist church around the block, closer to where the Whitteds lived. He wore a well-tailored, dark-blue suit, royal-blue shirt, and blue-and-black printed tie. The black dress shoes on his feet were shined and polished, and she tried to focus on her reflection in them, so she wouldn't have to look into his eyes.

To her dismay, he used a gentle finger to lift her chin. "I said, hello, Imani."

The low timbre of his voice stroked her much like his caress, and she realized she hadn't heard his initial greeting. She nodded and murmured a greeting in response. "Hi, Xavier."

An amused look on his face, he asked, "Is there something particularly interesting about my feet?"

She closed her eyes and willed herself to calm down. "Nice shoes," she said, trying to keep her tone casual.

"Thanks." He held the screen door open. "After you, sweets."

She did her best to ignore the term of endearment he'd called her in high school and strode past him into the house.

Inside, she expected him to sit down on her mother's pink chintz sofa and wait to be summoned when the food was ready. As if he were at home, he followed her into the kitchen. She cut her eyes at him, but he didn't seem to notice.

The kitchen hadn't changed much since she was a teen. The light-blue striped wallpaper, blue tiled floor, and her mom's collection of china teapots held memories of those days, some she wished she could dismiss. Her eyes fell on the old butcher-block table occupying its usual corner. She recalled sitting on that table, stealing kisses with Xavier on many occasions.

Alma had changed into a blue floral housedress and was tending a pot of fragrant turnip greens on the stove. "I made an extra pie for you to take home, Xavier," she said as she added a bit of garlic to the pot. She'd already set glasses of iced lemonade on the table.

Xavier's smile was wide and gorgeous. "I appreciate that, Ma Alma."

"Sit on down. The food will be ready in a minute." Alma continued her task, humming a tune.

Xavier pulled out a chair for Imani. She held back a sigh. There were so many unresolved feelings swirling around inside her, and seeing Xavier only made her feel more out of sorts. Rather than be rude in front of her mother, she sat. An instant later, he took a seat in the chair next to hers. Hanging her coat on the back of her chair, she rested her clasped hands on the tabletop and waited.

After Alma set plates filled with the turnip greens, roasted chicken, and buttered cornbread before them, Xavier volunteered to say grace. Imani closed her eyes and bowed her head.

"Dear Lord, for this food and the many blessings You have given us, we are truly thankful. We pray that You will feed the hungry, bless the poor, and soften the hearts of all Your children. Amen."

When he'd finished and she opened her eyes, Imani found him watching her intently. It occurred to her that his prayer for the "softening of hearts" was probably directed at her. Vowing not to let things get awkward, she started in on her meal.

A few moments passed in silence as they enjoyed the well-seasoned food. She raised her glass to drink the lemonade just as Xavier opened his mouth.

"Ma Alma, you know I intend on being your son-in-law."

The tart lemonade hit a speed bump on the journey down her throat as he spoke the words. The next thing she knew, she was coughing and gripping her chest.

Alma patted her back with a look of concern. "You all right, baby?"

Wiping her mouth with a napkin from the ceramic holder on the table, she nodded. A glance at Xavier showed him hiding a smile behind his own napkin.

As Imani glared at him, Alma said, "I'd be honored to have you, Xavier. And, Imani, stop scowling at the man."

She knew there was no point in arguing with her mother, so she turned her focus back to her plate.

Xavier continued. "I don't think she's going to make it easy for me."

"That's my baby. Stubborn as an old mule." Alma popped a piece of cornbread into her mouth.

Listening to them talk about her as if she weren't in the room got old very quickly. When her plate was finally empty, she stood. "Excuse me," she announced, and left the room as fast as her feet would carry her.

Upstairs, she went into her old bedroom and locked the door behind her. In the adjoining bathroom, she bent over the pedestal sink and splashed some cold water over her face. She couldn't shake the memories of their weekend at Georgia's wedding, but she knew deep down inside that their relationship could go no further. Her past held secrets, things she knew would harm his political aspirations. Aside from that, her father's violent death still haunted her. She was sure her mother still felt that pain as well. How could she get serious about someone who spent so much time with the kind of kids who'd left her fatherless and had widowed her dear mother? Despite her best efforts to keep things casual, Xavier had to go and ruin everything. If he could have kept his big mouth shut, they could have all enjoyed a nice dinner.

Looking at her reflection in the oval-shaped mirror, she laughed bitterly. Xavier might think he was enamored with her now, but he had no idea what she'd been up to while she was away at school. No one knew other than Maya, and Imani planned to keep it that way. She was nearly certain that if he knew, he'd turn tail and run, especially if he wanted to win his campaign for the city council.

The fact was Xavier was looking for an Imani who no longer existed.

―∼∼∼―

As Xavier watched Imani run off, he wished he'd been more subtle about declaring his desire for her. He looked across the mahogany pedestal table to Alma, who had a knowing smile on her face.

"Go on up there. Just don't make her mad, or she'll smack you for sure." Alma's brown eyes held kindness and humor as she spoke.

He nodded, rose from the table, and made his way up the stairs. When he reached her bedroom door, he rapped on the heavy, whitewashed wood.

"Yes?" Her voice was soft, and it sounded as if she might have been crying.

"Can I come in?"

Silence.

"Imani, please, let me talk to you for a minute."

She finally responded, but her tone was less than welcoming. "If I do, will you leave me alone?"

He shook his head. She rarely gave an inch, but he still cared for her. "If that's what you want."

He could hear her moving toward the door, and it swung open a moment later. Arms folded across her chest, she stood back a bit so he could enter.

Even though she wore a disapproving frown, she was still a beauty. The low-key jewelry and barely there makeup allowed her ethereal loveliness to shine through unhindered. He preferred her hair down but understood why she'd bound it for church. She was the product of a Southern Baptist upbringing.

Her dress, as solid and practical as she was, hugged her curvy frame, showcasing the hollow of her neck, the swell of her breasts, and the roundness of her hips. Looking at her made him harbor thoughts that were very inappropriate for a Sunday, especially while they stood in her mother's house.

She was watching him, he realized. "I thought you wanted to talk?"

He smiled. "I do. Did you get the package I sent?"

She nodded. "I did. Thank you."

He noted that she didn't appear moved by the gift in the least. "Did you like it?"

She shrugged, her face an emotionless mask.

Her indifferent show might have fooled someone else, but he knew her better. "My queen, when are you going to step outside of your ice palace?"

The angry flash in her eyes would have frightened a lesser man. "Xavier, what are you up to? I don't have time for games right now." She flopped down on the edge of her bed.

"This isn't a game, Imani. Not to me. I know I screwed things up, but I want the chance to redeem myself." He walked over to where she sat, careful not to encroach too much on her personal space.

"I thought we talked about this. Weren't we going to take things slow?"

He shifted his weight from left to right. "That was the plan. But as you know, plans sometimes change."

She dropped her head forward, directed her gaze at the floor. "Xavier. We can't get too serious right now. I mean, everything is so new. I've got my practice; you've got your business and your work with the kids…" She didn't finish the sentence, letting her voice trail off.

He ran a hand over his hair. "Okay, Imani. I see what you're saying."

She looked up, her eyes filled with emotion. "Then you understand what we have to do."

With a wry smile, he nodded. "I get it. We'll keep it nice and casual."

Her breath escaped her lips on a sigh of relief. "Thank you."

Seeing her there, atop the pale-pink bedspread he'd once made love to her on, gave him pause. He was pretty sure her mother didn't know about that hot summer evening following their senior year. Alma had been in church, and Xavier had been doing his best to persuade Imani, in the most intimate way possible, to go to a local college.

Shaking off the memories of that day, he watched her. She looked conflicted, torn. And while his mouth had agreed with her request to keep things casual between them, he knew his heart could not comply. He respected her and would do his best not to press her or make her uncomfortable. But with slow, deliberate actions, he would show her why she should give him a chance. He would do anything in his power to feel her in his arms again.

Imani embodied all the qualities he craved to help balance his life. No other woman he'd encountered had affected him the way she did. His ex, Jess, had been physically beautiful but a harpy inside. With Jess, he'd been foolish enough to allow his focus on her appearance to cloud his judgment. Never again. Imani, his Imani, presented the total package: grace, intelligence, kindness, and beauty. He knew Imani would always tell him the truth and that she'd never betray him the way Jess had.

A fat tear spilled down her cheek, and she dashed it away. "You think you know everything about me, Xavier, but you don't."

Seeing her cry tugged at him so strongly, he risked her wrath by touching her cheek gently. "I know enough, sweets."

She looked up at him, and the pain in her chocolate eyes was so vivid, he could almost touch it. "Xavier, please. Just go." Her voice was pleading and strained with unshed tears.

He had no idea why she was so upset, but if she really wanted him to leave, he couldn't remain. "All right," he acquiesced. As he eased toward the door, he glanced back at her. She'd lain down and was curled up in a ball, clutching a pink satin throw pillow. He gazed at her a few moments longer, then quietly slipped from the room, closing the door behind him.

Downstairs, he thanked Alma for the delicious food and took his foil-wrapped pie with him to the car. He'd been coming to Alma's for Sunday dinner for several months now, favoring it over his parents' traditional Sunday dinner and bridge game at his uncle and aunt's home. Now, he wondered if he should stop coming. Imani was home now, so Alma wouldn't be alone. Also, his presence seemed to cause her a great deal of distress, but he didn't know why. Imani had always been complicated and stubborn, but he couldn't recall her ever being this sensitive. Something was obviously bothering her, and he wanted to fix it more than anything. But with no way of knowing what the problem was, he had no idea how to help.

Backing his car down the inclined driveway, he cast a glance at her upstairs window. She stood there, watching his departure. Her tear-damp eyes met his for a few long, powerful beats. He stared back, letting his gaze tell her that he was determined to have her and intended to pursue her despite her protests.

Her eyes retreated from his. Then she turned away and disappeared from the window.

Confused and concerned, Xavier headed home. As he drove the familiar streets, lined with the showy red and gold branches of century-old oaks, he turned over her words in his mind.

You think you know everything about me, but you don't.

What in the world was she hiding from him?

With no answer to that question, he focused his attention on the road as he headed the car toward Tyrone's house.

As he left downtown and traveled down Glenwood Avenue in the direction of the tony neighborhood where his friend lived, he popped a CD into the car's disc player. The melodic sounds of jazz guitarist Earl Klugh filled the interior, providing a soundtrack to his thoughts of Imani. He'd never seen her look the way she had when he'd left her. The pained expression on her face had tugged at his heart, reawakening the old protective instincts he'd had for her since the first day they'd met.

When he pulled up to Tyrone's massive two-story mansion, he slid his sedan into an empty spot on the circular driveway and cut the engine. The front door was already open, and he could see the glow of the light inside flowing through the glass storm door. Letting himself in, Xavier crossed the foyer and entered the front parlor. Inside the cherrywood-paneled room, he found Tyrone leaning over the pool table, lining up a shot. Behind him, on an overstuffed, tan leather sofa, Maxwell Devers reclined, feet up, smoking a cigar. His black slacks had risen up to show the black socks he wore with his Stacy Adams wingtips.

Seeing his two frat brothers lounging helped to break his tension. He nodded to Tyrone. "Hey, T."

Tyrone made his shot, then stood to his full height. The black T and jeans he wore were his standard uniform when he was away from the law firm. "What's up, Xavier?"

Flopping down on the comfy sofa next to Maxwell, Xavier greeted his friend with the Theta handshake. "How are you, playboy?"

Maxwell exhaled a cloud of spicy-smelling cigar smoke. "I'm good, man. So we gonna talk campaign shizz tonight?"

The loud crack of two pool balls hitting each other signaled Tyrone making another shot. "Yes, we are, Max," he called over his shoulder.

Dropping the cigar butt in the crystal ashtray on the polished cherry table, Maxwell chuckled. "Y'all do remember me saying I was a silent partner in this thing. I just wanted to donate some bread to help my frat brother out."

"I still like to run things by you, man." Xavier ran a hand over his head. "Your funds went a long way in getting my campaign ads on television."

Waving his hand dismissively, Maxwell smiled. "I trust you, man. I wanted to help fund your quest to change the world. But I do enough strategizing at work."

Xavier knew that to be true. Without Maxwell's brilliant mind for strategy, however, Devers Architectural Development would never have existed. He appreciated his frat brother's help, in whatever capacity he wanted to give it, so he decided not to press him.

A clanking sound drew Xavier's attention, and he looked up to see Tyrone at the minibar. "What are you drinking, X?"

"Jack and Coke."

"Straight Scotch on the rocks for me," Maxwell called.

Tyrone prepared the drinks, then brought them over to his friends on a glass tray. He sat down in the fluffy armchair across from them and took a sip from his own drink. "Either of y'all heard from Orion?"

Maxwell swallowed a mouthful of Scotch. "Yeah, the Young'n called me last week. He's touring with one of the label's new groups. He was in Houston then. Who knows where he is now?"

Tyrone nodded. "Yeah. That's our little man. I did get a text message from Bryan today."

"He sent it to me, too." Xavier remembered seeing the message earlier in the day. "He's gone to close a distribution deal in Paris and won't be back for a few weeks. I appreciated him wishing me good luck, though."

Maxwell released a deep, rumbling chuckle. "That's the busy life of an industry executive. Who knew when we were knuckleheads back at Central that we'd be so successful as adults?"

Xavier shook his head at the memories of their college shenanigans. "I bet our professors didn't. I know I was slack-ass in most of my classes."

"So was I, but we always got our papers and exams in on time and on point." Tyrone tented his hands in front of him. "We got ourselves together where it counted."

Nodding his agreement, Xavier pushed away his lingering thoughts of Imani. Right now, he was on a mission to better his city. *After all, improving the community is what a Theta brother does best.* Leaning forward, he asked Tyrone, "So, what's our strategy for these last few weeks?"

"First things first, man. I know you got with your ex during the wedding festivities." Tyrone took a drink from his glass.

Xavier frowned. "Yeah, what does Imani have to do with the campaign?"

"Plenty. You can't be dating right now, X. You've got to put your full focus on the campaign. Remember what happened the last time you were involved with a woman during a campaign?" Tyrone fixed him with a stare as he referenced Xavier's first attempt at a campaign. He'd only gotten as far as declaring himself a candidate before he'd had to withdraw.

Having the incident with Jess brought up made Xavier groan. "I know, I know. Jess almost ruined my political career before I ended it with her. I haven't forgotten."

Maxwell added, "Ty is right. Better play it safe this time, man."

Xavier rolled his eyes. "Max, I thought you were a silent partner. And, Ty, don't go there with me on this. Imani is different."

Tyrone shook his head. "Man, I'm telling you. You've got to take it easy with her."

Xavier, taking a long sip from his glass, shook his head. "Like I said, Tyrone. Imani is different. Now quit lecturing me about her, and let's talk some real campaign strategy."

Chapter 4

"Dr. Grant?"

Imani snapped out of her reverie and back to reality. "I'm sorry, Mrs. Flynn. What were you saying?"

"I asked if you had any recommendations for treating my eczema." The petite woman reclining in the exam chair looked none too pleased with having to repeat herself.

Imani took a deep breath. She was only two patients into her first day at her new practice, and already she was losing focus. "Yes. Since it's mild, I'll recommend twice-weekly oatmeal baths. Make sure the water is warm, not hot, because that dries the skin more and exacerbates the condition."

Mrs. Flynn nodded, sweeping a wayward red curl away from her fair-skinned face. "Is there something you can prescribe for the rough patches on my elbows and knees?"

Nodding, Imani retrieved her prescription pad from the breast pocket of her lab coat. "This should help with the itching and dryness, and reduce the redness over time." She jotted the name and dosage of the drug, along with the dispensing instructions, onto a sheet and tore it off. "Give it about four weeks to work. If things don't improve, or they get worse, come back and see me, okay?"

Gathering her things, Mrs. Flynn took the prescription. "Thanks, Dr. Grant," she called as she left.

After her patient's departure, Imani glanced at her wristwatch. It was ten minutes to eleven, and she didn't have another appointment until eleven thirty. Rising from the revolving stool she sat on during consultations, she went to the break room for a much-needed cup of coffee. As she sat at the round table, waiting for the single cup brewer to make her hazelnut latte, Maya entered the room.

"Whoa, what's the matter?" Maya filled her ceramic mug with hot water and rifled through a box of assorted teas for a bag that appealed to her.

"Still recovering from Sunday dinner with Xavier, I guess." The timer sounded on her coffee, and she rose to grab it.

"I got it," Maya said. She retrieved the coffee, along with her own cup of tea, and brought them to the table. "Now what's the problem?"

Imani blew a puff of air over the coffee to cool it a bit, then took a small sip. "He was sitting at the table, making all these grand declarations about marrying me, and he and Mom discussed it as if I weren't even there."

Maya sighed as she drizzled honey into her mug. "Does he really annoy you that much, or are you just worried he'll find out about your…activities while you were away?"

Imani cringed at the mention of her secret. "Maya, I'm so ashamed of it, I just don't want anyone else to know."

"I know." Maya grasped her hand. "You should give yourself credit for what you've accomplished. Look, you did what you had to do, and there's no shame in that."

"I mean, even if I was feeling chatty about it, the gag order is still in effect." She released a long sigh.

"I was just a kid trying to pay for my education, you know? I didn't want to burden Mom, especially after Dad's death."

Maya gave her hand a squeeze. "It's okay, Imani. You have to remember, you didn't do anything wrong."

She responded with a watery-eyed smile. "Who would have thought taking on a secretarial job would lead to all this drama?"

"Not me." Maya winked, obviously trying to soften her cousin's mood. "Still, I think you should be honest with Xavier. He's a good guy."

Imani scoffed. "Yeah, but don't you think it might affect his campaign?"

"Only if someone else found out. And you know I wouldn't dime you out." Maya's soft smile held sympathy and humor. "Aunt Alma still doesn't know who spilled her hundred-dollar bottle of perfume, remember?"

Silence fell as she thought about the incident Maya referred to. The memory made her smile in spite of her mood. When she and Maya were younger, they'd loved playing in her mother's makeup and beauty supplies, even though Alma forbade it. They'd try on lipstick and eye shadow and, most of the time, managed to wipe it off before they were caught. One time, while rushing to escape the scene of the crime, Imani had knocked over a bottle of French perfume, spilling the contents. Even though Maya had witnessed it, she'd never turned her in. To this day, Alma thought she'd knocked over the bottle herself.

"I know I can trust you, Maya," she admitted. "You're the only one in my circle who knows, and I just don't think I can tell him. Besides, I won't have to if we don't get involved."

"You always were the type to play it safe." She finished her tea and stood. "If I were you, I'd just tell him. I'd bet good money he's willing to overlook it."

"I'll think about it." Her cousin usually gave sound advice, but for now, that was all the commitment Imani could muster.

"I gotta get back to the reception desk." With a wave, Maya departed.

Imani swung by her personal office to touch up her makeup. Looking at herself in the mirror, she could see the worry she felt so vividly. She quickly refreshed her lipstick and stood back to evaluate her appearance. Brushing a bit of lint off the black pencil skirt and lavender blouse she wore beneath her lab coat, she tried to "fix her face," as her mom would say. She relaxed the tense muscles in her jaws and forehead as best she could, and put on a smile she vowed to wear for the rest of the day. Just because she was in turmoil over something personal didn't mean her patients had to know. She needed to project an image of competence and professionalism if she wanted to build a regular clientele.

Leona, one of her two nurses, stuck her head in the open door of the office. "Dr. Grant, your eleven thirty patient is here."

"Put her in room two, please."

"Yes, ma'am."

After the nurse was gone, she took one last look in the mirror. Satisfied with her reflection, she went to meet her patient.

Imani did examinations, gave consultations, and

wrote prescriptions for her remaining four patients of the day. By four thirty, her last appointment was done, and she returned to her office to put the notes she'd taken into her computerized patient files. The nurses left at five, after the exam rooms were cleaned and prepared for the next day, leaving only her and Maya in the building. Around five thirty, Maya appeared with a stack of folders in her arms.

"Here's all the insurance and billing stuff for the day."

Due to limited space, the hard copies of patient files and financial records were being stored in three tall filing cabinets along a wall in her office. "Just go ahead and stick them in the file cabinet," she instructed, still typing into the computer's database. "We'll sort them all at the end of the week."

After putting the papers away, Maya asked, "How much longer are you gonna be?"

"About ten minutes. I'm almost done." Imani spoke without looking up from the computer screen as she entered more patient data.

"I'll wait for you up front."

When she'd finished her work and shut down the computer, she carried her purse out into the waiting area. Spying the silver picture frame still lying in the box on the reception desk, she took it out. As Maya looked on, Imani stared at the photo for a few quiet moments. Then she walked back to her office, set the picture on the desk next to the one of her parents on their wedding day, and walked out, closing the door behind her.

Maya was waiting with her fists propped on her hips. "What was that about?"

Imani shrugged, smiled with feigned ignorance,

and said nothing. Admitting to Maya that she'd given Xavier's gift a place of honor on her desk would only start a conversation she was loath to have right now. When it came to Xavier, things were just too complex for her tastes. A loving relationship was the thing she wanted most, but could never really have. At least not until she conquered the specter of her past.

Her cousin, wearing a look of amusement, shook her head, then followed her out into the fading light of dusk.

Xavier walked into the H. R. Revels Youth Outreach Center, letting the glass-and-metal door swing shut behind him. The center, affectionately dubbed "the Yoc" by the kids who frequented the place, served as a second home for him. When he wasn't in his office or doing things for his parents, he spent the bulk of his free time there. Volunteering gave him a sense of connection to the historic Oakwood community he'd been raised in. He felt an obligation to the young people coming of age in the area now and wanted to have a positive influence on their futures.

The building was a sprawling, two-level brick structure that had once been an elementary school. On the lower level, a common area dominated most of the space. The commons had a variety of comfortable seating, foosball and air hockey tables, and a cabinet stuffed with board games. Behind the commons was a small gymnasium, where the kids often gathered to play basketball, as well as a cafeteria where they were served healthy snacks. Between the cafeteria and the gym lay a large office area, where the dedicated staff that kept the place running had their cubicles. The upper level of the building housed eight classrooms; there was a computer lab in one of the rooms. The other rooms were used for tutoring in various subjects and for private counseling for kids who requested it.

As Xavier moved farther into the common area, he passed the bust honoring the center's namesake, Hiram Rhodes Revels. Mr. Revels, of nearby Fayetteville, North Carolina, had been the first African American to serve in Congress. Ironically, the seat Mr. Revels had filled had been previously occupied by Jefferson Davis, who became president of the Confederacy at the start of the Civil War. Xavier recalled the discussion he and the rest of the board members had had while trying to come up with a name for the youth center. While many potential names had been mentioned, they'd all eventually agreed that Hiram Revels didn't get nearly enough recognition for the role he'd played in American history.

It was just after one o'clock, so the center was nearly empty. In a couple of hours when school let out, the place would be filled with the bustling activity of twenty-five or more kids, ages eight to eighteen.

The sound of someone whistling cut through the silence. Xavier smiled, knowing exactly where the sound was coming from. "How are you doing, Kel?"

O'Kelly Barnes, the aged janitor, rolled his cart down the hallway and into Xavier's line of sight. "Pretty good, Xavier. How are you?"

"Can't complain. How bad was it back there?"

"The cafeteria? Not bad at all. You all do a pretty good job of reminding the kids to clean up after themselves."

Xavier nodded as O'Kelly strolled by with his cart.

A retired mechanic, O'Kelly worked part-time at the center, stopping by two or three days a week to keep it tidy. The old man had been a fixture in Xavier's life since his own youth, when he'd hung out at O'Kelly's auto shop after school, soaking up his encyclopedic knowledge of cars.

Xavier moved down the corridor to the office and made his way to his cubicle, along the back wall. The office setup was nothing fancy, as the donations and grants that kept Revels running were much better spent providing food and resources for the kids who used the place. Only two people worked as paid employees for the center, and neither of them were full-time. For now, he had the cavernous room to himself, since no one else was due to come in until two.

He settled into the seat behind the glass desk and set down his water bottle. Then he pulled out his ledger. His Thursday routine meant leaving his accounting office for lunch, then reporting to the center to go over the books. The limited funding available to the center made financial discretion a top priority, and his weekly checks of the records helped keep things on the right track. The largest monthly expenditures for the center were food and utilities. Since the five board members had each chipped in several thousand dollars to buy the building from the city, and added donations from local businesses, there wasn't a mortgage. Televisions had never been used in the center, since he and his board agreed that kids got enough TV elsewhere. Still, running the lights and computers, and feeding the kids healthy, organic snacks free of charge drained the center's coffers every month.

Xavier placed a couple of calls while he had the quiet on his side: one to the electric company to ask again if they'd consider giving the center a discounted rate, and another to a local warehouse club to negotiate whatever savings he could on food. The warehouse club was happy to give the center an upgraded membership at no charge, as well as a revolving line of credit. The electric company rep was much less helpful; all they could promise was that someone from regional management would get back to him within ten business days.

He'd just hung up with the warehouse club when Tori Gray strolled in. Tori, an education major at Shaw University, was one of the two paid part-time staffers. The petite blond, known for the sky-blue streaks in her hair, came in toting an armload of textbooks. "Hey, Mr. Whitted."

"Hey, Tori." He greeted her while making a note of his phone calls and the results inside the center's ledger.

"What's wrong with you? Your face is looking sorta long." Tori ducked into her cubicle to set down her books and purse, then came to stand by his desk.

"No luck with the electric company. They're still putting me off. But the warehouse club worked with me."

Tori nodded. "You're a magician, Mr. Whitted. I tried with them last week, and they wouldn't give me anything."

"Must be my natural charm and charisma."

Chuckling, Tori started walking toward the hallway. "I'm going to get the snacks set up for the rug rats. They'll be here pretty soon."

He looked at his wristwatch and saw that it was ten after two. "You're right. Any volunteers here yet?"

"Yeah. Rick and JoJo are already in the cafeteria." She glided out of the room.

Xavier sat back in his chair for a moment, to savor the few remaining minutes of silence.

Half an hour later, he stood at the front door of the center, holding it open and welcoming the kids inside.

Xavier spotted Trent Holmes, one of the kids he kept an especially close eye on. Trent wore his usual baggy jeans and blue sneakers. He also wore a black Wu-Tang Clan sweatshirt, with the hood drawn up to obscure his downcast face. With a gentle tug, Xavier pulled Trent out of line and off to the side, to keep him from clogging up incoming traffic. The thirteen-year-old frowned but knew better than to make a fuss. Trent stood by the door, basically pouting, until everyone was inside and the doors closed.

Xavier turned to his young charge. "What's up, T? Why did you come in here with your face dragging the ground?"

Trent pursed his lips and groaned. "Come on, Mr. W. Why you sweatin' me?"

Tugging the dark hood away from the youngster's face, Xavier shook his head. "I'm not sweating you, Trent. But I will if you don't tell me what's wrong."

Trent's eyes darted around, as if he were looking for an escape. Seeing none, he sighed. "Can we at least go upstairs, so everybody don't have to know my business?"

"Fair enough." Xavier crossed the common area and climbed the old cement stairs, with Trent close behind.

On the second floor, Xavier escorted Trent into a vacant classroom often used by the center counselors. It was equipped with a few armchairs and a desk.

Xavier sat behind the desk while Trent took an armchair facing him.

Xavier rested his elbows on the desk and tented his fingertips. "What's up, Trent?"

Trent's eyes were downcast. Studying his lap, he spoke quietly. "Man, I was by my locker, right? And Moms had gave me her EBT card this morning, so I could go by the store when I leave here and get some bread and stuff."

Xavier nodded, listening intently for the problem.

"Anyway, I was talking to some dudes between classes by my locker. Reached in my pocket to loan a dude a pencil, and the damn—"

Xavier cut him a look.

"I mean the dang EBT card falls out of my pocket and hits the floor. Next thing you know, dudes is clowning me because my moms gets food stamps and sh—I mean stuff."

"So your friends tried to clown you, and you don't like it. I get it. Did you cuff anybody?"

He shook his head. "No, I didn't start no brawl. But I wanted to throat punch one of them dudes, man. I mean, I wanted to real bad."

Xavier watched the way Trent's expression gave away his hurt and frustration, and he sympathized with the boy. He'd experienced his share of lean years as a child as well. "I don't know if this helps, but I really respect and admire you, Trent."

The boy's eyebrows knit, and he looked in Xavier's direction. "Why, Mr. W? I just stood there and let them make a fool of me."

"No, you didn't. You were mature enough to manage

your anger without knocking a dude out. I know it wasn't easy, but it does make you worthy of respect."

Trent straightened up in the chair, and some of the negative emotions in his features seemed to drain away. "Really? That's real nice of you, Mr. W."

"It's the truth. I know grown men sitting in jail right now because they didn't have enough self-control to squash it before things got out of hand. I'm proud of you, Trent."

"Thanks, man."

"No problem. And remember this: you shouldn't be ashamed that your mother is getting food stamps. Everybody goes through hard times now and then. Your mother is just doing what she has to do to take care of you."

A crooked half smile spread across Trent's face. "I guess you're right."

Xavier chuckled. "I'm always right. Now go on downstairs and grab your snack."

"Yes, sir." Trent, never one who needed to be offered food twice, got up from the chair. Slinging his book bag over his shoulder, he disappeared from the room.

Xavier remained behind the desk for a few moments, thinking about the conversation they'd just had. He knew he wasn't supposed to have favorites, but he was particularly fond of Trent. The teen was a talented sketch artist and smart as a whip, though he often hid his intelligence to fit in with his peers. Still, there was no doubt in Xavier's mind that Trent would grow up to do great things.

And Xavier was proud to be a part of helping Trent, and all the other kids at the center, grow into a bright and productive future.

Imani sat at her desk Thursday morning, an open copy of *News and Observer* spread out before her. The wall clock displayed fifteen minutes to nine, and she didn't have any appointments until ten thirty that day. She'd come in early out of habit, and in case any walk-in patients showed up before that time. Even if no patients arrived, she'd have a little time to tie up yesterday's loose ends and start her day out on the right foot. Maya was already at the reception desk, as she was every morning by eight. She could hear her cousin typing on the computer, likely surfing the Internet. She took a sip from her mug of sugar-sweetened black coffee and began reading an article in the local section about the city council race.

According to the article, the incumbent, Givens, was a fine, upstanding man, with a faithful wife and two perfect adult children. He'd served three terms on the council, had a degree in political science from North Carolina State University, and had championed lowering local taxes. She could see how that might make him popular with the citizens of his district.

Xavier, however, was portrayed as an upstart who had little chance of unseating the older man. He was single, which was apparently a detriment, and had no previous political experience. Xavier had helped build homes with Habitat for Humanity, operated a local youth center, and participated in food drives and fund-raisers all over the city. Despite his extensive and continual work with the poor and underprivileged population, local political analysts didn't place much stock in

Xavier's chance of winning. Reading the article made her want to chuckle.

She wouldn't allow her past to ruin Xavier's chances of winning the election. She had no doubts that if he won, the city would be better off.

As she moved on to another article about possible rate hikes for customers of a local power company, she heard footsteps in the tiled hallway leading to her office. Looking up, she saw Maya stick her head in the door.

"Imani, you've got a walk-in," she announced, brushing a strand of her long, wavy, brown hair out of her face. "Are you up for it?"

Imani nodded. "Put them in exam room one. I'll be there in a second."

As Maya walked away, Imani stood. Grabbing her white lab coat embroidered with the words *Dr. Imani Grant, MD, FAAD*, she slipped it on over her navy-blue pencil skirt and powder-blue blouse. Then she took the clipboard she kept new patient notes on from her desk, and left the office and eased down the hall to the examination room.

She knocked softly on the closed door, then took the patient intake form from the plastic holder and attached it to her clipboard.

A soft female voice called, "Come in."

Imani opened the door and stepped inside.

The room, with its lavender walls and close-up photos of Maya's violet orchids, seemed to close in on her as she saw the face of her patient.

Glancing at the chart to see the name written on it, she felt her pulse quicken. *What the hell is Cassidy Lyons doing here?* They hadn't seen each other in years, but she would never forget the face of her old coworker. Cassidy had worked as a secretary at the same firm Imani had, the place where Imani had experienced that…unfortunate encounter. The place she still strove to forget. Drawing a deep breath to compose herself, she spoke. "Ms. Lyons. What brings you here?"

"Hey, girl," the woman said, a wide smile on her face. "No need for that Ms. Lyons stuff. Just call me Cassidy."

"If you insist." Imani closed the door behind her and plopped down on the swivel stool next to the exam chair. Her mind raced as she tried to think of a way out of the situation she was in. Now that Cassidy had already been checked in, though, it would be unprofessional to kick her out because of a personal issue. She thought the best course of action was to keep things professional, so she looked over the intake form again. "I see that you're having some problems with rough skin?"

Cassidy's green eyes filled with a mixture of humor and understanding. "Okay, I get it. You don't want to talk about it." She flipped her long, straight, brown hair over her tan shoulder. "Don't worry. I'm not here to make waves."

Imani sighed. Cassidy Lyons had all the features of a beautiful woman: glossy hair, a petite figure, and impeccable taste in clothing. Back when they'd worked together, Cassidy had always been friendly. Still, seeing her brought back memories of a time Imani would rather forget. Lowering her voice, she admitted, "No one here knows about my days at Doyle and Callahan, and I'd like to keep it that way."

She nodded. "Like I said, I'm not here to make trouble for you. I really am here about my skin." She turned slightly and pulled up the hem of her orange sweater. "See?"

Imani inspected the thick, scaly patches circling Cassidy's small waist above the band of her dark denim jeans. The layer of dry, cracked skin was certainly cause for concern. A measure of relief spread through her as she scooted her stool closer. "Let me take a closer look at that." She moved away long enough to don a pair of gloves, then gently inspected the area with her fingers.

"What do I have, Doc?" Cassidy's question broke through her thoughts.

She tossed the gloves. "Looks like mild to moderate plaque psoriasis. It's pretty common, and I can prescribe you a corticosteroid cream to treat it. If that doesn't provide enough relief, we can try adding a topical vitamin D."

Seemingly satisfied, Cassidy let her sweater fall back into place. "Sounds good. You know, I never imagined I'd find myself in *North Carolina*." She emphasized the last two words, as if she preferred to be elsewhere.

Imani slid back to the desk and extracted the prescription pad from her coat pocket. "How did you end up here?" She hadn't seen Cassidy since her days at Spelman.

Cassidy shrugged. "I'm seeing someone, and he moved me up here recently."

"Hopefully our little city will grow on you. Besides, this man must be pretty serious about you to pay your moving expenses."

"Nah. He's serious about having me close by when he wants me." Sadness entered Cassidy's dark eyes as she spoke, but in a second, it was gone.

In response, Imani gave only a brief nod of

understanding. She knew the implications of Cassidy's words, but she also knew it was not her place to sit in judgment of another woman's choices. "Are there any other places where the scales have flared up?"

"Yes. On my arms." This time Cassidy rolled up her sleeves.

"I see." Imani noted that her forearms were dappled with the same irritated patches of skin. Knowing the best drug for the case, she reached into an inner pocket of her medical coat for a pen. Imani scribbled the prescription onto the top sheet, then tore it from the pad and handed it to her. "While you're here, is there anything else I can do for you?"

Cassidy shook her head. "I've been looking for someone to take a look at my skin for a couple of weeks. When I saw the advertisement in the paper last Sunday with your picture, I decided to come here."

"Thanks for the vote of confidence." Imani stood. "Fill the prescription as soon as you can, and use it for a couple of weeks. If you don't see any improvement, make sure you schedule a follow-up with me, okay?" She smiled and held out her hand.

Cassidy stood too, but instead of shaking her hand, she grabbed her and pulled her in for a hug.

Surprised, Imani returned the gesture.

"You did really well for yourself." Cassidy's voice was an emotional whisper. "I'm glad to see you doing so well."

As they moved apart, Imani said genuinely, "Thank you."

With a teary smile, Cassidy slipped from the room, leaving Imani alone.

In the silence that followed, Imani reflected on the two very different paths their lives had taken. Cassidy was a lovely, intelligent, witty woman, but it was obviously she was unhappy with her current situation.

Imani tucked her prescription pad back into her lab coat and gathered her clipboard. As she left the room, a favorite quote of her late grandmother, Helene, entered her mind.

There but for the grace of God, go I.

Chapter 5

ARMS LADEN WITH GOODIES, XAVIER SHIFTED HIS LOAD around until he had a free hand. Hauling three oddly shaped cardboard boxes while wearing a business suit wasn't the easiest of tasks, but he had a mission. It was the second Monday since her practice had opened, and he planned on brightening her day. Grabbing the metal handle of the glass-paneled door, he entered Grant Dermatology with a smile on his face.

Seated behind the reception desk was Imani's cousin, Maya. He knew her well, having hung out with her back in the day, when he and Imani were high school sweethearts. Over the years, he'd often crossed paths with Maya at Alma's house, and she'd always been pleasant.

Maya stood and smiled when she saw him come in. "Xavier. How have you been? Haven't seen you in forever."

"Good morning, Maya. I've been well, and you?" He moved toward the desk, careful to keep a tight grip on his boxes.

"Can't complain. Let me help you with that." She walked over to him and took the wide, flat box from him. "Carson's Bakery? Is this what I think it is?"

"It's two dozen specialty doughnuts," he answered, lifting the other two boxes, "and a couple gallons of coffee." Carson's, a family owned operation, was famous in the city for their handmade cupcakes and doughnuts, which were considered the best in town.

Maya placed the box on the lip of the reception desk and took a peek inside. Inhaling the fragrance of the freshly made doughnuts, she groaned. "Thank you, Xavier. You're now officially my best friend."

The remark made him chuckle. "I hope you and the staff enjoy them. Where do you want me to put the coffee?"

"Come on. We'll set this up in the break room." Picking up the box of doughnuts, she led him into the corridor and to the break room. Once they'd placed the food on the counter, they returned to the reception area.

Leaning against the reception desk while Maya took her seat, Xavier spoke. "I don't want to cause any interruptions to the office, but I was wondering if—"

Before he could finish his sentence, Imani emerged from the corridor. She was dressed in a blue dress, covered by her white lab coat. Her hair was wound up in a bun at the back of her head, revealing the lines of her soft features. Heels the same shade as her dress capped her long legs, and her attention was focused on a clipboard in her hand. "Maya, have you heard from the medical supply company yet?"

Maya, wearing an amused smirk, shook her head. "Not yet, Imani. But if you bothered to look up from your notes, you'd see you have a visitor."

Imani raised her eyes, looking first at Maya before her gaze swung to Xavier.

He stuck up his hand in a wave. "Good morning, Imani."

For a moment, she let her surprise show, then a slight

smile graced her cherry-red lips. "Morning, Xavier. What are you doing here?"

"He dropped off Carson's doughnuts," Maya announced as she rose from her chair. "And I'm about to get some before the other girls smell them and eat them all." She disappeared down the corridor.

Xavier silently blessed Maya for giving him a moment alone with Imani. "I hope you don't mind me stopping by."

She tucked the clipboard under her arm. "Since you brought the doughnuts, I'll let it slide." She winked.

Feeling relieved that she didn't seem too annoyed with the interruption to her day, he smiled. "I was hoping you'd join me for appetizers and drinks tonight."

She looked somewhat skeptical. "Is this a date?"

He shook his head. "No way. It's super casual."

"Oh really? How casual is it?"

"This is about as casual at it gets, Imani. I mean, I usually do this with Tyrone, and I'm definitely not trying to get with him."

She giggled. "That's good to know."

"Since he got married, he's always busy with Georgia." He stuck out his bottom lip in a mock pout. "So will you come with me to Salinger's, so I don't have to go all by my lonesome?"

Her giggle swelled into a full-on laugh. "Sure, Xavier. I'll be Tyrone's replacement so you don't have to sit there and look pitiful."

Letting the smile return to his face, he clapped his hands together. "Great. Wanna meet me there around seven thirty?"

She nodded. "Seven thirty sounds fine."

"Nice." He straightened. "See how casual I can be? I'm not even offering to pick you up because that might drift over into the dating zone." He winked.

She shook her head, directing a soft smile his way. "Shoo, Xavier. I've got patients to see."

He backed away from the reception desk. "As you wish. Until tonight, my lady."

She pursed her lips at him.

"I'm just kidding. See you at Salinger's." And with that said, he opened the door and strode out.

As he drove to his office, Xavier felt cheerful. He'd been honest and straightforward with Imani, and she'd been receptive to his offer. It was true that he and Tyrone had been spending less and less time together in the weeks since Tyrone and Georgia's marriage. Xavier didn't begrudge his best friend his happiness, but he did miss hanging out with his boy. Being with Imani would present a whole different dynamic, and Xavier knew that. Still, he looked forward to talking with her, and catching up more on what had been going on in her life during the years they'd spent apart.

He parked his car outside his office building, then entered his suite. Rita, his secretary, was already seated at her post in the outer office. "Morning, Mr. Whitted."

"Morning, Rita." He approached her desk and took the stack of message slips she handed him.

"You have three company reps coming in for audits today."

Audits weren't his favorite thing to do, but in his work, they couldn't be avoided. "Thank you." He strolled by her desk and slipped into his inner office. There, he flipped through his message slips, apprising himself of the calls he'd missed and which ones needed to be followed up on right away versus which ones could wait.

Shrugging out of his sport coat, he sat down behind his desk and reached for the handset of his desk phone, intent on returning some of the more pressing calls. Before he could pick up the phone, it rang. Lifting the receiver, he answered, "Xavier Whitted, CPA, speaking."

"Xavier! It's me, Tyrone."

Curious about the excitement he detected in his friend's voice, he asked, "What's up, Ty?"

"I just wanted to let you know we got the Weathers endorsement."

Xavier smiled, now sharing in Tyrone's excitement. "That's great! When did this happen?"

"Word just came in about an hour ago. I had the interns contact his people to confirm it, and it's true. Man, this is gonna be great for your poll numbers."

"You're right. Thanks for letting me know." Xavier fist pumped behind his desk, anticipating the immense positive effect on his campaign. Grover Weathers had served three terms in the North Carolina state senate and was extremely popular in his district, which included parts of Wake County.

"That's all I wanted, man. I'll let you get back to your number crunching. Later."

"Later, Ty. And thanks again."

"No sweat, man." He disconnected the call.

Replacing the receiver in the cradle, Xavier tucked his hands behind his head and leaned back in his chair, taking a few moments to let the good news soak in.

So far, his week was off to an excellent start.

—◁◁◁—

Pulling her peacoat tighter around her to ward off the coolness hanging in the air, Imani walked up the sidewalk leading to the entrance of Salinger's. She'd briefly gone home after leaving the practice but hadn't had time to change. Still clad in the blue sheath she'd worn to work, she regretted that. The thin nylon of her panty hose did little to protect her legs from the chilly breeze. Hastening her steps, she thanked a man who held the door open for her and slipped inside the sports bar.

It was easily fifteen or twenty degrees warmer inside Salinger's, and she sighed as the heated air touched her frigid skin. Weaving through the thick after-work crowd gathered around the hostess stand, she peered over the shoulders of some of the people around her, to see if Xavier was already there.

Finally she spotted him, sitting at a tall pub table adjacent to the bar.

Apparently he'd had a less busy evening than she had, because he no longer wore the suit she'd seen him in that morning. He'd changed into a black turtleneck and black jeans, along with a pair of black loafers. The turtleneck clung to the hard lines of his muscled upper body quite nicely, and she had to admit she liked what she saw.

He glanced in her direction and waved her over with a smile.

Weaving her way past the throng, she made it to the table and climbed up into the empty chair. "Hey, Xavier."

"Hey, Imani. Glad you could make it." He took a drink from a glass of iced water. "I haven't ordered anything yet, so take a look at the bar menu." He gestured toward the long, rectangular menu lying in the center of the table.

"Cool." She picked it up, perused it for a few moments. "Why don't we just get a sampler?" She spoke louder than she usually would, due to the volume of the conversations around them, as well as the televisions blaring various sporting events.

"I'm good with that." Xavier raised one muscled arm to flag down a waiter.

The motion made the scent of his cologne waft up and touch her nose. She closed her eyes as she inhaled the clean, masculine aroma of him.

God, he smells good. Before she could stop it, a sigh slipped from her lips.

He turned his gaze to her. "You okay, Imani?"

She blinked a few times as panic set in, then quickly covered her mouth with her hand. "Sorry. It's been a really long day." To complete the illusion, she faked a yawn behind her hand.

He chuckled. "It's okay. I feel you. Adulting all day is hard work."

She countered with her own laugh. "Right."

The waiter approached to take their order, and she felt relieved to have the distraction. What was going on with her? She didn't know, but she vowed to get herself together. Keeping this thing with Xavier casual had been her idea, and she didn't want to screw things up.

"What will you have to drink, ma'am?" The waiter's question broke through her thoughts.

"I'll have a glass of merlot and an ice water, please."

The waiter disappeared into the kitchen, and she

turned her attention back to Xavier, only to find him watching her. With a nervous giggle, she asked, "Do you stare at Tyrone like that when you come here with him?"

He shook his head. "No, although Tyrone isn't as attractive as you are."

She wagged a finger at him. "Xavier."

He winked. "I know, I know. Casual. So what do you want to talk about?"

She shrugged. "Why don't you tell me about some of the community work you do? My mom is always bringing it up, but I've never heard it straight from you."

He rested his elbows on the table and tented his hands. "I'm glad you asked me that. I never get tired of talking about the kids."

Sensing the hum of excitement rolling off of him, she settled into the springy cushion of her seat. "Tell me about them, about what you do with them."

"We started the center several years ago, in the old Sunnybrook Middle School building. I'm all about taking kids off the streets and giving them something productive to do when they're not in school."

She nodded. "What ages are the kids you work with?"

"They're between the ages of seven and eighteen. A lot of them come from pretty rough neighborhoods. I just want them to be aware of what's available to them."

"I've never been to your center. What services do you provide for the kids?"

He smiled. "Healthy snacks, homework help, and people skills. They learn how to work well with others."

The waiter appeared again, setting their drinks on the table. After promising to return soon with their appetizer, he left.

She turned her attention back to her handsome companion. "This all sounds wonderful but very expensive. How is the center funded?"

He unclasped his hands, scraped his fingertips over his chin. "We get some money from the state, some from private donors. Most of it comes from our creative fundraising efforts, though."

"That's a lot of work, especially when you're not getting paid."

He shrugged. "I don't do it alone. I have four other part-time volunteers that help. Plus, I'd argue that I do get paid for my work there. Instead of money, my dividends are paid in the success of my mentees."

"Wow, Xavier." She couldn't help smiling. His passion for his community work was contagious. "That's really amazing."

His smile broadened. "I'm glad you approve. You should come by the center and visit with the kids. We're always looking for volunteer mentors."

Hoping her surprise didn't show on her face, she said, "I'll see what I can do."

"Great." He reached across the table to fist bump her. "We always say the kids can't be what they can't see."

She was still turning his words over in her mind when the waiter returned to deposit the steaming-hot tray of appetizers on their table, along with two small ceramic plates.

"Enjoy," the waiter announced before slipping away again.

She inhaled, grateful to have something on the table that would both quell her hunger and dampen the heady, masculine scent Xavier exuded. Picking up her plate, she helped herself to a few mozzarella sticks, spring rolls, and fried mushrooms.

Across from her, Xavier followed suit, loading up his own plate. "So what had Ma Alma told you about my work?"

"Just that you were doing something very positive for the community and that she was proud of you."

He popped a mushroom into his mouth and grinned. "I'm glad to hear it. I consider that high praise."

Nibbling on a mozzarella stick, she couldn't help drawing a parallel between Xavier and her late father. Before he'd opened his hardware store, Richard Grant had spent more than fifteen years as a high school shop teacher. His love of young people had been a hallmark of his life, evident in almost everything he did.

"You got quiet. What's on your mind?" Xavier asked the question between bites.

She could feel the smile stretching her lips. "I'm just thinking how much Dad loved 'the youngsters,' as he called them. The work you're doing and the way you speak about your mentees just reminds me of him."

Xavier swallowed, his expression changing. His dark eyes held a quality of emotion she hadn't seen displayed there before. His voice was soft when he spoke again. "Wow. I'm honored that you would say that, Imani."

"It's true. I know he'd be really proud of the work you're doing." She blinked a few times, determined not to let the tears welling in her eyes fall.

As if he sensed her sadness, Xavier reached across the table to squeeze her hand. "I hope one day I can live up to the man your father was."

A few moments passed in silence, as they both

courted their own memories of the man Richard Grant had been. Drawing a deep breath, Imani brushed away the single tear that escaped.

When she looked up at Xavier again, she saw him smiling. "What?"

"I'm just thinking. Tyrone never cried when I brought him here." He paused. "No, I'm lying. There was that one time when Carolina lost to Pittsburgh."

She snorted. "Xavier!"

Between chuckles, he continued. "No, I'm serious. You should have seen him. Bawled like a baby after the last play."

Peals of laughter erupted from her mouth as tears filled her eyes, only this time, they were the happy tears brought on by imagining Tyrone crying over a football game.

Xavier laughed just as hard as she did, slapping the tabletop with his large, open palm.

When she recovered from her laughing fit, she looked across the table at him. Still smiling, she asked, "Was that true? Or did you just say it to cheer me up?"

He straightened up in his chair, locked eyes with her. "It worked, didn't it?"

Shaking her head, she leaned over and playfully punched him in the shoulder. "It did. Thank you."

"What are friends for?"

Feeling calm and at ease, she picked up a spring roll. She was starting to see the benefits of having Xavier back in her life. It was nice to know that even with their new relationship dynamic, he still knew how to draw her out of a funk and back into the light again.

A few days later, Xavier tugged the Windsor knot of his blue paisley tie, nestling it snugly against the collar of his shirt. He stood in the men's room at the Pine View Senior Center, making final adjustments to his appearance before what was to be a very important campaign speech.

Tyrone stood next to him, running a brush over his hair. "You ready to go out there and crush this speech, X-man?"

Brushing a bit of fluff off the lapel of his gray sport coat, Xavier nodded. "Yeah, I'm ready."

Pocketing his hairbrush, Tyrone turned to face him. "Ok. Remember what we talked about."

"I know. Stick to the talking points. Eviscerate Givens but keep it classy. Point out why I'm the better candidate." He rattled off the three edicts that had been drilled into his brain over the past several days.

"Good." Tyrone slapped him on the shoulder. "Let's do this." He strode to the swinging door of the men's room and held it open.

Feeling confident and ready, Xavier marched through the door and headed down the hallway toward the center's main room, where he was to give his speech. Tyrone stayed close behind him the whole way.

When Tyrone opened the door to the room and Xavier stepped inside, he was met with a rousing ovation. The crowd, consisting of seventy-five or so senior citizens from the Pine View neighborhood and surrounding areas of the city, was very welcoming. Xavier smiled as he crossed the front of the room, moving to the podium that had been set up for him.

He stood back for a few moments, with Tyrone by his side, as the director of the senior center gave a brief introduction. When the woman stepped away, he approached the podium.

Xavier looked out at the men and women in the room. Reaching into the inner pocket of his sport coat, he pulled out the index card that contained his notes. While he didn't believe in reading prewritten speeches, he always kept a card with him that was filled with phrases to help kick-start his memory on his most important points.

Taking a deep breath, he began. "Ladies and gentlemen, thank you for your warm welcome. I'm honored and humbled that you've taken time out of your schedules to hear me speak today."

"Make us proud, young man!" an elderly brown-skinned woman near the back called out.

He smiled in her direction. "I'll do my best, ma'am. I want to talk to you today about choices. About how the choices you make at the polls and, in turn, the choices made by your elected officials, affect your everyday life."

He paused, letting a few moments pass in silence so the elders could consider his words. "First, let's talk about our current councilman, Aaron Givens."

A few boos and jeers sounded in the room, echoing off the tile floor and the cinder-block walls.

Xavier put up his hand. "Now, now. I'm not here to bash Mr. Givens. I'm just going to run through his record really quick. In the last five years, Mr. Givens has, on three separate occasions, advocated against funding the expansion of this very senior center."

The booing returned, louder this time.

Xavier continued. "Beyond that, Mr. Givens routinely accepts money from pharmaceutical companies known to price their drugs in a predatory manner. And if that isn't bad enough, he routinely speaks out against the expansion of medical care and services for seniors."

"Givens is a greedy jackwagon." An older man, seated up front, made the comment with anger flashing in his blue eyes.

Behind him, Xavier heard Tyrone chuckle, then try to cover it with a fake cough.

Stifling his own amusement at the comment, Xavier cleared his throat. "I won't speak on Mr. Givens's character. After what I just told you, I'm sure you all can judge for yourselves. What I'm really here to do is let you know why I want to be your city councilman. Rest assured, though, this campaign isn't about me. It's about you, the citizens."

Applause met the declaration, and Xavier showed his most winning smile until it died down.

"When I look out at you, the seasoned constituents of this city, I see a proud heritage. I see my grandparents, family friends. I see the people who helped to make Raleigh what it is today. And that's why, as your councilman, I'm going to work to make your lives better. I've run fund-raising campaigns in the past to expand this center, as well as build new senior centers. I'll continue that important work. You'll also be glad to know that I have taken zero dollars from the pharmaceutical industry, and that I will work tirelessly to see that healthcare is expanded for seniors and the economically disadvantaged."

Xavier continued the speech, pausing as needed for applause or questions. By the time it ended, the room was in an uproar. Many of the attendees pressed forward toward the front of the room to offer their support and a friendly handshake. He accepted their support gladly, offering his genuine thanks in return.

As Xavier and Tyrone left the center in Tyrone's sedan, Xavier looked out the window, watching the scenery of his beloved hometown roll by. He always felt somewhat thoughtful after he gave a speech. More than anything, he wanted to win, so he could deliver on the promises he'd made to the people of Raleigh.

"You killed it, Xavier. That was one of the best speeches I've ever seen you give. I'm proud of you, man."

He glanced Tyrone's way, noting the broad grin his buddy wore as he navigated the car. "Thanks, man. You really think I got my message across?"

"Of course you did. You keep making appearances like that, and I guarantee the polls are gonna turn in your favor."

"We'll see." He tried not to think too much about the polls, as he'd been trailing Givens by five to seven points ever since he'd announced his candidacy back in January. Now, they were well into fall, and the campaign season would be over in a matter of weeks. If they didn't turn the tide, and quickly, he could kiss his chance at the council seat good-bye.

"Remember why we got in this race in the first place, Xavier."

He flexed his fingers. "Because Raleigh deserves better than Givens." To Xavier's mind, it was the gospel truth. Aaron Givens was selfish, shortsighted, and power hungry. Xavier's intense desire to get rid of Givens and free the citizens from his subpar leadership formed the bedrock of his campaign.

"Exactly." Tyrone took one hand off the wheel long

enough to give him a thumbs-up. "Buck up, man. We got this. Trust me."

Settling back into the leather seat, Xavier nodded but said nothing.

For the sake of his hometown and his neighbors, he sincerely hoped Tyrone was right.

"Oh, by the way, I meant to tell you earlier, but I can't go with you to Reedy Creek this weekend."

Xavier felt his brow furrowing. "Man, you're canceling our run?"

"I'm not canceling anything. I just can't go. Georgia's parents are gonna be in town this weekend, so husband duty calls."

Xavier chuckled in spite of his annoyance. "Well, at least I know you won't be having fun without me."

"Shut up, Xavier." Tyrone rolled his eyes. "Hopefully it'll be just this once that you have to run alone."

Xavier turned his gaze back to the window. "I'm not going to run alone. As a matter of fact, I have the perfect partner in mind."

Chapter 6

IMANI TUGGED AT THE ELASTIC AROUND HER WRIST, dragging it around her hair to secure it in a ponytail. Taking a seat on the wooden bench near the trail, she double tied the laces of her all-white sneakers.

Xavier stood a few feet away, near the Reedy Creek trailhead. Tapping his foot and making a show of impatience, he asked, "You ready yet, Imani? I want to make it back here before dark."

"Hush, Xavier." Getting to her feet again, she zipped up the jacket of her purple velour tracksuit. "I'm ready."

"Do we really have to walk? You know I usually run this trail with Tyrone." He shifted his weight to his right foot as he lifted his left behind him to stretch.

"Yes, Xavier. Like I told you, I'm not a runner."

"Fair enough. I do appreciate you agreeing to come out here with me, so we'll walk it."

Imani took in the sight of him, wondering how he could be out in fifty-five degree weather in that getup. He wore a long-sleeve gray shirt, and a pair of black shorts instead of long pants. While she didn't mind enjoying the view of his long, muscled legs, she still didn't understand his attire. "Aren't you cold?"

Shifting his weight again to stretch the other leg, he shook his head. "Nope. I guess I'm what you'd call hot natured. Once I get moving on the trail, I'll be sweating."

"Eww. Don't walk upwind of me, then." She pinched her nostrils together, feigning disgust.

He laughed, shaking his head. "Come on, woman. Let's hit this trail."

She took her time approaching the trailhead, smirking at him as he looked on in mock impatience. Once she reached him, he started heading down the path.

At first she had to jog, until she finally got next to him. Doing her best to match his long-legged stride, she chided, "Slow down. We're not running, remember?"

"Sorry." He shortened his steps a bit. "Better?"

"Yes. Thanks." Now able to comfortably keep up, she began pumping her arms.

The morning air was crisp but refreshing. The light breeze held the scent of pine and carried the sound of the water lapping at the banks of the creek that bordered the namesake trail. She rarely did things like this, but when Xavier had called her two nights ago to ask her to join him, she'd accepted. Being out here with him gave her a sense of peace and tranquility she hadn't felt in quite some time. It was a wonderful respite from her long, activity-filled days at the practice.

"Tell me about what you were doing while you were away at college."

His request simultaneously drew her back to reality and pushed her mind to unpleasant memories. Clearing her throat, she kept her tone light as she responded. "Sure. What do you want to know?"

"I know you and Georgia were pretty tight back then, when y'all were at Spelman together. She pledged Sigma Delta Alpha. Why didn't you?"

A modicum of relief came over her. *That's a question*

I can answer, thank God. "I never really got into the whole Greek culture, you know? Pledging was about the only thing Georgia did without me, because I just wasn't into it."

They crested a small hill and adjusted their gaits as they began moving down the other side of the slope.

"What is it about Greek life that turned you off?"

She thought about it for a moment, trying to decide how to phrase her opinion. "I was superfocused in those days. I did three things: went to class, worked, and studied. I didn't feel I had the time to be involved in sorority shenanigans."

At the bottom of the slope, he stopped to retie one of his sneakers. "Shenanigans? You know Greek organizations are all about community service, right?"

She shook her head as she paused to wait for him. "I know that now, but I didn't then. All I saw on campus was the stupid stuff they made the pledges do to get in. Like the year Georgia pledged, the Sigmas made her wear the same ugly brown jumper for a week and referred to her as a lizard. It just seemed like too much to go through just so I could wear matching jackets with a bunch of girls in the student union."

When he was done with his shoe, they started walking again.

"I guess it all depends on the chapter." He kept his eyes on the trail ahead as he made the comment. "When I pledged TDT at Central, we didn't have to do anything too bad."

"Really?" She felt a growing curiosity about his experience. "What did you have to do to get in?"

"For two weeks, we washed our big brothers'

laundry, carried their books from class to class, and made them breakfast."

"Sounds like a lot of work for guys who are supposed to be studying and going to class."

"It was. And did I mention we had to wear dresses and frilly aprons when we served breakfast?"

Her mouth fell open. "For real?"

He nodded. "Yep. And I'd do it all over again."

She scrunched her brow. "Why on earth would you sign up for that kind of humiliation?"

"What you see as humiliation was really about humility. Our big brothers were helping us build character, instilling in us the value of hard work and brotherhood."

She hadn't thought of it from that angle. "And you were happy about it?"

"Hell no. Those were the hardest two weeks of my life. But when it was over, I was brought into a brotherhood that's benefitted me at every stage of my life since."

She looked at him but didn't say anything, as she sensed he wanted to keep talking.

"I wouldn't trade my TDT brothers for nothing. Ty, Bryan, O, and Maxwell can be crazy at times, but I know they have my back. I don't have any natural brothers, but after everything we've been through, I consider them as good as blood."

"Wow." She stayed quiet, thinking about what he'd said. Up until then, she hadn't thought men formed the kind of close friendships women did. But listening to the way Xavier described his boys made her rethink that stance.

They rounded a bend, coming to the halfway marker on the trail. There, the path jutted out a bit, to a rocky overlook. He approached the edge of the overlook, which was about four feet above the banks of Reedy Creek. She joined him there, looking out over the rippling surface of the water.

"If I'd known all that, I might have pledged back then." The wind kicked up, and she brushed a few wayward strands of hair out of her face.

"You still can," he said sagely. "There are local chapters you can join right here in Wake County, and you don't have to be a student."

She turned his way, shielding her eyes from the sun as she looked up into his face. "Is anybody going to tell me what to wear or call me lizard?"

He laughed. "I doubt it. The folks in the chapters are too old for shenanigans. Your dignity is safe with them."

"I might look into it." Holding his gaze, she offered a soft smile. "Thanks for bringing me out here. It's beautiful, and to be honest, I needed this break from thinking about the practice all the time."

He moved a little closer, gave her shoulder a squeeze.

There was nothing sexual about the gesture, but when the warmth of his body touched hers, she felt a sensual tremor shoot through her entire being.

"I figured that. When Tyrone ditched me, you were the first person I thought of to come out here with me."

"I'm flattered." She kept her eyes down, worried that if she looked up at him, he would see how much she was enjoying his touch.

He released her, taking his warmth a few steps away.

She felt bereft but kept her disappointment to herself.

He formed his big hands into fists and started jogging in place. "All right. We've still got two and half more miles to cover before it gets too late."

She turned back toward the trail. "Cool. But don't leave me."

His expression earnest, he said, "Don't worry. I'm not leaving you behind, Imani."

In response to the truth she sensed in his words, her heart somersaulted in her chest. As far as she was concerned, he'd already proven himself to be a great friend.

Moving to his side, she grinned at him as they returned to the path to complete their walk.

"Where are you, man?" Xavier spoke the question into the cabin of his car so it could be picked up by the vehicle's Bluetooth system.

"I'm in the Starbucks in terminal two," Bryan's voice announced through the car speakers. "Where are you?"

"Looking for a parking space. I can't believe you've got me out here dealing with airport traffic when I'm not even flying." He scanned the huge lot he drove around, searching the nearby lanes for an empty spot.

"You know you love me, man."

"Whatever. Look, I'll be there as soon as I get a spot." He disconnected the call, placing his full focus on the tedium of circling the lot. After about ten more minutes of making laps, he found a spot. Depositing his car there, he took a Park and Ride shuttle to the terminal and, once there, entered the building to meet Bryan.

Xavier's jet-setting fraternity brother had called him the previous night, inviting him to come hang out with him before he boarded his flight bound for Paris. Crossing the tiled concourse, Xavier strolled over to the coffee shop, which occupied a storefront just outside of the security checkpoint. Spotting Bryan at a small table, with his black leather, rolling carry-on parked next to him, Xavier walked over to join him.

"You're the only person I know who likes hanging out at airports," Xavier remarked as he sat down in the chair across from Bryan.

Bryan took a swig from his cup of coffee. "No, I don't. I just hate missing flights, so I tend to come early."

"Yeah, but four hours? That's overkill."

"Whatever. You came out here, didn't you?" Bryan ribbed him.

"I came because it was an excuse to get out of the office on a Monday morning. Don't get cocky, Bryan." He stifled a yawn.

"Anyway, do you want a coffee or something?"

After a morning spent doing spreadsheets and running the airport gauntlet, he felt less than perky. "I could use a little pick-me-up."

Reaching into the inner pocket of his sport coat, Bryan handed him a shiny card. "Here. Use my gold card. Get whatever you want, man."

Taking the card, he got up. "Thanks. I'll be sure to get the most expensive thing they have." He walked away to the sounds of Bryan's insults, knowing they were all in jest.

At the counter, he ordered a dark roast coffee and a croissant. With his beverage and food in hand, he returned to the table and gave Bryan back his card. "I was just playing, man. It only cost like five bucks."

Bryan tucked the card away. "The board is sending me out on the road again. They want to roll out a new line in the spring, but we don't have a designer on deck yet."

"Is that why you're flying to Paris today?"

He nodded. "I'm meeting with two designers while I'm there, then visiting the company headquarters there for a bunch of boring-ass meetings. Really looking forward to that," he groused.

"Come on. I know the notorious B. R. J. isn't going to spend his entire time in Paris alone. I know you've got at least a couple of honeys there."

Bryan scoffed. "Of course I do. It's me, baby! But I gotta get through those meetings before I can see any of them. I'm going on the company's dime, so work comes first."

"I feel ya." Xavier knew that even though Bryan traveled to Europe and Asia on the regular for his family's company, Bryan's father rode him constantly about doing his best work.

"Hey, you never told me what happened with Imani. Y'all got together at the wedding, right?" Bryan eyed him expectantly.

"Not exactly." Xavier had no plans of going into detail about what had happened between him and Imani that fateful weekend. "We have been hanging out since then, but we're taking things nice and slow."

"Oh, so Ms. Imani put you in the friend zone, then?" Bryan grinned as he chided him. "Tough break, man."

Xavier rolled his eyes. "Nah. She doesn't want to get serious right now, and I'm cool with it."

"Yeah, you keep telling yourself that, bro." Bryan turned up his coffee cup, draining what was left of his drink.

Xavier knew Bryan was kidding, but he didn't really appreciate it. "Whatever, man. Just make sure you keep your girls' names straight, before one of them goes all *Fatal Attraction* on you."

"You could take a few pointers from me on how to get a woman to be more than friends. So don't hate. Appreciate."

Xavier was about to hit him with a stinging retort, but his attention was drawn to a buzzing on his hip. Pulling out his phone, he checked the screen. A smile spread across his face.

"What's up?" Bryan took a moment to toss his cup in the nearby trash can before turning his attention back to Xavier.

"Imani's texting me." He tapped the screen, scrolled to read her message.

"What, does she want you to pick up her dry cleaning? It's the friendly thing to do." Bryan chuckled, apparently amused at his own joke.

"No. She wants me to come over to her house and watch a movie with her." He took a moment to shoot back a reply. "Still think I'm trapped in the friend zone?"

Bryan looked impressed. "I stand corrected. Go work your magic, bro." He extended both fists, bumping them with Xavier's.

"Don't worry, man. I plan to." Xavier tucked his phone away with a smile. Something told him Imani was finally starting to come around.

—∾∾—

With a big bowl of freshly popped corn in her arms, Imani padded barefoot across her living room carpet. Setting the bowl down on her coffee table, she returned to her apartment's small kitchen to grab a second bowl, this one smaller and filled with candy-coated chocolates.

She'd just set the second bowl down next to the popcorn when the sound of someone knocking at her door drew her attention. Straightening the long-sleeved, lavender, boatneck top she wore with matching wide-legged pants, she went to answer the door.

Xavier stood on the cement stoop outside the door. Dressed casually in a tan sweater and dark denim jeans, he wore a ready smile. "Hey, Imani. Thanks for the invite."

She returned his smile, noting how often she smiled when she was in his presence. "Come on in. What's in the bag?"

He handed over the plastic grocery bag as he entered the house. "I brought over a bottle of wine. Consider it a hostess gift."

She closed the door behind him before taking a peek at his offering. "Nice touch," she commented before setting the bottle of 2013 Clos du Bois California Merlot on the counter. "And it's chilled already. Thank you." She felt touched that he'd remembered her favorite wine, and that she liked it cold.

"Only the best for you." He sat down on the couch, patted the cushion next to him. "Break it open and let's watch the movie."

Doing as her guest requested, she retrieved two wineglasses from her cabinet. Within a few minutes, she brought the two filled glasses to the sofa and sat down next to Xavier, leaving a few inches of space between them.

The television was already set up to stream one of their favorite movies of the nineties, Spike Lee's classic

Mo' Better Blues. As the opening credits rolled, Imani settled into the cushion beneath her.

"I can't remember the last time I watched this movie," Xavier remarked before popping a few of the chocolate candies into his mouth. "It's been too long, I'm sure."

"Yeah, I know. This was Denzel in his prime. I still think he should've gotten the Oscar for his performance."

"I'm with you on that."

They lapsed into convivial silence as the movie began in earnest. Before long, she found herself feeling a level of comfort with him she hadn't felt in more than a decade. She scooted a little closer to him, and when their thighs touched, he glanced her way. The shared a silent smile as he draped his arm over the back cushion, letting his hand rest on her shoulder.

Throughout the film, they chatted, and she couldn't help noticing how easily conversation flowed between them. Between mouthfuls of popcorn, they talked about their views on the themes presented in the movie, what had happened to the cast members in the decades since the film's release, and whether or not it should be remade.

"If it ain't broke, don't remake it," Xavier declared in response to that issue.

"I agree. Although I wouldn't be surprised if some producer tried it, since Hollywood seems to be fresh out of original ideas."

"True, true. Here's hoping they leave this one alone."

She settled into the crook of his arm for the remainder of the movie.

As the end credits rolled, she sat up straight, stretching her arms above her head. Staying in the same position for so long had left her body a little bit stiff, but her soul felt

as warm and cozy as a kitten wrapped in a fleece blanket. Xavier possessed a special quality, something she
couldn't name. Whatever it was, it made her feel safe,
cared for. After spending these last few weeks getting to
know him all over again, she felt certain she didn't want
to return to an existence that didn't include him.

"I was pleasantly surprised when you invited me over,"
Xavier said, bringing her back to the present moment.

"I'm glad you came. You've already invited me out
twice, so I figured it was my turn." She pulled her feet
up on the sofa, tucking her knees to her chest.

"You cold?"

"A little." She wrapped her arms around her knees.
"The heat's been on the fritz and my landlord says he
can't fix it until the end of the week. What about you?
Are you cold?"

He shook his head. "Hot natured, remember?" He
rose from his seat, grabbed the big woven throw she'd
tossed over the armchair earlier. "Here." Sitting next
to her again, he wrapped the big throw around her.
"How's that?"

"Better." She looked at him, letting her eyes connect
with his, hoping her gaze would tell him what she was
too shy to say aloud.

"How about this." He scooted close to her, wrapping
his arms around her blanket-wrapped body.

She released a contented sigh as his body heat
cocooned her. "Much better."

They sat together for a few quiet moments, while she
enjoyed the sensation of being held in his strong arms.

When she spoke again, her tone was soft. "I'm really
enjoying what we have together, Xavier."

"So am I." He gave her a gentle squeeze.

"Really? Because you were coming on a little strong there in the beginning."

"I know, and I'm sorry if I made you feel uncomfortable."

She waved him off. "I get it. You've always been a go-getter."

He released a brief chuckle. "Listen. I'd be lying if I said I don't still want something more serious with you. But if this is what you want, if this is the way I can be a part of your life, then I'm down."

She turned her face up to look into his eyes. "You mean you're just going to go along with this little arrangement for as long as I want?"

"Yes, I am. I remember what you said that night after Ty and Georgia's reception, and you're right. We've been apart for so long that it just makes sense for us to take our time and get to know each other for who we are now."

Hearing him say that and knowing that he understood her reasoning and respected her enough not to press her filled her with a sense of peace and contentment. "Thank you, Xavier. I really appreciate you saying that."

"I mean it."

She was about to say something else, but a yawn came out instead.

He released her from his grasp. "It's time for you to go to bed, Imani. It's getting late and we both have to work tomorrow."

"Aw, come on." She stuck out her lips in a mock pout.

He playfully wagged a finger at her as he got up. "Nope. You're yawning. That means you're tired. I'm going home to get some sleep and you should do the same."

On the heels of another yawn, she acquiesced. "You're right. It is past my bedtime."

She walked him to the door and opened it for him.

"Good night, Imani." He winked at her from just outside the door.

"Good night."

As he started to turn away, she reached out and placed her hand on his forearm.

When he turned back to see what she wanted, she leaned up and placed a soft, fleeting kiss on his cheek. Sharing the small, affectionate gesture with him felt natural, right.

"Sweet dreams," she whispered as she retreated back into the apartment.

The last thing she saw before she shut the door was his grin.

Chapter 7

IMANI ENTERED THE EXAM ROOM AND SHUT THE DOOR behind her. This time, she wasn't surprised to see Cassidy sitting on the edge of the exam table. She'd seen Cassidy's name on the schedule for a follow-up. Wearing the same congenial smile she greeted all her patients with, Imani sat down on her stool and eased it closer to Cassidy. "Good morning. So I'm guessing you're not getting the results you want with the corticosteroid?"

"Morning, Imani." Cassidy returned her smile. "And no, I'm not. The patches are still just as irritated. Not to mention my skin looks a hot mess."

She nodded. In many ways, Cassidy's personality hadn't changed from the young woman she'd been in college. Imani remembered how concerned Cassidy had always been with her appearance, and even now, she sensed that Cassidy was more concerned with the cosmetic dilemma posed by her psoriasis than anything else. "You realize that you haven't given the cream enough time to work. It's been less than two weeks since your last appointment."

"I know I'm a little impatient, but is there anything else you can do for me? Is there any way to reduce the scaliness while I wait for the medicine to kick in fully?"

"There is. I can give you some UVB light therapy." Imani had only used her phototherapy machine once since she'd opened her practice, but she'd already been impressed with the results it provided. "I can administer it right here in the office, and it should dramatically reduce your scaling."

Cassidy's smile brightened. "Great. That sounds like just what I need."

Standing, Imani used her tablet to make note of the procedure in Cassidy's electronic patient record. "Okay. I'm going to get a nurse to bring the equipment into the room. Since you have scaling in various places, we'll need you to put on a gown."

Cassidy's face fell. "Oh Lord. One of those hospital deals with my tail hanging out?"

With a chuckle, Imani pulled a paper gown out of the storage cabinet in the room. "Nah. It's paper and there's plenty of coverage."

Taking the gown, Cassidy blew out a sigh of relief. "Thanks."

"I'll step out, so you can change, and be back shortly." She eased out of the room into the corridor and shut the door behind her. Poking her head into the break room, she gestured for Leona.

"What's up?" The nurse asked the question around a mouthful of muffin.

"Can you wheel the phototherapy equipment into exam room one, please?"

Dusting off her hands and using a pump of sanitizer, Leona nodded. "Sure thing."

Once Cassidy was gowned and the machine was set up, Imani rejoined Cassidy in the exam room. She donned her gloves, then handed Cassidy a pair of goggles. "Put these on to shield your eyes from the light."

Both women donned a pair of goggles, and Imani had Cassidy lie on the table.

"Is this going to take a while?" Cassidy adjusted her position slightly.

"About twenty minutes or so."

"Do you mind chatting with me while you do this?"

"No." Imani knew that proper bedside manner meant she should meet patient's requests when reasonable. "Are you nervous? Because the procedure is painless." With a gloved hand, she opened one side of Cassidy's gown.

"I'm not nervous. I just hate to sit in awkward silence with someone I know."

"I understand." She used one hand to hold the gown aside and wielded the phototherapy wand with her other. Tiny beeps and flashes of light were emitted from the machine as she treated the patches just above Cassidy's pelvis.

"So, from the way you reacted to seeing me last time, I'm guessing seeing me dredged up some unpleasant memories from our days at Doyle and Callahan."

Imani blinked a few times behind the protective lenses of her goggles. "Straight to the point, I see. But you're right."

"I figured. Everybody has something in their past that they regret, especially during college. Be easy on yourself."

She offered a soft laugh in response. "It's a little more complex than that, but I understand what you mean." She completed treatment of Cassidy's lower abdomen and set aside the wand for a moment to run a soft bristle brush over the newly treated skin.

Cassidy jumped a little, as if tickled. "We were young

secretaries, working for a bunch of older men in positions of power."

Imani wanted to sigh but didn't. She also held back her comments about the toxic attitudes that had run rampant in the all-male firm. "I think the lawyers could have been professional, if they had wanted to. But some of them let the power go to their heads."

"I know. I can remember a few of them who were pushy as hell, always trying to get under our skirts." She shook her head.

"I remember." Parts of her wanted to say more, to say aloud what she'd been holding inside all these years. Cassidy only knew part of the story. The abuse she'd faced at the hands of one of the lawyers had altered the course of her life. But she knew her legal obligation was to be silent.

"Not for nothing, but I used some of that desperation to my benefit." Cassidy pursed her lips. "If they were gonna be jerks anyway, I figured I might as well get something out of it."

Imani didn't know exactly what Cassidy meant, and she knew better than to ask. She sensed Cassidy would be honest enough to tell her everything, in detail. Instead of dwelling on that, she moved the light wand to treat the patches on Cassidy's arms.

Cassidy continued chatting about various subjects as the treatment continued, but Imani found she didn't have much more to say. She acknowledged Cassidy's words but kept her responses short. By the time they were finished and she'd applied moisturizing cream to the places that had been treated, Imani felt somewhat relieved that the conversation would soon end.

Removing her gloves and tossing them in the trash bin, Imani stood. "We're done, Cassidy. Continue using the cream I gave you, and that should keep most of the patches away. And remember, we still have some other options if you need them. But give it a few weeks this time."

Cassidy nodded. "I will. Now that my skin looks better, I think I can be a little more patient."

"Good. If you need anything, just call us." Imani glanced at her watch, mindful of her patient waiting in the next room.

"Thanks."

With a smile, Imani left the room. Cassidy had given her plenty to think about, but she had more patients to see. Tucking those thoughts of the past away, Imani sanitized her hands and entered the next exam room.

―⁓―

Xavier got out of his car, walked around to the passenger side, and opened the door. "Have I told you how beautiful you look tonight?"

Imani giggled as she stepped out, moving away from the car so he could shut the door. "Yes, but you can keep the compliments coming."

He took in the sight of her again in the incredibly sexy outfit she wore: a slinky red tunic top over a pair of shimmery black leggings. The black leather boots she'd paired the outfit with were knee high, with block heels that added a couple of inches to her height. Her makeup consisted of black eyeliner and ruby-red lipstick, and she'd let her hair fall around her shoulders. The longer he stood there looking at her, the happier he was with his decision to ask her out for a night of dancing.

Taking his offered hand, she let him escort her to the door of Te Amo Corazon, one of the city's hottest salsa and merengue clubs. He'd had a membership to the exclusive club for several years now, having received it as a birthday gift from Maxwell when he turned thirty. He went once after getting the membership and had enjoyed the atmosphere of the place so much that he renewed every year. The campaign had left him little time for fun recently, and he looked forward to dancing the night away with Imani.

After they'd gone through the security gauntlet and she'd handed her purse off to the coat-check attendant, a club employee in a red blazer lifted the velvet rope, allowing them access to the club's VIP section.

She made a slow turn, taking in the scene. "Wow. This place is impressive. I didn't know you had this kind of pull."

"Let's just say I know a guy." He gave her an exaggerated wink.

"In any case, I'm impressed."

He knew she had reason to be. The club's VIP section was on the second level and boasted a bar made entirely of imported crystal, booths with leather-topped ottomans and red suede chairs, and a dance floor fitted with lights that illuminated the surface from beneath. The sound booth, perched on a high platform above the bar, was being worked by a lady DJ spinning nonstop salsa music.

"Wanna grab a drink?" She spoke into his ear to be heard over the pounding music.

He nodded and, still clutching her hand, led her to the sparkling crystal bar. There, they sat on the leather-topped stools and summoned the bartender. They both ordered Corona with lime, and a few minutes later, they were sipping from their bottles, their eyes turned toward the dance floor.

"This place is amazing. How did you know I love salsa music?"

Setting his bottle down, he answered her truthfully. "I didn't, but since I've been wanting to bring you here, I figured it was worth a shot to ask."

"Good call." She took a dainty sip from her beer bottle, then set it aside. "We are going to dance, right?"

"Soon as they play something you like."

As if on cue, the DJ switched records, shouting into her microphone. "I know y'all gonna get on the floor for this Celia Cruz!"

Seconds later, the opening notes of Cruz's classic "Quimbara" filled the room.

Imani's eyes lit up. "I love this song!"

Before he could react, she'd grabbed his hand and dragged him out onto the dance floor. As soon as they fit themselves into an empty space on the floor, she began swaying her hips to the rhythm of the music.

He joined her in dancing but never took his eyes off of her. The way she moved hypnotized him, holding him captive. With her lithe arms waving above her head and her body swaying and undulating to the music, she was seduction personified.

He placed his open palms on either side of her waist, guiding her back and forth in time with his own movements. Their gazes locked. Time seemed to stand still as he read the unbridled desire in her eyes.

He could feel the heat building between them. It

oozed from her pores, rising between them like thick, curling smoke. They kept moving, their bodies in unison, and he felt her inching closer to him.

When she spun around to face away from him and gently pressed the soft fullness of her hips against his crotch, he held back a gasp. He could not hold back his body's physical reaction to her nearness, and was powerless to stop the blood rushing to his manhood.

By the time the song ended, he had a full-on erection. That didn't stop her from continuing her slow grind against him as the next song began.

When he felt sure he would explode if she didn't stop, she spun again to face him. A light sheen of perspiration clung to her hairline. With a sexy smile on her face, she said, "I can see you like my dancing."

"Oh my God, Imani." It was all he could manage. He could not remember ever being so aroused, least of all in public, in the middle of a crowded dance floor.

"Don't be embarrassed. I'm not." She lifted her small hand, placing it along his jaw. With her hips still swiveling, she leaned in and pressed her ruby lips to his. The kiss was brief, but those few seconds of connection with her were enough to drive him mad with desire.

She grabbed his hands, placed them back on her body. When he eased them lower, to her backside, she responded with a smile. "One more song, then I'm taking you home, Xavier."

Sucking in a breath through his teeth, he joined her in the dance, moving his body in harmony with hers. Pressed as close as their clothing would allow, they moved across the floor under the spell of the music—and of each other.

When the second song ended, she said nothing. She simply stopped dancing, grabbed his hand, and tugged him away from the dance floor.

They were outside and leaning against his car a few moments later.

She had her back against the passenger side, and he was pressed against her, holding her, kissing her. He felt like a teenage boy having his first encounter with a woman, all raging hormones and questing hands. He was probably wearing her lipstick by now, but he didn't give a damn. He couldn't seem to get enough of her intoxicating kisses.

A blast of cold air hit him as the autumn wind picked up, giving him a moment of clarity. He broke the seal of their lips, and she whined in protest.

"Imani. Are you sure? Because if you aren't, we don't have to—"

"Shhh." She extended her index finger, laying it over his lips to quiet him. "I'm sure, Xavier. I want this." She swept her hand over his jawline. "I want you."

A groan escaped him as he speared his hands through the soft riches of her hair and captured her lips again. He held that kiss for a long moment, slipping his tongue into her mouth before drawing it out again.

She looked up at him, her eyes sparkling, her breath coming in heavy pants.

Curling his fingers beneath her chin, he whispered, "Let's go."

Once he had her safely tucked into his passenger seat, he climbed into the car and drove her home.

He planned on giving her what she wanted—and so much more.

———∿∿∿———

As Imani unlocked her apartment door, she swung the door open and backed inside. Xavier, his hands on her waist, moved inside with her, as if they were still dancing.

She tossed aside her small handbag, not caring where it landed, as they kissed and fumbled their way toward her couch. She felt heady, almost intoxicated. But she knew the sensation wasn't from the three sips of beer she'd had. No, the thing turning her mind to mush was Xavier and the raw male power he exuded.

She fell onto the soft cushions, pulling him down with her. The muscled hardness of his frame on top of hers felt like pure heaven.

She spent several long moments wrapped in his arms, enjoying his kiss and the feel of his big hands touring her body. Pulling back for a moment, she smiled up at him. Her voice came out as a sultry whisper when she spoke. "I think we're grossly overdressed."

"I agree." A wide grin spread over his face as he lifted himself up. Standing next to the sofa, he unbuttoned his shirt and kicked off his loafers. His eyes never left her face as he slipped out of the shirt and undershirt, then his trousers. Wearing nothing but a pair of red boxers, he leaned down to kiss her cheek.

Staring at the hard lines of his body, it was all she could do not to drool. His chest and arms were sculpted, as were his abdominals and the powerful thighs crowning his long, athletic legs. As for the part of his anatomy that made him male, she could clearly see the thick hardness of it, outlined by the thin, clinging fabric of his shorts. *Why did I wait so long to get with him?*

She had no idea why she'd hesitated before, but she planned on making up for that now. Reaching for the zipper of her left boot, she was surprised when he stayed her hand.

"Allow me, baby." He knelt, grasped the zipper, and tugged it down. He wriggled the boot off, then unzipped its mate. "These boots are so damn sexy."

"I'm glad you like them." As he began to slide his hands up her legs, then her thighs, she instinctively raised her hips off the sofa cushion. He reached around to grasp the waistband of her leggings and tugged them. The snug fit of the leggings made her panties slide down with them. When he tossed the bundle of fabric aside a moment later, she was nude from the waist down.

Wearing only her tunic and bra, she looked on with wonder as he lifted her legs, placing one over each of his strong shoulders. A shiver shot through her as his fingertips grazed the sensitive skin of her inner thighs. His touch moved higher and, before she could blink, boldly slid into her center. He parted her damp folds, and she felt a rush of liquid heat as the pad of his thumb teased her clitoris.

He kissed the inside of her right thigh, then her left. "I've been wanting to taste you for so long." He murmured the words into her trembling skin. "Can I?"

As his thumb and fingers continued their wicked play between her spread thighs, her head fell back against the cushion buoying her.

He repeated his question as the tip of his finger delved into her slick passage.

"Yes." A moan carried her answer to his ears.

He bent his head, and the moment she felt his tongue

against her flesh, her whole body shook with pleasure. He moved his hands, using his large palms to put firm yet gentle pressure on her inner thighs, keeping her open to his fiery ministrations. She struggled to hold on to her sanity in the face of the ecstasy he gave her, and failed. Soon, an orgasm bloomed inside of her, making her twist and writhe beneath him. Her back arched, her toes curled, and her mouth dropped open in a silent scream.

Seemingly satisfied, he climbed up from his knees, standing before her again. As the high from her orgasm began to wane, her desire for him only climbed higher. Sitting up, she fixed her bleary eyes on the hard prize just inches away from her. Her hands gripped the waistband of his boxers and pushed them down his legs.

"You ready, baby?" He kicked the boxers aside.

"Oh yes." Her hands reached out, encircling his erection. She worked her hands back and forth for a few torrid moments, loving the way his hips shifted forward to meet her touch.

A low groan escaped him. "Not like this, baby. I want to come inside you."

She watched as he moved away and grabbed a condom from the back pocket of his trousers. He sheathed himself with the protection, and the moment he finished, she dragged him down onto the couch. With her lips pressed to his, she guided him into a sitting position.

She rarely ever did this with a man, and she realized how out of character it was for her to want to be on top. But there was something about Xavier that made her feel bold, reckless.

His smile in the darkness made her skin tingle. "So you want to ride?"

By way of answering him, she straddled his lap. Centering her body over his erection, she raised, then lowered herself. Her entire body sang with joy as he filled her. His thickness and length fit her perfectly, touching all the right places inside.

She began her ride, slowly rocking her hips as his hands grazed over her body. He leaned in to take her hardened nipple into his mouth, then his open palms grasped her hips, squeezing her soft flesh.

She felt as if she were on fire, with his hands, lips, and manhood bringing her such ecstasy. Increasing her pace, she continued to move against him, grinding her hips to claim every drop of passion he wanted to give. Her soft cries and his deep grunts filled the room, rising in the silence.

His grip on her hips became tighter, and their bodies rose and fell together in the ancient rhythm of passion.

"God, Xavier!" She felt tears stream down her face as her body shattered into a million brilliant pieces.

He growled, punctuating the sound with one final upward thrust as he found his own completion. Moving his hands up along her sides, he encircled her with his arms and pulled her close to him.

Lying against his sweat-dampened chest, she never wanted to move, never wanted to break the contact of their bodies. With the glow of orgasm still filling her soul, she felt drowsy and content. The heat of his body warmed her, while his protective embrace made her feel safe and cared for.

Being with him now brought back sweet memories of what they'd shared long ago. Now that she was older and had experienced the many ups and downs life could dole out, she sensed something new, something deeper in their current connection. She didn't want to label what she was feeling, but she knew she wanted this current state of bliss to last forever.

He kissed the hollow of her throat, murmured something against her skin.

She wanted to ask him what he'd said, but before she could form the words, her heavy eyelids closed.

Chapter 8

GETTING OUT OF HER CAR IN HER PRACTICE'S PARKING LOT, Imani tightened her gray wool trench coat against the chilly October breeze. Only an hour or so had passed since sunrise. She'd come with the intention of getting an early start to the day, since paperwork had proven to be a major drain on her time. Even though she delegated as much as possible to Maya and her nurses, there were still many documents that required her approval or signature. Beyond that, no one else in the practice had the authority to write prescriptions.

A smile touched her lips as memories of her weekend with Xavier returned. He'd treated her to an erotic feast Friday night, then spent Saturday morning discussing current events with her over coffee and croissants. Returning to reality was a bit of a bummer, but a necessary one.

She leaned back into the car to grab her travel mug full of hot chocolate and slung her purse over her shoulder. Juggling the items into position, she closed her car door and started toward the building.

She'd made it about five steps before she noticed a glint of sunlight sparkling as it reflected off the broken glass littering the sidewalk.

Her eyes widened. "Oh my God."

Her travel mug clattered to the pavement as she rushed up to what remained of her glass door. It had been shattered, and most of the glass littered the sidewalk and the floor inside. Her eyes traveled down, toward a large, jagged stone that sat just inside the doorway. She surmised it had been the weapon used to break through her door.

A shiver ran down her spine as she recalled the scene at her father's hardware store on that horrible day. The kids who'd robbed and ultimately killed him had come early in the morning, before the store was open. As her father had worked alone to get the store ready for the day, they'd broken his window with a cinder block, rushed in, and...

Imani staggered back a few steps, feeling the rising panic that accompanied those painful memories. Her chest tightened, her breaths coming shallow and fast.

What if I had been here?

What would they have done to me?

She didn't want to go in, even though she could easily fit through the wide opening the stone had left. Having no idea what conditions were like inside, and unsure whether she could handle what she might find without some support, she reached into her coat pocket for her cell phone. Pulling it out, she first dialed emergency services, to report the break-in.

"Ma'am, it may be a few minutes before officers arrive. Right now they're responding to an auto accident a couple of blocks south of your location." The dispatcher's monotone voice filled Imani's ear. "We have to give priority to emergency situations."

"Okay, thank you." She disconnected the call. While it wasn't what she'd wanted to hear, she understood why the police department would make the decision to respond to an emergency first. Drawing a deep, calming breath, she dialed Maya's number. When she answered, Imani asked her to get over to the office as fast as she could.

Rather than stand out in the cold waiting for the others to arrive, Imani jogged past the remnants of her shattered travel mug and went back to her car. Once inside, she let the engine idle and cranked the heat to stay warm. She'd been sitting alone in the car for only a few moments before the tears began to flow down her cheeks. She thought of all the hard work she'd put into getting her practice open, and it frustrated her that someone else's selfish act could set her back so far. With a leather-gloved hand, she dashed the tears away.

An RPD squad car entered the lot. She watched the car pull into a parking space, the doors opening as a pair of officers stepped out.

She cut the engine and climbed out of her car. As she approached, she watched the two uniformed officers of the Raleigh Police Department speaking on the walk in front of her practice. One was male, while the other officer was a woman.

"Ma'am, are you Dr. Grant?" the male officer, a tall figure with striking, blue eyes and dark hair, asked.

She nodded. "I am. I called to report the break-in."

The officer tipped his hat. "I'm Officer Riley. This is my partner, Officer Suggs. We'll do whatever we can to help you."

Officer Suggs, a petite woman with dark skin and friendly, golden eyes, asked, "Have you been inside the building yet?"

Folding her arms over her chest, she shook her head. "No, Officer. I wasn't sure it was safe to go in."

Officer Riley gave her a small smile along with a pat on the shoulder. "Ma'am, you can never be too cautious with things like this. We'll comb the inside to make sure it's safe for you to come in. Then you can get a look at the damage for your insurance claim."

"Thank you." She unlocked the door, to allow them safer passage inside. Then she stood by as the officers entered the practice.

Just then, Maya's gold sedan tore into the lot. Imani was relieved that the police had already gone inside when she saw her cousin whip the car into a spot.

Maya got out of her car, slammed the door, and sprinted over to where Imani stood. "Oh man, Imani. This is bad."

Imani had to agree with that. "I know. The police are inside. They'll come tell us if it's safe to go in."

Reaching out, Maya engulfed her in a bear hug. "I'm sorry this happened. I'll do whatever I can to help with the cleanup, and I'm sure the nurses will too."

She returned the embrace, taking comfort in her cousin's unwavering support. "Thank you, Maya. I really appreciate you."

"Hey, I'm here for you, Cuz." Maya stepped back, tightening the belt securing the waistline of her coat. Her expression sad, she spoke softly. "This is like when Uncle Richard…"

Imani sighed. "I know."

They stood there for a few moments in silence, each lost in her own memories.

As if to break up the melancholy that had descended over them, Maya announced, "Damn, it's cold this morning."

"You're telling me. I've been out here for about thirty minutes." Imani shifted her weight from side to side, hoping the motion would help warm her.

Officer Suggs came to the door then, addressing Imani through the gaping hole in the glass pane. "We'd like you to come in now, Dr. Grant, and let us know what's missing or out of place. Try not to touch anything until the investigators have had a chance to come in."

Imani nodded, asking, "Can I bring in Maya as well? She's my office manager."

"Sure." Officer Suggs gestured for them both to come inside.

Maya grabbed the door handle, and she and Imani entered the practice. In the reception area, two of the ficus plants Imani had brought in for decoration had been upset, and the dark soil from the pots had been scattered and tracked across the tile floor. Imani frowned when she saw the dark footprints staining the Oriental rugs she'd carefully chosen to complement the office's decor.

The walk through the rest of the practice revealed a mess of colossal proportions. Imani put her hands to her face when she saw the cash drawer behind the reception desk had been tampered with, but it looked like it remained locked. The drawers of the desk, however, had been pulled out and emptied, and Maya's things were scattered all over the desktop and the floor.

Officer Suggs made a note of the condition of the area. "Looks like someone was searching for anything of value."

When they walked into her office, Imani gasped. "Holy shit."

The room looked as if a tsunami had hit. They had attempted to shatter the glass top of her desk. The heavyweight, tempered glass bore several long, jagged cracks but still remained in one piece. Papers littered the desk and floor. Her coffee mugs, family photos, dust collectors—everything had been tossed around the space in a haphazard fashion. Her bookshelves, filled with medical volumes, had been overturned, along with her file cabinets that contained patient records. Due to privacy laws, the filing cabinets were locked, so their contents remained inside. The only thing in the office that was still in place were her degrees, hanging on the wall where she'd left them. Trying not think about what a pain it would be to clean up, she listed the damage in the notes app of her smartphone.

As Imani entered the room fully, her first thought was to collect the footage from the security camera. The camera system was digital, capturing images and uploading them to an offsite server. The camera outside looked as if it had been damaged, but there were cameras hidden in small globular structures in the ceiling of every room inside the place. "I'll get the security company to release the footage to the police department."

Officer Riley stood in the doorway behind them. "Any valuables missing from here?"

Imani shook her head. "No. I use a laptop, but I take it home with me at night. Maya takes hers home as well."

He nodded his understanding. "Did you have a television in your break room?"

Imani sighed. "Yes, but I'm guessing it's gone."

"Yes, ma'am. They did leave you the mounting hardware though."

Maya rolled her eyes. "Well, aren't they just angels of mercy."

"I think you should get a look at your examination rooms and your storage closet," Officer Suggs offered.

Imani agreed, and the four of them made the rounds of the rest of the practice.

In all three examination rooms, the paper liners on her exam tables had been unraveled and shredded, but not much else had been damaged. To her mind, it looked like the work of a bunch of toddlers. In the storage closet, things had been rearranged, but the most valuable things remained. All of her blood pressure monitors, portable stands, and medical equipment looked untouched.

"Is anything missing here, Dr. Grant?" Officer Riley asked, his pen poised over a clipboard he'd been writing on.

"There were three tablets that my nurses were training to use so we could go paperless. They're all missing." Imani pressed her fingertips to her temple. Those tablets had set her back about fifteen hundred dollars. She hoped her insurance company would replace them without too much hassle.

Once Imani and Maya had done their part, the officers brought them into the reception area.

Officer Riley explained, "We've taken some photographs, and now we're going to call in the City-County Bureau of Identification. They'll come in to take fingerprints and collect evidence here, so you should be closed for a few days to let them finish their work."

Imani flexed her fingers. "I understand. Is there anything else we need to do?"

Officer Suggs shook her head. "Not for now. We'll hang around for a while, to collect the security footage from the business center's cameras and talk to the other folks who lease office space here. Once we've taken all the witness accounts and have some time to collaborate with CCBI, we'll get in contact with you."

Imani and Maya shook hands with the officers as they left the practice.

Maya, seated on one of the chairs, asked, "What now?"

Imani sighed. "Now we call someone to replace the door with something sturdier. We'll hold off on cleaning up until the investigators have done their thing."

"I'm on it." Maya pulled out her cell phone and opened her Internet browser.

Imani sank onto the cushion of one of the waiting room chairs, letting her head drop back. It had already been a rough morning, yet the real work was about to begin.

From his seat behind his desk, Xavier used the remote to turn on the small television he kept on a corner shelf. It was just past noon, and he figured he'd watch a little of the local news while he waited for his lunch delivery from one of the local delis.

He turned the volume up and set the remote down on his desk. Leaning back in his chair, he listened to one of the local reporters talking about the latest battle going on in the school board. He shook his head, thinking of how often the county's education budget had landed on the chopping block over the past few years. And yet the school board never seemed to do anything about it. As far as Xavier could tell, they were more interested in arguing among themselves and clashing with angry parents and frustrated teachers.

His ears perked up when the anchor announced breaking news. The anchor's voice-over continued as the images on the screen shifted from the studio to live video coverage of a break-in. Xavier sat straight up in his chair when he realized where the crime had occurred.

"This is the scene at Grant Dermatology in west Raleigh, where police have told us there was a break-in overnight." The female anchor looked into the camera, her handheld station microphone positioned in front of her. "Not many details are available in this ongoing investigation, and police have asked that we do not enter the suite. Earlier, we spoke to Maya Grant-Arrington, the business manager of the practice. Here's what Mrs. Arrington had to say."

A brief taped interview aired next, with Maya acting as a spokesperson for the practice. She looked very poised, considering the situation. "We're going to spend some time cleaning up and assisting police in any way we can. I'll be contacting patients to reschedule their appointments. Dr. Grant and I, as well as the rest of the staff, apologize for any inconvenience this may cause our patients. That's all I can tell you right now."

By now, Xavier was on his feet. The live coverage continued, with the female anchor positioned in front of the practice. While the anchor spouted statistics about rising crime in the city, he looked past her, to Imani's suite. He could easily see the extensive damage done to the exterior and part of the reception area. He could only assume the rest of the inside looked just as bad. The door had been shattered, and there was glass scattered everywhere. The security camera perched above the door dangled from its wires, as if the culprits had attempted to disconnect it. And the decorative planters on either side of the entrance had been overturned, the dark soil spilled all over the floor, the leaves of the plants trampled.

He curled his hand into a fist, pounded it on the edge of his desk. He'd never known anyone as conscientious and hardworking as Imani, and he knew how important opening her own practice was to her. She didn't deserve this, and it angered him to know that someone had violated her property and disrupted her ability to earn a living. Crime prevention was a top issue in his campaign, and this incident made him want to work even harder to make the city as safe as it could be.

He wanted to go over there right now and see what he could do to help. Knowing Imani, though, she'd send him away. She was so put together, so independent and capable. Even though she must have been terrified to find her office that way, she'd soldier on as if she could handle it alone. He could see right through her, though—she needed him just as much as he needed her.

He thought of Tyrone and Maxwell, how they'd urged him to cool things off with Imani in the interest of his campaign. Imani had also emphasized her desire to take things slowly. That had all changed Friday night, when she'd taken him back to her place and made love to him. Their connection had been electric, undeniable. Something inside him, coupled with the passion they'd shared, made him want more with her. Between the memories of their loving and his hope for their future together, he was having a difficult time reining in his pursuit of her.

This wasn't just about him, though. He knew she needed time, especially in light of what had occurred at her practice. The break-in had likely left her angry and frightened; going over there now might ruin everything he hoped to build with her.

His stomach emitted a loud and insistent growl, bringing his mind back to the present and the lunch delivery he still hadn't received. *What's taking them so long?* He grabbed his desk phone, intending to place a call to the deli. He'd dialed the first three numbers when a knock on his door got his attention. Putting the handset back in the cradle, he went to open the door.

The smell of olive oil, fresh baked bread, and roasted turkey filled the office as he took the paper bag from the delivery guy. After giving the young man cash enough to cover his meal and a reasonable tip, Xavier closed the door again and took his lunch to the desk. He'd been working on client statements since seven that morning, and by now his stomach was ready to stage a coup. It took him less than ten minutes to polish off the ten-inch Italian turkey sub and the accompanying bag of plain potato chips.

His hunger satiated, he reached for his drink. He popped open the ice-cold can of Cheerwine, his thoughts going back to Imani. No matter how much she claimed there was nothing between them, he couldn't help worrying about her. She must have been devastated to come in to work and find her practice in such a condition. There had to be something he could do, something that would help her without setting her off. He picked up his cell phone from the corner of the desk, deciding he'd have a better outcome if he called her instead of just showing up unannounced.

He dialed her number from his contacts, then propped the phone against his ear with his shoulder.

It rang three times before she answered. "Hello?"

He noted how weary she sounded. "Imani, it's me. How are you doing?"

She sighed. "Hey, Xavier. I've been better."

"I saw the news coverage. I'm sorry to hear about the break-in."

Silence.

His brow creased. "Imani, are you still there?"

"I'm still here." Her voice cracked, giving away her sadness.

His heart clenched in his chest. "Is there anything I can do to help out? Anything at all?"

She sniffled. "I'm not sure, since the police think someone from your center may have been involved."

His eyes widened. "The youth center? Why would they think that?"

"I don't know, Xavier. They collected a lot of evidence earlier but didn't give me many details. But I know they suspect one or more of your wards."

His face crinkled into a frown. He didn't like the way she'd referred to his kids as "wards." "Imani, I don't know if that's the case or not, and it doesn't really matter. Just let me know what I can do to help."

"How can you say it doesn't matter?" She barked the question at him. "If those little hoodlums did this, I plan on seeking justice to the fullest."

He placed his fingertips against his temple. "Imani, I'm gonna need you to stop insulting my kids. Even if someone from the center was involved in this, that doesn't give you the right to put all of them down."

She scoffed. "Whatever."

His jaw tightened. Loosening his tie, he spoke again. "Look. If the police contact me or the center's staff, we'll cooperate fully. Until then, I'll look into things at the center, just to see what any of the kids might know about the break-in."

"You do that." She all but shouted the words into his ear before hanging up on him.

Placing his phone back on the desk, he tilted his head from side to side, hoping to alleviate some of the tension there. His feelings for Imani notwithstanding, he couldn't accept the way she'd slandered his kids. She probably felt helpless, angry, and frustrated, and he could understand that. Still, he had to draw the line somewhere, and she'd toed that line with her disdain for the kids at the center. He didn't have any children of his own, and he didn't know if he ever would. The kids who came to Revels were very near and dear to his heart. Most of them were growing up in circumstances far less than ideal, and he and his staff were determined to have some positive impact in their lives. He wouldn't stand for having them categorized as hoodlums, not by Imani or anyone else.

On the television, the midday newscast had ended. Now the theme of some cheesy soap opera filled the office, so he used the remote to flick the television off. His lunch break was over and there were piles of work he needed to complete by day's end to keep from falling behind.

Despite that, he took a moment to send a quick text message to Tori, who acted as activities coordinator at the center. The kids were overdue for a community service project. Center policy dictated that they complete one as a group at least every sixty days. He had the perfect project in mind for them, and he couldn't wait to see the look on Imani's face when she realized just how wrong she'd been about them.

The message sent, he turned to his computer and dove back into the day's work.

───∞∞∞───

Imani, dressed in a black tracksuit, slid her key into the new lock on the door of Grant Dermatology. She'd had the entire door replaced after the investigators finished their sweep of the premises. She'd paid out of pocket for the locksmith and the glass, but she expected her insurance company to reimburse her soon. She would have preferred to have the insurance pay for it, but she couldn't just leave her business completely unprotected. She had no interest in dealing with any other would-be thieves who might decide to strike while her security was still nonexistent.

Inside the office, she closed the door and locked it behind her. Some of the glass and dirt from her planters had been swept up yesterday, but a lot of work still remained. She expected Maya and her nurses to arrive within an hour to help her finish cleaning the place up. She went into her office, set her purse down on her bookcase. Averting her eyes from her damaged desk, she pulled her hair back with an elastic band. She reached into the plastic shopping bag from a local home improvement store, grabbing one of the pairs of thick gardening gloves she'd bought.

She slid her hands into a pair of gloves and started up the hall toward the reception area.

A knock on the door startled her, and she jumped. Realizing it was probably Maya or one of the nurses, she took a deep breath to calm herself.

She rounded the corner with her gaze on the glass door, expecting to see one of her employees.

Instead, she saw Xavier standing there.

Through the full-length glass pane, she could see all of him. She took in his smiling face, the bright-orange long-sleeved T clinging to his muscled torso, and the jeans gripping his powerful thighs like a second skin.

A sensual chill raced through her body at the memory of his hard thighs nestled between her own.

She rolled her eyes, tried to push those thoughts aside. The last thing she needed right then was for him to show up. Thinking about their relationship would be a major distraction at a time like this. Deep down, she knew their connection went much deeper than she wanted to admit, but if they were going to take it slow, she couldn't allow herself to tap into those feelings.

As she moved closer to the door, intending on opening it just long enough to tell him to get lost, she noticed that he wasn't alone.

There were two young men flanking him, and a few more teenagers standing behind him. Unsure what to make of that, she unlocked the door and opened it a bit. "Xavier, what are you doing here?"

"Good morning to you, too, Dr. Grant. I brought some of my *wards* to assist you with cleanup."

She noticed the way he drawled the word "wards" and recognized the dig. Folding her arms over her chest, she looked up into his dark eyes. "Are you serious?"

He looked back at her unflinchingly. "Yes, I'm

serious. The youth at Revels participate in at least one community service project every two months. Today, your office is our project."

She didn't really know what to say to that and she wondered if her shock showed on her face.

He smiled. "Are you going to stand there with your mouth hanging open, or can we come in and get to work?"

Embarrassment heated her cheeks, and she stepped back to allow them entry. "Come on in."

They filed past her in a neat line, with Xavier leading them. She counted nine young men and women. Like Xavier, all of them wore bright-orange shirts that said *H.R. Revels Youth Center*, as well as a pair of protective gloves. They didn't make a sound as they stood in the reception area all in a row, as if waiting for instructions.

Xavier sidled over to her. "We came ready to work, so just let us know what needs to be done and we'll take care of it."

She looked from him to the kids and back. "What made you decide to do this? I wasn't exactly charitable when I spoke to you yesterday."

He leaned close to her. "I figured the best way for you to see what kind of people they really are is to show you. Before the day is out, you're going to see how off base you were to call them hoodlums."

She swallowed the lump of guilt forming in her throat. She knew she'd been short with him yesterday. The pain and anger of the break-in had still been fresh; however, that didn't excuse what she'd said. In the light of a new day, she realized how wrong she'd been to make such broad generalizations. "I'm sorry, Xavier. I was really emotional yesterday, but I shouldn't have said that."

He watched her silently, as if waiting for her to elaborate.

She sighed. "This whole thing just brought up a lot of bad memories for me about Dad's death. It was wrong of me to make that kind of generalization, and I hope you can accept my apology." She'd pointed out how his passionate support of the city's youth reminded her of her father, and she felt ashamed that she'd insulted Xavier for possessing a quality she respected.

He patted her on the shoulder. "I'll let you slide this time. Just don't insult my kids again and everything's cool."

She nodded, feeling somewhat relieved. "Okay."

"So what do you need us to do?"

She scratched her head. "There's still a lot of glass and soil to sweep up in here, lots of papers and more broken glass scattered around my office, unraveled exam table liners in the exam rooms..." She rattled off the list of things to be done, realizing just how much of a mess the culprits had left her with. Emotion welled inside her again, and before she could rein it in, a tear slid down her cheek.

Xavier gave her shoulder a squeeze. "I'll handle it, okay?"

She nodded. Brushing away the tear, she went to one of the chairs behind the reception desk to sit down.

He turned to the kids. "Everybody, listen up. We're going to split into teams of three and work our way through the office. By the end of the day, I want this whole place looking as good as new. Who are we?"

"Revels Youth!" The enthusiastic reply of the children echoed through the suite.

Imani watched as Xavier broke the group up into

teams, shaking her head in amazement. She grabbed a tissue from the box on the reception desk and dabbed at her damp eyes. Xavier had one of the biggest hearts of anyone she'd ever known, and his presence at the moment confirmed it. Nothing obligated him or his helpers to be there; they were only there out of a sincere desire to help her.

Xavier asked her, "Where are your cleaning supplies?"

She pointed toward the hallway. "The broom closet is the door between my office and the first exam room."

"Gotcha." He dazzled her with another broad smile before disappearing around the corner with the kids in tow.

Sitting there, Imani felt her heart swell with gratitude. Xavier had taken time out of his own schedule to make this grand gesture. He'd succeeded not only in making her feel foolish for misjudging his mentees, but also in reminding her of what a good heart he had. All this time, she'd been insisting that they only see each other on a casual basis. Now, she was starting to think of him in a much more serious way. Maybe Xavier was too good a man to date casually.

Maybe I should give in.

Maya entered then, the door swinging shut behind her. "Hey, Imani. Feeling any better today?"

Drawn out of her thoughts, she smiled. "A little. Xavier brought some of the kids from the youth center over to help with the cleanup."

"Great. That must be their passenger van in the parking lot. It's so sweet of him to do that. Don't you think?" Maya traipsed over to the reception desk, resting her elbows on the marble top.

Imani nodded her head. "Yes, it is."

Maya said nothing but looked down at her with an "I told you so" expression.

Pursing her lips, Imani groaned. "Don't start with me, Maya. Just go in the hall and help them out."

"What do you need me to do?"

"Make sure all the paperwork they find is put in one place, so we can sort it later. Whoever did this got into some of my notes and patient files. That stuff is scattered all over the place."

"Got it." Maya backed up, gestured to her light-blue sweat suit. "I came ready to work and I'm going to. But you need to get your head outta your butt and give that brother some play. He's a good one, and you know it."

Imani rolled her eyes. "Bye, Maya."

Her cousin chuckled as she walked around the desk and into the hallway. "Whatever, girl. You know I'm right."

She knew Maya had spoken the truth; Xavier had always been a good guy. His generosity and caring spirit made it hard for her to keep pushing him away, especially after the gesture he'd made showing up there to help today. His good guy ways were precisely the problem when it came to becoming involved with him. Xavier was far too good for her; Imani knew that, but he didn't.

Seeing no use in dwelling on that now, she drew a deep, cleansing breath. She sat back in the chair, feeling some of the tension leave her body. With Maya and Xavier supervising the kids, she could take a moment to get her bearings after what had been a hectic twenty-four hours.

Chapter 9

XAVIER LOOKED ACROSS THE TABLE AT HIS PARENTS, FEELING the smile spread across his face. He'd brought them to their favorite restaurant, McPhee's Steak House, to celebrate their fortieth wedding anniversary. To his mind, such a milestone warranted a party. Edwin and Carol Whitted, in keeping with their simple, laid-back personalities, had requested the quiet dinner instead of a big gathering. So here they were. As an only child, Xavier did his best to honor his parents' wishes.

"Thanks again for bringing us, Son." Edwin raised his wineglass toward Xavier. "It's been a while since we've come here."

"You're welcome, Dad. I'm glad to do it. After all, this is a pretty big anniversary."

Xavier felt his smile widen in response to their banter. His father was a tall, broad-shouldered man. He kept his dark hair and his mustache trimmed close. Both were touched with shades of gray on the verge of turning white.

His mother, Carol, was tall as well, standing mere inches shorter than her husband of four decades.

Xavier admired the love and genuine affection his parents shared. Carol's eyes still lit up when Edwin paid her a compliment, and they still held hands most of the time. Theirs was the kind of love Xavier aspired to, and more than anything, he wanted to share that love with Imani.

"How long has it been since the last time we came here, baby?" Edwin's question, directed at his wife, broke the silence that had fallen over the table.

"Oh Lord, I don't know. I guess it's been a year or more." Carol sipped from her glass of Cabernet.

Xavier popped one of the soft, buttery yeast rolls into his mouth to soothe his rumbling stomach. The rich scents of roasting meat, herbs, and spices permeated the air, making him wish the waiter would show up with their meal.

"Xavier, I saw in the paper that Imani's clinic was broken into." Carol's hazel eyes displayed her concern. "Is she all right? I know you've been over there to see about her."

Xavier washed down the roll with a swallow of water. "Yes, I've been over there. She's fine. She wasn't there when the break-in happened."

"That's good to hear," Edwin remarked. "It's a shame what society is coming to these days. Folks just don't respect other people's property and hard work."

With a solemn nod, Xavier agreed. His father had owned a small tailor shop, Whitted's, for more than forty-five years. Xavier knew Edwin felt a sense of kinship with other small business owners, especially those of color.

Carol clasped her hands, rested them on the white-clothed tabletop. "Is there anything she needs? Maybe I can have some of my students come over to help her with cleanup in exchange for some extra credit." Carol taught English at Saint Augustine's University, located two blocks from the family home in the Historic Oakwood neighborhood.

Xavier smiled. "I beat you to it, Mama. I already took some of the kids from Revels over there a couple of days ago."

Edwin, looking pleased, asked, "How did things go?"

"I think they went very well. It took us about five hours, but we got everything back in its rightful place. Once Imani's insurance claims are settled, I think she'll be back on solid ground and ready to reopen."

Carol reached over to squeeze her son's shoulder. "I'm proud of you, Xavier. That was awfully sweet of you, and I am sure Imani appreciated it."

Xavier thought about telling his parents that he'd been partly motivated by the opportunity to serve her up a large slice of humble pie, but he decided against it. He'd done a good deed and his parents were proud of him. He saw no reason they should know Imani had slandered his kids.

"Good job, Son. And how do you think this is going to affect your quest to win her heart again?" Edwin asked, his eyes locked on his son's face.

Xavier stared back at his father, trying to remember if he'd mentioned that to his parents. "Did I tell you that?"

A chuckle left his mother's mouth. "Baby, you didn't have to tell us. Ever since you ran into her at that wedding, that's all you've been talking about. Imani this, and Imani that."

Leaning back in his chair, Edwin folded his arms over his chest. "Your mother's right. It's plain as day that you want to rekindle what you had with her back in the day."

Xavier shook his head at how transparent he'd been. Then again, his parents had always been very perceptive when it came to him. He could remember many times during his childhood and formative years when he'd been stopped from doing something wrong before he even had a chance to get his little plot off the ground. Since they were talking about Imani, one memory in particular stood out in his mind: the night he'd lost his virginity. He'd come home that night on time, not even a minute past his curfew. Still, the moment he'd shut the door behind him, he'd made eye contact with his father. Edwin, reclining on the couch with his pipe, had held his son's gaze for at least a full minute. Then, he'd given Xavier a slow, solemn nod, as if he somehow knew that his son had just taken that major step toward manhood.

Xavier was snapped out of his memories and back to the present by the sound of his father's voice.

"She's in your heart, Xavier, and we both know why. When a woman is in your blood, you don't really have a choice but to give in to it." Edwin punctuated his words by reaching over to place a kiss on his wife's cheek.

Xavier felt his brow furrow. Had they both been thinking back on that fateful night at the same time? Whatever the case, his parents were right again.

"I'm not trying to embarrass you, but she's been a part of you ever since that night. You know the night I'm talking about."

Xavier shook his head, amazed. "Dad, don't."

Edwin waved him off. "I'm not going to put your business out in the streets, but you know what I'm talking about. Your mother and I didn't hassle you about it because you were old enough to make your own decisions about that sort of thing."

Carol interjected, "And it didn't hurt that we liked Imani. We knew she was a good girl and that the two of you fit together."

Xavier let his parents' words sink in. Their perceptiveness seemed unending, at least when it came to their only child. He recalled the way they'd raised him to be independent, chivalrous, respectful, and kind. Edwin and Carol had given him a levelheaded talk about the birds and bees and seemed more concerned with him being safe than with holding him to some parental fantasy of purity. Looking back, he realized he had a great appreciation for their methods. They'd provided a guiding hand and had his best interests at heart without making demands on his autonomy as a young man. He surmised that was why he had such a close relationship with them even in adulthood.

Clearing his throat, Xavier announced, "You're right, but I'm sure you already knew that. I can't let go of what we had or of what our future together could be."

Carol squeezed his forearm. "Then don't let go, baby. If you really love her, you have to go after her."

"I have been going after her—dates, the whole nine." Xavier felt his frustration rising as he spoke about his efforts. "I know she still has feelings for me. I can feel it. But she keeps pushing me away and I don't know why."

"Sounds like she's dealing with something, something on the inside." Carol placed a hand over her heart. "She's got to heal herself before she can accept your love."

Edwin nodded his agreement. "Listen to your mama.

She knows what she's talking about. Keep doing what you're doing, but give her time. She'll come around."

As he looked between the only two people he loved more than Imani, he sincerely hoped they were right.

The waiter strolled up bearing two large trays laden with steaks, lobster tails, and cracked crab.

Xavier watched as his plate and all the accompaniments were set before him. When the waiter left, the three of them joined hands to bless the meal.

As Edwin gave the prayer, Xavier added his own supplication that Imani could find peace, so that she could accept all the love he had waiting for her.

Standing by her coffeemaker, Imani yawned as she waited for her morning caffeine to be dispensed. The open shade at her kitchen window allowed warm sunlight to pour in, the glow dappling her floor tiles. The rich scent of her favorite dark roast coffee emanated from the machine, rising with the steam as the hot beverage filled her mug.

She picked up her mug, inhaled the scent, and sighed. Once she'd doctored the coffee up with some sugar and a hint of milk, she took it to her small table and sat down.

It was just after seven, and on a weekend morning, there was no good reason she should be up. But ever since the break-in at her practice several days prior, she'd been restless and on edge. When she'd cracked her eyes open around dawn this morning, she'd tried to go back to sleep. After a good forty-five minutes spent staring at the ceiling, she'd given up and gotten out of bed to seek her coffee.

She'd just swallowed her first wonderfully warm sip when a banging on her front door startled her. Setting down her mug, she shuffled her slipper-clad feet in the direction of the sound.

Checking the peephole, she pursed her lips when she saw Maya standing there, fully dressed and looking as perky as ever.

She opened the door for her cousin. "Maya, what are you doing here?"

Maya slid past her and into the house, closing the door behind her. "Good morning, sunshine. I came to get you out of this house."

Imani looked down at her cotton pajama top and pants, printed with tubes of lipsticks in various shades, and the pink bunny slippers on her feet. Looking back up at her cousin, she frowned. "Do I look like I want to get out of the house?"

Maya snickered. "No. I could tell you what you actually look like, but I'm guessing you don't want to hear it."

She shook her head. "No, Maya, I don't."

By now, Maya was moving into the kitchen. Imani followed her long enough to sit back down to her coffee.

Maya, standing by the counter, spun the carousel holding the individual pods for the coffeemaker. "Ooh, mocha."

Imani sipped from her own mug. "Go ahead, Maya. Help yourself."

"Thank you, Cousin." Maya slipped the pod into the machine, then took a clean mug from the cabinet above the counter. Once her drink was brewed and in her hand, Maya took a seat next to Imani at the table.

"I know you've been superstressed since the break-in, so I think you need a little getaway to take your mind off things." Maya puckered her lips, blowing away some of the steam rising from her cup.

Imani sighed. "And do I have any say in this, or have you already decided?"

Maya shrugged. "I told Aunt Alma I was taking you to the beach today. She liked the idea, so..."

Another deep sigh escaped Imani's lips as she realized she didn't have a choice. Her mother would no doubt have plenty of questions for her if she didn't go on this little excursion with her cousin. "Let me finish my coffee and I'll get dressed. How long are we staying?"

Maya patted her on the back. "That's the spirit. And it's just a day trip, so you only have to bring what you'll need for the day."

"What did you bring?"

Maya tapped her index finger on her chin as she spoke. "A magazine, a book I've been trying to finish, some snacks, and a cooler full of drinks."

Imani looked at her cousin over her coffee cup, brow hitched. "What kind of drinks?"

"Water and those little travel-size bottles of chardonnay."

"Wine? Girl, why didn't you say so?" Imani finished up the last bit of her coffee and got up, with the sounds of Maya's laughter following her as she went to her room to change. She decided on a pair of white jeans and a long-sleeved black T. Pulling on a pair of black knee-high boots, she brushed her hair into a low ponytail. She tossed a couple of magazines, a book, and a few

BACK TO YOUR LOVE

other odds and ends into a large tote bag, then she met Maya by the door.

Maya, who'd worn a pair of black jeans with a Run DMC sweatshirt and sneakers, looked her over. "You're wearing boots to the beach?"

"Yeah. It's October, and I don't want to be shaking that cold, wet sand out of my shoes like you're going to be doing." Imani giggled while gently jabbing Maya with her elbow.

Maya jabbed her right back. "I brought a pair of sandals, so it's all good." With the house secured, they both climbed into Maya's small sedan and hit the road.

As her cousin drove, Imani could feel the sleep she'd missed coming back to find her.

Maya shook her awake once she'd parked the car at the boardwalk at Carolina Beach.

Coming awake, Imani rubbed her eyes. "We're here already?"

Maya snorted a laugh. "Yeah, finally. I've been listening to you snore for the last two and a half hours."

"Sorry." Imani yawned on the heels of her sheepish apology. She climbed out of the car and she and Maya headed for the beach.

The blue sky and bright sun belied the chill in the air, as temperatures hovered around fifty-five degrees. They picked a spot a good distance away from the water's edge, where Maya laid out a large blanket. Soon, Imani was comfortably seated, wrapped in the throw she'd brought from home, with her book in her lap.

Before she dove into the novel she'd been trying to finish for months, she looked over at Maya. "You mean you're not going to talk my ear off?"

Maya, who lay on her stomach with her face in the pages of a fashion magazine, shook her head. "Nope. I brought you out here to relax, so relax."

For the first time that day, Imani felt a real smile touch her lips. She took out her bookmark and let herself get swept back into the mythical world of her fantasy novel.

She'd breezed through three chapters and several changes in position on the blanket when her phone vibrated against her hip. She flipped the book over, slid her phone out of her jeans pocket, and answered it. "Hello?"

"Hello, I'm trying to reach Dr. Grant." The male voice on the line sounded vaguely familiar.

"This is she."

"Hi, Dr. Grant. This is Detective Clark with the Raleigh Police Department. I've got some information regarding your case."

Hearing that, Imani bolted to an upright position. "Okay, what do you have for me, Detective?"

"We've received several tips, in addition to the evidence we gathered on the scene, that point to the break-in being perpetrated by one or more youths with a connection to H. R. Revels Youth Center. My partner and I will be going by the center on Monday to question a few of them."

It disappointed her to hear that, because she knew how highly Xavier regarded the kids he mentored at the center. "How sure are you?"

"Very. Now it's just a matter of weeding out the guilty parties, which we hope to do without much adverse effect on the center or the kids there who weren't involved."

"I understand. Is there anything else I need to do?" Imani noticed that Maya had stopped reading her magazine and was looking straight at her. Imani guessed her demeanor must have given away the serious nature of the phone call.

"You'll have to decide how you want to pursue the case once we've identified the culprits. It will be up to you whether you want to press charges, so think about it."

"I will." She didn't know what else to say to that.

"All right. Thank you for your time, Dr. Grant. I'll reach out to you again early in the week."

When Imani disconnected the call, Maya was still staring at her.

"What was that all about?" Maya's questioning eyes were wide.

"It was the police. They're almost positive that some of the kids from Xavier's center were involved in the break-in. They're going over there Monday to question people."

Maya frowned, shaking her head. "That's unfortunate. I can't imagine it was any of the kids who came to help with the cleaning. They were all very helpful and well-mannered."

"They were." Imani had to agree with her cousin's assessment of the group. Still, she had no idea how many other kids frequented the center or what any of the rest of them were like. This whole situation was unfortunate for everyone involved.

"I wonder if they've notified Xavier." Maya tapped her chin, her gaze drifting out over the blue-gray waters of the Atlantic.

"Probably. I don't think they can just show up unannounced for something like this." Imani wished Maya hadn't mentioned Xavier. Every time someone spoke his name, she felt her heart contract in her chest. The feelings she'd had for him all those years ago still lingered inside of her. She wanted to push them aside, to tuck them away until she felt ready to face them.

Xavier was a good guy. He worked hard at his center and at doing other things to improve the community. Now that he was in the running for the city council seat, he finally had a real shot at getting into a position of power. Imani didn't doubt for a second that he'd be a good steward for the city and do his best to effect positive change.

With a secret like the one she harbored, she knew that getting serious with him was out of the question. Even though her feelings for him were intensifying, she couldn't stand the thought that she might be a detriment to his political career. The city shouldn't lose out on a truly great leader just because she lacked self-control.

But the passion they'd shared last weekend had rekindled the sparks of romance—sparks she'd thought had been doused by time and distance. Every moment she spent with him, she could feel those old feelings returning. Resisting him had always been difficult, but after his last gesture of helping with the cleanup at her practice, it was next to impossible.

"You never get over your first love," Maya voiced sagely, as if reading her thoughts.

Imani closed her eyes, shutting out the bright sunlight and the crashing waves that smacked against the beige sands. The sounds of the water and the calling gulls overhead, as well as the scent of salt in the air, stayed with her.

She had to find a way to get over Xavier before things got any more complicated. He thought he loved her, but he didn't really know her, not the way he thought he did.

"Maya, I never told him what happened to me in Atlanta. He doesn't know because I can't bear to tell him." She said the words with her eyes still shut, not wanting to see her cousin's expression. "And after last weekend…"

Maya's brow hitched. "What happened last weekend?"

She hesitated. "We, uh… Well, you know…" She let her expression tell the tale.

"Y'all got busy!" Maya clapped her hands on each syllable to emphasize her words.

She nodded, letting the warmth of the memories take over for a moment. "It was amazing. He was amazing. And I just can't stand to ruin it."

Maya's voice rang clear as she answered, "You're going to have to unburden yourself one day, Imani. If he's going to be the man in your life, he needs to know."

She knew Maya was right. One day, Xavier would know everything.

But for now, she wanted to put that day off for as long as she could.

"Just be honest with him, Imani." Maya's eyes held sympathy. "Let the truth set you free, girl."

Imani shook her head. "I can't. I mean, with the gag order and everything, my hands are tied on saying too much. What if he doesn't believe me? I'll have ruined our friendship for sure. And you know this can't go beyond that because when the press digs it up, it will destroy his political career. I can't do that to him, Maya. I just can't."

"So you admit you want this, that you want him in your life?"

She sighed. "Of course I do. But I just don't see a way this can work out. I was terrified when Cassidy showed up in my office. What if they sent her, Maya? What if they're out to get me?"

Maya got up from her spot and joined Imani on the blanket, folding her arms around her. "Imani, what happened wasn't your fault. You've got to stop doing this to yourself."

Tears began to spill down Imani's cheeks as she laid her head on Maya's shoulder. "Xavier has been the one bright spot in my life. How can I pull him into my mess and ruin things for him?"

Maya squeezed her even tighter. "It's not a mess. The people who told you that were assholes, caught up in victim shaming and vitriol. Don't let this rule you anymore, Imani."

Sniffling, Imani closed her eyes against the painful memories. "I'll try."

Maya grabbed her shoulders, made her look her in the eye. "You can do this."

A teary-eyed Imani nodded. "I love you, Maya."

"I love you, too, girl. Now get yourself together before you have me out here crying," she teased.

The two of them shared a laugh before settling back in to enjoy the day together.

—⁓—

Despite repeated attempts to calm his nerves, Xavier found himself pacing the floor of the office at Revels. Around him, the center bustled with the noise and activity typical of any autumn Monday. But something very atypical was about to take place in about thirty minutes, when detectives from RPD would show up to question several of his mentees.

One of the kids scheduled to be questioned was Trent. When Xavier had called Trent's mother, Stacy, she'd been stoic as ever as she promised to accompany her son to the center at the appointed time. Despite her manner, Xavier had detected the sadness and frustration in her voice.

By the time Xavier escorted the detectives, parents, and the small group of kids upstairs to one of the vacant classrooms, he'd managed to tamp down his agitation to a degree. Both the detectives were white men and over forty if Xavier's guess was correct. In a situation like this, he needed to set a good example for the kids in how to handle stress. Aside from that, he knew better than to appear hostile or otherwise suspicious around police officers. As a black male growing up in the South, he'd dealt with that reality his entire life.

In the hallway, Xavier spoke briefly with the detectives. "You can conduct your interviews in this room. I'll wait with the other kids and parents in the classroom next door."

One of the stern-faced detectives gave Xavier a stiff nod of acknowledgment. The other detective said, "Thanks."

Ignoring the prickling discomfort that ran down his back, Xavier took the parents and kids into an adjacent classroom. The room was used as a study hall for the center's patrons and had the traditional classroom setup. Everyone took a seat, with Xavier at the big desk in the front of the room and the others sitting in the smaller desks positioned around the space. Xavier kept to his seat, remaining quiet as the two detectives called the kids into the other classroom one by one. Each young man went in with only his parents, if any were present. Of the five boys that had been chosen for questioning, four guardians had made themselves available. One of the boys, sixteen-year-old Peter "P-Dawg" Goings, had no guardian show up to accompany him. Xavier had tried to reach out to someone in the household but had had all his calls go unanswered. Three of the boys were interviewed in succession, one with his mother, another with his father, and the last with his grandmother.

As Trent and Stacy went in with the detectives, Xavier held his breath. He could see the budding intelligence and immense promise in Trent, and he hoped and prayed the boy hadn't been involved in the break-in. To keep himself from pacing the hallway, Xavier returned to the chair behind the big oak desk and planted himself on the seat.

Only Xavier and Peter remained in the study hall room, which meant Peter would be interviewed last. Peter stood by one of the old, wood-framed windows, gazing out at the gray evening sky. Xavier sensed the young man wasn't feeling particularly chatty, so he kept quiet. He knew it wasn't his job to press the kids. All he could do was make himself available to them, so they could talk to him on their own terms.

In the silence, he listened to see if he could hear any of what was transpiring in the next room. The old building, with its brick construction, had withstood over fifty years of use. That made the place great for longevity but terrible for eavesdropping. He could only make out a few muffled sounds. He thought he heard Stacy crying but couldn't tell for certain.

When the interview finally concluded, Xavier had his answer as he viewed Stacy's tearstained face.

He stepped into the hallway, and when he saw the handcuffs binding Trent's wrists behind his back, his heart sank. "What's going on?"

The more talkative of the two detectives answered. "We're taking young Mr. Holmes in for additional questioning after we've spoken to Mr. Goings."

Xavier looked to Trent, saw the boy's stoic manner. He had to know what was going on. "Trent, what did you tell them?"

Stacy answered for her son. "He confessed to the break-in. They know he didn't do it alone, but he won't say who else was with him." The bewilderment and sadness she felt were evident in her tone.

Xavier shot a look at Trent. "Is that true? Why would you do that?"

Trent's frowning lips parted. "I ain't no snitch, man."

Touching his fingertips to his temple, Xavier took a deep breath. "Are you telling me you'd rather do time than be a snitch?"

Trent said nothing—just cast his eyes downward.

The saltier detective cleared his throat, looked toward Peter. "Do you have anything to say, Mr. Goings?"

Barely turning his attention from the window, Peter groused, "No."

Stacy demanded, "Peter! If you were a part of this, you'd better speak up. My son shouldn't have to go down for this alone."

Peter shrugged, his eyes downcast. "Whatever, man."

Xavier bristled, turned serious eyes on the detective. "Why don't you just level with me? I'm sure you've probably got fingerprints and who knows what else on the culprits."

By now, the detective was crossing the room toward Peter. "You're right. We just wanted to see if young Mr. Goings would admit his involvement."

Xavier could see it all now. There was always a method to this sort of thing. It became clear why Trent and Peter had been interviewed last. The police already had what they needed to bring them in; this whole setup had likely been some sort of Scared Straight attempt at keeping the other boys on the straight and narrow. Xavier shook his head, folding his arms over his chest as he watched Peter get his own set of iron bracelets.

Peter cursed, rolled his eyes. "Damn, Trent! Now you got us both in trouble."

Trent, still standing there in handcuffs, responded with tears in his eyes. "P-Dawg, c'mon, man! I didn't say anything. I swear!"

Peter said nothing else, just let his jaw fall into a hard, defiant set as he was guided toward the corridor.

The detective leading Trent joined his partner. "We're going to have to continue this downtown."

"Oh, we're going to." Xavier had been trained all his life to de-escalate, but he wouldn't just give this guy the okeydokey. Not now, not when it came to his kids.

Xavier fell into step behind the detectives as they escorted the kids into the hallway, with the still weeping Stacy in tow. He couldn't remember the staircase ever seeming this narrow and confining before, and he attributed it to the mood of the moment. He worked his ass off to keep these kids out of trouble, to give them an alternative to getting caught up in the streets. This time, his efforts had proven inadequate.

As the somber procession reached the first floor, all activity stopped. Games were paused, conversations dropped off, and all eyes turned to watch Trent and Peter being led away in handcuffs, Trent's mother and Xavier on their tail.

In the parking lot, Trent and Peter were loaded into the back of a patrol car and closed in.

Stacy stepped forward. "I'm going with him. You're not taking my son anywhere without me."

"You can follow us in your car, ma'am." One of the detectives shut the rear doors of the squad car. As Stacy climbed into her older model sedan, Xavier approached the window. He made a gesture with his hands, forming it into a phone to let her know to call him. She nodded and followed the patrol car as it drove away.

Xavier stood there in the cold until the taillights of Stacy's car faded from sight. Then he grabbed his phone from his pants pocket, dialing Tyrone's number.

When his friend and campaign manager answered the call, Xavier said, "I'm going to need some legal advice."

Tyrone laughed. "What have you done?"

Xavier kept his hard gaze fixed on the horizon, wishing things could have been different this time. "It's not for me. It's for two of the kids at the center."

Tyrone's tone turned serious. "Then let's talk."

Xavier gave him a brief summary of the day's events. When he'd finished, he asked, "What can we do?"

Tyrone cleared his throat. "Because of their ages,

the boys will land in the North Carolina juvenile justice system. That's not really my area of expertise, but I've got a friend who can help us out."

"At a low rate, I hope." Xavier knew Stacy didn't have the resources to pay for her son's defense, and no one from Peter's household had even bothered to show up. He'd offer up some of his personal funds without hesitation, if it came down to that.

"Don't worry. We'll work something out." Tyrone was already on his computer, typing, the sound of the keystrokes being picked up by his phone's speaker.

"Keep me posted, man. I'm headed downtown to see what I can find out."

"I'll call you back as soon as I get in contact with him."

"Cool. Thanks, Ty."

"Hey, man. I got your back. Thetas stick together." Tyrone's smile registered in the tone of his voice.

Taking a deep breath, Xavier disconnected the call. When he exhaled, creating a cloud of steam on the cold night air, he fished his keys out of his pocket. Then he ducked his head inside the door to let Tori know he was leaving.

With a promise to keep the center staff updated on what was happening with the boys, he climbed into his truck and drove off.

Chapter 10

"MOM, I'LL HAVE TO CALL YOU BACK. THE CLINIC IS slammed today."

Speed-walking down the corridor of Grant Dermatology, Imani tried again to get her mother to disengage. For some reason, Alma was feeling particularly chatty today.

"Okay, baby. I'll tell you the rest of the story later." Alma's tone held a hint of humor.

"Can't wait. Love you. Bye, Mama." Balancing the phone to her ear with her shoulder, Imani shifted the patient files in her hands, so she could open the door to her office.

"Bye, sweetie."

Alma disconnected the call as Imani slid into her office, kicking the door shut behind her. Setting the patient files down on top of her new solid mahogany desk, she checked the wall clock. Ten twenty a.m. She grimaced at the thought of the jam-packed two hours standing between her and a lunch break. As things stood, she had about ten minutes to catch her breath before her next patient came in.

Next to the wall clock hung her nature scenes calendar, and glancing at it reminded her again of today's date: October 20. Today would have been her father's sixty-eighth birthday. Today, more than any other day of the year, she missed her father and wished those young men who'd robbed his hardware store on that fateful day had made a different choice, a better choice.

She drew in a deep breath and sank into her desk chair. Grabbing a tissue from the box atop her desk, she dabbed at her damp brow. All the running she'd been doing this morning had her feeling pretty warm—almost warm enough to ditch her medical coat. The professional code dictated she keep the coat on, sweltering though it might be. To give herself a little relief, she opened the buttons securing the front and flapped the open halves back and forth, generating a breeze. When she felt a bit cooler, she let her head drop back against the headrest and closed her eyes.

The blissful calm lasted only a minute or two before a knock on her office door snapped her back to reality.

Unable to keep the weariness out of her voice, she called, "Come in."

Maya stuck her head in the door. "There's a Miss Cates here to see you."

Confusion knit her brow. "My next appointment is with Mrs. Neilson."

"I know. Miss Cates doesn't have an appointment. She just wants to speak with you. She promised to be brief."

Imani didn't recognize the woman's name and had no idea what she might want, since she wasn't a current patient. "Can it wait? We're swamped today."

"I know that, too, and she says it can't wait."

"And you're sure she's not a pharmaceutical rep or somebody trying to sell me something?"

Maya nodded and watched her, waiting for a response.

Imani looked at the wall clock again. "Okay, but I'll need her to say what she has to say in five minutes or less."

Maya disappeared, then returned with a petite

brown-skinned woman wearing a black sweatshirt and dark denim jeans.

When Imani invited the woman into the office, she took slow steps, as if she were nervous or afraid.

"Hello, Ms. Cates. What can I do for you?"

The woman swallowed. "Hello, my name is Stacy Cates. My son, Trent, was arrested for being involved in the break-in here last week."

Imani felt her brow furrow. She'd heard from the police about Trent and about their knowledge that he hadn't acted alone. "Yes, the police mentioned him to me. Has he turned in any of his accomplices?"

Stacy's face tightened, as if she took offense. "Dr. Grant, my son was not the ringleader. He did something foolish, yes, but I know this wasn't his idea."

Imani said nothing, instead observing the woman's body language. The tension in her stance was noticeable.

Stacy spoke again. "Anyway, no, Trent hasn't given any names because he thinks he's being a good friend by not 'snitching.' I've tried to explain to him how silly that is, but at his age, he's hardheaded."

"I see." Looking across at the woman, Imani sensed her discomfort.

Stacy swallowed again, then spoke. "I came to apologize personally for Trent's foolish actions."

Imani laced her fingertips together. "I appreciate that, Ms. Cates. And while I accept your apology, I'd really like to hear it from your son."

Stacy nodded, looked away. "I understand that, and that's definitely going to happen. Please remember that Trent is covering for somebody. He's not the main one."

"That may be so, but he did confess. Hopefully, he'll

tell the truth about who else was involved, or the other parties will come forward."

"I'm hopeful about that, Doctor." She wrung her hands. "I don't want to take up much more of your time. I just came by to apologize."

Imani stood from her desk, knowing her time until her next appointment was running short. "Again, I appreciate you doing that. Now, if you'll excuse me, I have a patient coming in. Good-bye, Ms. Cates."

Taking the hint, Stacy pulled open the office door and started to leave. She stopped, turned toward Imani. "Look, my Trent is a good boy. Smart, too. I don't know what possessed him to act this way." She paused, the sadness showing plainly on her face. "Please. Just know that this isn't like him."

Imani nodded.

Stacy turned and walked out.

Imani stood in her office alone for a few minutes, trying to get her bearings before she saw Mrs. Neilson. Her feelings on the situation with Trent were mixed. While she understood his mother's fierce urge to protect him, she also felt he should face some kind of punishment for his actions. She shook her head; she didn't have time to think about it now.

Instead, she got Mrs. Neilson's patient file, tucked it under her arm, and walked down the hall to exam room two.

The rest of the day continued in a blur of appointments, paperwork, and the constant ringing of the office telephone. By the time Imani shut the overhead lights off, it was nearly six thirty, well past the practice's five o'clock closing time. Darkness had begun to fall.

Maya, closing up her station behind reception, pulled on her fleece jacket and matching hat. "Finally. The nurses left an hour ago."

"I just had a few loose ends to tie up. Now I want to get over to the cemetery before it gets too dark out there." Imani thought of the silk arrangement she'd purchased the previous day to place on her father's grave. It was made up of carnations, roses, and poppies in varying shades of blue, which had been his favorite color.

Maya offered her a wistful smile. "I got Uncle Richard flowers, too. Would you mind taking it over there?" Maya pulled a small wreath of blue blooms out from beneath the reception desk.

Imani took it, shaking her head. "You know, you could just come with me."

Maya recoiled. "You know I don't do graveyards. Too depressing. If I go with you, we'll both end up sitting on the grass in tears."

Imani didn't press the issue with her cousin. Maya had been that way their whole life; she'd never attended any graveside event or visited a graveyard, no matter whom the deceased was.

"Are you going to be okay out there by yourself?"

Imani nodded. "I'll be fine. I never stay too long."

Maya surprised her then by grabbing her and pulling her in for a tight hug. Imani shifted the wreath to one hand to keep it from being crushed, but accepted the hug gratefully.

When they separated, they got the rest of their things and left. Once the place was locked up and secured, Imani and Maya went to their separate vehicles and parted ways.

The drive to the cemetery lasted less than ten minutes. While Imani didn't enjoy working late, at least it meant she didn't have to deal with the height of the city's rush hour as she made her way to pay her respects.

Once she'd parked her car along the street bordering the cemetery, she got out. She noted the relative quiet as she carried the two floral arrangements through the gate and up the rise, toward the grave. There were the distant sounds of traffic and horns honking, but not much else to impinge on the solitude. She could hear her footsteps crunching over the dry autumn grass beneath her boots.

Arriving at the top of the hill, she knelt next to her father's headstone. With gentle, loving hands, she placed the two arrangements atop the grave, arranging them in a way she found attractive.

"Happy birthday, Daddy." She said the words aloud, as she often did when she visited the grave. "One's from me and the other's from Maya."

She leaned on the granite marker, letting the side of her forehead rest on the cool surface. Her fingertips played over the engraved letters of her father's name and the dates that represented the beginning and end of his life. The old, familiar pain rose again. Tears filled her eyes, blurring her vision, and she closed them. Rather than release the pent-up sob, she inhaled deeply and hummed the tune of the old hymn "Because He Lives." The song had been his favorite.

"Imani." A deep, silky voice called her name, cutting through her pain to reach her ears.

She opened her eyes, raised her gaze to see the face of a tall figure standing before her. The scent of his cologne, rich and masculine, touched her nostrils.

He squatted next to her, his hand reaching out to touch her shoulder.

Looking into her eyes, he asked, "Imani, are you okay?" His voice conveyed much caring and concern.

Through the tears, she managed to ask, "What are you doing here, Xavier?"

———

Xavier fought the urge to pull Imani into his arms, not wanting to press her. Finding her in tears this way made his chest constrict; it physically hurt him to see her weep.

Her watery eyes searched his face, waiting. She wanted an answer to the question she'd asked, he realized.

So he gave it. "I'm here for the same reason you are. I brought flowers for Mr. Grant." He gestured to the small bundle of violets in his hand.

She blinked a few times, her eyes wide. "You remembered my father's birthday?"

"Of course I did. I've been here a couple of times over the years. Seeing you again at the wedding brought it back to the front of my mind."

She looked down at his offering now, as if seeing it for the first time. "That's really sweet, Xavier."

He nodded. Then he placed his flowers atop the grave.

She watched him in solemn silence; he could feel her eyes on him.

Reaching into the inner pocket of his sport coat, he extracted a handkerchief.

She reached for it, but he held it back.

Instead of handing her the linen handkerchief, he dried the tears clinging to her face. He used as gentle a touch as her delicate skin and fragile mood demanded. By the time he was done, she seemed to have calmed somewhat.

"Thank you." Her words were so soft he might not have heard her if they weren't in such a peaceful place.

"You're welcome." He tucked the handkerchief away again, still longing to hold her. He would not do it, though, unless she asked for his comfort. She mourned her father even after all this time, and he respected that. He would never want her to think he was coming on to her or pressuring her in any way, especially at a time and place like this.

After a few silent moments, she got to her feet, brushing away the bits of soil and brown grass clinging to her slacks.

He followed her lead, standing to his full height.

She raised her chin and looked into his eyes. "I could use a cup of tea. Would you join me?"

Shocked but pleased by her invitation, he nodded. "Yes. Just name the place."

She started walking down the hill, away from the grave. "Do you know Cathy's Coffee, right there on Martin Street?"

"Yeah, I know the place. It's only about five minutes from here." He shortened his usually large stride in order to keep pace with her as they strolled toward the curb where their vehicles were parked.

"Good." She sniffled, drew her coat closer around her body.

He waited near his SUV until she'd climbed into her sedan. Getting into his truck, he started the engine and swung out of his parking space.

Within twenty minutes, the two of them were tucked into an overstuffed sofa in the rear of Cathy's Coffee.

Imani sipped from a ceramic mug of peppermint tea, a sigh of pleasure escaping her lips. "Cathy's has the best peppermint tea in town. Even when I make it at home, it's never as good."

Drinking from his own mug of hot, spiced cider, he smiled. He enjoyed the feeling of having her body close to his. "Cider's not bad, either." He took another deep draw, relishing the sweetness of apples and the spicy kick of cinnamon that tickled his taste buds.

She scooted closer to him on the cushion, until the sides of their thighs touched. Her expression earnest, she said, "Thank you for coming here with me, Xavier. I know you probably have other things you need to be doing."

Sensing that she wouldn't mind, he draped his free arm loosely around her shoulder. "That's true, but there isn't anything else I'd rather be doing." And there wasn't. His campaign strategizing work would still be there tomorrow morning. Right now, she needed someone, and he felt honored to be able to be there for her.

"I'm still surprised that you remember Dad's birthday."

He couldn't help smiling at his memories of Richard Grant. "Mr. Grant was a good man, and probably the closest friend my dad ever had. I really looked up to him."

Her face brightened, and for the first time that night, a hint of a smile showed on her beautiful face. "Really? I remember that you three used to go fishing, but I never knew you thought of him so fondly."

"What you don't realize is that fishing is the ultimate in male bonding. I learned a lot on those trips, and because my dad was, well, my dad, I got plenty of advice from Richard."

She looked genuinely interested. "I didn't know any of this. I guess fishing is to men what shopping and manicures are to women."

He shrugged. "I guess. Your father had a big impact on me during my teenage years. I would talk to him when I felt weird about going to my own dad. I'll always be grateful to Richard."

Her head dropped to the side, resting on his shoulder. "I appreciate you telling me that."

"No problem. You may be an only child, but he helped raise a lot of the young men in the neighborhood. He's one of the folks who inspired me to do the work I do with the kids now."

Her smile widened. "Wow, Xavier. I'm really glad to hear that, and I think he would be very proud."

It relieved him that she didn't bring up the break-in or say anything negative about his center kids. Despite what Trent and Peter had done, he didn't want her to view all of them through a set of tired stereotypes of inner city youth.

"You're a good guy, Xavier. I really can't thank you enough for coming here with me and for sharing with me like you just did." She clasped his hand and gave it a brief squeeze.

The warmth of her touch radiated throughout his body. "You know how I feel about you, Imani. I'm always going to be here for you."

She tensed a bit at the mention of his feelings; he could feel it. Still, she didn't pull away from him, so maybe that meant he was making progress with her. Or maybe she just needed to be held right now, due to her vulnerable state. Either way, he would continue to hold her for as long as she allowed it.

The sounds of Dinah Washington's rich alto emanated from the sound system in the coffee shop. Other than the two baristas working the counter, Xavier and Imani were the only people in the place. Dinah's impassioned crooning, along with the dim lighting and the quiet, semiprivate atmosphere, began to have an effect on him.

He shifted around, so he could look into her eyes.

To his surprise, her soulful, dark eyes were there, waiting.

For a long moment, their gazes locked and held. He set his mug aside, then let the tips of his fingers graze her jawline.

She shivered at his touch but didn't back away. Instead, she eased closer to him, her head tilting ever so slightly upward.

He bent and let his lips brush against hers. At first, he kept it brief, in case she didn't want to take it there.

She remained receptive after the first quick brush of his lips, so he repeated it once more, then again.

She reached up, her hand coming to rest against the back of his neck, and pulled him in. At that point, he knew she wanted the same thing he did: to share a kiss worthy of the affection flowing between them.

He gathered her in and pressed his lips to hers, with full force this time. Her lips parted to accept his searching tongue, and he felt his whole body tingle when she released a soft moan into his mouth.

She let her hand fall from his neck and shifted a bit. Feeling her pulling away, he followed her cue and broke the seal of their lips.

When their gazes met, he could see the flush of

heat coloring her cheeks. Her eyes were pensive, unreadable.

He could sense that she'd become uncomfortable, or at least unsure of what she was doing. "I've kept you out late enough. Will you be all right getting home, or should I follow you?"

Seeming relieved, she shook her head. "No, I'll be okay. I'll send you a text when I get in."

He stood. "Sounds good. Look, if you need something or you just want to talk, give me a call."

She got up, setting the mug on the short table in front of the sofa. Slinging the shoulder strap of her purse on, she gave him an easy grin. "Thanks, Xavier. For everything."

He touched his brow in mock salute. "At your service."

She hurried toward the coffee shop door and tossed a hasty good-bye over her shoulder.

He waved and watched her disappear into the cool night.

Monday morning, an arrangement of white roses arrived at Grant Dermatology. It was followed by a second arrangement just after lunch. They continued to arrive daily, and by that Thursday, Imani had to admit she was taken by his persistence. Xavier was proving harder and harder to resist as the days went by. Add that to the fact that Maya was picking up on Imani's growing feelings for him, and it was almost too much to handle. Even now she was smiling to herself, though she knew it would be a bad idea to get in deeper with Xavier. She would never forgive herself if her past caused him any harm.

As Maya entered her office with yet another bouquet, she jumped up from behind her desk. "Maya, I told you we can't accept any more of these flowers. We're running out of places to put them." Even as she complained, a smile curved her lips.

Maya shook her head. "You know we can't just send them back. Look at them. Aren't they beautiful?" She admired the eighteen snow-white blooms and greenery in the crystal vase before setting them on the desk.

Imani sighed. "Yes, but this is a medical practice, not a greenhouse." The first few vases were now decorating the waiting area, but she had precious little room in her personal office. Xavier's gesture, while incredibly sweet, had left her with enough roses to build a parade float. She absentmindedly scratched her head with the tip of her pen, wondering where she could put this one.

"Look at you, over there, grinning." Maya pointed her index finger at her with mock accusation. "Just admit you like it. Every girl loves to get flowers."

Imani rolled her eyes, but the smile remained on her face. "Yes, of course I like the sentiment, and the flowers are beautiful. But if he keeps sending them, there won't be any room left for us." She chuckled as she imagined herself unlocking the door of the practice only to be taken out by a literal avalanche of snowy-white blooms.

"If you just give in to the man, he'd probably stop sending them." Maya's voice broke into her thoughts.

"I don't want to get into a relationship with him. I keep saying that, but no one is listening." She laid her forehead on her desk in defeat. "Not you, not Mom, and least of all Xavier."

"That's because the rest of us know y'all are meant to be together."

She looked up for a moment to say, "Maya, get out of my office." She intended to sound stern, but a look at her cousin's Cheshire-cat expression made her smile instead.

"I will, as soon as you admit that you have feelings for Xavier."

Imani pursed her lips. "Maya, don't start with me."

Maya folded her arms over her chest and leaned her shoulder against the doorframe. "I'm not going anywhere until you say it out loud. Tell the truth and shame the devil, girl."

Letting her head drop back, Imani blew out a breath. "Okay, okay, I admit it. I want Xavier. I want him bad."

"Hallelujah!" Maya threw her hands up. "She's seen the light, Lord. Now why don't you stop running from the man and let him catch you? I mean, look at what he did for you the other day, bringing the kids over to help with cleanup. And he must have spent about a grand on flowers this week alone."

A wistful smile spread over Imani's face. Her cousin was right. "I know, I know. One day, when the time is right, I promise I'll stop running. But for right now, I've gotta keep my sneakers laced up." She pointed at the corridor. "Now quit pestering me and go do some work, girl!"

With a giggle, her cousin did as she asked but left the flowers for her to deal with. Imani let her forehead rest on the coolness of the glass topping her desk again and sighed.

There were still five patients for her to see before she could go home for the evening, and she was already tired. The nights since the one she'd been out with Xavier had been rough on her. Falling asleep had been taking much longer than usual, and when she did sleep, he haunted her dreams like a specter. No matter how she tried to fight it, her body called out for Xavier's touch. Her soul craved the feeling of safety only he could provide. She hadn't been this sleep deprived since her father's death.

Imani smiled a bit at the memory of her father. Richard Grant had been a formidable man and a constant source of love and support for her. She knew she could always count on him for advice, a hug, or whatever else she needed.

Richard was so hardworking and determined, Imani had been convinced he'd go on forever.

Without the steady comfort of her father's presence, sometimes life seemed too much to bear. She knew that if he were still alive, she could count on him not to take sides or make judgments, but to give her sound advice that she could use. While everyone else seemed bent on pushing her and Xavier together, she knew her father would have looked at things with a more objective eye. Even if Richard thought she and Xavier belonged together, Imani knew he wouldn't push the issue. It just wasn't his way, and that was part of why she'd loved him so much. Her father had provided guidance but also trusted her judgment.

Raising her head, she stood behind her desk and stretched. Straightening her lab coat and the brown slacks and white blouse beneath it, she left the office to see her next patient. Even as she approached the open door of exam room three, she could smell the heady scent of expensive perfume. Surprised that anything could overpower the aroma of eight dozen roses scattered about the practice, she stepped inside the room. There, she found a short, wide woman with fair skin waiting for her. Auburn curls framed a face that was probably very lovely twenty years ago but now showed the ravages of stress and time. The woman's expensive-looking black suit and pumps were a stark contrast to her skin tone.

"Hello, Mrs. Givens." She greeted her patient with a cheery smile. "I'm Dr. Grant. You're here to talk about antiaging products?"

"Yes," the older woman agreed. "You see, my husband is in politics, and I'd like to keep my looks up, since I'm often on camera."

She nodded. "I see. So what are your main concerns?"

Mrs. Givens launched into a lengthy description of her wrinkles, sagging neck, and other complaints. Imani listened for key words in what she was saying, but the rest went underwater as she wondered what to do about Xavier. He'd brought so much joy into her life, and thoughts of him seemed to flood her mind with every breath.

"So, what would you recommend, Dr. Grant?"

Dragging herself back to reality, she gave the woman some information about the importance of daily skin care, weekly exfoliation, and professional facials. Then she continued, "There are a few creams containing retinols and some botanical ingredients that I could prescribe to you. These will take several weeks to work. Also, if you're seeking more noticeable results, you may want to consider visiting a cosmetic surgeon for injections."

She appeared to mull things over for a moment, then

said, "I think I'll do a little of both. Could you recommend someone?"

Producing a business card from a plastic holder on the exam room's small desk, she handed it to Mrs. Givens. "Rachel Turner was a classmate of mine at Meharry. I'm sure she can be of assistance to you."

Mrs. Givens expressed her thanks and, with her newly written prescriptions in hand, turned to leave. As she did, she dropped her purse.

"Let me help you with that." Leaning down, Imani picked up a few of the spilled contents of the bag, including a vinyl holder full of wallet-sized photos. The top photo depicted Mrs. Givens with a slightly taller, dark-skinned man with gray around the temples. The man's face was so familiar to her that she asked, "Is this your husband?"

"Yes, that's my husband. Councilman Aaron Givens. You've probably seen him on television." She beamed with pride as she accepted the handful of dropped items Imani offered. "We've been married twenty-six years." With a smile and wave, Mrs. Givens departed, along with the invisible cloud of musk fragrance surrounding her.

A stunned Imani remained on the small swivel stool she'd been perched on for a few long moments.

She had seen that man before, but it had not been on television. No, she'd seen him in person, wearing a dark suit similar to the one he'd been wearing in the photograph.

And thinking of the place where she'd met him made the bile rise in her throat.

It seemed the universe had presented her with another sign that her past would continue to haunt her.

Maybe Maya was right.

Maybe the time had come to tell Xavier the truth.

———⌇———

Xavier swung open the door to the youth center, sticking out his free hand. "Bryan. Thanks again for doing this for me, man."

Removing his dark sunglasses, Bryan entered the common area and let the door swing shut behind him. "Hey, no problem. We're brothers, right?" He tapped his index finger against the green-and-silver TDT tie tack he wore.

"That we are." Xavier glanced at his own TDT cuff links. "You're a little early, so let's get you set up before the kids get here. Want a soda or something?" He began walking toward the office, with Bryan following him.

"I'll take a bottle of water."

Xavier fetched two bottles from the mini fridge in the rear of the office, tossing one to Bryan. "So, are you ready to do this?"

"I don't know. Speaking in front of kids about my job isn't something I do often." He twisted the cap off his bottle and took a long swig of water.

Xavier smiled. Career Day was a quarterly occurrence at Revels Youth Center, and he expended a lot of effort in finding speakers who would expose the kids to a wide variety of career options. "I know. But trust me, you'll do fine. You know your business inside and out. I'm sure that'll come through in your talk."

Bryan adjusted his collar. "We'll see how it goes."

Hearing the front door open and the chatter and laughter of the first of the kids to arrive, Xavier slapped his friend on the back. "The kids are here. You're on, B."

With a smile, Bryan finished the bottle of water. "I'm ready, X."

The two men left the office, moving through the center's lower level until they returned to the common area. The arrangement of the space had been changed to allow everyone to sit and watch today's presentation. Most of the furniture had been moved, and the chairs had all been set up to face the wooden podium.

As the kids filed into the room, watched over by Tori and Xavier, they took up residence in the chairs. Bryan straightened his tie and took his place behind the podium, awaiting his cue to begin.

Xavier chose a seat near the back, next to Tori. With everyone in place, Xavier raised his hand toward Bryan, signaling to him.

"Good afternoon. My name is Bryan James. Mr. Whitted asked me to come and speak with you all about my work for your Career Day, and I'm happy to be here."

"How do you know Mr. Whitted?" The question came from a young man in the back.

"Xavier and I went to college together, and we're fraternity brothers." Bryan shifted his weight, resting his palms on the sides of the podium. "I work in the clothing industry. I am the CMO, or chief marketing officer, of Royal Textiles."

Xavier chuckled. When Bryan said he didn't usually speak to kids about his work, he hadn't been kidding. So far, he was coming off way too formal for this crowd. In order to get Bryan to relax, Xavier got up and walked to the front. He stood next to Bryan long enough to speak quietly into his ear. "Lighten up, dude. The kids aren't expecting Shakespeare."

Bryan nodded as Xavier walked back to his seat. "I want this to be an informal conversation. I didn't come here just to talk at you about the boring day-to-day details of my job. I'll give you the basics; then I'll open up to questions."

Xavier watched and listened as Bryan rattled off some of his responsibilities as an executive in his family's company. He also gave something of a motivational speech, encouraging the youngsters to pursue their goals relentlessly. The kids seemed to get a kick out of hearing about the famous designers that had their clothing manufactured by Royal Textiles, and the atmosphere in the room lightened significantly as Bryan ran down the list.

"Does anybody have questions for me?" Bryan's eyes scanned the room for raised hands. Seeing one, he pointed to the girl sitting on the second row. "Go ahead."

"So, are you rich or something? I mean, how much money do you make?" The girl sat forward in her chair, as if particularly interested in his answer.

Xavier noticed a lot of the kids' ears perk up at that question.

Bryan smiled. "I don't know if rich is the term, though I make a very good living. My salary is in the middle six figures, but I'm not pulling down Jay Z money or anything like that."

Laughter met that answer. Xavier laughed too, but he appreciated his friend's honesty. He didn't want the kids getting a false impression.

"Yo. I got a question," Corey, one of the boys, spoke as he raised his hand. "I'm not trying to be in your personal business, but I don't know about a lot of straight dudes in the fashion industry."

Xavier cut a serious look in the boy's direction and was about to tell him how rude the query was, but Bryan smiled, taking the question in stride. "You're right, young brother. There's not a lot of straight men in the industry, at least not in positions that have high visibility. I'm straight, though. I guess I'm out there blazing a trail." He shrugged.

More chuckles met that answer.

Xavier shook his head. There was never a dull moment when he was with his kids, and he'd just been reminded of that.

From behind the podium, Bryan spoke. "I don't normally do talks like this. But I really do want to encourage some of you to think about getting into the fashion and textiles industry. Right now, it's not very diverse, and that's especially true when you reach the executive level, where I'm at."

A hush fell over the room, and to Xavier, it looked as if some of the kids were considering what Bryan had just said.

Bryan spoke again, pointing out a girl on the front row. "Like you. What's your name?"

Quietly, she answered, "Shelly."

Bryan walked over from the podium to where she sat. "Stand up, Shelly. Turn around so your peers can see you."

Shelly did as she was asked.

"Now look at Shelly's shirt and bag. You made these, didn't you?" He gestured to the airbrushed, deconstructed T she wore and her multicolored handbag.

Shelly nodded. "Yeah. I painted the shirt, and the bag is made out of candy wrappers and stuff."

Bryan clapped his hands. "See what I'm talking about? This sister is talented. She's already got the natural skills she would need to thrive in my industry. How old are you, Shelly?"

"Fifteen." She blushed. "I'll be sixteen next month."

"Well, you're already showing a knack for design. And if it's okay with your parents, you're welcome to come and intern at Royal during the summer."

Shelly's eyes widened. "For real?"

"Yeah, for real." Bryan gestured to her chair. "I'll leave my card with you."

Xavier cheered. Not only had Bryan given a great talk, but he'd also related to the kids on a personal level and taken the time to point out Shelly's talent to her peers.

Bryan returned to the podium. "I'm done talking, unless you all have more questions. But remember what I said. There is no limit on the things you can do. Just follow your heart, capitalize on your talents, and never give up."

As Bryan walked away from the podium, the kids burst into a boisterous round of applause. Xavier met him at the front of the room, shaking his hand and giving him a manly half hug. "Thanks a lot for this, man."

Bryan grinned as he glanced at his watch. "I was happy to do it. Gotta get back to the office now. Make sure to give Shelly's parents my card."

Xavier smiled, grateful for his friend's willingness to help. "You were serious, weren't you?"

Bryan shrugged. "What can I say? She's got the chops." With a wave, he headed for the door.

Xavier shook his head as he watched him go. Of all his frat brothers, Bryan was the most business-minded, so he wasn't surprised that he was rushing back to work. Still, he really did appreciate what he'd done. He glanced at Shelly, who appeared to be looking at her handbag with new eyes.

Xavier had spoken to Shelly about her wearable art-work before, encouraging her to pursue it profession-ally. She'd always dismissed him, however, claiming that she only made the things she wanted that her parents couldn't afford to buy her. He could understand how that encouragement seemed far more valid when it came from a fashion industry executive.

Odds were, Bryan had just given her a brand-new perspective on who she was and what she could be.

And for that, Xavier would always be grateful to him.

Chapter 11

FRIDAY MORNING, THE NEXT BOUQUET OF ROSES ARRIVED, and they were not brought in by Maya or a deliveryman but by Xavier himself.

As he walked into her office, she straightened up in her chair and pushed a fallen lock of hair out of her face. "I hope that's the last vase of flowers you plan on sending here. I'm beginning to run out of space to house them." She laughed nervously, hoping he wouldn't take offense.

He chuckled, running his free hand over his chin. "That depends."

Taking in his handsome face and the well-cut dark suit clinging to his muscular frame, she sighed. "On?"

"Go out with me again and I'll stop."

She studied him. "Seriously? All of this to get me to go out with you again?"

With a sly smile, he shrugged his broad shoulders. "Hey, whatever works."

"Don't you have clients you should be working for right now?" Despite her efforts to appear upset, she couldn't stop the smile that spread across her lips.

"Of course. But those spreadsheets can wait."

She shook her head ruefully. This man was too much. Looking at him standing there with those flowers in his arms, she made a decision. It was obvious he wasn't going to leave her alone. And honestly, she didn't want him to. She'd give this thing a chance, but he could never know her secret. As much as she knew she should tell him, she couldn't. Not now, anyway. Maybe later, when the time was right. Bracing herself, she announced, "All right. I'll go out with you. Again."

His face brightened with a wide grin as he set the flowers down on her desk. "Great."

She let a small smile lift the corners of her mouth. He moved around the side of her desk, and she could feel a shiver go down her spine.

Leaning down, he whispered, "You won't regret this, sweets." Then his lips brushed against the shell of her ear, and the warmth of the contact touched her very core.

A soft sigh escaped her lips as he kissed her earlobe, the crook of her neck, then the underside of her jaw. Finally, his lips met hers, and she let her mouth drop open as their tongues mated and played.

When he drew away a few moments later, she was left breathless, dazed, and wanting more.

He straightened to his full height. With glittering eyes, he said, "Until tonight. I'll pick you up at eight."

Her mind hazy with sensation, she nodded at his softly spoken words. By the time she'd come back to her senses, he'd slipped out of her office and was gone.

The rest of the day, she did her best to keep her focus where it was needed—on her patients and paperwork. Thoughts of Xavier and whatever he had planned for her were with her through it all. She left early, around two thirty in the afternoon, to take her mother to a doctor's appointment. Though she didn't enjoy hanging around in the waiting room, she would be grateful to have something else to occupy her mind besides Xavier.

As she drove to pick her mother up, she wondered whether or not to tell Alma about their first date. Now that she'd agreed to go out with him again, she supposed her mother might as well know.

As Alma settled into the black leather of the passenger seat, she asked, "How was your day today, baby?"

For a moment, Imani thought about telling her of Xavier's visit. She knew how her mother's mind worked, and Alma would jump from deciding Imani and Xavier were an item again to planning their wedding and naming her grandchildren. Not wanting to excite her and raise her blood pressure right before a doctor's appointment, she changed her mind. "It was a pretty good day." She said nothing more.

In the office of Dr. Lyle Tillman, she listened intently to what he was saying. Her mother sat next to her and appeared to be taking in the doctor's words as well. Alma had been through a battery of tests, complaining the entire time about being "poked and prodded," so she would probably do whatever he requested just to avoid a repeat of the day's trials.

The older man, with his gray-streaked brown hair, blue eyes, and ready smile, had been her mother's doctor for several years. "If you can keep up with your insulin doses and blood pressure meds, Alma, I think you'll do well," he said, jotting notes on his clipboard. "Are you going to follow my orders this time?"

A sheepish-looking Alma nodded. "Yes. I let myself get too wrapped up in my church work, but even the Lord would want me to take care of myself."

Hearing that gave Imani a measure of relief. She'd still hired a nurse to help her mother out for a few hours each day, in the name of precaution, but she was happy to hear her mother's words.

Dr. Tillman seemed satisfied as well. "Good. Then I'll send your prescription over to your pharmacy for you to pick up later today." He stood and shook both their hands. "Make an appointment for six weeks from now, and I'll see you then." With a smile and a wave, he was gone.

Imani gathered their things, so she could take her mother back home. "I hope you'll be good about taking your medicine this time, Mom."

Alma waved her off as she got to her feet. "Don't lecture me, baby. I learned my lesson the last time." She swept a hand over her short salt-and-pepper curls and gestured to the door. "Let's go. I've got some pies to bake for the church bake sale."

They left the hospital, and she drove her mother home. After Alma was safely inside, Imani said, "I've got to go, Mom, but I'll swing by tomorrow and check on you."

"You're not staying?"

She shook her head. "You'll be happy to know I'm going out with Xavier tonight."

Seated on the aging pink sofa, her mother clapped her hands gleefully. "Finally! Be sure to give the man a fair chance. He's done some good work in the community."

She nodded. "I will, Mom. He's sent me flowers at work every day for more than a week. How could I resist?"

Her mother beamed. "He's the one, I just know it, and I'm glad you're coming around."

She chuckled. "Slow down, Mom. I didn't say all that. We're just going on a date."

Alma shook her head. "I don't know why you've been playing hard to get with him this long. He's a good man." Every time she'd visited or called while she was in college, her mother had regaled her with the latest news on Xavier's volunteering and fund-raising for one cause or another. To hear Alma tell it, the man spent all his free time helping disadvantaged neighbors.

Imani cringed as her secret rose within her again. "Maybe too good," she remarked, her voice barely above a whisper.

"What's the matter, baby?" Alma's expression filled with genuine concern. "You know you can tell me anything, Imani. We've always had an open, honest relationship."

Drawing a deep breath, Imani fixed her face, not wanting her mother to worry. "It's nothing, Mom. Just a little predate jitters, I guess. But like I said, no need to make wedding plans just yet."

Alma's expression conveyed that she thought differently, but she deferred to her daughter on the matter. "Whatever you say. Have a good time, baby."

She felt her cheeks warm as she kissed her mother's caramel-colored cheek and left with a wave.

―∾―

Tonight is the night.

Xavier slipped his cell phone out of the pocket of his slacks and dialed Imani's number. Knowing her, she would appreciate some hint about what she should wear tonight. He hummed to himself as he waited for her to answer.

"Hello?"

"Imani, it's me."

"I know." A soft chuckle accompanied her statement. "What is it that couldn't wait until we see each other in a few hours?"

Keeping his tone light, he answered, "I just wanted to let you know that I'm wearing something formal. I didn't want to leave you in the dark about the dress code."

"Let me guess. You're still not going to tell me where we're going tonight, right?"

"Right." A smile touched his lips. "Our destination is still a surprise."

Another giggle. "Okay. I'll dress accordingly."

"I can't wait to see you. I know you'll look gorgeous in whatever you choose."

Her tone was flirtatious as she spoke. "You're quite the sweet talker."

"Just you wait, baby. This night is going to get way sweeter."

The line fell silent for a moment before her soft response. "Let me go get ready. I'll see you later, Xavier."

"Until tonight, sweets."

As he disconnected the call, he felt his smile broaden. She really had no idea what she was getting into with him, but all would soon be revealed.

Xavier straightened the gold bow tie that had come with his tuxedo rental and checked his reflection in the mirror. He ran a small amount of pomade over his close-cut hair, slipped into his jacket, and stepped into the black wing tips. He'd promised Imani he wouldn't come on too strong, but that didn't bar him from looking his very best. To his mind, this was what she deserved as the woman he loved.

The night he had planned for her would surprise and delight her—or at least he hoped so. He'd done a great deal of planning that week to make sure the evening would go exactly as he wanted. The many floral arrangements he'd sent to her office were just the beginning. Imani Vivian Grant had captured his heart years ago, and the passage of time hadn't changed that. Now he was going to capture hers. Humming to himself, he grabbed his keys and wallet and headed out to his car.

As he drove from his house in Oakwood to hers in Cameron Village, he wondered about what she would wear tonight. He hadn't had the privilege of seeing her formally dressed since Tyrone's wedding. She'd been a vision of beauty in her bridesmaid's attire, and his memories of that day increased his anticipation for seeing her.

He parked his car in a spot beneath her second-story unit and got out of the car. The evening was crisp and clear, and the complex was quiet except for the distant sound of music from someone's stereo. He fired off a quick text message to let her know he was outside. As he glanced up, he could see movement in her front window. A lamp clicked off, dousing the window in darkness. Moments later, he heard her door open and close. He waited at the foot of the stairs for her to make an appearance.

When she finally did, his breath caught in his throat. She was wearing an ankle-grazing blue dress. The fabric clung to her ample breasts and shapely hips like a second skin as she descended the steps. He could hear the click of her pumps echoing on the concrete in the silence. Around her neck was a string of pearls that matched the studs in her ears. Her hair cascaded down around her shoulders. Her brown eyes held a smile that was just for him, and he could feel his manhood stiffening as she came near. "Evening, Xavier," she said easily.

Doing his best not to stammer, he returned her greeting. "Good evening, sweets." She was a vision of feminine beauty, and he was having a hard time keeping his composure.

She pulled a printed blue wrap from her purse and swept it around her shoulders gracefully. "I hope you like it," she remarked as she went around to the passenger side of his car.

Following her and opening her door, he assured her, "You look sensational, and I'm honored to escort you tonight."

She sank into the seat, and he closed the door behind her. A chilly breeze blew through the lot, nipping at him. Grateful, he let the breeze cool the heat building within him. He didn't want to embarrass her with the very obvious proof of just how desirable he found her. A few moments passed, and when he'd willed his body to cooperate, he got into the car and drove them away from the apartment.

He focused on his driving as best he could while he guided the vehicle to their destination: the Staff and Cape Inn. The old, upscale hotel, just a few steps from the campus of North Carolina State University, had a wonderful menu in its dining room. There was also another reason he wanted to take her there, though.

As they pulled into the brick-paved driveway, she said, "I remember this place. This is where we came after prom."

He smiled. "Your memory is just as good as mine, sweets."

He parked and helped her out of the car. As they crossed to the entrance, she said, "I wonder if it's still the same."

With a shrug, he said, "I don't know. I do know it's changed hands since the last time we were here."

Inside, he led her by the hand to the Marquis, the lounge in the hotel's lobby. The host seated them near a window looking out onto Hillsborough Street, then departed.

The sound of classical piano music filled the well-decorated room. Taking in the floral drapes, the napkins folded into swans, and the fine crystal and china set on the tables, he realized the place hadn't changed much since the late nineties. That was a good thing, as he appreciated the subdued atmosphere. It would give him and Imani the peace and privacy they needed.

Imani perused the menu silently, then remarked, "It's pretty quiet in here."

"It was the only place I could think of that wouldn't be too crowded on a Friday night." He sipped from his glass of ice water, his eyes never leaving her face. Her glossy lips, softly moving as she read the menu in silence, beckoned for his kiss. Her lips had always twitched like that when she read, but tonight, it was driving him crazy with desire.

She looked up, eyes questioning and innocent beneath the fan of dark, lush lashes. "What is it?"

He remembered his vow not to come on too strong, so shook his head, letting his gaze drop to his own menu.

A short, brown-skinned waiter, wearing a starched white shirt and black trousers, approached. Once he'd taken their orders and their menus, he disappeared into the kitchen, leaving them alone again.

Xavier reached across the table to capture her hand in his. As he caressed the silky skin, he said, "Thank you."

"For what?" Her soft-spoken words barely broke the silence.

"For giving me a second chance."

She smiled, and the sight melted his heart. "I just decided to see where this thing goes."

Nodding, he drew her hand to his lips and kissed it. "Anything you want, sweets." The lingering scent of her perfume teased his nostrils with its sensual notes of flowers and fruit.

Before the words died on his lips, he heard a brusque voice behind him demand, "Where is the host?"

As the host rushed over to the stand in the doorway, Xavier turned toward the voice. As soon as he saw its owner, he cursed under his breath.

"What's the matter?" Imani's voice cut into his thoughts.

He turned back to face her. "That's my opponent in the city council election, Aaron Givens." He found looking at her very much preferable to looking at the old blowhard now making his way into the lounge. Irritation caused a painful twinge in the muscles running along the back of his neck. Of all the times to run into Givens in public, he'd have preferred anything to this. Knowing the councilman would approach, he waited but kept his focus on Imani.

As predicted, Givens sidled up to the table, his doting wife clinging to his arm. "Good evening, Mr. Whitted. How nice to see you."

Doing his best to relax the tightness in his jaw,

he extended his hand. "Good evening, Councilman. Mrs. Givens."

The two men shook hands, and Givens's eyes swung to Imani. "And you are?"

Xavier immediately didn't care for the way Givens looked at her. The old man's gaze was hard, almost hostile. Mrs. Givens also looked decidedly displeased with her husband's demeanor.

Choosing to class it up instead of knocking the man down, he replied, "This is my companion, Imani Grant. Imani, this is Councilman Aaron Givens."

Givens offered a stiff "hello, ma'am" in response.

It was only then that Xavier noticed that Imani was staring, wide-eyed, at Givens, as if they'd had some previous unpleasant contact. Her hand trembled as she drew away from Givens.

"We don't wish to delay your meal," Xavier announced. "Do enjoy it."

With a terse nod of parting, Givens escorted his wife away.

Xavier turned back to Imani, who still looked somewhat stricken. "What's wrong? Do you know Givens?"

The question seemed to take her by surprise. "Uh... no," she murmured, taking a sip from her water glass. The ice clattered and clanked as she set the glass down, a side effect of her still shaking hand.

He watched her intently for a moment, but she said nothing else. He let the issue drop, but in the back of his mind, he wondered what had just happened between Imani and Givens.

―⁓―

Imani willed her hands to stop shaking with everything in her. She couldn't believe they'd run into Aaron Givens here. Her short encounter with his wife had been difficult enough to get through, but seeing him was almost impossible to take. And sitting there with Xavier, the timing was the worst it could possibly have been. Knowing Xavier had been watching while Givens gawked at her with those greedy, lascivious eyes—it was something she never wanted to experience again.

She hated lying to him, but it was better if she kept the information to herself, in the interest of his campaign. She didn't want to tarnish his reputation or jeopardize his chances of winning in any way.

She looked up from her water glass and found Xavier watching her. His face was etched with concern. To ease his mind, she said, "I'm all right. I just can't believe the man was so rude to me."

Nodding his understanding, he chuckled. "Me either. Here's hoping Mrs. Givens boxes his ears when they get home."

The silly joke drew a laugh from her—a laugh she dearly needed. It helped her put the unpleasant memories of her former life and the secret she sheltered out of her head for the time being.

In a short while, the food arrived. The savory garlic shrimp and Alfredo-drenched pasta she ordered made her taste buds do a two-step. "Mmm," she groaned around a mouthful. Swallowing, she added, "The food here is excellent."

"It is," he agreed, cutting into his chicken breast. "We should have eaten here on prom night."

She shook her head. "We'd already eaten at the Barn,

and besides, we didn't come here for food." She couldn't finish her sentence. The memories dredged up by the words she'd just uttered captured her mind all at once.

He seemed affected by her words, too. With heat-filled eyes, he finished the thought for her. "We came here for a room."

The warmth rising inside her affected her so much, she could feel beads of perspiration forming on the back of her neck. She sipped from her water glass, hoping to cool the fires he was stoking, but his gaze was just as hot as the August sun over Jordan Lake.

"You were so beautiful," he breathed, his hand capturing hers. "So sweet." He stood and came around to her side of the table.

The trembling set in again, this time worse than before. He drew her to stand and, before she knew it, pulled her into the circle of his arms. His lips brushed against the shell of her ear, and a sigh slipped from her throat.

"Xavier, remember your promise," she whispered, even as she melted under the fiery touch of his lips.

"I remember," he whispered back. "Tell me you don't want this and I'll take you home right now."

His deep voice reverberated in her ears. Turning her face up to look into his eyes, she saw sincerity there. Deep down, she knew her body could no longer stand being denied the touch of the only man who'd ever brought her to the heights of pleasure, who had ever captured her heart. "I want to stay," she admitted with much more boldness than she felt.

He didn't even wait for the check. Extracting a hundred-dollar bill from his wallet, he dropped it on the tabletop. Leading her by the hand, he escorted her to the front desk.

A petite blond woman wearing red-framed glasses and a burgundy uniform looked up from the computer. "May I help you?"

She heard him ask, "Is room 1201 available?"

She felt her body tingle at the mere mention of the room.

The woman, typing and peering at the computer monitor, said, "Yes, sir, it looks like it is. How many nights would you like to stay with us?"

In a voice edged with confidence, he replied, "One night is enough."

It was all she could do to stay on her feet. Leaning against the steadying strength of his shoulder, she drew a deep breath.

Once the transaction was completed, he led her through the back door of the lobby, into the inn's courtyard. It was a beautiful night, with stars twinkling like fireflies in the clear, dark sky above. The five-story brick building beyond the main building, with its wrought-iron scrollwork, was a familiar sight. Trying her best to be calm, she followed him until they reached the room. Sliding the card key into the lock, he swung the door open and stepped back so she could enter ahead of him.

Stepping into the room was like going back to the past. The wallpaper and bedding had been updated, but other than those small changes, the room remained the same. He hit a switch near the door, and two glass sconce lamps on either side of the bed illuminated the room. Her eyes fell on the bed. It was a king-size four-poster and so intricate she assumed it must have been carved by hand. The cream floral bedspread draped over the hulking piece of furniture added a touch of softness to the dark wood.

She heard the door close, and then a heartbeat later, he was behind her. He fit his muscular frame against hers, and she felt the trembling begin anew as his strong arms encircled her waist.

His breath was warm on her neck as he said, "You won't regret this, sweets."

The soft-spoken promise moved her so much, and she knew he was right. Fighting him had been so difficult, making this even sweeter. She turned in his arms and raised her chin for his kiss.

His lips crashed down on hers, and they fed on each other with all the urgency and pent-up passion inside. She ran her hands up and down his arms, and he drew away for a moment to strip out of his jacket and shirt. As their lips joined again, she relished the feel of his hard, muscular arms and chest beneath her caressing hands. He was a gorgeously made man, and she wanted to savor every moment.

He broke the seal of their lips again, this time to lead her farther into the room, toward the bed. She sat on the edge and waited for him to join her.

Instead, he knelt on the floor in front of her.

She shivered. He'd knelt before her in just the same fashion on that night so many years ago. The heat glittering in his dark eyes as he pushed her dress up around her thighs filled her with a sweet anticipation. It was obvious Xavier intended to skip the sightseeing and go right to the main attraction.

He kissed the inside of one bared thigh, then the

other. "I've been waiting to touch you again," he murmured as his big hands slid beneath the rucked-up dress. His thumb brushed over the tiny bud between her thighs, pressing against it through the thin fabric of her silk panties. She gasped, and as he continued to stroke and entice her, her hips rose and undulated to the rhythm of his caress.

Deftly, he slipped the panties down her legs and tossed them aside. She felt his breath on her as he spread her thighs apart. A second later, she felt his tongue, and her head dropped back like a rag doll. Sheer pleasure radiated from her very center, and she could barely breathe from the joy of it.

A strong arm pulled her forward, until she was dangling off the bed's edge, but she didn't care. His other hand opened her even farther as he treated her to scalding licks, sucks, and kisses that were driving her closer and closer to insanity. She could hear her own guttural cries echoing through the dimly lit space. In that moment, he was the whole world; there was nothing beyond the sweet fire he was building inside her. The flames rose higher and higher still, and as an orgasm gripped her, she let out a hoarse scream, feeling the tears streaming down her cheeks.

Hearing Imani's cry, he eased away from her sweetness. Watching her weep and twist as an orgasm swept over her was the most beautiful sight Xavier had seen in many years. She was the woman who filled his very soul, and to his mind, she deserved to be pleasured this way on a daily basis. He was so hard, he knew standing would be difficult to impossible, looking at her lovely face as she took her pleasure.

When she quieted, he stood. Shucking away his remaining garments, he gently sat her up and helped her out of her dress, white lace slip, and blue bra. Bared for his eyes, she lay back on the bedspread, presenting an erotic sight he would remember forever. Fiddling around in his pants pocket, he found the foil packet he sought. Once he'd covered himself with the protection, he joined her on the bed.

Looking into her smiling, damp eyes, he asked, "Are you ready?"

She nodded, drawing him on top of her. Soft hands stroked his chest, his waist, and his hips. "Yes, Xavier," she whispered.

Her surrender fueled his desire even more. Eyes locked with hers, he rose a bit between her open thighs and slid inside her. Bit by tantalizing bit, he edged in, hearing her gasp with each advance. He held himself in check as he moved deeper, seeking all she could give him, until he filled her completely. Her eyes closed, and as he began to move, she wrapped her long, lithe legs around his waist.

As much as his body would allow, he took his time. The channel gripping him was so tight, he struggled to keep his strokes slow and even. Her sighs and soft moans spurred him on, so he increased his speed. Grasping her luscious hips in his hands, he let loose and thrust into her with all the pent-up passion he felt.

Her moans grew louder, more guttural. He could hear his own grunts competing with the sounds she made.

"So good," he ground out, his hips moving like a piston.

He could feel her shaking beneath him. Then, in a pleasure-filled voice, she called out his name. Her muscles gripped him even tighter. She was coming, crooning and shivering beneath him. Her reaction was so tantalizing, he couldn't hold back any longer. With a roar, he succumbed to his own powerful orgasm.

Only their harsh breathing broke the silence in the room as he let his body drop to hers. Resting on her soft curves, with the last remnants of pleasure still lingering, he felt more relaxed than he could remember feeling in a long while. He could feel the lure of sleep calling to him.

"Xavier?"

"Hmm?"

"You're crushing me, honey." Her voice was quiet and laced with humor.

Hearing her refer to him that way made him smile. Chuckling, he rose so she could scurry from beneath him. While he pulled back the covers and crawled between them, she stood beside the bed, waiting.

She was a vision of loveliness, standing nude in the dim light, with a light sheen of perspiration glistening on her silken skin. With a finger, he beckoned to her. She didn't protest. Sliding into the bed next to him, she pressed her back flush against his chest and settled in. He threw the covers over them and relished the feeling of having her where he most wanted her to be: in his arms. The ice around her heart seemed to be melting, and he wanted her warming his bed for the rest of his life.

Chapter 12

IMANI'S EYES FLUTTERED OPEN, AND SHE KNEW RIGHT away she wasn't in her own bed. The mattress beneath her felt as soft and light as a cloud. Beyond that, a strong, muscular frame pressed up against her body.

A sliver of sunlight flowing in between the floral curtains across from her fell on Xavier's face as he snored next to her. His big arm lay draped over her in a possessive fashion.

Memories of last night's loving broke through her morning bleariness. The remembered sensations of his touch still singed her skin, and a sleepy smile spread across her face. The feeling of waking up with him, wrapped in his embrace, made warmth bloom in her belly and radiate out to her limbs. She felt safe, cared for, and, most of all, satisfied.

Still a bit groggy, she slipped from beneath his arm and stood. She stretched and padded across the carpeted floor to the bathroom. Once she'd taken care of her morning needs, she returned to the bed...

And found him sitting up watching her.

Feeling heat rush to her cheeks, she got back into the bed and used the sheet to cover her nudity.

He laughed in response to her show of modesty. "You don't have anything to be ashamed of, sweets." His gaze swept appreciatively over her, even as she held the sheet up beneath her bare shoulders.

"I'm not the one-night stand, walk-of-shame kind of girl."

His right eyebrow went up. "Trust me, this was no one-night stand." He scooted closer, raised her chin for his kiss. His lips brushed fleetingly against hers, and more memories of the night they'd shared rose in her mind. Breaking the contact, he asked, "Are you hungry?"

She nodded. "Starving, actually. And with good reason," she chided, softly elbowing him in the ribs.

He wore a look of feigned innocence. "I'll order room service." He turned away to use the phone on the nightstand next to him, and she sank back against the stack of pillows behind her.

As he placed their breakfast order, her thoughts spun in several different directions. Regardless of where their interlude led, she could not deny that she'd enjoyed his thorough, skillful loving. The few encounters she'd had in college had been marginal at best. When she'd entered medical school, she'd become celibate, so she'd have no ties to distract her from her studies. Her passionate interlude with Xavier on that warm summer night had broken a long chain of nights free of physical gratification. After almost four years of going without, being with Xavier was quite a refreshing experience.

He placed the phone back in its cradle and turned toward her. "Should be here in forty-five minutes."

She peered over the edge of the bed, saw her underthings and dress strewn around. "I'd like to be dressed when they get here."

Apparently he agreed, because he got out of bed and began searching out his own tossed-aside clothing. They dressed in relative silence, and as she slipped into her clothes, she continued to replay her memories of last night. Letting things between her and Xavier progress naturally was the only thing that made sense. He brought a lightness into her life, a sense of joy that she craved. Another smile touched her lips, because she knew her feelings toward him were growing in intensity. She was now willing to admit that she was falling in love with him. She couldn't remember ever being so thrilled to have been wrong.

So much for keeping things casual.

As if reading her mind, he announced, "You realize you're mine now."

She looked in his direction and found him fully dressed except for the coat and bow tie. Heart racing, she nodded.

He appeared pleased with her acquiescence. Sitting down at the circular wooden table occupying one corner of the room, he grabbed the remote and flicked on the television. She smoothed the wrinkles out of her dress as best she could and sat down on the edge of the bed to await the breakfast delivery.

They watched a few minutes of a program on a sports network before a knock sounded on the door. "Room service," the visitor announced through the whitewashed wood.

He rose to open the door, and a short, young, blond girl, dressed in the same uniform as the waiter in the Marquis the previous night, carried in a tray laden with food. As she set the tray down on the table and presented Xavier with the slip to sign, she gazed up at him with wide eyes. "Aren't you Xavier Whitted?"

Smiling, he signed the slip. "Yes. Do I know you?"

"I've seen your campaign commercials and signs all over town," she gushed. "Wow." Her eyes fell on Imani, as if she'd just noticed her presence in the room.

Imani saw a gleam in the girl's eye that made her downright uncomfortable, but she offered a quick wave anyway.

The young girl nodded to her. "Ma'am. Have a nice day." Taking the slip and pen from Xavier, she left in a hurry.

After she'd gone, Imani sat down at the table across from him. "There was something a little weird about that girl."

He shrugged as he looked beneath the lids covering the plates. "Probably a little starstruck. If she's a potential vote, I've got to be nice."

She supposed she understood that, but the look in that girl's eyes still lingered in her mind. There was something suspicious about the girl, something almost predatory. Who knew what was going on behind that creepy stare of hers?

Turning her mind away from Ms. Creepy Hotel Employee as best she could, she opened the lid on the plate Xavier had set before her. Inside were strips of crisp bacon, a pile of scramble eggs covered with shredded cheese, seasoned potatoes, and a fat biscuit slathered with butter. "What a feast," she commented as she grabbed a fork.

"There's fresh fruit, too," he said between mouthfuls. Lifting the lid on the last remaining dish, she found it filled with bright, dewy strawberries, sliced oranges, green apples, and chunks of pineapple.

Starting in on her own food, she couldn't help smiling. Pushing away all other thoughts, she concentrated on enjoying the food and the company.

When they'd finished eating, she wiped her mouth with a white linen napkin. "I'm stuffed."

He nodded his agreement. "It's almost checkout time. Are you ready to go?"

A glance at the digital clock on one of the nightstands confirmed his words. "Sure. Just let me grab my purse."

They gathered their things and left the room. As the door closed behind them, she felt a small amount of disappointment at having to leave their private paradise. She didn't linger on the feeling because she knew there would likely be many more pleasurable interludes in their future.

He kept his eyes focused on the road as he drove her home. Still, the atmosphere in the car held a charge. It was different from the anticipatory air of last evening but noticeable nonetheless. Breaking the silence, he said, "I'd love to introduce you to my campaign staff."

She was taken aback by that. "Really? Why?"

"Because I've been talking about you for weeks, and I'm sure they're curious." He glanced at her long enough to wink before turning his eyes back to the road. "Besides, what man wouldn't want to show off a woman like you?"

His words flattered her, and she could feel her face warming. She offered a soft smile. "Maybe. I'll think about it."

"That's all I ask."

She sat back in her seat and watched the familiar scenery go by.

As they passed the shopping center at Cameron

Village, she saw a large woman step out of one of the boutiques, laden with bags and packages.

It was Lorna Givens.

Their eyes met for a split second, and the older woman's glare made her displeasure very plain.

Shaking off the chill that went down her spine, Imani turned away from the window.

At eleven thirty Monday morning, Imani knocked on the door of Xavier's office suite. Flattery had gotten him everywhere with her, because she'd given in to his request that she meet his campaign staff. The office suite he leased for his accounting business had several rooms, one of which currently housed his campaign headquarters.

The Whitted Accounting suite had an exterior entrance shaded by the branches of two weeping willows. She stood on the sidewalk by the door, tightening her coat to fend off the October chill, which intensified with the breeze. Blue and green signs posted on the windows flanking the office door were emblazoned with the slogans "Win with Whitted" and "Whitted for City Council." Her eyes raked over the signs as she waited for someone to open the door.

The door swung open, revealing Xavier's smiling face. "Hi, Imani. I'm so glad you could make it, sweets."

She returned his smile. "I knew you'd keep pestering me if I didn't come by, so here I am."

"Whatever works. Come on in." He linked arms with her and led her inside, letting the door swing shut behind them.

While they walked the corridor, she enjoyed the

view—not of the office decor, but of her handsome escort. He wore a coal-black tailored suit with a canary-yellow shirt and black-and-yellow patterned tie. Clearly, he possessed impeccable taste, because every well-cut suit he wore seemed to thrill her. She swallowed, not wanting to be caught drooling.

I've got to get myself together. Between the raging hormones brought on by being in Xavier's presence and the nervousness she felt about meeting his campaign staff, she knew the odds were pretty good that she'd do or say something she'd regret. Taking a deep breath, she clung a bit tighter to Xavier's arm.

"Campaign headquarters is in here." He made the announcement as he guided her toward the last room on the right side of the carpeted corridor. The door was propped open, and she could hear muted conversations from inside.

She stopped abruptly.

Xavier stopped as well, turning confused eyes on her. "What's the matter?"

She looked up into his eyes, stammering, "I…I'm not sure if I'm ready to meet them yet."

He grazed his fingertips over her jawline. "Trust me, it will be fine. Why are you so nervous, sweets?"

Her mind raced. In his quest to find out what troubled her, he'd essentially given her the opportunity she needed to come clean, to tell him what she'd been keeping from him for so long. She drew a deep breath. "Xavier, I have to tell you—"

"Hey, Mr. X! Who's the newbie?"

Imani's mouth snapped shut. Both she and Xavier turned toward the source of the question.

A young man had appeared in the doorway and now watched Xavier expectantly. He looked to be about twenty-one, with light-brown hair, deep-blue eyes, and an average build.

Xavier chuckled. "Hold your horses, Kevin. We're coming in."

"If you say so." Kevin ducked back into the room.

Turning back to Imani, Xavier quipped, "As you can see, my staffers are nosey. So come on in and meet them, or else they'll all find a reason to come out here."

Imani nodded, taking a deep breath. What she had to say would just have to wait. "Okay." Her arm still linked with his, she let him lead her into the room.

The space was of reasonable size, large enough to accommodate a ten-person conference table. The long, rectangular table was centered in the space. The walls were papered with campaign signs similar to the ones she'd seen outside, as well as an array of charts and graphs she assumed to be pertinent election-related data.

Only four of the seats at the table were occupied, and Imani was grateful for that. At least she didn't have to worry about being gawked at by an entire room full of people.

"Imani, this is my campaign staff—well, all the full-time people, anyway." Xavier continued to hold on to her arm, using his free hand to gesture at the folks around the table. "You already met Kevin, the go-getter. This is Sam, Jacki, and Katrina."

"Hi, it's nice to meet all of you." Imani offered a smile and wave to the group.

Katrina, pushing a pair of round glasses up her nose, asked, "Is Imani joining the campaign?"

Xavier chuckled. "In a way, but no. She's my—"

"Old friend," Imani interjected, lest Xavier start tossing around labels. "But Xavier definitely has my vote. I know he's going to do great things for Raleigh."

Katrina and Jacki exchanged a look, but neither of them spoke.

Xavier and his staff began chatting, and Imani could feel the twinge of anxiety speeding through her body as she observed their interactions. Did he expect her to just hang out with them for the rest of the day? She had to be back at her practice after lunch; she had three more patients to see before the day ended. Rapidly tapping the toe of her black pump on the carpeted floor, she waited for this official meeting to be over.

Xavier stopped talking and turned to her. His expression told her that he sensed how uncomfortable she was. "Okay, y'all. I'm sure Imani needs to get to lunch. I just wanted to make sure you all met her."

The youngsters around the table waved as Xavier and Imani departed.

In the hallway, Imani commented, "Wow. Your staffers are really young."

"As they should be. They have the energy and the drive to really move this campaign, and they keep me on my toes." Xavier gave her shoulder a squeeze.

"Are they all over eighteen? Jacki looks like a high school kid."

He chuckled. "She's nineteen, and she's the youngest."

Imani shook her head, sharing in his laugh. "Hopefully now that I've met your extremely young staff, you'll quit bugging me…" Her words trailed off as she noticed two women walking toward them.

The blue-eyed woman in the front, sporting a blunt-cut blond bob, had a press pass dangling around her neck. She was followed by another woman, dark-skinned, with a fierce afro. The second woman had two things around her neck: a press pass and an expensive-looking camera.

Oh crap.

Imani's eyes darted around the corridor, seeking an easy escape route. But before she could duck into an empty office, the blond woman spoke.

"Xavier Whitted? I'm Cara Carson from the N&O. This is Renee, my photographer. We were hoping to get a few shots of you and your staff, and a few quotes for the paper. Got a minute?"

Turning on his megawatt smile, Xavier nodded. "Sure, but it'll have to be brief."

Renee raised her camera, and Imani barely managed to shield her face with her hand before the flash went off.

Lowering the camera, Renee remarked, "Sorry, didn't mean to startle you, miss…"

Xavier stepped in then. "This is Imani. She's not on my campaign staff. She's…" He looked to her for guidance.

She tightened her lips, signaling him that she'd rather not air her personal business.

"She's a good friend of mine, and she's camera shy." He gestured toward the open door of the campaign room. "Why don't you ladies head on into the war room? My staff is already in there, and they're feeling really chatty today. I'm sure they'll give you the good stuff."

"Awesome." Cara clapped her hands together and started toward the office, with Renee following her.

Once they were alone in the hall again, Imani lifted her gaze to his. "Thanks. I'm just not ready to be making announcements and all that."

He waved her off. "Don't worry about it. I get it. I'm sorry about that. I didn't know any reporters were coming today. That's the fun part of running a campaign. You never know what's going to happen."

The two of them moved down the corridor and around the corner that led back to the entrance. As she placed her hand on the door handle, he stopped her.

"Thank you for coming by, Imani. It means a lot to me."

She smiled. "I know. That's why I came."

He reached for her, splayed his fingertips up the back of her neck until they were buried in her hair. Then he turned her face up and pressed his lips to hers.

Her eyes slid closed, and she saw fireworks as his tongue eased between her lips. She gave herself over to the kiss, letting the hunger she felt inside have its way. When he finally released her, she felt dazed, breathless.

"I've got to get back to work. I'll call you later, sweets."

And with that, he and his intoxicating presence disappeared around the corner.

She glanced around, wanting to make sure no one had seen them.

It was only then that she noticed the reception desk, tucked in a corner to the far left of the door. But the receptionist appeared absorbed in a phone call, so she assumed they hadn't been spotted. Gathering her wits, Imani pushed down on the door handle and slipped out of the office suite.

—◆—

A whistling Xavier strode into his office Tuesday morning, his suitcase in hand.

Rita, seated in her usual place behind the reception desk, greeted him. "Good morning, Mr. Whitted."

"Good morning, Rita." He noticed the slight frown on her face. Because his secretary was a sunny person by nature, he knew something was up. "What's going on?"

She hesitated for a moment. "Mr. Fields is waiting for you in your office."

"Oh boy." Whatever Tyrone had come to discuss would not be good. Rita's face told all. "Well, wish me luck."

She nodded, and he straightened his tie and went down the hall. As he came to his open office door, he saw Tyrone sitting stiffly in a chair in front of his desk. Bracing himself, he walked in and set his suitcase on the desktop.

"Good morning, Tyrone." He dropped into his leather chair and waited for the reckoning to begin.

His scowling friend scoffed. "Not as good as you think, Xavier." Extracting a newspaper from his briefcase, he opened it and tossed it onto the desk.

Curious and confused, he picked up the paper. It was the local section of the *News and Observer*. He scanned the page for a moment but couldn't figure out what Tyrone wanted him to look at, so he shrugged.

Arms folded across his chest, Tyrone stated tersely, "Center page, about three quarters of the way down."

When he looked again in the place Tyrone indicated, he cursed. He read the headline aloud in an anger-filled voice. "'City Council Candidate Rekindles Old Romance'!"

Tyrone nodded solemnly. "You know nothing is private when you run for public office. What was Imani doing in the office yesterday?"

"I asked her to come by and meet the staff."

Tyrone rolled his eyes. "Dude. We talked about this. You can't be dating right now, not in the middle of the campaign. And you certainly can't be bringing women here to meet the staff."

Xavier sighed. "Ty, I already told you. There are no similarities whatsoever between Imani and Jess. She's not going to do me wrong, man. I know it."

"I can't believe you let them get all these photos of you. Look at this one, with you two kissing in the office. And look at this one—are you two coming out of a hotel? What the hell were you doing there?"

Xavier raised his eyebrow. "You know what I was doing, man. But I can't see how this got out so quickly." He thought about it for a moment, then remembered his encounter with Aaron Givens in the hotel restaurant. "Wait a minute. Imani and I saw Givens and his wife in the hotel lounge."

"He's not the source."

"What?" He was sure if anyone wanted to sabotage him, it was Givens. So who else would have gone to the papers?

Tyrone shook his head. "It wasn't Givens. Like you said, he only saw you eating with her and there's no scandal in that." He paused, pointed to the paper. "I read the article. The source was a young girl who works room service at the hotel."

He smacked his palm against his forehead. Imani had mentioned that there was something odd about the girl, but he'd dismissed it. Never again would he ignore his lady's intuition. "What could she possibly have to gain from going to the papers with this?"

"Turns out she moonlights for the Givens campaign." Tyrone leaned back in his chair, his face finally relaxing out of the scowl. "I'm willing to bet the campaign gave her a fat check for this little tidbit."

"You're probably right." Xavier ran his hand over his eyes and groaned. "Imani is not going to like this. She's not a girl who likes the spotlight."

"We're just lucky there's not a racier photograph to go with the story." Taking the paper back, he tucked it away again. "Besides, it's not her you should be worried about. They didn't say all that much about her. The voters aren't going to take kindly to a story like this so close to Election Day."

This was the part of the campaign he loathed most: having to be so careful about everything he said or did. "I'm a single man. Am I supposed to be celibate while I'm running for office?"

Tyrone chuckled. "No, but you'd damn well better make it look that way." He ran a hand over his head. "Look, man, I know you're a modern thinker but this is still the South. Taking a girl to a hotel for a night is not proper behavior when you're on the campaign trail."

His shoulders slumped, because he knew Tyrone was right. "But this isn't a fling. Imani means everything to me. We just got caught up in the moment."

"How is the public supposed to know that?" Tyrone stated. "I've already checked the damage, and we are down ten points in the polls." Smoothing his jacket front and slipping a pair of dark shades over his eyes, he got up to leave. "If you want that council seat, you've got to cool it with Imani—at least until the votes have been cast. All right?"

Xavier pressed his hand to his forehead. "You're not serious, Ty. How can you ask me to do that when you know everything I've gone through to get her back?"

Arms folded over his chest, Tyrone shook his head. "You won her back once. You can woo her again. *After* the election."

Xavier groaned, burdened by the truth of his words. With a terse nod, he acquiesced. "Fine."

After Tyrone left, Xavier got up and stood by the large window behind his desk. Outside, the sunny scene belied the chill in the air. The bright-green leaves of the oak near the window rustled in the breeze.

Damn. Imani is going to hate me for this.

He realized what he'd just agreed to do and how hurt Imani would be. Tyrone had told him straight up that dating her would be detrimental to his campaign, and now that he'd seen the story in the paper, he believed him. Tyrone had always been a truthful friend, which was why Xavier asked him to be his campaign manager in the first place. There was so much work he wanted to do in the community, and the council seat held the key to doing those things. To him, this wasn't about politics. It was about making Raleigh a better place for all its citizens, especially the elderly and the disadvantaged.

Telling Imani that he couldn't see her for a few weeks was the last thing he wanted to do right now, but he saw no other choice. He didn't want to cheapen the special bond they shared by sneaking around with her, and he knew she wasn't ready to become a candidate's fiancée and step out into the limelight with him. After she saw the article, he knew Imani would lash out at him, and he couldn't really blame her. He'd spent all this time chasing her, and now he was about to push her away, just when she'd surrendered to him.

He hoped that room service girl was happy, because she'd just ruined the most important thing in his life: his relationship with the woman of his dreams. Turning away from the window, he sat back down at his desk to tackle accounts payable for one of his clients. Even as he began running the spreadsheet, thoughts of Imani and how he would explain the situation to her crowded his mind.

The buzzing of his cell phone alerted him to a text message. Picking it up, he opened the message from Maxwell. Saw the paper. Don't worry. The Thetas got your back.

That gave him a modicum of comfort. The backing of the Epsilon Alpha chapter of Theta Delta Theta meant more to him than any other endorsement he'd received. Plenty of people and groups had supported his campaign in one way or another, but the Thetas were special. Every step of the way, they had lived up to their fraternity motto: Gentlemen, Leaders, Brothers.

He could only hope Imani would be as understanding as his friends when he broke the news to her. Somehow, though, he doubted it.

———

Imani stretched her arms above her head, then tightened the scarf she'd tied around her hair to protect it from the dust. A glance outside the window showed the sunny

Monday evening becoming a bit overcast as clouds rolled in from the south. Blowing out a breath, she trudged back into the closet and pulled out yet another old box.

Alma stuck her head in the open bedroom door. "How's it going in there, baby?"

She sighed. "With any luck, I'll be done by Christmas."

Her mother chuckled. "I've been asking you to clean out this bedroom since before you started your residency."

"Now you see why I've been putting it off so long." She slid the heavy box across the wooden floor, toward the bed, and flopped down on the edge of the mattress. "I've held on to way too much."

"I brought you a soda." Setting the icy beverage on the nightstand, Alma turned to leave. "I'll be downstairs. Good luck."

After her mother left, Imani grabbed the glass and took a long sip. Then she set it down and brushed away some of the grime on her hands. It shouldn't be a surprise that pulling out all these things would kick up a cloud of dust. After all, they hadn't been touched in a decade. But her mother wanted a functional guest room, and it really was time. She was a grown woman now, in the process of building a medical practice. She knew she no longer needed the things that reminded her of her teenaged days, so she'd come over right after the practice closed and waded in.

Part of her wanted the cleaning to last long enough for her mother to fall asleep. She knew that as soon as she finished, her mother would want to play twenty questions, and the topic would be her date with Xavier. With a groan, she opened the last box she'd pulled out of the closet.

She recognized the contents immediately.

The box was full of stuffed animals, silk roses, and letters she'd received from Xavier. Looking through the box led her back down memory lane, and in light of her newly revived relationship with him, she decided to leave everything in the box and take it with her to her apartment. A smile spread over her face as she thought of how he'd react when he found out she'd held on to mementos from the old days, just as he had.

Those were the days. Life was so much simpler then, back when her biggest concerns had been home-work, extracurricular activities, and her social life. She remembered the Saturday nights spent on group dates with Xavier and a bunch of their schoolmates, seeing the latest releases at the movies or hanging at the mall. Remembered her Dad handing her the keys to his old Buick and a couple of twenty-dollar bills so she could hang out with her friends. "Be back by eleven or else," he'd said.

"I will, Daddy," was her constant reply. A few words and a smile, and all was right with the world.

Adult life had proven to be much more complex and nuanced.

She thought back on the article she'd seen in Sunday's paper and the pictures of her and Xavier appended to it. The flash of light she'd sensed when he kissed her at his office Monday had apparently come from a flashbulb, though at the time she'd thought it was her body's reac-tion to him, making her see fireworks. He exuded a raw male power, and somehow it managed to overwhelm her whenever he was around.

The article had spoken of their "rekindled romance"

in mainly positive terms, but it still made her uncomfortable to think about the reporters lurking around, waiting to document Xavier's every move. The more involved she got with him, the more likely that those same folks would become curious about her past. And there were parts of her past that simply couldn't be known by the public.

There was one last box to be opened, so she sat down on the floor and lifted the flaps. Inside were many of her old textbooks and items from her Spelman days. She had fond memories of attending the all-female HBCU and credited the experiences she'd had there with preparing her so well for medical school and business ownership.

Near the bottom of the box, she found a familiar blue journal. It was a simple, leather-bound book she'd kept as her personal diary during her college days. Back then, she'd faithfully recorded everything of note that happened to her. Every evening, she'd sit down and pour out her thoughts in the book, which she'd kept hidden away at all times. Her meticulous documentation of her entire college experience was both a treasure and a curse.

Recorded within the journal's pages were accounts of the awful harassment she'd endured during her time in the secretarial pool at Doyle and Callahan, up to and including the day she'd been assaulted. Seeing the journal again brought a tear to her eye, just as seeing her attacker again had brought fear to her heart. But parts of her couldn't let go of the journal, because of all the happy memories it contained. It was her life in words, and for years since college, she'd held on to it, taking the bitter right along with the sweet.

She stacked the college box on top of the other one

and stood. Doing her best to tamp down the anxiety she felt whenever she thought about those days, she made a decision.

She'd take both boxes home with her.

And at the first chance she got, she'd get rid of that damn journal.

With the room vacuumed and dusted, and her boxes of possessions moved downstairs, she ventured into the kitchen to get something to eat. She saw her mother sitting at the table with the day's *News and Observer* spread before her and a mug of her favorite mint tea. The spicy aroma permeated the air, competing with the fragrant smells of Alma's cooking.

Seeing her mother sitting there made her want to turn and flee. But her stomach protested that idea with a loud, angry growl. She sidled over to the stove and lifted the lids off the blue ceramic pots her mother had cooked in. Inside them she found smothered steak, fried corn, and green beans seasoned with turkey bacon and onions. She pulled a paper plate from the stack on the counter, filled it, and took a seat across from her mother.

She lifted a forkful of the corn to her mouth. As she savored the buttery, pepper-seasoned corn, her mother's voice broke the silence.

"You know, you're gonna have to tell me how your date went eventually." Alma took a sip from the cream-colored mug of hot tea. "May as well get it over with."

Nervous butterflies flapped crazily inside her chest. There was no getting out of it, but she vowed to spare her mother the details of her steamy encounter with Xavier. "It was nice. We ate at the Marquis Lounge inside the Staff and Cape Inn."

Alma nodded, her eyes on the newspaper. "Was the food any good?"

"Yes, it was excellent. I really enjoyed myself."

"Did you enjoy Xavier's company?"

The pointed question made her cringe. This wasn't a conversation she wanted to get into with her mother. "Yes, Mama, I did. You'll be happy to know that we're back together."

Raising her gaze to meet her daughter's, Alma smiled. "Good. Xavier's a good man, and he's got a good heart. With all that work he does for the wayward youths, he's proven himself honorable."

Her smile mirrored the one her mother wore. "I know. I've come around." Hard as she'd fought to deny the attraction she felt for him, being in his arms and experiencing his skilled loving again had melted her resolve like an ice cream cone in July.

"Some folks ain't gonna like it, though," Alma added, turning the paper to a new section. "Women have been sniffing around him like hounds on a fox since he came back."

She'd heard her mother speak on that subject before, but had never really been concerned about it. At least, that's what she'd told herself. But now that she and Xavier were trying to give their relationship another shot, the last thing she wanted was to have to fend off a bunch of meddling, jealous women. "I guess I'll just have to deal with that." She shrugged, showing her mother far less concern than she actually felt.

"You'll be fine." Alma waved her hand dismissively. "No woman has ever been able to turn his head but you, baby."

Heat rushed to her cheeks at that declaration. He'd professed desire only for her, and now her mother was corroborating his story. She wondered if things could really be as wonderful as they seemed. Her practice was off to a great start, adding new patients every week. Now Xavier was back in her life. Could she really have it all: the career, the stability, and the man of her dreams?

A smile touched her lips. She knew that whatever lay ahead for her would be infinitely sweeter as long as Xavier was by her side.

Chapter 13

LEANING AGAINST HIS CLUB LIKE A CANE, XAVIER WATCHED his father set up for his next shot. Edwin stooped low, taking great care in pressing the sharp end of the plastic tee into the soil, then positioning his golf ball atop it.

Golf wasn't among Xavier's favorite pastimes, but his father enjoyed it. In order to get in some all-important time with his father, Xavier had taken off the whole day from work. Being at the country club instead of at his desk on a Wednesday morning felt somewhat foreign, but refreshing nonetheless.

Edwin straightened, then readied his nine iron. "Watch this, Son. This is how you do it."

Xavier nodded, keeping his eyes on the golf ball. They'd now reached the fourth hole, and he couldn't remember the last time he was this bored.

Edwin smacked the ball with a powerful swing. The tiny white orb went flying, landing on the ground mere inches from the hole.

As they watched, the golf ball rolled in a semistraight line toward the hole...and then kept rolling right past it.

Edwin snapped his fingers. "Dadgum. Almost had it."

Xavier patted his father on the shoulder. "Don't be so hard on yourself. It's the first shot you've missed today, and it's way closer than any of my attempts."

At that, Edwin chuckled. "You're right about that. Despite my best efforts, boy, you are terrible at golf."

Xavier knew better than to deny that. He couldn't think of anybody worse at golf and had pretty much abandoned all hope of getting any better at it. That wasn't why he'd come to the course with his father. Male bonding aside, his main motivation was distraction.

Adjusting his golf gloves, Edwin eyed him. "Son, why are we really here? Sure doesn't seem like you're interested in improving your game."

As always, his dad could see right through him. "I'm not. I don't think I'll ever be any good at it." He wasn't even sure where the problem lay. Did he lack coordination? Aim? Or did he just not have enough patience to learn the rules of the game?

"So why are you torturing yourself? And don't say male bonding because we could easily do that at the house over a beer."

Xavier groaned aloud. "I know. I'm just looking for creative ways to spend my time that don't involve Imani."

Edwin's gray brow furrowed. "Why? You two have a falling out?"

He shook his head. "No, but Tyrone wants me to cool things off with her until the election is over. After that newspaper story, he got all bent out of shape."

"That's what campaign managers are supposed to do." Edwin tucked his iron into his golf bag. "But as your friend, he oughta know better than to think you can stay away from her."

Xavier followed his father's cue and put away his own club. "Does this mean the game's over? It's only the fourth hole."

Already on his way to get his ball, Edwin called back,

"We both know you'll be way happier if we end it now. We can chat in the clubhouse."

Xavier didn't bother to hide his smile.

Once they'd put their gear away, they got a table in the clubhouse cafe. Oakwood Acres, one of the nicest golf clubs in Raleigh, boasted a five-star clubhouse, complete with a pro shop, well-appointed locker rooms, and a few flexible spaces that were often rented out for private parties and other events. The crown jewel of the place was the cafe, which served high-end lunch, dinner, and specialty drinks.

"I know you're miserable without her," Edwin remarked over his steaming cup of coffee.

"I am. But I can't really argue with Tyrone because he's right. I need to keep my nose clean if I'm going to unseat Givens." Xavier drank from his own glass of iced tea.

"It's not going to be long. You've only got about ten days before Election Day."

He nodded. Logic told him that the next eleven days would speed by, but to his heart, the time felt like an eternity. Stretching his arms over his head in an attempt to release some tension, he turned his head to the left, looking out over the cafe's interior.

His gaze landed on Imani and he frowned. She looked beautiful in a long black skirt, tall boots, and a red sweater. She had her arm looped through that of a tall, light-skinned brother standing next to her, and the two of them were smiling and laughing.

Xavier's frown deepened. He'd never known her to play golf, so what would she be doing here? And who in the hell was that guy with her?

Edwin seemed to notice his son's staring. "What are you looking at?"

Xavier eased his chair back from the table. "Dad, am I crazy, or is that Imani over there?" Rather than point, he jerked his head in her general direction.

Edwin's eyes swung in that direction, scanning until he found her. "Sure does look like her. But you know what they say, everybody's got a twin."

Xavier sincerely hoped the woman was Imani's doppelgänger because he did not like seeing her with another man. No, she wasn't his wife—yet. But that didn't mean he was okay with other men pushing up on her.

He started to get up from his chair.

Edwin's hand shot out. "Son, don't. We're not even sure it's her."

"I only know one way to find out." His felt his frown deepen into a full-on scowl as he zeroed in on the brother, who had just brushed a lock of hair away from her face.

"Oh, come on. Think about it. If it's not her, you'll have embarrassed yourself for no reason. And if it is her, what do you think you're going to accomplish?"

"Giving that guy a piece of my mind." Jealousy rose within him, doing battle with his good judgment.

Edwin scoffed. "Oh really? So you're going to do what? Punch that perfect stranger in the face? How many brownie points do you think you'll get with her by being a brute?"

The reason of his father's words finally penetrated Xavier's anger. Drawing a deep breath, he dropped back down into his chair. "You're right, Dad."

"Of course I'm right. I've lived seventy years on this

earth, and I haven't gotten this old by being an idiot, you know." Edwin lifted his mug to his lips again, taking another drink of coffee.

Xavier dragged his gaze away from the pair by the counter, looking out of the window instead. The table was positioned next to a wall made entirely of glass, allowing him an unencumbered view of the rolling green lawns of the course. There were a few golfers out walking on the green, as well as a few driving around in carts.

Edwin spoke, breaking into his thoughts. "I know you love her. But it's up to her whether she wants to be with you. Right now, try to take a step back. You've got a lot on your plate, and after the election, you all can straighten things out."

"You sound mighty certain. It's almost like you know something I don't."

Edwin shrugged. "I know things always work out the way they are supposed to. Just let it be for now, Son. Everything is going to be fine."

Looking across the table at his father, Xavier realized how much his reassurance meant to him. Even as a grown man, he found it to be a priceless gift. "Thanks, Dad."

Only a nod and smile came in reply as Edwin opened the golf magazine on the table.

Xavier went back to looking out of the window, and while he watched the passing carts and strolling golfers, he did his best to push aside any thoughts of Imani and what she might be doing.

Because as much as he loved her, she wasn't his pet or his property. He had no claim on her, and it was time he accepted things as they were, not as he wanted them to be.

The couple who'd been standing by the counter strolled by, still arm in arm.

As they passed, Xavier got a better look at the woman, and when he saw it wasn't Imani, he felt the tension leaving his body.

Edwin didn't look up from his magazine. "See? I just saved you from making an ass of yourself."

Xavier chuckled. "Thanks, Dad."

The experience taught him a crucial lesson. It turned out that Tyrone's assessment was correct. Imani was a huge distraction for him. He couldn't even focus on a glass of iced tea when it came to her, so how could he be involved with her and remain focused on his campaign?

That solidified his decision to go along with Tyrone's edict. He wasn't going to tell Tyrone he'd been right; Lord knew he'd never hear the end of it if he did that. But he would do his best to stay away from Imani, at least until the votes were cast and counted. After the election was off his plate, he would revisit their relationship.

"Hey, Dad, how about some stumping?"

Edwin looked up from the glossy pages of his magazine. "You mean, go around with you and shake hands so you can get the golf club vote?"

With a laugh, Xavier stood. "Yeah, that's exactly what I mean."

Edwin closed the magazine, winked at him. "Then lead the way, Son."

～

Using one of her bright-orange oven mitts, Imani opened her oven door and slid out the pan of lasagna she'd put in forty-five minutes prior. Setting it on top of the stove, she closed the oven door, then lifted the foil to check it. The aroma of tomatoes, garlic, and basil wafted up from the glass pan, and she smiled as she looked at the layer of bubbly, perfectly browned cheese on top.

Replacing the foil, she left the lasagna and headed to the refrigerator to grab the ingredients for the rest of the meal. As she spread the thick, crusty slices of French bread with olive oil and spices, she thought back on the call she'd received earlier from Xavier. He'd asked if he could come over to have a talk with her, and she'd agreed, suggesting he stay for dinner. If they were going to give this relationship a shot, the least she could do was make him a nice meal on a Friday evening.

After she'd toasted the garlic bread and shredded the lettuce for her Caesar salad, she opened her tool drawer to search for her salad tongs. The ringing of the doorbell interrupted her search. Wiping her damp hands on the front of her apron, she untied the strings and tossed it on the counter, then went to open the door.

Xavier stood on the cement porch with a single yellow rose in hand. He wore a pair of dark-blue jeans and a green sweater. "For you." He smiled as he extended the rose in her direction.

With a smile of her own, she took it. "Thank you. I'm glad to see you finally got the message that I don't have room for any more huge arrangements."

That drew a chuckle from him. "I did, and I'm glad you like it." He paused, inhaled deeply. "Mmm. Something smells great in here."

"You mean besides me?" She posed the question in a teasing tone.

He leaned down, placed a soft kiss on her neck. "You always smell like heaven on earth, sweets."

A small tremor of pleasure ran through her at the contact. "Simmer down, Xavier."

"I mean, what's cooking in here? My stomach is already growling."

She stepped back to allow him entry. Once he was inside, she shut the door and locked it. "I made lasagna and garlic bread. I was finishing up the salad when you rang the bell."

Still walking as if following the scent to the kitchen, he said, "Is it Caesar salad? You know that's my favorite."

She winked. "Of course it's Caesar. I remembered."

As he moved into the kitchen, he clapped his hands together. "Need any help?"

She shook her head. "All that's left is to mix the salad." Grabbing a large slotted spoon as a replacement for her lost tongs, she went to the bowl of salad she'd left on the counter and tossed the ingredients until everything was well coated.

Before she could turn to place the bowl on the table, she felt his strong form press against her back. "Look at you—smelling great, looking gorgeous, making my favorite food. A man could get used to this."

She gave him a Mona Lisa smile. "A man should be so lucky."

He stepped back, allowing her to put the salad and the rest of the meal in the center of her small, round kitchen table. She'd already set the table with plates and glasses of iced tea.

He pulled out her chair, and she sat. "Dig in, Xavier."

Sitting on the other side of the table, he quipped, "You don't have to ask me twice."

They filled their plates, and the two of them enjoyed a little small talk as they ate the meal. As time went on, though, Imani noticed that something seemed off between her and her dinner companion. He'd asked to come here so they could talk, and even though he'd been there over an hour, he'd made no mention of what he wanted to discuss.

Xavier raised a forkful of lasagna to his mouth, but before he could eat it, the fork dropped from his hand and clattered to the tabletop.

Imani looked up from her plate. "Sorry, did I get olive oil on the silverware?"

He shook his head as he recaptured the fork. "No, I'm just clumsy. Let's just say your food is so delicious, I can't think straight." He chuckled.

She noticed his laugh lacked the bright humor it usually held. No, this laugh sounded more like it was driven by nervousness instead of humor. Deciding not to press the issue, she continued eating her dinner.

When they'd finished the meal, she stood and started to gather the dishes.

"I'll do that," Xavier offered. He took their plates to the sink, and just as he arrived there, dropped them. The ceramic plates clanged loudly against the interior of the metal bowl of the sink.

Imani's head jerked in the direction of the sink. "Xavier, what's up with the butterfingers? Am I going to have to give you your dessert on a paper plate?"

He laughed again. "No, no. I'm sorry. I'm good now."

She smiled, but inside she had her doubts. *What is going on with him tonight?* The Xavier she knew exuded charm, confidence, and sex appeal, making this bumbling version of him very unnerving.

Once he was back in his seat, she brought over two small plates containing slices of apple pie a la mode. "I hope you like it. And full disclosure, I didn't make the pie." She set his slice before him, then set down her own. "Would you like some coffee?"

He nodded. "Decaf, if you have some."

"Sure. That's the only kind I drink this time of day." She moved around the kitchen, making preparations until she returned to the table with two steaming mugs, cream, and sugar on a tray. Setting the tray down between them, she returned to her chair.

Xavier took a sip from his mug. Apparently he liked the brew black, because he smiled after the first sip went down. "Italian roast?"

She nodded while she added cream and sugar to her own mug. "Yep. It's my favorite."

"Mine, too." His eyes were focused on her. He raised the cup for another sip, but this time when he went to set it down, he completely missed the table. The mug crashed to the floor, shattering and leaving a puddle of dark liquid on the light-gray tile. "Damn it. I'm sorry, Imani."

Imani stood, rushed around the spill to get a towel.

He took the towel from her hands and squatted down to soak up the spilled coffee. She retrieved the dustpan and a small brush and began sweeping up the broken pieces of the mug.

"Xavier, what is going on with you? I think you'd

better tell me what you want to talk about before you break any more of my dishes."

Most of the mess cleaned, he raised himself back up into his chair.

She stood, leaving the dustpan full of broken mug on the floor. Looking into his eyes, she could see that something was wrong.

He sighed. "You're right, Imani. We have to talk."

Sensing the conversation would soon turn very serious, she flopped down in her seat. Propping her elbows on the table, she rested her chin in her hands. "Okay, what is it?"

He drew a deep breath, then launched into a speech. "So, you know when we first got together at Tyrone's wedding, you were talking about needing your space, so you could focus on your business? And how you didn't want to be involved right now because the timing was bad, and you thought it would be better if—"

"Xavier, stop."

He opened his mouth, then clamped it shut.

"I've known you a long time, and I've never known you to string together that many words without stopping. Why are you rambling?"

He looked away, as if he felt guilty—or at least uncertain. "Well, Imani, I just want to make sure I say what I have to say in the best possible way, because—"

"Rambling again, Xavier. Just say what you want to say, boo." The term of endearment slipped from her lips unexpectedly, effortlessly, as if she'd always referred to him that way.

He swallowed. "I think you were right about us needing to be cautious and take things slow. Maybe we should—"

She sighed loudly, knowing exactly where this conversation was going. "So I guess you know about it, then."

—⁓—

Xavier felt his brow furrow. The nervousness he'd been feeling the entire evening was washed out by confusion as he tried to process Imani's cryptic statement. "Know about what?"

She took a sip of her coffee. "Come on, Xavier. You must have found out about the harassment case by now."

"Imani, I don't know what you're talking—"

"Yes, you do. That's why you're fumbling through this whole, 'it's not you, it's me' break-up speech you're doing right now." She sat back in her chair, her expression one of resignation.

In opposition to her gesture, Xavier leaned forward in his seat. "Imani, I have no idea what you're talking about, but it seems like you have something you need to tell me."

She folded her arms over her chest. "I don't want to do this, Xavier."

He watched her, waited.

Her expression softened, and she appeared to be searching his face. "You mean you really don't know what I'm talking about?"

He shook his head slowly, hoping she'd believe him this time.

Her eyes widened. "Oh my God."

"Yeah. I'm gonna need you to start talking, Imani." He thought back on her words the day they'd had dinner at Alma's house.

You think you know me, but you don't.

Imani closed her eyes, released a long sigh. "I can't talk about this right now, Xavier."

"I don't really know what's going on. But is there something I need to know?"

She said nothing but looked away.

"Does it have anything to do with my campaign?"

She shook her head. "I can't tell you that."

"I'm at a loss here, Imani."

"I really can't get into this with you, Xavier. We're having such a nice night. Let's not ruin it."

"So, that's all you're going to say?"

"Xavier, I'm not about to rehash all the ghastly details. To be honest, the whole ordeal is something I'd much rather forget."

"Imani—"

"Xavier, please. This whole mess is mine to deal with. I don't want it interfering with any of the things you're trying to accomplish."

"Why were you so determined to keep this from me?"

She rolled her eyes.

He tented his fingers, resting his elbows on the table.

He sensed her discomfort, and with everything in him, he wanted to know what the problem was, so he could fix it. But after everything he'd gone through to get to this point with her, he knew she'd flee if he pushed. She was silent for a few moments, as if thinking about what he said. Finally, she pressed her fingertips to her temple. "Xavier, I'm really tired. We've had a lovely evening but I think I need to get to bed early."

His protective instincts kicked in again. "Are you okay? Do you feel sick?"

She shook her head. "Just a little headache. I'll be fine, but I'd really like to just go to bed."

"I understand." He didn't, really, but he sensed she'd already made her decision. Standing up, he made his way toward the front door. "Call me if you need anything."

"I will. Thanks." She reached for her glass, took a sip.

"Good night, Imani."

After hearing her quiet reply, he slipped out of the apartment and closed the door behind him. Outside, as he got into his truck, he wondered what had just happened. Something wasn't right with her, but he knew trying to force her to talk would be a mistake.

His mind still ticking through the possibilities, he backed out of the parking space and drove away.

———

On her lunch break on Monday afternoon, Imani popped a slice of Granny Smith apple into her mouth. Chewing, she washed down the tart sweetness with a sip of cold water.

Joining her nurses and Maya in the break room was not something she usually did, but she felt she could use the company. It had been a long, miserable weekend since she'd fought with Xavier, and now all she wanted to do was sit in a dark room and feel sorry for herself. Being around other women seemed to lift her out of her funky mood.

She reached for another apple slice off the fruit and cheese tray Maya had brought in for lunch. They were all watching the noon news on the small flat-screen television mounted on the break room's apricot-hued accent wall. The surrounding walls were painted a muted shade of yellow and were decorated with small, square, framed images of Maya's orchids.

Maya sipped from her bottle of diet soda. "I'm glad you decided to eat with us today. You needed some social interaction."

Imani had to agree, so she nodded. "I'm glad I did, too. We should do this more often."

Tara, one of the two nurses working, added, "There's nothing like good food and good company to heal the spirit." In her muted, solid-colored scrubs, and with her long black hair in a bun, Tara was a pretty mellow character.

"Amen to that!" echoed Leona, the other nurse. Leona was the opposite of Tara, preferring a short, spiky hairstyle and neon-colored scrubs.

Imani was about to comment on Leona's lime-green ensemble when Maya tapped her shoulder. Imani turned. "What is it?"

Around a mouthful of crackers, Maya said, "Look at the TV."

Imani followed her gaze. Grabbing the remote on the table, she turned up the volume.

An image of Aaron Givens was on the screen as the lady reporter spoke. "Councilman Aaron Givens took time away from the campaign trail today to visit a home for the mentally disabled in Rocky Mount."

Maya's face twisted into a frown of distaste. "This is really gross. It's blatant pandering at the expense of those disabled people."

Imani nodded, her mood solemn. If she never had a reason to root for Xavier to win the election, she certainly had one now. Aaron Givens was a horrible person.

On the decency scale, he ranked somewhere between pond scum and possum crap, and growing up in North Carolina, she'd encountered her share of both.

As she ran a hand through her wavy dark hair, Maya cursed. "I don't believe this guy. Xavier's definitely got my vote."

Imani lowered her voice before speaking again. "What really sucks is that the general population has no idea what a scumbag Givens is," she lamented. "I'd love to inform them, but—"

Maya finished her sentence. "You don't want your business out in the street." Her arms were folded across the front of her red sheath dress, and she wore a knowing look.

Imani sighed. "Even if I did, I still have to contend with the gag order. You know me too well."

Maya hooked arms with her. "I wouldn't worry about it, Imani."

Imani asked, "How can I not worry about it? I don't much care about politics, but do we really want someone like Aaron Givens to stay in power?"

Maya shook her head. "Let it go, Cuz. Karma will bite him in the ass, you'll see."

As she sipped from her bottled water, Imani dearly hoped her cousin was right.

A man like Aaron Givens deserved to have his dirty deeds exposed.

Imani found she no longer had much of an appetite. She could still see Xavier leaving her apartment, still feel the sting of guilt from being evasive with him. From the day she'd seen Xavier at the wedding, she'd tried her damnedest to get him to leave her alone. He'd chosen to pursue her anyway, and she was pretty sure he regretted the choice now. As she thought of him and how confused and hurt he'd looked that night, she could feel the tears well up in her eyes. She'd tried in vain all weekend to convince herself that she was fine, that not telling Xavier everything was best. Her head told her it was better this way.

Her heart vehemently disagreed.

Despite her protests, being with him the past few weeks had changed her. He'd worked his way into her heart, opening the places occupied only by him, places she'd thought she'd locked away forever. The old feelings of first love were revealing themselves again, and now that she'd become so deeply involved with him, she had no idea how to put them under lock and key again.

As she tried to shake off the nagging thoughts of Xavier, she looked up and found Maya watching her.

With serious eyes, she stated, "Call him, Imani."

Imani smiled wearily, shaking her head. "Trust me. Xavier isn't going to talk to me."

<hr />

Raising his mug of beer to his lips, Xavier took a long drink. He was sitting at the bar in Rizzo's, one of his favorite places to go for a cold one.

Bryan, sitting on the next stool, was enjoying a cold brew of his own. "I love Rizzo's house brew. Can't get anything this good anywhere else in the world."

"You should know." Xavier set down his now-empty mug, wiped away foam he felt clinging to his lips with a napkin. "It's taken me way longer than I thought to buy you a beer, because you're never in town more than a hot second."

Bryan sighed. "That's true. My travel schedule has been outrageous lately. I think I'm gonna try to stay at the office more, do some remote work."

Xavier felt his brow hitch in surprise. "I thought you liked the travel? Besides, if you stay home, how are you gonna hook up with your squadron of international honeys?"

With a groan, Bryan shook his head. "I'm not. After what I went through in Paris, I turned in my player's card."

Now Xavier was really confused. "Dude, what are you talking about?"

"Oh, that's right. I didn't tell you when I came to the center, because I was rushing back to work, and I haven't seen you since then." Bryan drained his mug and set it down. "Let's just say I got burned, and badly."

Tenting his fingers, Xavier gave his friend his full attention. "I gotta hear this. Tell me about this legendary woman who took you down a peg."

Bryan frowned but continued. "Her name is Marielle. Every time I've visited Paris for the last two years, she and I have met up for a little…adult activity. This time, we did the same. She left my room one morning without even leaving a note. I saw her in a café that same day, and she wasn't alone."

"Dude. Y'all weren't exclusive or anything, so what's the big deal?"

He shook his head. "Listen. I saw her, but she didn't see me. And I stood a little distance away, listening to her clowning me to another man."

Xavier scratched his chin as he took in the tale. "Are you sure she was talking about you?"

"Man, who else do you know with a dragon tattooed

on his upper left thigh? Not only did she make fun of my tat, but she was dissing my equipment."

Xavier sucked in a breath. "Ouch. She's cold-blooded, man." That was a pretty low blow and seriously detrimental to a man's ego, no matter how confident he might be.

"You're telling me. I just can't do it with these women anymore. I don't even want to think about what the rest of them might be saying about me behind my back." Bryan gestured to the barkeep to refill his mug. "I'm telling you. From now on, it's all business for me. No more playing the field."

"Wow. I never thought I'd see the day." And he hadn't. Xavier could recall Bryan's way with the ladies back when they were in college, and apparently his charms had only intensified with age, at least as far as most women were concerned. Hearing Bryan swear off women was odd, kind of like when he found out Pluto had been demoted and was no longer considered a planet.

"I'm serious, X. I'm done with dating. At least Dad will be thrilled. He's always complained that I wasn't focused enough on company business. Now there's nothing competing for my attention."

"For what it's worth, I'm sorry she did that to you." Xavier gave Bryan's back a reassuring slap.

Bryan shrugged. "I appreciate you, man. You've already helped me out by bringing me here and footing the bill for my favorite brew."

Xavier waved to the bartender for a refill. Once his mug was filled again, he raised it, careful not to spill the foamy head. "Hey, what are friends for?"

Bryan struck his mug against Xavier's, and then the two men took drinks.

"But enough about my troubles. What's up with you and Imani?"

Xavier shifted on his stool. "Who knows? This is all turning out to be way more complex than I thought it would be."

"What do you mean?"

"Well, I went to her place for dinner the other night. She makes a mean Italian meal. But when I started to tell her about how Tyrone's been riding me to cool things off with her, she said something off the wall."

Bryan said nothing, but his brow creased with confusion.

"She started to admit something to me, then she walked it back. No matter what I said, she wouldn't tell me anything. I don't know what's going on with her."

Shaking his head, Bryan chuckled. "Women. Just ain't no understanding them, man."

Xavier laughed, but deep down, he could see the truth in Bryan's words. There were so many things about Imani that he didn't understand. As much as he cared for her, he knew he was going to need some clarity before things with her progressed.

"You ready?"

Imani tightened her charcoal wool peacoat against a cold breeze before answering Maya's question. "I'm ready to get out of this cold air."

She and her cousin were on the steps of the Wake County Courthouse, in advance of today's proceedings.

The air held the chill of the approaching winter, even as the sun sat high in a cloudless blue sky.

The two young men who'd been charged with breaking and entering for the crime they'd committed at her medical practice were appearing before a judge today for a hearing.

"Me, too." Maya climbed onto the landing and swung open the glass door, holding it open. "Let's go in."

The two women went inside, and Imani immediately felt the relief of the building's heated interior.

"I don't know about you, but I still think it's a little crazy that these boys' hearing date fell on Halloween." Maya made the remark as she emptied her pockets and purse for the metal detector by the entrance.

Imani handed over all her cargo to the stern-faced deputy. "It is a little weird. But I'm just ready to get this whole thing over with."

Maya passed through the metal detector first, then stood still for one of the deputies to pass a wand over her. Imani endured the same tedium, and when they had their items returned, they went on their way. A quick elevator ride delivered them to the second floor, where they made their way to the hearing room.

Inside, Imani found two vacant seats near the rear and gestured to them. She and Maya slid into the chairs. Imani's rear end immediately protested when it came in contact with the stiff wooden seat.

Maya shifted, as if trying to get comfortable. "Damn, these chairs are hard. Sorry we couldn't get closer to the front."

"Don't worry about it. This just means we'll be able to get out quicker when it's over." She gestured to the exit doors on their right.

Maya set her purse on the floor, her eyes scanning the room. Then she jabbed Imani. "Look, there's Xavier."

Rubbing her arm to soothe the pain brought on by her cousin's sharp elbow, Imani rolled her eyes. "I expected him to be here to support Trent and Peter. They are his charges, after all."

"You sound a li'l salty there. I know you've got better sense than to blame Xavier for what they did."

"I don't blame him. I'm not that petty. I just wish it hadn't happened in the first place, that's all."

Maya pursed her lips. "Well, I'm glad to hear you say that because ain't nobody else responsible for what those boys did."

Imani shushed her cousin, then whispered, "Stop lecturing me so we can hear the proceedings."

Maya shook her head and folded her arms over her chest but remained silent.

Thankful her cousin had finally zipped her lips, Imani looked to the front of the room, in anticipation of the hearing. The wall clock behind the judge's bench gave the time as four minutes to eight, so things were bound to start soon.

Imani watched as Trent and Peter were led to a table in the front of the room. She assumed the tall man with them to be their legal representative. The boys cleaned up nicely, and she noted how presentable they looked in their dark suits and solid-colored ties.

Their lawyer, who didn't look much older than they were, wore a suit in navy, with a smart paisley tie. A pair of black-rimmed glasses perched on his nose, he wore an easy grin that contradicted the seriousness of the occasion. Imani thought the lawyer had a whole Malcolm X/Dwayne Wayne thing going on.

Behind the boys and their lawyer, Stacy Cates entered. Trent's mother had dressed in a green suit and pulled her hair back into a conservative bun. Stacy's gaze swung in Imani's direction, and they locked eyes for a moment.

Imani gave her an almost imperceptible nod.

In response, Stacy frowned, then hurried to a seat in the front row.

Imani supposed she could understand Stacy's frustration and didn't begrudge the woman her opinion. Still, someone had to be held responsible for all the damage done to her practice, not to mention the loss of income and sense of unease she'd experienced in the aftermath. The police had informed her of the boys' arrest and subsequent temporary custody. Though she didn't have children, Imani guessed that had been a stressful situation for both the boys and their parents.

The judge, a stout woman with curly white hair, emerged from the chambers and took the bench. Her voluminous black robe enveloped her petite figure. With a bang of her gavel on the wooden block, the judge commanded silence in the room. Under her unwavering gaze, conversation in the room quieted, then ceased.

Listening to the proceedings, Imani learned the judge's name: Philomena Caprese. Judge Caprese spoke at length with the man who'd accompanied Trent and Peter; he was indeed their lawyer, Seth Douglas.

"We recommend mediation in this situation, Your Honor. The boys' actions, while regrettable, are an indication of bad judgment more than anything." Seth paced the floor in front of the bench as he made his argument. "There was no real malice in the act."

"Mr. Douglas, the plaintiff in this case has filed a formal complaint with the Department of Juvenile Justice. You're right about the bad judgment, but lack of malicious intent does not affect the outcome of their actions." Judge Caprese shuffled through a stack of papers on the high desk in front of her. "Dr. Grant suffered significant damage to her property, as well as loss of income and undue stress."

"I don't deny the facts of the case, Your Honor. I'm simply asking for a chance at redemption for my clients. This youthful indiscretion, while serious, should not ruin their chances at success down the road."

Imani, with her hands folded in her lap, had to admit she agreed with Mr. Douglas's assessment. Peter and Trent were still young, and while she wanted them to pay a penalty for their deeds, she wasn't sure she wanted the penalty to ruin their lives.

Maya shook her head. "Those boys are about to have their futures destroyed, all over a stupid decision."

Drawing a deep breath, Imani rose to her feet. "Your Honor, I'm Dr. Imani Grant. May I speak, please?"

Judge Caprese acknowledged her with a nod. "Dr. Grant. Yes, you are entitled to speak as part of this hearing."

"I agree with Mr. Douglas. I don't want these young men to have their futures taken away from them. It's important that they understand they did something wrong, but I don't want to ruin their lives."

Stacy, seated near the front, turned in her seat to stare at Imani. Unshed tears stood in her eyes.

Imani glanced Stacy's way, letting her gaze reassure the woman. "I'm willing to drop my complaint if the boys are willing to do some community service."

Seth Douglas smiled but still kept his expression serious. "Well, Your Honor, if the plaintiff is willing to do this, my clients will be happy to cooperate."

Judge Caprese folded her arms over her chest and sat silent for a moment. "I'll allow it. But I expect full and complete cooperation from you two young men. Is that understood?"

"Yes, ma'am." Trent and Peter stated their agreement in unison.

"Mr. Holmes, Mr. Goings, I'm going to sentence you to fifty hours each of community service. And I don't want to see your names come across my desk again." Judge Caprese banged her gavel again.

As the bailiff called for the next hearing, Imani watched the boys shake hands with their lawyer. When she saw Trent clutch his mother in a tight hug, Imani felt a smile lifting the corners of her mouth.

Maya patted her on the shoulder. "You did the right thing, girl."

Looking at the scene unfolding in front of her, Imani sighed. "I hope so."

Chapter 14

Rising from his seat, Xavier looked toward the back of the courtroom. Imani stood there, gesturing with her hands as she conversed with Maya. He couldn't hear whatever they were speaking about, but honestly, he didn't much care, because Imani had his full attention regardless.

It had been over a week since he'd gone by her apartment for dinner, since she'd started to open up to him about her life during the years they'd spent apart. He knew there was more to the story, but she'd apparently revealed more than she'd wanted to. He supposed he shouldn't complain about the turn of events; after all, he'd gone there with every intention of taking a break from their budding relationship. In a way, she'd made the task easier.

What hadn't gotten any easier, though, was the misery of being away from her. Tyrone was thrilled that Xavier hadn't had any contact with Imani recently. Tyrone thought Xavier's full focus was on the campaign, but Xavier knew better. He'd been phoning it in, because he missed her terribly.

He contented himself to stay where he was for a moment, admiring her beauty. She wore a dark-gray coat, cinched at the waist, over a conservative pair of navy-blue slacks. The outfit obscured her figure somewhat, but not from him. He had intimate familiarity with the soft, womanly curves that lay beneath her clothing. She'd pulled her hair back, revealing the soft lines of her face. She'd forgone heavy makeup in favor of just a touch of lipstick, and he didn't mind at all. She was gorgeous, and seeing her now made him want to stride over to where she stood, take her into his arms, and kiss away the ruby-red color staining her lips.

He knew that if he didn't get out of there fast, he'd be unable to control his urges. Still, he needed to speak with her for a moment, so he could communicate his gratitude for what she'd done. He gathered his strength, then began moving in her direction. Maneuvering around the chairs and the people who still remained in the room, he kept moving until he entered her personal space.

Maya, as perceptive as ever, smiled at his approach. "I'll go warm up the car. Meet me outside."

Imani's eyes widened, and she looked as if she wanted to stop Maya from leaving. But before she could formulate a sentence, Maya had already snatched Imani's keys and disappeared through the double doors.

"Hello, Imani." He tried to look into her sparkling, dark eyes, but her gaze fled from his.

"Xavier." She gave him a sidelong glance, then looked away again.

If she chose to inspect her shoes while he spoke, he didn't care. "I just wanted to thank you for what you did. I know you could have easily let the judge throw the book at the boys, and I just wanted to tell you I appreciate your decision."

She drew her purse strap onto her shoulder and lifted her gaze. "I just did what I thought would be fair."

He waited, sensing she had more to say.

"I had to be honest with myself. When I looked at Trent and Peter, I saw the faces of the young men who murdered my father. But I can't hold them responsible for that. Your kids still have a chance to avoid going down that path, and I want this to be a learning experience for them, not a life sentence."

He nodded. "That's a very mature way of looking at things."

A small smile touched her lips. "Thank you. In the end, I think it's what Daddy would have wanted me to do."

He noticed she still didn't look directly at him; she appeared to be looking past him. "Listen, Imani. About what happened the other night—"

She raised her hand to stop him. "Xavier, look, I'm sorry I can't give you the total transparency you want from me. I really am. But I'm just not there yet. Can you understand where I'm coming from?"

He touched her shoulder. "I'm willing to try."

She exhaled through rounded lips. "I appreciate that. I'm in a complex situation when it comes to my past. But if we just let it go for now and don't speak of it, everything will be fine. I promise I'll tell you everything when the time is right. But, Xavier, you've got to give me time."

He looked into her eyes, saw the sincerity and the unshed tears. She was struggling with something, and if he truly cared about her, he had to let her work through it in her own way. Abandoning her was out of the question. "Sweets, don't worry about it. We'll figure it out together."

Wearing a teary smile, she leaned up to place a soft

kiss against his cheek. "Thank you," she whispered into his ear.

He held her close for a few seconds, aware of the prying eyes all around them. Stepping back, he said, "I won't hold you up. I know Maya's waiting for you, so I'll give you a call. Okay?"

"Okay." Still wearing that soft smile, she tightened her coat and walked away.

He watched her leave, and as the doors swung shut behind her, he could feel the warmth of her kiss still clinging to his jaw.

Someone tapped him on the shoulder, drawing his attention. He turned to see Stacy standing there with a sheepish-looking Trent in tow.

She reached out to shake his hand. "I'm so glad Dr. Grant came around." Her eyes were still watery, but she appeared much happier and calmer than she'd been earlier.

He offered a small smile. "So am I."

Stacy linked arms with her son. "Now I'm taking my boy home, so we can have a long chat about making good choices. Right, Trent?"

"Yes, ma'am." Trent looked at Xavier. "See you later, Mr. Whitted."

Xavier offered a wave as the two of them departed.

~~~

Imani stared out the window of her father's study. Outside, it was a beautiful fall Saturday afternoon. Some of the young children in the neighborhood dashed by on their bikes, stirring up the gold and crimson oak leaves littering the sidewalk. The sun shone bright, unencumbered by the thin, wispy clouds overhead.

The scene blurred as her eyes filled once again with tears. She was overwhelmed by such a volatile mix of emotions that even the simplest tasks seemed daunting. Parts of her were ecstatic that she and Xavier had made up, and she wanted to give him the complete honesty he craved. But deep inside, she clung to the fear of what that would mean. Would he really be able to accept what she told him as truth? Would Xavier take her word over the word of someone so powerful?

In the past, she'd gone to her father for advice whenever she found herself in a complex situation. So, this morning, she'd donned an old pink sweat suit and gone to her parents' home, seeking whatever solace she could find in her dad's study. Her mother spent most Saturdays at the church, doing auxiliary work, so Imani knew she wouldn't be disturbed.

Easing over to her father's desk, she fell into the big brown leather chair and let her gaze sweep the familiar surroundings. The walls, painted her father's favorite shade of midnight blue, were filled with things he'd collected during his life. His secondary education degree from Shaw University was displayed directly behind his desk. The opposite wall was filled with pictures of Richard and his students at Millbrook. During his teaching years, he'd been very popular with the students, some of whom looked up to him in place of their own absent fathers. The smile he'd worn when surrounded by his students was telling: he'd loved his work.

On the tall mahogany bookcase that occupied the corner next to the window, books on topics ranging from accounting to woodworking filled the shelves. Richard had been an avid reader in his free time. The top two shelves also held some things Alma had kept from the hardware store. A framed photo of the three of them on the day Excalibur Hardware opened, as well as the first dollar the store had made and the old cash register her father had used occupied the space.

Leaning back in the chair, Imani felt the tears running down her face again and didn't bother to wipe at them as they ran down to fill her ears. She missed her father now as fiercely as the day he'd died and wondered how long it would be before the pain finally subsided, or at least waned. She closed her eyes and pictured his handsome, smiling face. If he were there, what would he tell her to do about Xavier? Her father had never steered her wrong, and she dearly wished he could be there to offer the sage advice she so desperately needed.

Imani had always known she couldn't keep her secret from Xavier forever. What bothered her was the growing feeling that she wanted to be with Xavier, needed to be with him. She'd been career focused, thinking of romantic entanglements as a distraction from achieving her goals. Yet here she was, weeping and wondering if she would have to live all alone for the rest of her life.

Her stomach growled loudly, but she ignored it. While her body might crave food, she was too mentally exhausted to want anything to eat. She'd choked down some wheat toast this morning, but even that had been an ordeal. She didn't intend to eat anything else until she could shake the anxiety that plagued her.

Imani knew her mother would eventually come home and find her sitting there, but she had no desire to rush to her own apartment to avoid her mom. Since her world was falling apart anyway, her mother might as well know her secret. She'd tell her when Alma got back from church. The conversation would not be a pleasant one, but Imani knew her mother loved her. As Southern and Baptist as she was, Alma wasn't the type of woman who would disown her only child for something that wasn't her fault.

Exhausted, Imani tipped forward, resting her forehead on the coolness of the polished mahogany desktop.

She didn't realize she'd fallen asleep until she heard sounds of movement downstairs. As her eyes slid open, she saw the color of sunset painting the room around her. Soon after that, she heard Alma's voice calling her name.

She lifted her head long enough to call back, "I'm in here." Then she let it drop right back down on the desk. Moments later, the door to the study opened, and her mother stepped inside.

"Imani? I saw your car in the driveway. What's the matter, baby?"

Hearing the concern in her mother's voice brought on a fresh round of tears. She sat up, focusing her watery eyes on her mother.

As she stood there in a pair of khaki pants and a yellow long-sleeved T, Alma looked worried. She made her way over to the desk and wrapped her arms around Imani's shoulders. "Tell me what's bothering you."

Imani took a deep breath. "Do you know how I paid my tuition to Spelman, Mama?"

Her mother looked confused. "You worked. And I'm proud of you." She searched her eyes. "What are you getting at?"

"It was a settlement, Mama. I worked, but it was

an out-of-court settlement that really paid my tuition."
Imani's flat tone covered the immense shame she felt as
she said the words out loud.

Alma stiffened but didn't withdraw her embrace.
That gave Imani a measure of comfort as an awkward
silence fell between them.

Finally, Alma asked, "Settlement? For what? Baby,
you have to tell me what happened."

"I was a receptionist for a small law firm." She looked
up into her mother's eyes, so she would know she was
telling the truth. "And one of my bosses thought I should
be doing more for him than just filing and answering
his phones."

Alma gasped. "Oh no."

Tears were already sliding down Imani's face. "I tried
to get away from him. I really did. But he was stronger.
He held me down…" Her words were extinguished,
fading into a sob.

"Oh no. Not my baby." Alma's embrace tightened
as she spoke in a tear-strained voice. "I'm so sorry that
happened to you, Imani. So very sorry."

Imani rocked side to side in her mother's arms, letting the motion soothe her. Somewhat recovered, she
continued. "It was just the way things were done in that
office, I guess. But nobody told me that. When I went to
Human Resources, he tried to turn things around on me,
tried to act like I came on to him. He threatened to sue
me for harassment."

Alma loosened her grip, so she could sit back and
look into her eyes. Wiping the tears from her daughter's
face with her fingertips, she sighed. "Let me guess. You
took a settlement rather than be publicly embarrassed."

Imani nodded. "And under the terms of my settlement, I'm under a gag order. I can't publicly discuss the details until after his death."

Shaking her head, Alma touched her hand to her temple. "Who did this to you, Imani?"

With an expression of utter disgust, she muttered his name. "Aaron Givens."

Alma's hand flew to her mouth. "Not the same Aaron Givens on the city council!"

"Yes, the same one."

Alma's face creased into a frown. "Well. I can't remember the last time I've been this disgusted."

Imani shook her head, trying to rid herself of the image of Givens's face. "The worst part is, I can't tell anyone what kind of person he really is. The city of Raleigh deserves so much more from its leaders."

"Baby, I'm so angry and so hurt that this happened to you. But knowing what you went through and that you've still managed to accomplish so much just makes me even more proud of you." Alma squeezed her daughter's hand.

A smile spread across her face, despite the tears that still fell from her eyes. Only now, the tears were happy ones. Unburdening herself to her mother felt good, better than she could have imagined. She stood and embraced her mother. "Thank you, Mama."

"Does Xavier know about all this?"

"Yes and no." Imani could feel the fear growing inside once again. "I told him that I'd been harassed and that I was under a gag order, but not much else."

"Why haven't you told him the full story?"

"Mama, Givens is a powerful man. If the truth comes out, I know he'll come after me. With Xavier's campaign going on, I just can't bring myself to drag him into this. Beyond that, I don't have any assurance Xavier will even believe me."

Alma's expression conveyed her intent listening.

"What if he thinks I had an affair with Givens and that I was just trying to cover it up by going to HR?"

Alma looked thoughtful. "I can see why you're nervous, but I don't think Xavier is like that."

"I don't know, Mama. I just don't know how he'd take it."

"I understand. Do what works for you, but if you're going to be with Xavier, he needs to know what happened. Just promise me you'll think about it."

"I will, Mama."

Alma nodded, seeming satisfied for now. "Come on downstairs. I'll make you something to eat."

"I'm not really hungry."

Her mother cut her a look that told her she would eat whether she wanted to or not.

Knowing better than to argue, Imani followed her mother out of the study and closed the door behind her.

When Imani entered Copeland Jewelry, she was surprised to see how thin the crowd was. Though it was early November, the store was already decked out in Christmas finery and displaying signage touting their holiday specials. It was holiday shopping that had brought her there. With everything going on in her life, she needed a little retail therapy, so she'd decided to take some time to shop for Christmas gifts for her mother and Maya.

Copeland was the best place in town for custom jewelry, especially tennis and charm bracelets. It occupied a storefront in Brier Creek Commons, the upscale shopping center abutting the wealthy neighborhood of the same name. Fighting traffic from the other side of the city to reach Copeland's wasn't something she enjoyed, but she'd been shopping at the family-owned store for years and wouldn't dream of purchasing from one of those cookie-cutter chain stores.

Imani moved toward the tennis bracelet display, eyeing a setting she'd been thinking of getting for her mother. Bracelet settings were available in a variety of metals and finishes. The store allowed buyers to customize the bracelet with their choice of stone, and Imani wanted to have one made for her mother that contained three birthstones: Imani's, Alma's, and that of Alma's late husband.

She was still eyeing the selection of settings when someone walked up next to her and rang the bell on the counter. Turning toward the sound, she was surprised to see Cassidy standing there. "Hi, Cassidy."

Cassidy turned her way with a smile. "Oh, hey, Imani. How are you doing?"

"Pretty good. Just trying to get a jump on the Christmas shopping. How about you?"

Cassidy's smile brightened, her lashes fluttering dramatically. "I'm picking up a little gift from my man."

Imani smiled but didn't say anything. She remembered how Cassidy had spoken of her mystery man when she'd first come to Grant Dermatology. Since the details of Cassidy's relationship were none of her business or concern, she chose to simply mirror Cassidy's expression.

A clerk appeared, and Cassidy gave her name. "I'm here to pick up an order that was placed for me." She produced identification from her small handbag.

"Ah yes. I have it for you right here, ma'am." The male clerk turned to remove a long box from a locked cabinet and handed it over to Cassidy. "We hope you'll find it satisfactory."

Imani watched as Cassidy opened the box. The gold-and-diamond tennis bracelet inside had so much bling, Imani found herself squinting.

Unable to hold back, Imani said, "That's one hell of a bracelet."

Cassidy squealed in delight. "I know! But you know what they say about diamonds being a girl's best friend and all." She snapped the box shut and slipped it into her purse.

Imani continued to stare in Cassidy's direction as she signed for the bracelet, not knowing what to say. Whoever Cassidy was dating right now apparently made very good money. Still, Imani couldn't imagine why a man who'd dropped that kind of cash on a piece of jewelry wouldn't want to be with his woman when she received it.

Cassidy turned back toward her as the clerk departed. "You know, back in college, I dreamed of owning some-thing like this. Who knew I'd get it from my man with-out even having to break a sweat?"

Imani released a little nervous laugh. "Yeah. Who knew?" She couldn't help thinking how the brightness in Cassidy's voice seemed false, even rehearsed.

"I've gotta go. It was good seeing you again. Good luck with the shopping."

"Thanks." It was all she had a chance to say as Cassidy strolled out of the store. Shaking her head, Imani went back to picking out her mother's gift.

Chapter 15

FRIDAY EVENING, IMANI RECLINED ON HER SOFA WITH A magazine. As she flipped through the pages, a knock sounded at her door. A smile touched her lips as she went to answer it.

Xavier stepped inside a few moments later, bringing with him the spicy, masculine scent that always clung to him. He wore a pair of black slacks and matching loafers. A kelly-green shirt covered his muscular torso, and he loosened the knot of his solid-black tie as he spoke. "Hey, sweets. I got your text and I came straight here from work."

She gave him a peck on the cheek. "Nice suit. But where's the sport coat?"

"In the car." He entered the living room fully, using his foot to push the door closed behind him. "I didn't want to waste any time."

"What do you mean?"

By the time the last word of her question left her lips, his strong arms were encircling her. "I've been thinking about making love to you all day long."

She pressed her open palms against his chest, felt his muscles flex beneath the soft fabric of his shirt. "Xavier, that sounds wonderful, but we have to talk."

He lifted one hand from her waist. Spreading his fingers, he speared them through her hair and tilted her head. "We can talk after."

His lips crashed down against hers, and in an instant, she forgot everything she had planned to say.

He eased her back toward her tan couch. "I've missed you so much," he murmured into her neck, placing his warm kisses there.

As they fell down on the soft fabric, she felt her resistance waning. "Xavier, I should have been more open." Her voice sounded weak in her ears, but she was putting up all the fight she could muster at the moment.

"I agree." His hot eyes held hers as he undid the buttons running down the front of her blouse. "And you will be. Later."

Imani started to form another weak protest, but his full, warm lips touched hers, and all thoughts dissolved into the haze of desire. He teased her a bit, placing short, fleeting pecks on her lips. As passion grew, he followed the curve of her mouth with his tongue until her lips parted. Her arms wound around his neck, pulling him closer as she fed on the potency of his kiss.

When he pulled away to slip the now-open blouse off her shoulders, she could feel herself trembling beneath his touch. Heat filled her blood as the heady, attractive aroma of his cologne wafted up her nose, increasing the heady nature of her desire for him. He let his palms graze her nipples through the thin white camisole and white lace bra she wore, and they answered his call by hardening with need.

A loud, persistent buzzing momentarily broke the spell. "Xavier. Is that your phone?"

"Don't care." The words were punctuated by his caress, moving over her torso like a whisper. "God, I've missed you."

The buzzing ceased, or at least she didn't hear it anymore.

Her eyes slid closed as he eased the camisole down around her waist, then reached around her to unhook her bra. When his fingertips grazed the bared nipples, a moan slid from her throat. His lips replaced his hands, and as he delighted the hard peaks of her breasts with slow, hot kisses and licks, her back arched in response.

The buzzing started again.

This time, Xavier only murmured "I'm busy" against the bud of her taut nipple. That said, he continued to work his magic.

He finally moved away from her damp, pleading breasts, but before she could catch her breath, she felt his lips trailing humid kisses down the plane of her stomach.

She could hear her own sultry croon echo in the silence as he raised her hips, freeing her of the pushed-down camisole. Next, he unclasped her slacks and, swirling his tongue around her navel, tugged them down. Her white satin panties soon joined them, and she was left nude and buzzing with arousal and anticipation.

His phone buzzed a third time. Xavier, his jaw tight, reached into the pocket of his slacks. "I'm turning this damn thing off." Once he did, he tossed the phone to the floor. It bounced as it hit the carpet.

He stepped away to strip out of his own clothing, and she tried to gather herself. Imani knew how good Xavier was at this, and that made it hard to contain her anticipation. This interlude seemed more like a slow, deliberate attempt to render her insane, or at least mindless enough that she would do whatever he asked.

With little effort, he lifted her up onto the padded back of the sofa, so that she sat atop it. He knelt on the sofa's seat, parted her thighs with gentle but firm hands, and leaned in.

Her head fell back as his mouth made contact with her most intimate place. She clutched the cushions around her to maintain her upright position as he licked, sucked, and loved her with such ardor, she could barely breathe. Her soft sighs soon turned into cries of ecstasy as he pushed her closer and closer to the edge of her sanity. His big hands reached around to cup her behind, and he pulled her closer to allow himself even more access to her treasure. She could feel herself shaking under the fiery stroking of his tongue. The power and majesty of it grew and grew until an orgasm ripped through her. Shivering and crying out his name, she bloomed in the sunlight only he could give.

She felt him tugging her down and let him do it. Whatever this man wanted, he could have. He laid her on her belly on the sofa, with her knees resting on the plush taupe carpet.

"You're mine, Imani," he whispered as he kissed the indentation of her spine. "All mine." He fiddled around in his pocket, and she heard the foil packet tearing.

She felt his hardness probing her. Welcoming the iron feel of him, she arched her back, raising her hips in welcome. Before her next heartbeat, he filled her, and she moaned low in her throat, relishing the feel of every inch of him inside her.

He began to move, and the glowing bliss radiated from her very center. Her nipples ached, hardening as she met him stroke for stroke. He was so wonderfully thick and filled her so well, she didn't think she could hold out much longer.

She heard him grunt as he wrapped a strong arm around her waist and began stroking her harder, faster. The rhythm built and grew, his hips pistoning until she was sure she was impaled on the root of heaven itself. Everything in her world centered on his loving, and she never wanted it to end. Never.

She felt the searing, persistent opening notes of orgasm building inside her, and before she could react, she was gone. The force of her ecstasy ripped a hoarse scream from her throat as her world exploded into brilliance.

He kept up his pace until a few moments later, when he stiffened and groaned. The low, rumbling sound filled the room around them.

Xavier let his manhood slip from her, then sank onto the floor.

Too sated to do anything else, she followed him and let his arms encircle her.

When she came around again, she was still sprawled naked across her living room carpet, but she was alone.

She sat up, looking around for any sign of Xavier.

He emerged from the hallway with one of her teal bath towels wrapped around his waist. Droplets of water clung to the rippling muscles of his chest and arms. "I took a shower. I didn't think you'd mind."

She shook her head. "I don't mind." Getting up, she gathered her scattered clothing and scurried to her bedroom.

He followed her. As she tossed the clothes in the hamper and pulled a sleeveless cotton nightgown out of her drawer, he stood in her doorway. "Imani, you said you wanted to talk."

Imani's heart pounded in her ears. She slipped into a pair of panties, the nightgown, and then went into the closet for her robe. He was right; they did need to talk. But he had no idea of the subject matter they were about to cover. "I agree. But you should dress first."

"Why?"

She didn't want to tell him it was because she was afraid he'd storm out the minute he heard what she had to say. Dread rose within her, but she knew she'd put this off long enough. "Because I won't be able to concentrate with you wearing nothing but my towel." It was a true statement. She would need her wits about her to tell him her secret.

He chuckled with obvious male satisfaction. "Fair enough." He left to retrieve his clothes from the living room, and she pulled on her robe and tied the belt tight around her waist. Barefoot, she went back into the living room and waited on the sofa for him to cover his muscular, distracting frame.

While he dressed, she spoke. "You know, I really want to try to be open and honest with you. I understand now that's what you need from me."

"I'm glad to hear it." He made the remark as he buttoned his slacks.

"That's why I wanted to talk to you about something really important."

From its spot on the floor, Xavier's phone buzzed again.

Now dressed, but with his shirt still hanging open, he squatted to retrieve it. The move gave her a wonderful view of his powerful thigh muscles, flexing beneath his slacks.

His brow furrowed. "Excuse me, Imani."

She watched him disappear into the hallway, wondering what had suddenly taken his attention away from her.

~~~

Standing in Imani's bedroom, Xavier swiped his fingertip across the screen of his phone. Once it unlocked, his eyes grew wide at the number of notifications waiting there.

Nine missed calls and fifteen text messages? All of them were from Tyrone, and the sheer number of times his friend had tried to reach him was concerning. He swiped over the screen again, scrolling through the texts.

The phone buzzed in his hand with an incoming call. He answered immediately. "Tyrone. What the hell is going on that has you calling me this many times on a Friday night?"

"Didn't you read any of my texts?" As always, Tyrone's tone of voice conveyed his mood. He sounded agitated, on edge, and ready to snap.

"I was trying to, but you called."

"What the hell have you been doing all night?"

Xavier rolled his eyes. "Handling my business. Now what's going on? Somebody need bail money or something?"

Tyrone sighed. "I wish it was that simple. You need to get over to the *News and Observer* website right now and search Imani's name."

He felt his brow hitch. "Why?"

"An article came out today about her, and you need to see it. I would have called you earlier, but I was tied up in court until past seven."

"Ty, are you sure it's all that serious?" Xavier chuckled, hoping he could get Tyrone to lighten up. It was the weekend, after all.

Tyrone's answer was flat, lacking any humor. "Xavier. Read the article." Without another word, he disconnected the call.

Xavier shook his head. Rather than go back into the living room, he took a seat on the edge of Imani's bed and opened the Internet browser on his phone. Navigating to the newspaper's website, he ran a search for Imani's name and sorted it by most recent.

Two articles came up. One was the one he'd seen a few weeks ago, published after she'd made her visit to his campaign headquarters. But the other, newer result had a title that made his heart stop.

Dr. Imani Grant—Power Player or Pariah?

He clicked the headline and began scanning the text. Several phrases jumped out at him, and by the time he reached the third paragraph, his jaw tightened.

Dr. Grant, while well-off in her own right, seems to always place herself in the company of men in power. Before her current romance with city council hopeful Xavier Whitted, Grant is believed to have carried on an affair with current councilman Aaron Givens. Records of Grant's association with Givens were discovered when

Givens's personal finance records were accessed in accordance with campaign rules, and a harassment suit between Grant and Givens, with a subsequent settlement, was revealed. The Givens campaign couldn't be reached for comment, but pollsters expect the incumbent's numbers to suffer in light of these revelations. The settlement amount is undisclosed...

Xavier's grip on the phone went lax, and he almost dropped it. Closing his hand around it again, he got up and stalked back into the living room.

Imani remained on the sofa, sitting with her legs tucked beneath her. Looking up at him, her smile faded.

Apparently she could read his stormy mood from the expression on his face.

Her tone cautious, she asked, "Xavier? What's wrong?"

He held up his phone, the article still displayed on the screen. "You were involved with Givens, and you didn't tell me?"

Her eyes grew large, round. "Involved with him? I was never—"

"That's not what the paper says, Imani." Xavier could feel the blood boiling in his veins. He tossed the phone at her and sat on the arm of the sofa farthest away. Arms folded over his chest, he gave her a few moments to read what was there in black and white.

"Oh my God. Who would do this?"

"Why didn't you tell me, Imani? I can't believe you would keep something like this from me."

She let the phone drop from her grasp. "I couldn't because I'm under a gag order."

Xavier shook his head. "Do you really expect me to believe that now?"

"Xavier, this is the truth. We were never involved. He…assaulted me." Her voice wavered, and tears stood in her eyes, shimmering like jewels. "I reported him to Human Resources and he tried to pin the whole thing on me."

"A gag order means you can't speak on something publicly. There was no reason for you to hide this from me." Anger burned so hot inside him, he feared he might explode. "Givens…touched you?" He could hear himself shouting but couldn't seem to reel in his emotions.

She shouted back through her tears. "He forced me! Whether you believe me or not, it's the truth." Her eyes glistened as they filled again.

He recoiled. How could she have kept this from him? With the election just days away, this was the last thing he needed. "Imani," he murmured.

Her head down, she wiped at the tears that splashed down the front of her robe now. "This is why I didn't want to tell you. I was ashamed."

He didn't speak, just stared at his hands resting in his lap.

"I knew you would react like this. I tried to tell you to stay away from me." She turned her back to him.

"If it really was an assault, why would you keep it from me so long?" He didn't bother to hide the disbelief from his tone. He looked up, and she spun back to face him again.

She blinked rapidly, appearing stung by his words. "What are you saying? You don't believe me?"

He shrugged, his jaw tight. "I don't really know what to believe, Imani."

Her eyes hardened. "I don't believe this. You have no right to accuse me of anything. I tried to warn you off, but you wouldn't listen!"

Never in his life had he felt so duped, so betrayed. His cold, distant gaze met hers. "You won't have to worry about me bothering you anymore." He stood up, grabbed his suit jacket from the back of a nearby chair, and stalked toward the door.

She didn't follow him. When he looked back, he saw her lying over the arm of the sofa, weeping.

Anger flared within him, warring with a deep sense of betrayal. Unable to put his feelings into words, he knew there was nothing left for him to do but make his exit. He left her apartment and didn't bother to say good-bye.

As he drove away, at first not even knowing his destination, he cursed a blue streak. His mother would undoubtedly faint if she could hear the obscenities pouring from his mouth like a waterfall. He could not believe Imani and her deceitful ways. He'd just made love to her, for God's sake. How could she hurt him this way after what they'd shared?

This was not the sweet, innocent Imani he knew. He'd always loved the virtue in her, the upright and elegant way she carried herself. But now, his perception of her had been tainted by the harsh reality of her secret. Never, not in ten lifetimes, would he have thought she was that kind of girl.

He had to go home. He wanted a drink, but Imani had already endangered his campaign, and he wasn't about to make matters worse with public drunkenness.

He made his way home on autopilot, taking the turns that had become second nature to him without much thought. When he pulled into the driveway of his modest one-story home just off of Oberlin Road, he got out of the car and trudged inside.

Xavier tossed his jacket over the back of his brown sofa and walked straight to the tall wooden cabinet occupying a corner of his living room. He extracted a humidor, then opened it to select one of the fine cigars inside. He couldn't recall the last time he'd smoked one, but something about the spicy bite of the aged tobacco seemed to calm his nerves. A compartment of the humidor held a book of matches and a stainless steel cutter. Flopping down on the couch, he used his cutter to snip the end of the cigar, then lit it. The first draw made him cough a bit. Soon he relaxed into a comfortable position and tried to let thoughts of Imani float away from his mind like the curling smoke rising above him.

He'd just begun to get into the cigar's complex flavor when his cell phone vibrated on his hip. He slid it out of his pocket and demanded, "Hello? Who is this?"

"Hello, Mr. Whitted." The voice on the other end belonged to Aaron Givens.

"How did you get my private number, you prick?" He waited for an answer.

In response, Givens snorted. "Easily. I have my ways."

"What do you want?" He was in no mood to talk to the old blowhard, but he'd already answered the call. He wondered why he never looked at the damn caller ID.

"I'm just checking in with you. Have you been reading the paper lately?"

Xavier could detect the note of condescension in Givens's voice. "What's your point?"

Givens chuckled. "I'm offering you a little friendly advice. Drop out of the race, before you embarrass yourself." He paused for a moment. "Ms. Grant has quite a past, and the word is out now."

Anger sprouted anew, and Xavier wanted to punch something. Was this asshole threatening him? "Save it, Givens. I'm not dropping out of the race."

On the other end of the line, Givens sputtered "You'll regret this!" and disconnected the call.

Tossing his cell phone aside, Xavier took another long puff from the cigar. When he'd smoked his fill, which was only about halfway down the cigar's shaft, he extinguished it in the metal ashtray on his side table. Exhaling the last curl of smoke, he let his head drop back on the pillows behind him.

Before he'd let Imani seep back into his heart, he'd never had to go through things like this. The presence of the lit cigar in his hand spoke volumes about his stress level.

He told himself that it didn't matter, that he was through chasing after Imani.

But a part of him knew that when it came to the two of them, it was never really over.

Xavier didn't realize he'd drifted off until a loud banging on the front door startled him. Grumbling, he got to his feet and stumbled in that direction, shouting, "Who the hell is it?"

"Max and Tyrone, man," came Tyrone's reply.

Xavier flung the door open, leaning on it for support. "What are y'all doin' here, banging on my door like the police?" He'd been just starting to get into his impromptu nap, and he hadn't appreciated the loud knocking.

Maxwell, dressed in a brown designer suit, stepped past him into the house. "We were supposed to have a poker game." He looked his friend up and down. "Man, it smells like a cigar shop in here."

"I know. I had one a while ago." Xavier gestured toward the remains of the cigar resting in the ashtray.

Tyrone closed the door behind them as he slipped out of his black trench coat, revealing the navy suit beneath. Waving a hand in front of his face, he wrinkled his nose. "Damn. Are you sure you only smoked one?"

"The smell lingers." Xavier shrugged. He was a grown man in his own house, and he'd do as he pleased.

"X, I haven't seen you smoke in years." Tyrone's voice held a mix of irritation and concern. "What the hell is going on with you?"

"Imani." His tone was bitter as he said her name. He dropped down onto the couch again, reached for the still-open humidor. Maxwell pulled it away.

"Oh, no," Maxwell insisted. "You know I hate the smell of those damn things." He punctuated his complaint with a couple of fake coughs.

Xavier rolled his eyes but closed the humidor. After returning it to the cabinet, he sat down on the couch again.

Tyrone took a seat on the love seat across from them. "So I'm guessing you read the article." His brow furrowed.

"Yeah, T." Xavier rubbed a hand over his eyes. "We made love, and now I find this out."

Maxwell's brow hitched in confusion. "What are we talking about?"

"She had some kind of involvement with Givens

back in the day." He shook his head at the memory of her words.

Tyrone settled back in the chair. "I guess you know she might endanger your chances at winning the council seat."

"It's more than that. She lied to me, T. She kept it from me all this time." The sting of betrayal hit Xavier again, tightening his chest. He wanted to finish his cigar, but he didn't want to deal with Maxwell's dramatics about the smell.

Maxwell remarked, "I don't know why y'all let women get under your skin like this."

Tyrone shook his head. "Spoken like a true Casanova. You'll meet your match one day."

"We'll see about that." Maxwell folded his arms over his chest.

Xavier shook his head at the two of them. Tyrone and Maxwell often took on a lecturing tone with him when he did something they didn't approve of. He supposed he understood Tyrone's ways; as the oldest of the group, he probably felt a certain responsibility for them, like a big brother. Maxwell, however, was the same age as Xavier. As far as Xavier could tell, Maxwell just liked being the contrarian of the group.

Xavier admitted, "I don't feel like I can trust her anymore. So I'm through chasing after her."

Tyrone looked sympathetic. "Then you should have no problem sticking to our agreement to stay away from her until after the election this time."

His eyes cast down toward where his bare feet rested on the area rug, Xavier nodded. "No problem whatsoever."

As far as he was concerned, everything he'd shared

with Imani had been reduced to ash by her lies, just like the smoldering remnants of his cigar.

———— ∾∾∾ ————

After Xavier's departure, Imani remained prone on her sofa for what seemed like hours. She wept bitter tears, her sobs echoing in the room until hoarseness rendered her silent. The teardrops fell, staining the fabric of her sofa until she had no tears left to shed. Finally, she dragged herself up, trudging to her bedroom.

What bothered her most was that she couldn't nail down why she'd cried so hard for so long. Were her tears brought on by Xavier's anger or by her own shame? For weeks now, she'd been trying to get him to walk away from her and from whatever emotional connection they shared. She felt certain she'd finally succeeded in her quest as of today, but the victory felt hollow. There was no sense of triumph at having been right or relief at having him out of her life. No, today felt decidedly sad. It was almost as if she were mourning for their lost relationship.

Inside her bedroom, she dragged her bare feet across the carpet until she reached her closet. She took a few steps inside and grabbed the edge of the big cardboard box she'd brought over from her mother's house.

Once she pulled the box out of the closet, she slid it to the foot of her bed and sat down there. She rifled through the box for a few moments, sniffling as she touched these physical manifestations of her past. There were so many things in there from Xavier, things she had no need of now. At least, that's what she told herself. She closed her eyes and sighed.

In the empty room, she gave voice to her thoughts. "I need to let go of him. How can I get him out of my system?"

The empty room offered no response, but an idea popped into her head. Maybe some catharsis would help here, some symbolic activity to rid her of all the feelings Xavier stirred inside her. Determined to bring an end to this madness once and for all, she went back to the closet to get dressed.

Within thirty minutes, she'd donned a pair of jeans and a Spelman sweatshirt, hauled the box out to the trunk of her car, and gotten on the road. Her destination was Maya's house, set far off the beaten path in the wilds of Wake County.

The drive proved long, as usual, and contemplative. She took the back way to Maya's house, down a narrow two-lane road bordered on both sides by towering pine trees. As she navigated the winding roadway, the brilliant sunlight of the morning penetrated the canopy of pine branches to dapple the asphalt. With each passing mile, she pushed away thoughts of last night, when she'd given herself to Xavier with such abandon. He'd been an attentive lover, and she would miss the feeling of his strong hands on her body. But as she'd been trying to tell him all this time, what they shared was better left in the past.

She arrived at Maya's house and pulled her car into the long gravel driveway, parking it behind Maya's sedan. Getting out of her car, she hiked across the neatly trimmed grass and up the three steps to the wide sitting porch that wrapped around the single-story house. There, she rapped on the door.

The door swung open, and Maya appeared in the frame. Still clad in her typical weekend ensemble of lime-green bathrobe, bunny slippers, and pink flexi rollers, Maya fixed her with a confused stare. "Hey, Imani. What are you doing out here, and why didn't you call so I could get dressed?"

Imani offered a small smile. "Sorry, Maya. Coming out here was kind of a spur-of-the-moment thing."

Maya stifled a yawn. "Good thing I love you and you're always welcome. Do you want to come in?" She swung open the screen door and stepped back.

Imani shook her head. "No, not really. I just want to use your fire pit."

Lips pursed, Maya folded her arms over her chest. "You're not trying to get rid of a body or anything, are you? What's next, getting a ticket to Tijuana?"

Despite her sullen mood, Imani giggled. "No, nothing like that. Just throw on some sweats or something and meet me in the back."

"Okay, but if it turns out to be a body, I'm not going to jail for you."

Imani shook her head at her cousin's silliness. When Maya stepped back inside the house and let the door swing closed, Imani sat down on one of the brown wicker chairs on the porch. For a few minutes, she enjoyed the near-silent surroundings of her cousin's property. She could smell the sap from the pine trees scenting the air and heard the distant mooing of a cow. Maya lived in the heart of farm country, though she and her husband never grew anything except azalea bushes, like the white ones currently blooming around the porch.

Maya returned a short time later in a black tracksuit with a hot-pink stripe. "Okay, what are we burning, Cuz?"

Imani got up and gestured for Maya to follow her. "Come on, I'll show you. By the way, where's Fred, anyway?"

Maya, trailing behind Imani as they walked toward her car, shook her head. "Still asleep. He was up half the night last night playing poker with his boys."

Imani used her remote to pop the trunk. As the lid swung up, she gestured to the box inside. "See, no body. I've just got some stuff I need to get rid of."

"Like what?" Before she could even finish asking the question, Maya had already begun digging through the box's contents. "Looks like a lot of stuff you got from Xavier."

"That's right."

Maya shot her some side eye. "Imani, don't tell me you drove all the way out here to set some letters and teddy bears on fire. Isn't that a little petty?"

Imani pursed her lips. "Maya, don't start with me."

Maya rolled her eyes. "Whatever, girl. I rescind my previous statement. It's not a little petty; it's a lot petty. What are you, seventeen?"

Smacking her lips, Imani folded her hands into fists and propped them on her hips. "Come on. It's not about being petty. It's about being symbolic. It's time for me to move on."

"I'm assuming you two had a fight." Maya remained bent over at the waist, still digging through the box.

"You assume right, and it was the big one. He knows about my harassment suit, and it's over between us." She pulled in a deep breath, trying to draw strength from the fresh country air. "I need to get rid of these things and the feelings they evoke. You know what they say: when in doubt, kill it with fire."

Maya snorted, both her hands buried in the box now. "Imani, you are not burning stuffed animals in my fire pit. I will not be party to the petty."

"Why not? I just told you what I'm trying to do here."

Maya pulled something out of the box. Straightening, she held it up for Imani to see. "If you're going to kill anything with fire, it should be this. Why in the hell do you even still have it?"

Taking in the sight of the journal she'd written in all those years ago, she sighed. "To remind me of how hard I worked to get where I am."

Maya shook her head slowly. "I call bullshit. This old, ratty book only reminds you of keeping secrets and feeling ashamed. This is what belongs in the fire pit, Imani. It's time to kill the shame and the secrets with fire."

Imani looked into the kind eyes of her cousin and knew she was right. Maya was her only female cousin on her father's side and the closest thing she'd ever had to a sister. In all the years they'd been together, Maya had always looked out for her.

"Did you bring matches, or do I need to get some? Because we are turning this thing to ash today, girl." Maya tucked the journal under her arm, then used her free hand to close the trunk. "Have I ever steered you wrong?"

Imani blew out a breath through pursed lips. "There was that time you told me to get the Halle Berry haircut, and I came out looking like a dude."

Maya cut her a look. "Other than that, crazy."

"All right, all right. Other than that, you've given me

pretty solid advice." She reached into the pocket of her jeans, pulling out the book of matches she'd tucked in there earlier.

"Good." Maya started walking toward the backyard. "Then let's have us a bonfire."

The two of them circled around the right side of the house, until they reached the fire pit. The pit was just a round indentation in the soil, filled in with sand and surrounded by a circle of large stones. A patio made of flat stepping-stones bordered the pit, and two white Adirondack chairs sat on the flat surface.

Maya handed the journal off to Imani, then grabbed a bottle of lighter fluid from the grill station a few feet away. Returning, Maya waited for Imani to toss the journal in the pit before handing off the lighter fluid. "Go ahead, Imani. Douse it good so it'll go up right away." She flopped down in one of the chairs to watch.

Taking the plastic bottle, Imani turned and anointed the journal with a liberal squirt. Then she gave Maya the bottle back and went for her matches. Striking one, she dropped in into the pit. The fabric caught immediately, and Imani backed away to take up residence in the other chair.

The two of them watched the leather, ink, and paper burn in silence.

Imani saw the pages disintegrate in the dancing yellow flames, smelled the gray smoke rising from the pit. Inside, she felt something happening, as if her soul were turning over. She projected the shame, the secrecy, and the pain she'd been holding on to into the pit, with the journal. As the smoke curled and rose toward the sky, she imagined those negative emotions floating away with it on the November wind, never to be seen again.

Maya's voice broke into her thoughts. "Feels good, doesn't it?"

Never taking her gaze off the plume of rising smoke, Imani nodded. "Yes, it does."

"What about Xavier? Does he know now?"

She sighed. "Yes, and I'll probably never see him again."

Maya shook her head. "I'm shocked. I thought Xavier was the understanding type."

"After he saw that article in the paper, he started making all kinds of assumptions. I probably just lost the best thing that ever happened to me, all because I held back when I should have just been completely honest." Imani dashed away a tear.

Maya reached over the arm of her chair, clasping hands with her cousin. "I'm sorry, girl."

"Me, too." Lying back in the chair, Imani tried to push her thoughts of Xavier away. Because now, she saw no way they could ever mend their broken love.

Chapter 16

ON THE DRIVE TO FIRST BAPTIST CHURCH, XAVIER LOOKED at his eyes in the rearview. He was relieved to see the redness of the previous day gone. Satisfied, he directed his attention back to the road.

As he pulled into the church parking lot, he found a spot and slipped the truck into it. Soon, he was standing by the side door, where he'd agreed to meet Tyrone. As the minutes ticked by, he still saw no sign of his campaign manager. When Tyrone finally jogged up, thirty minutes before Xavier was supposed to speak, he gave him a look like he wanted to pop him upside the head. "You cut it way too close. Don't pull this crap on me again."

Tyrone nodded, looking apologetic. "Sorry about that, X."

"And what's your excuse for being this late? You're usually such a stickler for the schedule."

Tyrone didn't bother hiding his grin as he answered. "Remember, I'm still a newlywed."

Xavier shook his head, trying not to think about how much he missed having Imani's body next to his. "Whatever. Let's just get inside, so I can make my speech."

Tyrone dialed it back. "Fine. Now let's go in there and wow them. We've only got five days to convince the good citizens of this district they should let you have Givens's seat."

"Speaking of which, I got a call from that jerk Friday night."

"What was he doing calling you?"

"Trying to intimidate me again into dropping out of the race." Just remembering Givens's snide tone and his threats made him angry all over again. Clenching his fists, he reined in his temper. They were on church ground, after all.

Tyrone shook his head. "Still up to those shenanigans."

Xavier said, "If he calls me again, I should record it. I'm sure his constituents would be interested in hearing how childish and petty he really is."

The thought of embarrassing Aaron Givens brought a smile to Xavier's face. As he and Tyrone entered the church, they were shown to a room behind the pulpit, where they could wait for his turn to speak. The room, papered with children's drawings and brightly colored Bible verse posters, reminded him of his own Sunday school days.

A ghost of a smile crossed Tyrone's face before he shook his head. "No, Xavier. We're running this campaign with class, remember?"

Xavier sighed, knowing his friend was right. "Yeah, I remember. Taking the high road sucks."

Tyrone chuckled, patted him on the shoulder. "Don't worry. Guys like Givens always step in it on their own. Always." He handed him a folded sheet of paper. "Here's your notes."

Xavier opened the paper, taking a few moments to compose himself. When he looked up, he saw Tyrone eyeing him curiously. "What, man?"

"Did you ask her about the article? Give her a chance to explain?"

"T, drop it. You run my campaign, not my personal life." He fought to keep his tone even.

Tyrone made a face but let the matter drop. "Okay, I won't press you, then."

He sat at the rectangular table centering the room, and Xavier followed suit. As Xavier's eyes fell back to the notes, the door to the room swung open. Reverend Fitts, the pastor of the church, walked in. Following him was a sour-faced old woman Xavier didn't recognize. Her bright-pink dress, with its large red-and-yellow flowers, was a direct contrast to the muted royal blue of the reverend's pastoral robe. Even though Xavier had no idea who the woman was, he noticed she was glowering at him with a mixture of disapproval and disgust.

Tyrone asked, "What can we do for you, Reverend?"

Reverend Fitts looked decidedly nervous. "I'm afraid we've replaced Mr. Whitted in today's program. I've only just learned of this from Marie, our church secretary." He gestured to the mean-faced woman accompanying him.

Tyrone stood, obviously surprised. "Why is that?"

As if he'd spoken to her, the scowling Marie declared, "We only want speakers of high moral character here at First Baptist." She reached into her gigantic brown purse and slapped a folded copy of the paper down on the table. It was open to the local section and the recent unflattering article that referenced Xavier's association with Imani.

Xavier could feel his jaw tighten. How dare this woman judge him based on some trashy gossip in the local paper? He ignored Marie and turned his attention to the minister. "Reverend Fitts, is this what your congregation wants? To cancel my speech because of what was written in that article?"

Still looking nervous, Reverend Fitts started to open his mouth when Marie cut him off.

"Yes, Mr. Whitted. We don't want our church associated with that kind of behavior." She folded her arms across her chest and appeared quite satisfied with herself.

Tyrone just stood there, as if stunned by the woman's out-and-out rudeness.

Xavier rose from the table, refolded the speech, and placed it in one of the inside pockets of his sport jacket. He shook the minister's hand. "Reverend Fitts, I wish you the best of luck with your fund-raising." He wanted dearly to put the smirking Marie in her place, but he'd been taught to respect his elders. To that end, he said, "As for you, sister, you might want to reread Proverbs 20 verse 19. I always try to follow it."

The stunned expression on her face was the last thing he saw as he strode out, with Tyrone close behind him.

As they stepped into the sunshine once again, Tyrone asked, "What does the verse say?"

Gazing out at the lush, manicured grounds of the state capitol across the street, he recited the verse: "A gossip betrays a confidence; so avoid anyone who talks too much."

A chuckling Tyrone followed him into the parking lot.

———※———

Hands wrapped around the steering wheel, Imani steered her car into the parking lot of Buttercup's Cafe. Her eyes scanned the crowded lot for a spot.

"The doctor said my A1C was looking good today." Alma's voice cut into her thoughts.

"I know, and I'm happy about that." She glanced at her mother sitting in the passenger seat for a moment before refocusing on parking. Navigating the car into a spot between a monstrous extended-cab pickup truck and a haphazardly parked motorcycle, she cut the engine. "As soon as you get your blood pressure down, you'll be golden."

"I'm working on it. Watch, I'm not going to be eating any salt today." Alma grabbed her purse from the floor and opened her door.

Imani got out of the car, pleased to hear her mother's vow. She would probably still keep an eye on her during their lunch, out of habit and concern. "All right, but I will confiscate the saltshaker if I have to."

She linked arms with her mother. Using the remote to lock the doors, Imani then escorted Alma inside the restaurant through the double doors at the main entrance.

The place bustled with the usual lunchtime crowd, and there was a short wait for a table. Imani had anticipated that, as places with prime downtown Raleigh locations and great food always filled up like this during the weekday lunch rush. Hordes of state employees, along with folks working at the civic center and the bevy of banks, colleges, and hotels in the area, flocked here to feed their faces before heading back to complete their workdays.

Once they were seated in one of the cozy booths by the window, Imani picked up the single-page menu and looked it over. Spending the morning at the doctor's office with her mother had left her feeling a bit sleepy, so she decided to stick with something light in hopes of staving off the afternoon nap she felt coming on. It was rare that she took a day off from the practice. Today, she'd cleared her schedule so she could accompany her mother to her follow-up.

"What are you going to get, baby?" Alma casually posed the question.

"Probably a grilled chicken salad. I don't want anything heavy." She stifled a yawn with her open palm.

"I think I'm gonna get a grilled shrimp salad. Haven't had any shrimp in a good little while." Alma pushed her glasses up the bridge of her nose as she laid her menu on the table.

The waitress came around to take their order, deposited two glasses of ice water on the table, then departed with their menus.

Alma said something, but Imani couldn't hear her over the rising din of conversations.

Imani cupped her hand to her ear in an attempt to make out her mother's words. "What did you say, Mama?" She glanced over her shoulder and saw the reason the space had grown so loud. A large group of suit-clad men had just entered and were carrying on a rather loud conversation at the hostess stand a few feet away.

Alma raised her voice and repeated herself. "I said, there's Xavier. Behind you."

When she heard that, she almost wished she hadn't asked her mother to repeat herself. Shifting her torso, she took another look over her shoulder, hoping her mother had been mistaken. *No such luck*. There, in the center of the group of loudmouth businessmen who'd just entered, stood Xavier. She assumed the other men must be clients of his accounting firm, since she didn't see Tyrone in the mix. If the other men were voters or campaign contributors he wanted to schmooze, she knew his campaign manager would have been present.

"You see him? He's looking good, too. Then again, he always did clean up nice."

Imani agreed with her mother. Taking in the sight of his tall, broad-shouldered handsomeness draped in a well-fitting navy-blue suit, she felt a familiar stirring in her lower regions. After everything that had transpired between them, seeing him threw her way off kilter. Her heart somersaulted in her chest, and a sound escaped her lips.

Alma's brow furrowed. "What do you mean, 'ugh'?"

"It's nothing, Mama. We're not on good terms right now." That was a gross understatement, and she knew it. "I'm pretty sure he's out of the running to be your son-in-law."

"Is this about that article in the paper?"

"It's complicated, Mama." Imani looked down at the tablecloth, feeling the tears rising in her throat. "Basically I screwed it up, and I'm sure he never wants to have anything to do with me again."

"Mmm-hmm." Alma pursed her lips, folded her arms over her chest, but said nothing further.

Though she withered beneath her mother's accusing stare, Imani felt a modicum of relief that she'd avoided a lecture, at least for the moment. If the hostess escorted Xavier and his lunch companions to the left, she could avoid all eye contact with him and continue with her day in peace. She crossed her legs and fingers beneath the table, offering a silent prayer that this potentially awkward confrontation would be avoided.

Alma's expression brightened. Looking past Imani, she announced, "Look, they're coming this way."

Imani sighed. *Today is just not my day.* She didn't dare turn to look behind her again. To avoid her mother's gaze, she instead stared at the red leather of the booth next to Alma's head.

The group moved closer, still chatting. The warring scents of half a dozen different colognes wafted up Imani's nostrils, threatening to overwhelm her. One scent, familiar and altogether attractive, stood out above the rest.

When the men came abreast of her table, they moved on en masse—all except Xavier. Imani cringed when she heard his deep voice.

"I'll be over to the table in a minute," he said. His tall figure cast a shadow over the table as he stopped beside it.

Still staring at the red leather seat back, Imani blinked several times. She was so aware of Xavier's eyes on her face, her cheeks burned with heat.

"Hello, Imani." The greeting sounded stiff, formal.

"Xavier." She gave him a brief nod, matching his tone.

He spoke again. "Hey, Ma Alma. It's always good to see you. How are you?"

"I'm good, Xavier, but what on earth is going on between you and my daughter?"

Imani's heart pounded in her chest like a hip-hop bass line, and she swallowed.

"It's kind of complicated," Xavier answered with a slight smile.

Alma offered a soft smile. "Oh, come on, now. You haven't been over to the house to see me in a while. I miss seeing you."

He grinned. "I'll try to stop by this week. Have a good day, Ma Alma. Imani." He looked at her again, then strode away.

As his heady presence moved away from the table, Imani took a long sip from her water glass, hoping to calm her frayed nerves. When she looked up, she saw her mother looking straight at her.

Her face locked in a deep frown, Alma asked, "What is going on with you two?"

Bracing herself for an epic lecture, Imani informed her mother of the fight she'd had with Xavier over the weekend. "I think it's all over for us, Mama. I knew it was too good to be true."

"Really? You think you don't deserve happiness?"

"Mama, I—" Imani shut her mouth as the waitress returned with their salads. Once the plates, silverware, and the tiny containers of dressing were left on the table and the waitress left, she finished her sentence. "I don't know. But after the things he said to me, it's pretty clear he doesn't trust me, and without trust, we don't have anything."

"Hmph." Alma dressed her salad, her face still tight with displeasure. "The two of you were probably angry, and I'm sure you both said things you didn't mean. The bottom line is that the two of you belong together. I can't believe you didn't tell me about this."

Frustration got the better of her, and she snapped, "Why? So you could tell me how I was wrong and how I should beg his forgiveness? You always take his side."

Alma looked up at her daughter. "Now I know you've lost your mind. You'd better watch that tone with me, Imani."

Imani remembered herself and straightened up. "I'm sorry, Mama. I'm not trying to be disrespectful, but I'm really frustrated. All this time I've been thinking of what was best for Xavier and his aspirations. I just can't take his political future away from him. That's why I told him." For the life of her, she couldn't figure out why no one ever gave her any credit for taking the noble road. She was willing to set aside her own desires to do what was best for Xavier and his campaign, so why was she constantly being attacked for it? Did any of them realize how painful a sacrifice this was for her?

"Have you really been thinking of him? Or have you been thinking of how embarrassed you would be if he found out what you'd been keeping from him?"

A lump of emotion formed in Imani's throat. With some effort, she held back her tears. Her mother's perceptiveness had dredged up that sick feeling in the pit of her stomach, that feeling she thought she'd rid herself of when she'd set fire to her journal. "It's not as if what happened to me is something to be proud of, Mama. Can you really blame me for not wanting him to know?"

"No, I can't. But I'll tell you something. You overcame that. And that proves you can do anything, even make things right with Xavier, if you set your mind to it."

Imani sniffled. "I'm not sure, Mama."

Alma reached across the table to grab her hand. "Well, I am."

A tear escaped, sliding down Imani's cheek. She brushed it away and took a deep breath. "Thank you for that."

Alma offered her a teary smile. "I'm proud of you,

baby. You've accomplished so much. I know Richard is proud of you, too."

Holding hands with her mother, Imani felt a lightness enter her spirit.

No matter how hard he tried, Xavier couldn't put Imani out of his mind. The last three days had been hell on earth for him—first, the fight with her, then the embarrassing incident at the church to top it all off. After the weekend he'd had, Monday didn't seem half as daunting as it usually did. All he wanted now was to forget the events of the past several days.

A loud, obnoxious tapping broke into his thoughts.

He looked to his left and saw Tyrone tapping his metal pointer on the table. "I don't mean to bore you, but try to pay attention, Xavier." His annoyance was plain.

Xavier sat up straight in his seat, ran a hand over his weary eyes. He scanned the small conference room, looking at the faces of his campaign staff. They'd come today, three days before the election, to decide on a strategy for a final push. He knew they were down to their last chance to convince his fellow Raleighites that he was the best choice for the council seat.

Tyrone's tone was terse as he spoke again. "As I was saying, the latest polls from Friday have us up two to four points." He gestured to the image of the poll results projected on the wall next to him. "Givens is suffering because of the things that have come out about his past. That means we have a pretty good chance of winning this thing, if we can drive home that Xavier is the best candidate for the job."

"Or if Givens does something incredibly stupid," offered one of the volunteers.

Chuckles filled the room, and Xavier laughed in spite of his stormy mood.

Tyrone shook his head. "That would be nice, but Givens is too smart for that. He's held on to his seat for three terms already, and for good reason. He's a shrewd politician."

Loosening the blue-striped tie around his neck, Xavier spoke up. "So, what do you have in mind for these last few days, T?"

With a sly look, Tyrone retracted his pointer and placed it in his shirt pocket. "Well, you have potentially damaging information on Givens."

Xavier shook his head. "I'm not going down that path." And he wouldn't, no matter how much they badgered him. His parents had raised him better than to participate in mean-spirited gossip, even if the information was true. Besides, he didn't want to drag Imani back into this. His anger at her lying ways aside, he knew it would crush her to have that part of her past become fodder for the local news.

Tyrone rolled his eyes. "You keep saying you want to be the bigger man, but you know good and well if Givens had this kind of intel on you, he'd drop a dime on you in a hot second."

Xavier met his friend's gaze. "Don't you get it? That's why I'm keeping it to myself. If I release the information, I'll be no better than him."

Sighing in resignation, Tyrone turned to face the staffers present. "Well, our candidate has spoken. So what's on the schedule to keep the clean campaign going?"

Vera announced, "Xavier's booked for a meet and greet at the Museum of History tomorrow, and he'll be inspecting the progress on his community center Wednesday. News 14 is going to cover both events."

Tyrone's tight-lipped expression relaxed a bit. "I really think holding off on announcing the building of this community center was a good idea. With Givens out trying to convince the populace he's the Second Coming, this will be our ace in the hole."

Xavier chuckled at his friend's use of "the Second Coming." "What's Givens up to that's got you pissed off?"

Tyrone announced, "All right, people. You're dismissed. See you at the museum tomorrow."

As the small contingent of staff exited the room, Tyrone eased into the chair next to Xavier. "You haven't seen the news today, I'm guessing."

He shook his head. "No. What did I miss?"

Tyrone's face scrunched into a disgusted expression. "Givens had a camera crew follow him to a homeless shelter. The footage has been playing all day."

Xavier shook his head in amazement. "He's really laying it on thick, huh?"

Tyrone nodded. "He even took the opportunity to bring up your inexperience while he was there, as if that had anything to do with the people he was supposedly visiting."

"This guy is a real piece of work." Xavier wasn't surprised Givens was out spreading goodwill this close to the election. But to use those homeless people to sell himself to the public was pretty low, even for a man like Givens. Obviously he lacked morals, scruples, and good taste.

Tyrone stood. "I'm headed out, man. I'm supposed to meet Georgia for dinner."

Xavier exchanged a quick hug with his old friend. "I'll see you tomorrow, T."

"Later."

After Tyrone left, Xavier sat in the empty conference room, trying to rein in his thoughts. Was he really so bent on running a clean campaign? Or was it more about sparing Imani from very public embarrassment? A voice inside his head reminded him that she'd lied by keeping her past a secret. But had she really? She'd told him months ago that she didn't think his being involved with her was a good idea. She'd come up with myriad excuses about bad timing, being too occupied with other things, and not wanting to get serious with him. She'd tried her best to shake him, but he'd been so determined to be with her, he'd ignored her every attempt to push him away. She'd obviously been aware of the damage she might do to his campaign if word of her harassment suit got out. Now that everything was out in the open, he wished he'd listened to her then.

Parts of him wanted nothing more than to see Givens exposed for what he really was: a philandering, dishonest, lazy politician who cared more about status than his constituents. If he went public with what Imani had told him, Givens would go down in flames for all to see.

As much as he felt betrayed that she hadn't been honest with him, he missed her. He'd been dreaming of having her in his arms again for a decade, and just when the dream was a reality again, things had gone terribly wrong. Unfortunately, he couldn't simply turn off his feelings for her, even in the midst of his red-hot anger.

Immediately, he pushed the thought away. There was no way he could love someone like her, someone he didn't trust.

Getting up, he gathered his briefcase and strode from the room.

Chapter 17

IMANI RECLINED ON HER SOFA, READING OVER A PATIENT FILE. Wearing an old, comfortable blue strapless dress and a black silk cap on her hair, she stretched out and sank farther into the cushions. She'd already completed her usual Tuesday-night routine of giving herself a pedicure, and the foam toe separators remained in place. She knew Maya wouldn't have approved of her doing paperwork when she was supposed to be relaxing, but she saw no reason she shouldn't get some work done while the orange polish on her toes dried.

As Imani used her red ink pen to make a note on the file, a pounding at her front door startled her.

Turning her upper body toward the door, she scrunched up her face in annoyance. Who in the world would be beating her door down after nine o'clock?

The knocking came again, followed by a shouted greeting. "It's Maya. Let me in!"

A bit perturbed, she put the file on the coffee table and made her way to the door. When she swung it open, Maya stood on the other side of it, grinning widely. Her cousin looked gorgeous in her silver-sequined cocktail dress and sky-high black pumps. Her wavy hair was twisted and pinned low on her neck.

Eyes wide, Imani took in her cousin's attire. "Maya, what are you doing here? And where are you going dressed like that?"

Maya threw her head back and laughed, her chandelier earrings dancing. "We're going out. So go get dressed."

Imani folded her arms over her chest and shook her head. "Uh-uh. It's Tuesday night. I'm not going anywhere."

Pushing her way inside, Maya waved her off. "Spare me the 'it's a school night' speech. You sound like my mama." Perching on the arm of the sofa, she stared expectantly.

"I'm not going anywhere." Imani tried to be firmer as she repeated herself.

"Yes, you are. We saw our six hundredth patient today, and we've been in business less than six weeks." Maya smiled widely. "I'd say that's reason to celebrate. Wouldn't you?"

Six hundred patients? Imani hadn't had a clue she'd seen that many. With everything going on with the break-in, and then with Xavier, she'd been less than focused the last few weeks. Looking at her cousin, she saw her waiting, tapping her toe on the carpeted floor. It was pretty obvious that Maya was not taking no for an answer, and Imani supposed the milestone was worth celebrating. "All right. Just let me find something to wear."

Seeming satisfied, Maya stood. "That's better. Me, Tara, and Leona will wait for you in the car. Make it snappy." That said, she went out the door, closing it behind her.

Imani sidled into her bedroom. In the small closet, she rifled around for a suitable outfit. Her cousin had gone all out, so she supposed she would as well.

She slipped into a show-stopping lemon-yellow wrap

dress that fit her figure like a second skin. After adding strappy gold high-heeled sandals, gold hoop earrings, and a plethora of gold bangles, she moved on to her hair. She placed a yellow flower near her left ear, and let her hair hang loose, grazing her shoulders. With a touch of pink lip gloss and a bit of shimmery gold eye shadow, she looked at her reflection in her bedroom mirror and declared herself ready.

A few minutes later, she descended the stairs from her apartment. The nip in the air, common in early November, made her wish she'd grabbed a sweater. Knowing her cousin had probably grown impatient, she tried to ignore the chill as she approached Maya's dark-blue sedan.

Sliding into the passenger seat next to her cousin, she closed the door behind her. "Is this acceptable, Maya?"

Her cousin nodded approvingly. "You look pretty damn hot, girl. With that bait, you might just catch a big one."

Imani wanted to tell her that after what had happened with Xavier, she wasn't interested in hooking up, but she thought better of it. She offered her cousin a quick smile and turned to greet Leona and Tara in the backseat as Maya navigated the car out of the parking lot.

During the ride, Imani found herself getting drawn into the infectious excitement the other women gave off. If Maya was correct about the patient count, then her practice was indeed thriving. A successful practice had always been her goal, so she let the jubilant spirit take hold of her, pushing away thoughts of Xavier and past events that couldn't be changed.

The popular and long-standing local R & B station,

K97.5, blasted from the speakers of Maya's radio. The DJ announced a throwback track, and then the familiar opening notes of Mary J. Blige's "Real Love" filled the cabin of the car.

In typical Maya fashion, her cousin yelled, "Oh, that's my jam!" She removed one hand from the steering wheel and waved it wildly over her head.

Imani shook her head at her antics, but soon enough, they were all belting out the lyrics. She had fond memories of many an awkward middle school dance being made less awkward by the common love of Mary's music. Mary J. Blige could always be counted on to fill up a dance floor.

As they arrived at their destination, a local twenty-five-plus nightclub called Cagney's, Imani got out of the car and followed her cousin and friends to the door. Once they'd paid admission and made their way inside, they all took seats at side-by-side stools running along the glass-topped bar.

"What'll it be?"

Imani glanced up to see the darkly handsome, blue-eyed bartender's gaze fixed firmly on her. His attention was a little lower than she preferred, but she decided not to make a fuss. "I'll have an appletini, please."

He smiled broadly. "Coming right up." He took the other ladies' orders, then went to prepare the drinks.

Maya whistled. "Go ahead, Imani! We haven't been here five minutes and you already got the bartender drooling!"

Imani could feel herself blush, even as she stifled a chuckle. "Shut up, Maya." Her cousin's outrageous behavior soon had her laughing once again.

When the drinks arrived, Leona raised her glass. "A

toast, to Dr. Grant—the best boss a girl could ever have, who's on her way to astronomical success."

As they clinked their glasses, Imani smiled, touched by the kind words. "Thanks, ladies. I really appreciate you all doing this for me." She'd been surprised by Maya's sudden appearance at her door and the impromptu celebration. Still, she needed to get out of the house, and a little enjoyment would go a long way in helping her put pesky thoughts of Xavier out of her mind.

Imani had neared the bottom of her glass and was starting to feel the effects of the alcohol when she felt an insistent tap on her shoulder.

Turning, she came face-to-face with Cassidy Lyons. Her long brown hair looked disheveled, as did her red halter top and white miniskirt. Her green eyes glistened with the effects of liquor.

"Hey, Imani," Cassidy trilled, slurring the words a bit. She grinned like the Cheshire cat.

"How are you, Cass?" Imani smiled back, waiting to see what she'd say next. Maya, Tara, and Leona seemed similarly inclined, because they were all watching Cassidy.

"I came out to celebrate my independence." Cassidy flopped down on a stool next to her. "So I'm doing great. How 'bout you?"

"We're celebrating the success of the practice," Maya volunteered.

Cassidy looked pleased. "Good, good. I always knew you were going to do well for yourself, Imani."

"Thank you." Imani's eyes locked with Cassidy's, and for a moment, her old friend's eyes became as clear as day.

"I left you-know-who," Cassidy whispered. "And tomorrow, everything is gonna be set right."

Imani nodded, aware of the significance of Cassidy's words. "That's great, Cass."

Cassidy slid from the barstool and turned to leave. "You ladies have a good night," she called. Then, she walked away, disappearing into the crowd on the dance floor.

After she'd gone, Tara announced, "Well, that was weird."

A collective murmur of amusement rose from the group, but Imani looked in the direction Cassidy had gone for a long while.

With a root beer in his grasp, Xavier made himself comfortable on his sofa. His evening plans included nothing but snacks and watching Thursday night football. On the coffee table in front of him, he'd set down a big bowl of pretzels and a tray of hot wings. He'd turned the big screen television in his living room to the day's gridiron matchup between Carolina and Tampa Bay, and looked forward to watching the game. He felt certain the action on screen would distract him from thinking about Imani.

He settled in to listen to the talking heads make their usual pregame commentary. Before he could absorb any of it, the sound of someone pounding on his front door captured his focus. With a grunt, he got up from his comfy seat and went to the door. As he got closer, he heard familiar voices coming from outside.

He swung the door open to find Tyrone, Maxwell, and

Orion on his doorstep. All three men were carrying plastic grocery bags and food containers. "What y'all want?"

Tyrone ribbed him. "What do you think we want? We wanna watch the game on your big screen."

Orion, wearing his trademark grin, said, "Yeah, and we brought grub, so let us in!"

"Even Max?" Xavier jerked his head in Maxwell's direction. While O and Ty were decked out in Carolina gear, Max, in his typical contrary fashion, wore a Tampa Bay jersey.

Max moved his sunglasses to the top of his head. "I brought wings, so I know you're not going to leave me out here."

Pretty shady of Max to prey on my wing weakness. Shaking his head, Xavier stepped back to allow his frat brothers entry into his house.

The three of them filed in, heading straight for the kitchen. Xavier followed close behind and helped them empty the bags and unwrap the bounty of snacks they'd brought.

As he removed the plastic dome lid from Max's extra-large tray of buffalo wings, Xavier asked, "Where's Bryan this time?"

Orion dumped a bag of potato chips into a plastic bowl. "He texted me last night. He's in Italy, meeting with some industry people. Said he couldn't get out of the trip. Something about Italian silk."

It amazed Xavier how hard it was these days for all five of them to be in the same place at the same time. He didn't think too much about it, because he would never begrudge his brothers their successful careers.

They spent a few moments preparing food and drinks,

ferrying them into the living room. The sounds of their footsteps tramping back and forth across the hardwood floors echoed around Xavier. He flopped down on the sofa and turned up the volume on the television, so he could hear the commentary over their marching.

Finally, everyone took a seat. Tyrone joined Xavier on the sofa, Orion took up residence in the matching armchair, and Maxwell copped a squat on the ottoman. The low coffee table in the center of things was completely covered with food. Looking at the hot wings, chips, pretzels, cheese balls, and more, Xavier could see the benefits of his boys coming over to watch the game with him.

The game kicked off just after one, and the men alternated between stuffing their faces and cheering for their teams. Everyone in the room, except for Max, repped Carolina. At every field goal, touchdown, or interception that favored Carolina, the room would echo with shouts of jubilation. And when the tide turned in Tampa Bay's favor, Max found his cheers drowned out by the groaning complaints of the other men.

Halftime saw the two teams tied at fourteen. As the action on the screen segued to former players in suits voicing their opinions about the day's matchups, Xavier stifled a yawn. He'd eaten no less than a pound of hot wings, so he decided to back away from the food for a bit while his stomach settled. Taking a swig of root beer from his mug, he sank back into the padded cushions behind him. He couldn't remember the last Thursday he'd been able to relax like this, and he relished it.

Next to him, Tyrone opened his mouth and fractured

his sense of peace. "What's going on with you and Imani, man?"

Xavier groaned. "Ty, I don't want to talk about her. I just want to enjoy the game."

Orion quipped, "Whatever, man. Just level with us."

Xavier's brow cocked. "*Et tu, O?*"

"It's the half. We've got some time to kill." Orion shrugged.

Maxwell, his expression flat, popped a cheese ball into his mouth. "You might as well tell us. Ty is gonna ride your ass until you do."

Xavier rolled his eyes. "Seriously, Ty. There's nothing to tell."

Three sets of male eyes were trained on him; all looked unconvinced.

"She lied to me, I can't trust her, and it's over between us."

Tyrone shook his head. "You're really going to hold this against her?"

Xavier groused, "Stop hassling me. I thought you'd be happy. Weren't you the one who said she was endangering my campaign?"

Tyrone guzzled from his glass of cranapple juice. "Yes, I did say that. But that was before I knew what you'd be like without her."

Puzzled, Xavier asked, "What are you talking about?"

"I'm talking about the last two events you did for the campaign, since you had this argument with her. You barely smiled, and you all but growled your answers when people asked you questions." Tyrone punched him in the shoulder. "Without Imani, you're kind of an asshole. People don't usually vote for assholes."

Xavier said nothing, keeping his eyes focused on the television. He hoped that would signal his friends that he was done having this conversation.

It didn't.

"You should know that we're looking into the harassment suit she filed. We don't have confirmation yet, but everything seems to be on the up and up. I don't have any indication that she lied."

"You don't have any indication she's telling the truth, either," Xavier muttered.

Orion said, "You're not being reasonable. You're acting as if she was wrong to do what she had to do to take care of herself."

Turning angry eyes on the youngest member of the group, Xavier snapped, "Who asked you, O? You're the least experienced in the group."

Tyrone snorted a laugh. "Well, I'm the most experienced, and I say O is right. Stop acting like your past is so perfect, like you've never done anything less than ideal."

Folding his arms over his chest, Xavier lapsed into sullen silence. He kept his eyes on the television, ignoring Tyrone's ribbing and the comments flying past him from all three of his friends. He didn't care what they thought, which was why he hadn't asked their opinion. All he'd wanted to do today was enjoy the football game in peace. They'd ruined that by bringing up the topic he least wanted to talk about. If he were inclined to clean up their mess alone, he'd have kicked their asses out of his house right then.

To his amazement, they continued to debate his now-defunct relationship with Imani even after the second half of the game started. Between plays, they traded barbs, and while he heard everything they were saying, he didn't open his mouth to contribute. *I don't care what they say. I'm done talking about her.*

During a commercial break, Maxwell snapped his fingers, as if to indicate a flash of inspiration. "Look, we're getting nowhere with the lunkhead here. Why don't we appeal to Imani? She's got to be the more reasonable party."

Xavier's jaw tightened. Surely they weren't serious about interfering in his love life.

Tyrone leaned forward in his seat. "Actually, that's not a bad idea. And I think I've got an approach in mind. Are you in, O?"

Orion nodded.

Oh, hell no. "Y'all can't be serious. I don't want anything to do with Imani, and I don't want you meddling—"

Tyrone cut him off midsentence. "I'm going to need to stop by one of those sign places, where they make custom banners and all that."

Xavier groaned aloud. So now they were going to ignore him. "Fine. Do what you want, but I'm a grown-ass man and I'm going to do what I want."

His three friends paused their plotting long enough to look at him, then went right back to their conversation.

Asses. Xavier got up from his seat and disappeared into the kitchen to refill his mug.

Imani leaned down to tie one of her sneakers, then straightened. Her feet sank into the damp grass as she walked from the driveway around the side of her mother's house. It was a bright Sunday afternoon, and her mother had asked her to come over and help clean out the garden beds in the backyard and prepare them for the coming winter. Not one to turn her mother down, Imani had dressed in a long-sleeve T and yoga pants and come prepared to work.

She swung open the chain-link gate to the backyard, letting it close behind her. Alma knelt on the ground next to one of her three raised beds, her back to her daughter.

"Hey, Mama," Imani called.

"Hey, baby. Thanks for coming over to help me out." The response came from beneath the wide brim of Alma's straw sun hat.

"What do you need me to do?"

Alma used her glove-clad hands to steady herself as she stood up. "Go over to the patio and get a pair of gloves and a trowel out of the storage box there."

Imani went to do as her mother had asked, returning a short while later wearing a pair of her mother's floral-printed gardening gloves and carrying a plastic trowel.

Alma gestured to the left-most bed. "I need you to root up those potatoes in that bed. You can toss 'em into that plastic barrel so we can wash them off."

"Got it." Imani knelt in the dirt next to the bed her mother had indicated. Above the soil, the bushy leaves of the potato plant were beginning to turn brown around the edges, a sure sign that the spuds were ready for harvest. Using the trowel and her gloved hands, she dug into the depths of the soft, dark soil in search of the fingerling potatoes her mother had planted several weeks prior.

The two of them worked in convivial silence, with Alma weeding the center bed while Imani pulled heaps of the tiny potatoes from the left bed. She had the plastic barrel about three-quarters full when she heard someone opening the gate. Glancing over her shoulder, Imani saw Carol Whitted walking toward them.

Her brow furrowed. *What is Xavier's mother doing here?* She'd known the two women to be social with each other, but she couldn't remember the last time she'd actually seen them hanging out together.

"Hello, Alma. Imani, it's so nice to see you again." Carol closed the gate and made her way toward them, taking small, delicate steps.

"Hey, Carol. Come on back." Alma waved, welcoming her visitor.

As Carol drew closer, Imani noted her attire. Carol wore a melon-colored pantsuit with a pair of taupe suede flats, and she'd accented the outfit with gold jewelry in her ears and around her neck and wrist. Imani brushed the loose soil from her pants and sighed. Carol had not come here to help with the gardening; that couldn't be more obvious. She sensed some serious meddling about to take place.

Alma's voice cut into her thoughts. "Looks like you've got most of the potatoes. Let's take a break and have a little chat with our visitor, baby."

"Yes, ma'am." Imani spoke the only logical answer to her mother's request. Removing her gloves, she set them on the rim of the bed and dusted off as best she could. With that done, she followed her mother and Carol to the round wrought-iron table on the patio. She hadn't paid much attention to the table when she'd come, but now she saw that her mother had set out a plastic pitcher of iced tea, along with a small stack of plastic cups.

The three of them took seats around the table.

Alma poured them each a cup of iced tea and passed them around.

Imani sipped from her cup, letting the sweet liquid slide down her throat while she awaited the onslaught. Her mother and Carol might consider themselves clever, but Imani knew exactly what they had up their sleeves.

Carol folded her hands on the tabletop in a demure fashion. "So, Imani, did your mother tell you I would be stopping by?"

Imani cut a look at her smiling mother, then answered, "No, I'm afraid she didn't."

Carol took a brief sip of tea. "Okay, then I may as well tell you and get on with it."

Imani sighed, feeling her irritation rise. Her ire emboldened her, and she asked pointedly, "Are you two really going to tag-team lecture me about Xavier? Because I'm not interested in hearing it."

Eyes wide, Carol stammered, "Imani, that's not why I—"

Alma's eyes narrowed to slits. "Now you wait just a minute, Imani."

She stilled when she heard her mother's stern tone and snapped her mouth shut.

"That's more like it," Alma groused. "I don't know what kind of meddling old biddies you take us for, but that's not what we are here to talk about."

This time, it was Imani whose eyes widened. "It's not?"

Folding her arms over her chest, Alma pursed her lips. "No, it's not. Contrary to what you might think, our lives do not revolve around you and your relationship troubles. Now you apologize to Carol for being so rude."

Imani looked down, wanting nothing more than to

have the patio open up and swallow her, chair and all. She couldn't remember the last time she'd put her foot quite so far down her throat. "I'm so sorry, Carol."

Carol, classy as ever, said, "It's all right. The reason I'm here is that I'm head of the youth committee at church, and I wanted to ask you to speak to the kids about your career as a doctor."

"Really? When?"

"The last Sunday of the month, we're having a youth program." Carol leaned back in her chair. "The theme of the program is Aim High, Achieve More. We want to motivate them to dream big about what they can be. Would you be willing to do it?"

"Yes, I'd be honored." Imani didn't hesitate to accept Carol's gracious invitation. After the way she'd just behaved, she felt lucky Carol hadn't rescinded the invitation before she'd given it. "And again, please forgive my incredible rudeness."

Carol lifted a graceful hand and waved her off. "It's not a big deal, honey. Although…"

Imani drained her tea glass, waiting for Carol to complete her sentence. "Although, what?"

"The fact that you brought Xavier up and then went immediately on the defensive does mean you still have feelings for him."

"She's right," Alma said. "There's no way you'd go off the way you did unless you still care about him."

Dropping her head onto the tabletop, Imani sighed. She'd walked right into that one and had managed to bring up the one topic of conversation she'd been most eager to avoid.

Alma chuckled. "You might as well pick your head

up before you end up with that paisley pattern imprinted in your forehead. You brought Xavier up, not us."

Lifting her head to face her mother, Imani groaned. "Don't remind me. I'm already kicking myself for it."

"Don't. It's like I told you. Carol and I are not going to lecture you about him." Alma sat back in her chair, looking casual.

Carol added, "That's right. There are two main reasons for that. First of all, your mother and I are active women with lives of our own. And second of all, true love will always win out in the end."

Imani took in the older woman's words, wishing she could be as confident. After everything that had happened between her and Xavier over the past several months, she didn't feel any degree of certainty. Now that he knew her secret, the one she'd carried in ashamed silence for so many years, she didn't think things could ever be the same between them. No, now there would be a new normal, and it might not be the one Imani had always wanted.

Because she didn't want to sit and dwell on it anymore, Imani rose from her seat. "Carol, just tell me what time and I'll be there for the church program."

"We want the speakers there by five thirty. Program starts at six."

"I'll be there." Imani pushed her chair beneath the table and reached for her gloves. "Mom, I'm going to finish rooting your potato bed, okay?"

"That's fine, sweetie."

Imani strode back to the potato bed, all the while feeling the heat of two sets of female eyes watching her retreat.

Chapter 18

Seated in the leather chair at his desk Monday morning, Xavier pored over the sloppily handwritten balance sheet of one of his clients. For the life of him, he couldn't read the chicken scratch, and he set the paper aside. He'd have to call the client and tell them he needed a typed copy of the document, or they'd be out of luck. As he reached for the phone, it began ringing, the shrill sound filling the office. He lifted the receiver to his ear. "Hello?"

"Xavier, it's Tyrone. You've got to get over to city hall right now." His friend's words came out in a rushed tumble, and he sounded out of breath.

The clock on his desk read twenty minutes until ten, and he couldn't imagine what had Tyrone so excited this early in the day. "Why? What's going on? You sound like you just ran there from Durham."

"There's about to be a press conference in fifteen minutes, and you'll want to see this."

Xavier shook his head. "A press conference about what, T? I've got a ton of work to do here."

"Givens is about to go down in flames on national television, man."

That statement piqued his interest. Standing, he said, "I'll be there in ten minutes."

Dropping the phone back into the cradle, Xavier shrugged into the gray suit jacket he'd worn to work that morning, grabbed his briefcase and keys, and jogged out of the office.

In her usual manner, Rita called out to him as he dashed by the reception desk. "What's going on, Mr. Whitted?"

With a smile, he called back, "Givens's shit is about to catch up with him." He didn't stop but turned back long enough to see the satisfied smile cross his secretary's face.

He drove the short distance to city hall as fast as the speed limit would allow. The last thing he needed was to get a speeding ticket the day before the election. He noticed several news vans from local stations parked at the curb as he circled around to park. When he found a spot in one of the downtown parking decks, he darted across the street at the earliest opportunity, then climbed the steps and entered the building.

He scanned the crowded lobby, looking for Tyrone. There were so many cameramen, reporters, and press-pass-wearing journalists milling about the lobby, Xavier wondered what was going on. Judging by the throng of press, he guessed it must be pretty damn big.

Even though Tyrone's back was turned to him as he spoke to a group of reporters, he recognized him anyway. Striding over, he hung back a bit and waited for his campaign manager to finish what he was saying.

Tyrone noticed him and raised his hand, palm out, to deflect any further questions. "Excuse me, folks. I need to speak with my candidate."

The gaggle of reporters around him broke up and drifted away, and Tyrone turned to Xavier. His wide smile held an edge of mischief.

Eyebrow raised, Xavier asked, "T, what is going on?"

"I got a call early this morning from a reporter at News 14," he said, his voice hushed. "She gave me a tip that a woman was about to come forward today who claims to be Givens's mistress."

A rush of feeling hit Xavier at the idea that Aaron Givens was about to be exposed. "Seriously?"

Still grinning, Tyrone nodded. "Yep. The political gods have smiled on us, my brother."

Xavier shook his head in awe. He'd made a decision at the beginning of this race to run a clean campaign. Even after what Imani had told him, he'd held fast to his integrity. Now, Aaron Givens would pay for his lack of good sense and morals, and Xavier's hands would be clean. Knowing that filled him with glee.

A crush of people began moving toward the double doors that led to the first-floor auditorium, where public hearings were usually held. Tyrone began moving in that direction, and Xavier followed. Once they pushed their way inside and took seats near the rear, Xavier folded his hands in his lap and waited.

Cameras and microphones were trained on the main podium in the front of the cavernous room, which was already set up for television broadcasts. People milled about the room, waiting for the show to get underway.

The almost-deafening din of conversation quieted.

Xavier cast his eyes toward the front of the room in time to see a tall, dark-suited white man escorting a petite white woman with dark-brown hair to the podium. The woman, wearing a dark suit and shades that would've been appropriate for a funeral, stood back as the tall man adjusted the microphone. Then, the man stepped up and spoke.

"My name is Victor Young, Esquire, of Young, Turner, and Brown. This is my client, Cassidy Lyons. Ms. Lyons will make a brief statement, and then we are leaving. There will be no questions taken, and anyone who badgers my client, know that we will consider it harassment and act accordingly."

Xavier watched as the tall man readjusted the microphone, then Cassidy stepped up. "As my lawyer said, my name is Cassidy Lyons. I'd like to come forward with some information I have, which I believe the public should know before they cast their votes." Her voice wavered, and she paused to compose herself. "I'm Aaron Givens's mistress. We have carried on an affair for five years now, and he visited me regularly in Atlanta until recently, when he brought me here to North Carolina. He's been paying rent for a townhome for me for thirteen months now." She paused again, drew a shaky breath. "I know he'll deny everything I'm saying, so I've been recording our conversations."

Xavier turned to Tyrone, and his friend's jaw was pretty much in his lap.

"The more I saw Aaron out on the campaign trail, touting his honesty and his perfect marriage, I knew I had to come forward. The people of Raleigh deserve better."

A loud, gut-wrenching sob echoed in the near silence.

Xavier turned back toward the sound.

In the doorway, a stricken-looking Lorna Givens stood. Tears streamed down her face, streaks of black mascara flowing to her chin. Covering another sob with her hand, she backed out of the room and retreated.

Dabbing her eyes with a handkerchief her lawyer passed to her, Cassidy Lyons stepped back and said no more. Victor Young spirited her out a side entrance, even as the shouted questions of journalists filled the air.

Xavier turned back to Tyrone, who was now shaking his head, a look of pity on his face. "No wonder Givens didn't show up. If he got wind of this and knew his dirty laundry was about to be aired, my guess is he hopped the first thing smokin' out of town."

Though he had no regard whatsoever for Aaron, Xavier did feel sorry for his wife. Such public embarrassment would be hard for anyone to deal with.

As the now-solemn crowd of people moved toward the exit, Tyrone stood. "Well, I guess that's that. You'll take the election now, without a doubt."

Xavier knew his friend was likely right. Once the news reports and footage of Cassidy Lyons's speech began circulating, the citizens of Raleigh would discover the true nature of their long-serving councilman.

"What's more," Tyrone continued, "the reporter turned over the redacted records of that harassment suit to me. Imani's on the up and up, man. Apparently Ms. Lyons recorded some of the interactions between Imani and Givens, back when they worked together at the law firm. If you want, I can show you the papers."

Blowing out a pent-up breath, he stood and followed Tyrone through the throng.

The following evening, Xavier and his campaign staff were camped out in his office conference room. The flat-screen television that occupied one wall was set to the local twenty-four-hour news channel. Informal polls taken all day had been leaning in Xavier's favor, but he wasn't about to declare victory yet. Regardless of the events of the previous day, he preferred to wait for official confirmation. Sipping from his third cup of coffee, he leaned back in his chair and waited.

Just after eleven that night, the news came in. A blond reporter delivered the results. "In Raleigh's District C, newcomer Xavier Whitted has unseated three-term incumbent Aaron Givens." She went on to talk about the scandal, but Xavier didn't care. He was too busy shouting and being slapped on the back by his friends.

"Oh yeah! The frat brothers are gonna throw you an epic party, man!" Tyrone grinned widely at him as he shook his hand. "You did good, X."

As the revelry quieted, a tired Xavier flopped back down into his chair. He'd done it. He'd won the city council seat, and he vowed to use his position to do as much as he could for the disadvantaged in his community.

Parts of him cheered, but other parts of him remained somewhat melancholy.

What is wrong with me? His goal had been accomplished, and now all that was left was to get to work at bettering his hometown.

Still, an echoing emptiness remained inside him.

He let his head drop back against the chair, and his eyes slid closed.

A vision of a radiant, smiling Imani shimmered in his mind.

And just like that, it hit him as if he'd walked into a glass door.

She was the missing piece of the puzzle.

In order for him to be truly happy and at his best, he needed Imani by his side.

—〰—

Imani gripped her red Betty Boop coffee mug with both hands, sipping the hazelnut latte she'd just brewed in the break room. The warm mug heated her hands as she drank. Setting the cup down on her desk, she leaned back in her chair and blew out a long, exasperated breath. The nurses had been chattering excitedly about their plans when she'd come in this morning. The way she found herself missing Xavier had sucked the anticipation for the weekend right out of her. From where she sat, staring at the large photograph of a group of fiery-orange orchids hanging on her office wall, it didn't even feel like Friday.

Every day since she'd fought with Xavier, she'd been plagued by a sense of melancholy that was hard to shake. A part of her wanted to pick up the phone and call him, but another more stubborn part of her refused to do so. After all, she'd tried to push Xavier away, tried to let him know that a relationship between them would lead to nothing but heartache. She crossed her arms over her chest as she thought of his hardheaded nature. He'd made the choice to pursue her, and now they were both paying the price. He was angry, but he had no idea how ashamed and hurt she felt.

Maya breezed into the office through the partially open door. The long bell sleeves of her aqua-and-brown maxi dress swayed as she reached out to lay the newspaper on her desk. "Have you seen the paper this morning?"

Directing her gaze to the copy of the *News and Observer* in front of her, Imani shook her head. The headline emblazoned across the front read "City Council Newcomer Whitted Defeats Givens." Even though the election had happened a few days ago, it continued to dominate the local news cycle because of Cassidy's bombshell. A smile lifted the corners of her mouth, but only for a moment. She was pleased Givens had lost his seat, because she knew what kind of person he really was. Aaron Givens didn't deserve to hold public office. She didn't really know how to feel about Xavier's win. She knew he would likely be good for the city, but she doubted the win would have any effect on their now-nonexistent relationship. It was a selfish perspective, and she knew it.

Looking up into Maya's expectant face, she mumbled, "I'm glad he won the election."

Maya scoffed. "You sure don't sound glad. When are you guys gonna make up? I haven't seen your face this long in years."

"We're not going to make up, Maya." Imani picked up the paper off the glass surface of the desk and handed it back to her cousin.

"He was just being a man, being pigheaded." Maya flopped down into the consulting chair on the opposite side of the desk, making herself comfortable. "They react first, then think later. I'm almost positive he misses you now that he's had some time to cool off."

Imani stared down into her lap. She saw a spot of coffee on the fabric of her lab coat and grabbed a tissue from the box on her desk to dab at it before she stained the fuchsia sheath dress she wore beneath. "If he misses me so much, why hasn't he called?"

"Another typical male trait." Maya chuckled, brushed a lock of wavy hair away from her face. "They hate to admit when they're wrong. Besides, there's nothing stopping you from calling him."

"Yes, there is. Good sense." Imani could feel her righteous indignation swelling up inside her, pushing aside the hurt she'd been feeling. "Why would I want to be with someone who has made it clear he doesn't trust me?"

"Excuses, excuses." Maya waved her hand dismissively in front of her. "The point is, you're miserable, and he probably is too. So you have to decide if you wanna be two miserable people, fighting their attraction, or two happy people who embrace it." She shrugged her slender shoulders. "The choice is yours, Imani."

Imani sighed. She hated it when her cousin went all philosophical on her. "Sheesh, Maya."

"Listen. I'm not saying he's right for not believing you. What happened to you was awful, and you're entitled to deal with it in the way you see fit. Just think about it, okay?"

"Don't you have some duties to attend to at the reception desk?"

Maya smiled and stood. Her tone a mixture of humor and resignation, she declared, "Fine. Throw me out. But you know I'm right." With a rustle of fabric, she was gone.

Alone in the office again, Imani dropped her head, resting it on the cool glass surface of her desk. Continuing to sulk tempted her something fierce, but she had patients to see. Raising her head, she stood and checked her reflection in the oval gold-framed mirror hanging on the wall to the right of her desk. After she'd brushed away a few wayward mascara flakes, she applied a bit of lip gloss.

The day passed quickly—she saw patients, wrote

prescriptions, and filled out insurance forms. She had lunch in her office and left the practice right at five, before Maya had time to harass her. All through the day, thoughts of Xavier filled her, haunting her.

At her apartment, she checked her messages, finding nothing but a few telemarketers and an appointment reminder for her upcoming dental checkup. Kicking off her shoes, she hung her peacoat on the brass peg near her front door and headed to her bathroom.

As she stood beneath the rushing water of a hot shower, she let her mind drift. The water pounding against her back felt wonderful, like the caress of a skilled lover. If only Xavier could be replaced so easily, she wouldn't be nursing a broken heart.

She slipped beneath her covers a little while later and sighed as she sank into the depths of the soft cotton. Exhaustion got the best of her, and she was carried away by sleep within moments.

Her dreams were filled with visions of Xavier. He appeared a short distance away from her, smiling at her and declaring his love. His arms were open to her, and she craved his embrace. But just as she moved toward him, wanting to be held, he disappeared, fading into a puff of smoke. Quickly, her sweet dream became a nightmare, and she wandered around a dark space, searching for Xavier.

By the time the morning sunlight touched her eyelids, her bedsheets were soaked with sweat.

Around eight, she grew tired of tossing and turning, so she released herself from the damp cocoon of the sheets tangled around her and plodded to the bathroom. After she'd taken care of her morning essentials and showered away some of the stress of her night, she slipped into a clean pair of silk pajamas and went to the kitchen in search of some much-needed caffeine.

She rummaged in the cabinet above her sink until she found her Minnie Mouse mug, and set it on her single cup brewer. With her coffee pod in place, she engaged the machine and waited for the magical results.

She was leaning against the counter, waiting for the coffee to brew, when she saw something odd through her window.

A frown furrowed her brow, and she crossed to the window for a better look.

Her jaw dropped when she saw what was happening outside.

Maxwell and Bryan were sitting in lawn chairs in the grass in front of her building. The thing she'd seen in front of her window was a banner. The banner was stretched out, pegged to the ground, and facing up, and she could clearly read it from her second-story unit. It read "Imani Grant: Come to Xavier's Party or We're Not Leaving."

"Ugh!" She had no idea what party they were referring to, but she couldn't believe they'd set up in front of her home like this. Fists balled at her side, she spun around and retrieved her coffee, then stalked downstairs, mug in hand.

When Bryan looked up and saw her, he gave her a jovial smile. "Good morning, Imani. How are you on this beautiful day?"

Imani rolled her eyes and took a long draw of the still-warm coffee before she spoke, hoping the caffeine would temper her irritation. "My day will be great when you and Max get away from my apartment."

Max's answering chuckle sounded amused and a bit condescending. "I'm sure you can see the sign from upstairs, honey. We're not leaving until you agree to come to the party."

She took a deep breath and drank again from the mug. "I don't know what party you're talking about, and I'm not interested."

Maxwell called out, "We've been planning a party for Xavier for weeks now. We wanted to congratulate him on his hard work in the race, even if he lost."

Bryan spoke up. "Xavier won the council seat. You had to have seen it in the newspaper or heard about it. Anyway, we're celebrating." He sipped from a bottle of water in his hand. "It won't be much of a celebration for him if you're not there."

An old, familiar feeling rose inside of her, but she pushed it away. Downing the rest of the coffee, she shook her head. "No. If he wants me there so badly, why isn't he here convincing me?"

"He's giving you your space, but we're under no such obligation." Max stretched out his arm and looked at his gold Rolex. "Party starts at eight tonight. We'll be here for the next six hours or until you change your mind. Then the shift will change, and Orion and Tyrone will take over."

Dangling the empty mug from her index finger, she crossed her arms over her chest. "You've got to be kidding. I'll call the property manager."

Max, still looking unfazed, reached into the pocket of his khaki pants. "We already did. Got ourselves a permit to set up here for the day." He handed the folded form over for her to inspect.

Looking at the paper, on the property stationary and bearing the "approved" stamp, she stomped her foot. "If you want to sit out here in the cold, go ahead. But I'm not going to any damn party."

Bryan chuckled. "Imani, come on. We all know Xavier's acting stupid, but y'all love each other."

Imani rolled her eyes. "You guys are nuts."

Max yawned.

So exasperated she wanted to scream, she stomped back up the stairs, went into her apartment, and slammed the door behind her.

<center>~~~</center>

Xavier crossed the crowded parking lot of the swanky Barrington Hotel, closing his coat around him on the way. He'd had the heat blasting in the car, but the chilly November winds reminded him he'd left his coat open on the ride. As his breath formed white puffs in front of him, he did his best to enjoy the moment. It wasn't every day a man got the honor of being elected to serve the citizens of his hometown, and he wanted to remember it. So, despite the cold, he stopped for a moment on the sidewalk in front of the hotel and took in the view. The hilltop location allowed him a beautiful view of the Raleigh skyline, painted pink and purple in the twilight. The lights of the tall buildings downtown twinkled in the distance, and just below him, traffic on U.S. 70 whizzed by. It was Saturday evening, and the city was alive with activity. Looking out over it now, he was proud the people had chosen to let him serve.

When he'd gotten the call that his fraternity brothers were throwing him a party to congratulate him on his city council win, he hadn't expected anything this big. What he'd thought would be a casual gathering at Tyrone's or Maxwell's house had instead turned out be an affair held in a ballroom of one of the most expensive hotels in Raleigh. Not wanting to be late to his own party, he turned away from the beauty of his city and entered the golden double doors of the building.

Inside the opulent, Baroque-style lobby, he took in the golden crown moldings, sparkling crystal chandeliers, and heavy velvet draperies in shades of cream and burgundy. The wine-colored carpet beneath his feet was so soft, his wingtips sank in as if he were standing in damp soil. He'd only been there once before, and that was to apply for a part-time job when he was a struggling college student. That day, the staff had been less than courteous.

It appeared times had changed now that he was a duly elected politician, because a white man in the Barrington uniform of burgundy blazer, white shirt, and black slacks was headed in his direction, grinning from ear to ear.

The smiling man extended his hand to Xavier and gave him a firm handshake. "Councilman Whitted, we're so happy to have you here for your celebration. Congratulations on your election, sir."

Xavier returned the handshake with a smile. "Thank you. I appreciate that."

"I'm Oscar, and Mr. James and Mr. Devers insisted that I see to your every need. Should you require anything at all, just ask for me." He gestured toward the wide corridor ahead of them, past the gilded marble of the front desk. Behind the desk, two smartly dressed employees offered mirror images of Oscar's congenial expression. "Your event is this way, sir. Follow me, please."

So, Bryan and Maxwell were behind all this. Still somewhat taken aback by all the fuss, Xavier followed Oscar down the corridor, to a ballroom whose double doors were propped open. Inside, he could see his friends seated around a central table. "Thanks, Oscar. I've got it from here."

With a quick bow, Oscar left, and Xavier slipped inside the ballroom.

As soon as he did, he was met with loud applause and cheers. Around the table his friends were occupying, several more round tables had been set up. The decor was as fancy as he would expect for an event at the Barrington. The tables were draped in gold and cream tablecloths and set with china and shimmering crystal goblets. In the crowd, he saw his parents, his campaign staff, and a few unfamiliar faces he assumed were his new constituents. A long buffet had been set up along one wall, and a line of black-and-white uniformed waiters waited behind the gleaming silver serving dishes. He could feel the broad smile spreading across his face as he approached the table where his fraternity brothers sat.

Extending his hand to Maxwell, he shook his hand. "You didn't have to do all this, Max."

"Sure I did. How often do you actually win at something?" Maxwell punched him playfully in the rib cage. "Besides, my secretary did most of the work."

He rolled his eyes at Maxwell's smart remark. Snark was part of the man's DNA. Turning his attention to Bryan, he slapped his old friend on the back. "Bryan. When did you get back in town?"

A chuckling Bryan pulled him in for a quick hug.

"This morning. When Tyrone called me with the good news, I knew I had to be here."

Xavier went around the table hugging his brothers and thanking them for their roles in putting this together. Then he stepped back and stood for a moment, just drinking it all in. He looked at the faces of the people he cared about: his mother, dabbing at her eyes, his father, beaming with pride. All his fraternity brothers—Ty, Max, Bryan, and Orion—were together; a rare treat. His campaign staffers, who'd worked long, arduous hours for the last eighteen months trying to get him elected and somehow still liked him enough to come to this event. Seeing all these people gathered to honor him made for a moment of sheer perfection.

Almost.

There was one face missing, a presence so important to him, he could not ignore the sting of her absence.

Imani.

He drew a deep breath and steeled himself. He missed her like he'd never missed anyone or anything in his life before, but he hadn't wanted to push her. He'd tried that already, staying in her face until she'd finally given in. Right now, he was surrounded by friends and family who'd gone through an awful lot of trouble and expense to throw him a party, and he wasn't about to be an ingrate and run off after Imani. His mama had raised him better than that.

So he went to the podium that had been set up near the front of the room and stood behind the microphone. As he looked out over the assemblage, they gave him another enthusiastic round of applause, then gradually quieted to hear him speak.

Xavier cleared his throat to push away the lump of emotion he felt. "I'll keep this brief because, frankly, I'm hungry and I want to know what's on that buffet." The quip drew a smattering of laughter before he continued. "I want to extend my most sincere thanks to everyone who had a part in planning this and to everyone who supported me on this long journey. As councilman, I vow to serve the people of Raleigh to the absolute best of my ability."

His mother, still dabbing her eyes, jumped to her feet, clapping furiously. The rest of the people in the room joined in, until he was taking in the sights and sounds of a full-scale standing ovation.

He didn't consider himself a sensitive person, but at that moment, as sheer happiness and bottomless emptiness collided inside him, he found himself holding back a tear.

His eyes swung to the double doors he'd entered, and his heart jumped in his chest like a caged rabbit.

Standing there, in the most beautiful gown he'd ever seen, was Imani. She'd styled her hair up, revealing the delectable feminine curve of her neck and shoulders above the silver, strapless gown's fitted bodice. Long feathery earrings dangled from the lobes of her ears, sparkling in the light as they grazed her collarbone. The swell of her breasts was on tempting display for his hungry eyes. From head to toe, she was glowing and shimmering, just as he was inside now that she was here.

Her eyes locked with his, and he could hear his heart thumping loudly in his ears.

He left the podium and moved toward her as fast as his feet would carry him.

She moved toward him as well, and when they met, he swept her into his arms and crushed her lips with his.

The room erupted into hoots and applause, but he ignored it as he held the woman he loved close to his heart and kissed her with all the adoration he felt inside.

When she finally pulled away, looking breathless and flushed, her glossy lips curved into a smile. "Hi, yourself."

His voice conveying the wonderment coursing through him, he caressed her face, tracing his fingers along her jawline. "How? Why?"

"Let's just say your fraternity brothers can be very convincing." She gestured to their table they were all looking on from. "They camped outside my house until I agreed to come here."

"What?" He glanced at his buddies, who were giving him goofy grins and thumbs-up. He couldn't remember when he'd thought them more awesome than he did right then.

"Yeah. Max stayed for six hours." Imani clasped his hand, lacing her delicate fingers with his. "How could I say no? A man with friends like that obviously has good judgment."

He lifted her hand to his lips and kissed the tender skin of her palm. "I'll be sure to thank them later."

She gestured to the podium. "Don't you think you should get back up there? Your constituents want to hear from you. Don't worry. I'm staying."

He couldn't hold back his grin. "I'm going. But you should know, I can't wait to get you out of here and out of that dress so we can make up properly."

She nodded. "Go on, Xavier."

Releasing her hand, he returned to the podium and, after a brief apology, continued his speech.

After he spoke, he spent the next two hours greeting guests, shaking hands, and accepting congratulations. Imani remained by his side the entire time, and he couldn't help but be impressed with her. The way she carried herself made him realize that she'd already fallen comfortably into the role of political wife. Her charm and intelligence won over everyone they spoke to, and by the time the last party guest filtered out, he couldn't deny the incredible asset Imani would be, both to his life and his political career.

By ten o'clock, no one remained in the ballroom besides Xavier, Imani, and his fraternity brothers.

Xavier stopped by their table with Imani on his arm. "I gotta thank you guys again. You put on a hell of a party, and I owe you big time."

"I'll be sure to convey that to my secretary." Max offered a smile and a wink.

The men stood to exchange fist bumps and brief hugs with Xavier and to kiss Imani's hand.

Bryan looked at Xavier and asked, "What the hell are you still doing here with us? Go handle your business, man!"

Xavier turned to Imani. "Sorry I've kept you out so late. I'll take you home."

"Good night, boys." After speaking her parting words to his friends, she grabbed Xavier's hand and tugged him toward the door.

Outside in the hotel corridor, he whispered in her ear, "I can't wait to get you home, baby."

She winked, producing a hotel key card from her small clutch. "I'm not going home tonight."

A sound conveying surprise and pleasure escaped his throat. Holding tight to her hand, he smiled. "Lead the way."

Chapter 19

HER HANDS TREMBLING, IMANI INSERTED THE KEY CARD into the lock, and Xavier swung the door open. She felt as antsy and giddy as she had when she'd given him her virginity all those years ago. The main difference was that now she knew just how skilled a lover Xavier was. Thinking of what was to come had her moist and flowing in her most secret place.

A few of the lamps had been left on, allowing them to see as they entered the room. The space was beautiful, but she had little time to take in the scenery as he caught her up in his embrace again, pressing his body close to hers. With only the fabric of their clothes between them, she could feel the hard promise of his excitement flush against her stomach.

Between feverish kisses, she did her best to talk, to explain. "I'm sorry…" His lips smothered her next words.

His tongue searched the depths of her mouth, and she welcomed him. Soft moans escaped her as his hands cupped her behind through the fabric of her gown. She was melting, drowning in desire.

He freed her lips for a moment and lifted her into his arms. Her legs instinctively wrapped around his waist as he carried her toward the large bed. "I'm sorry. I shouldn't have overreacted the way I did." He laid her gently on the soft surface of the bed.

As his fingers opened the fastener of his trousers, she

trembled in anticipation. She knew he was about to give her everything she'd longed for in the time they'd been apart, and she could barely keep her composure.

She waited there, her chest heaving with each breath she struggled to take as he took off his jacket. Before he continued to disrobe, he paused to remove something from a pocket inside the dark sport coat. It sparkled in the circle of light cast by the bedside lamp, and he held it out to her.

"I saved this for you."

For a moment, she was confused, but she sat up to take the object from his hand. It was a chain fashioned of white gold. On the chain dangled a familiar object. "The promise ring you gave me? I tossed this into the creek the day I left for college." Her voice was filled with all the awe she felt at seeing the ring again.

He only smiled. "I knew we were meant to be, Imani. So after you left that day, I fished it out of the creek. It took me hours to find it, but it was time well spent." He sat down on the bed next to her, and his dark eyes locked with hers. "I've had it all this time. I've just been waiting for you."

Her free hand flew to her mouth as the fat tears began to run down her cheeks.

"Ten years. So much has changed since then." She'd been through a lot in the past ten years, enough to see what a loss she'd suffered the day he left her.

"Not everything. I still love you, baby." He reached out, caressed her cheek, and she covered his hand with her own.

Before she could form another word, he pulled her to his kiss. The waves of passion rose anew, threatening to consume them both. She snatched his shirt open, popping off some of the buttons in the process, but he didn't seem to mind or even notice. He busied himself with reaching around her to unzip the back of her gown.

They continued that way, alternately kissing and undressing each other, until they were both bare. He laid a gentle touch on the sensitive flesh between her breasts as he guided her down onto the bed.

The kissing continued, their lips crushing together in a frenzy of heated desire. She pulled him atop her, fervently running her hands up and down the long, muscular lines of his body. God, how she'd craved this man. His fingertips seemed to singe her skin in every place he gifted her with his touch.

Just when she thought she'd die from wanting him, he nudged her thighs apart and entered her in one slow, delicious stroke. The feel of him buried deep inside her was wholly sensual, almost magical. Her body rejoiced at their joining.

She looked at him and saw that his eyes were shut tightly as he moved above her, each stroke pushing her nearer and nearer to paradise. Everything within her was enraptured in the sensations he gave her. She wound her arms and legs around him, pulling him closer, deeper. He responded by increasing his pace. His eyes fluttered open for a moment, and he cupped her breasts in his big hands. Sparks of electricity emitted from the pads of his thumbs as he circled them over her tight, pebbled nipples.

The pleasure glowing in her womb grew, expanding until it radiated out to the very tips of her fingers and toes. She could hear her own throaty cries echoing in her ears, as well as his short, deep growls as he moved in and out of her. Then it all became too much, and an orgasm swept over her, so good her toes curled and her body shook with total abandon. Above her, he continued to grind his powerful hips until he found his own release and fell on top of her, his breaths short and raspy.

As she lay beneath him, their sweat-dampened torsos pressed against each other, and she kept her arms around him. She'd pushed him away so many times, but this time she knew better. She vowed then and there to never let him go again. Enjoying the feel of his body so close to her own, she closed her eyes and tried to catch her breath. The aftermath of her orgasm still warmed her insides, and she wanted to enjoy it as much as she could before sleep claimed her.

He had other plans, though, because before she could sink into dreamland, she felt something. He was still inside her, and he was hardening again. She could feel his manhood growing by the second, stretching her inner walls with an insistent, delicious pressure.

She opened her mouth to protest, but before she could, he slipped out of her. "Turn over, Imani."

While she did as he asked, he positioned her to his liking, with her knees bent and hips angled upward. She arched her back as he plunged inside her once again.

As he drove her toward ecstasy again, she had one last cogent thought—this man, and no one else, was her soul mate. And as he loved her so thoroughly, he stole her breath, and she knew it was a fact that would never change.

Xavier stood near the window, looking out at the scene below him. From his vantage point in one of the guest rooms of the newly built home he and Imani now shared, he could see the people gathering in the backyard for the day's celebration. After all they'd been through, together and separately, he'd been afraid this day would never come. Now that it had, he found himself very impatient to make Imani his wife. He supposed part of that stemmed from the wedding gift he would give her today. He and his fraternity brothers had put a lot of planning and hard work into it, and he couldn't wait to see her reaction.

Straightening his orange silk tie, he turned from the window and checked his reflection in the glass. The gray suit fit him perfectly, and the snow-white shirt and sunset-colored tie accented it well. He had everything he was supposed to have, except for the boutonniere. He tried to remember who had it the last time he'd seen it.

He swung open the door and nearly bowled over his mother. Carol dabbed at her eyes with a handkerchief, just like she'd been doing all day. Despite her red-rimmed eyes, she looked beautiful in the cream-colored suit and matching pillbox hat she'd chosen for the occasion.

Extending the orange rosebud and a straight pin, she sniffled. "I brought your boutonniere, baby boy. Let me pin it for you."

He stood still as she went about the task. "Mama, stop crying. It's a happy day."

"I know, baby. These are happy tears." On the tail of her words, she let out another sob. "I'm going on outside." Still wiping her eyes, she walked down the hall and descended the staircase.

He stood in the doorframe, watching her go, then stepped back inside the room. Ma Alma had given him strict instructions not to come downstairs until one of his boys came to get him, and he wasn't about to upset his future mother-in-law by disobeying a direct order. So he dropped down into the wing chair just inside the door and waited.

Edwin entered the room, a broad smile on his face. "You clean up nice, Son."

"So do you, Dad." Xavier smiled as he hugged his father. "Everything's going according to plan out there, right?"

He nodded. "Fine, fine. I'm just here to chat with you for a minute."

"Ah. Do you have some words of wisdom for me, Dad?"

"Of course I do. I've been with your mother forty years, and I'm going to tell you the most important thing I've learned about marriage."

Xavier leaned in, bracing for a lengthy speech. "I'd love to hear it."

"She comes first. As long as you remember that and never put anything before her, you'll be all right."

He turned his father's words over in his mind. It was much simpler advice than he'd expected from his father; Edwin Whitted could be quite wordy when he chose to be. *She comes first.* Xavier didn't anticipate having any trouble with that. "That's it?"

"Yes, that's it. Don't let your friends or your work or anything come before her. Even when you have kids, your priority is your wife. Understand?"

"I got it, Dad." In all honesty, he looked forward to putting his soon-to-be wife on a pedestal, where she belonged.

Edwin patted him on the shoulder. "Good. Then I'll see you out there."

Xavier watched his father stroll toward the door. "Dad?"

Edwin stopped and turned his way. "What is it, Son?"

"Thanks. For everything. I love you."

A smile stretched across Edwin's aged, brown face. "I love you, too." Humming, he departed.

Xavier returned to his seat to await his release. Judging from the position of the sun outside the window, he knew it wouldn't be too much longer. Imani wanted a sunset wedding, and that meant timing was everything.

Before long, Maxwell appeared. As he came up the steps, he checked the gold watch on his wrist. "It's almost showtime, brother. Are you nervous?"

"Not at all." He stood as Max entered the room, shaking his hand. "I've known for years I wanted Imani to be my wife, and now it's finally going to happen."

"That's what's up." Max stroked his hand over his jaw, as if thinking. "I don't know if settling down is in the cards for me, but I wish you luck, my man. With a sister like Imani by your side, I'm sure you'll do well." He slapped him on the back. "Come on. Ma Alma gave me permission to take you out back."

Xavier caught his friend in a tight hug. "I never really thanked you for what you did, convincing her to come to the party and all. Thank you, man."

Max chuckled. "It's cool, X. I'm just glad I could help." Max strode from the room, and Xavier followed him. They went down the stairs, through the formal dining room and kitchen, and out the glass doors, onto the stone patio. The doors had been propped open, and when he stepped out into the cool air, he was thankful for the beautiful weather. It was the end of February, an unpredictable time for North Carolina weather, but the chance they'd taken by scheduling an outdoor wedding on this date seemed to be paying off. The sky was blue; fat, puffy clouds were floating overhead; and it wasn't too cold. If it did rain, the large white tent that had been set up in the yard would provide shelter for the assemblage. A quick glance at the weather app on his phone showed the temperature right at sixty degrees. He hoped it would hold.

They entered the tent through the open flaps and walked slowly down the center aisle. It was lined with cream-colored rose petals, with the twenty or so round tables filled with guests sitting on either side. Many of those present offered greetings, smiles, and kind words as he passed by them. White lights twinkled above his head, and towering floral arrangements filled every available corner. The pianist played the familiar tune "In a Sentimental Mood." As he made his way toward the front, where their childhood pastor stood under a rose-draped arch, his heart thumped in his chest. It was obvious someone had worked very hard to make everything look so nice, and he made a mental note to thank the setup crew. Still, his main focus was on his bride. He couldn't wait to see her. His anticipation grew stronger by the second.

The flaps of the tent behind the altar were tied back with lengths of cream-colored satin ribbon. The pale glow of the setting sun flowed through the opening, and Xavier took a moment to view it as his fraternity brothers moved into place beside him. Xavier shifted his eyes toward Tyrone, his best man, who opened the jacket of his suit and patted the inner pocket, his way of indicating that he had Imani's ring. Satisfied, Xavier redirected his attention to the aisle.

The pianist began to play Luther Vandross's romantic classic "Here and Now." Xavier linked his hands in front of him, watching as Maya and the other bridesmaids walked down the aisle and took their places. Two of Imani's young cousins, acting as ring bearer and flower girl, came next. The little girl sprinkled a thick carpet of orange- and cream-colored rose petals on her way.

When he saw Imani enter the tent on the arms of her uncle Clive, the sight of her took his breath away. Her dress was a form-fitting lace number, with a high neckline that grazed her chin, and long sleeves. The dress ended just above her knees, giving him an unencumbered view of her long bronze legs, capped in sky-high cream-colored pumps. A small satin bow at her waist flared into a full train, dragging on the rose petals as she walked. She'd foregone a veil. Her hair lay sleek and straight around her shoulders, crowned with a band of rosebuds and baby's breath. Her eyes were damp, and the serene smile on her face made her glow with love and light. He'd never seen a more beautiful sight in his life.

He let his eyes fall to her legs, just for a moment, as he took her hand from her uncle Clive's. Trying to push away the anticipation of having those long legs wrapped around his waist, he turned to face the pastor. They spoke the words to one another, and as he held both her hands in his, he put his whole heart into his recitation. Every word felt sacred to him as he promised her forever. With everything in him, he meant those words, and he planned to spend the rest of his life showing her.

When the pastor finally gave the go-ahead, Xavier pulled his wife against him and sealed their vows with a passionate kiss, just as the sun sank below the horizon.

Imani relished the feeling of Xavier's hand cradling hers as the two of them moved around the tent's interior, greeting their guests. Now that darkness had fallen, the space was aglow with the light from the paper lanterns strung overhead, and the hurricane lamps sitting in the center of the tables. Ambient heaters in all four corners of the tent helped to chase away the chill that accompanied the rising darkness. Imani barely felt the coolness. The knowledge that she was now Mrs. Xavier Whitted warmed her very soul.

When they sat down at the long table reserved for them and their wedding party, she sighed with happiness. Turning her head, she found her husband watching her.

"You look stunningly beautiful, Mrs. Whitted." He lifted her hand to his mouth and placed a soft kiss there.

"I'm glad you approve, baby." She eyed him in his well-cut suit, not bothering to hide the desire from her gaze. "And you are looking mighty delicious yourself."

A broad smile spread across his handsome face as he eased nearer to her. Draping his arms around her waist, he leaned in and spoke so that only she could hear. "I can't wait to peel that dress off of you and make you scream my name."

Feeling the heat rush to her face, she stifled a giggle

behind her hand. Then she rewarded his naughtiness with a quick peck on the cheek. As she looked over Xavier's shoulder, she could see Maxwell eyeing them. Her husband's fraternity brother wore an amused expression as he regarded them.

Soon the space quieted as Tyrone stood to make his toast. They laughed at Tyrone's anecdote-laden speech, and Imani dabbed at her eyes with Xavier's handkerchief when Maya gave her matron of honor toast. As Maya walked by to return to her seat, Imani stopped her and gripped her in a tight hug. Imani was thankful to have such a wonderful person in her life.

Dinner was served then, and Imani took her time savoring the surf-and-turf meal. She thoroughly enjoyed the well-seasoned steak, buttery grilled lobster tail, and the accompanying vegetable medley. She washed the food down with several long sips of chilled champagne from her glass.

The pianist played the opening notes of "What Are You Doing the Rest of Your Life?" and Xavier grasped her hand and escorted her to the center of the tent. There, as the music filled the air, she waltzed around the space in his arms. She couldn't recall feeling happier. Her spirit felt as light as a feather, and her love for Xavier made her feel as if they were floating.

The song came to an end, and the pianist stepped away from his instrument so the DJ could take over. Once the young fella hit the turntables, folks began to rise from their seats to fill the empty space in the center. Soon, tables were pushed back, leaving a wider area of grass to act as a dance floor.

Imani reached down to unhook the train from her

dress. Tossing the satin over the back of a chair, she pulled Xavier along by the hand. "Let's dance!"

He obliged, and they joined the revelry surrounding them.

The music, the champagne, and the good company all enhanced the celebratory atmosphere of the reception, and Imani lost track of time. By the time she and Xavier rushed off to their limousine in a shower of bubbles and confetti, dawn was beginning to paint the sky with ribbons of orange and pink.

Inside the warm interior of the limo, Imani snuggled close to Xavier's side. Taking his hand in hers, she looked at his cuffs. "Do you like the cuff links?"

He nodded, his gaze settling on the solid-gold theta symbols she'd given him as a wedding gift. "I love them. Thank you."

"You're welcome." She laid her head on his strong shoulder, loving the feel of being in his arms.

"Now it's time for me to give you my gift."

She looked up into his eyes, meeting his mischievous gaze. "I'm looking forward to it."

He played his fingertips through her hair as the limousine rolled on through the city streets.

As the ride stretched on, she wondered where they were going. Since she was so caught up in the enjoyment of being wrapped in her husband's embrace, she decided not to ask questions.

The limo finally came to a stop, and Xavier tapped her on the shoulder. "We're here, baby."

She peered through the window at the unfamiliar surroundings. "Where is here?"

The driver opened the door, and Xavier stepped out.

With a smile, he remarked, "You'll see." He extended his hand, reaching inside to help her out of the limo.

Careful of her gown, she climbed out and stood. She joined hands with Xavier as she took stock of their location. They were standing in a cleared field, surrounded by a stand of pine trees. Confusion knit her brow. "It's a construction site."

"Yes, but not just any construction site." With his hand firmly wrapped around hers, Xavier began walking.

They'd only taken a few steps before the wood-and-steel frame of what would soon be a very large two-story building came into view. A lone worker was present, and even he seemed out of place, since it was so early on a Sunday morning. Clad in a red-plaid shirt, jeans, work boots, and a hard hat, the man was standing in front of the frame structure, as if waiting for them.

When they approached, Xavier swung out his free hand and shook with the worker. "Harold. Thanks for coming out here so early."

The man smiled. "No problem. Just doing a final check to make sure there weren't any hazards to interfere with your tour." He touched the brim of his hat, nodded in her direction. "Congratulations to both of you."

"Thanks." Xavier started moving again as Harold walked away from them, up the rise.

Thoroughly confused, Imani asked, "Baby, what's going on? What is this place?"

He led her through an opening she assumed would remain a doorway, and inside the framed structure's first floor, speaking to her as they walked. "This is the new location of Hiram Revels Youth Center."

She let her eyes sweep over the site again, as far as

she could see. "Wow. This is going to be a great space for the kids."

They moved into a very large room, and in the center of it, Xavier stopped. "Here we are. This is what I wanted you to see. It's going to be the largest room in the center."

"I can tell." She looked up at what would likely become the high ceiling. While she was happy that Xavier's beloved charges were finally getting a new and improved space, she was still trying to figure out why he'd brought her here, especially when they were both so eager to get the honeymoon underway.

He stood behind her, resting his palms on her shoulders. "Imani, my love, this is my wedding gift to you, my beautiful bride. Welcome to the Richard Grant Center for Economic Empowerment."

Her hands flew to her mouth as tears flooded her eyes. "You named this after my father?"

His velvet voice answered from behind her. "Yes, baby. Here is where the kids will come to learn hands on. We'll teach them trades, basic auto and shop skills, and financial literacy. This will be your father's legacy."

She turned around, letting his embrace envelop her. "This, and all the babies I plan to give you."

He kissed her cheek. "Do you like your gift?"

She squeezed him tightly as fresh tears filled her eyes, blurring her vision of his handsome face. "This is the best, most thoughtful gift I've ever received. Thank you, Xavier. Thank you so, so much."

He cupped her cheek with his palm, tilted her face up for his kiss. "Anything for you, Mrs. Whitted."

And as she let herself be swept away by his kiss, her heart soared with all the happiness she felt inside.

*Keep reading for a sneak peek of the next
book in the Brothers of TDT series*

Couldn't Ask for More

STRETCHED OUT ON THE FLOOR OF HER LIVING ROOM, ALEXIS Devers flipped through the pages of her sketch pad. Sunlight flooded through the bay windows of her downtown Raleigh condo, illuminating the images she'd created. The soft, white carpet beneath her cradled her body, threatening to put her to sleep. It was only the sheer thrill of artistic expression that had kept her awake for the three hours she'd been lying there, in the same spot.

She smiled. The sketches filling the book's crisp, white pages represented the final iteration of what would be her first independent fashion line. She already had the perfect name for it: Krystal Kouture One. She planned to keep it simple, numbering her lines and using her company name, to keep her brand top of mind with fashion consumers as well as movers and shakers in the industry.

Alexis hadn't left her house for four days, she was so wrapped up in getting the pieces in the line just right. She'd barely slept, unable to stop visualizing her designs. She'd entered her kitchen maybe twice, and that was to get coffee or water. Everything she'd eaten had been delivered to her door, courtesy of the many nearby restaurants.

Seeing the completed sketches made all her hard work worthwhile. Pride surged through her, because she knew she'd created something sorely missing in the fashion world. Her clothes would blur the line between sexiness and practicality, giving women the option to cover up their bodies without losing any of their natural allure. This line would be perfect to launch for Fall Runway Week in New York City, as chilly air encouraged people to layer clothing and shield themselves from the elements.

She blew out a breath, anticipating the time crunch she and everybody at Krystal Kouture would soon enter. In order to get the One line ready for launch at Fall Runway Week, they'd have to make samples, test and photograph them on the fit model, do preliminary press... Thankfully, she knew her small but brilliant staff would be fully capable of pulling it off. It just meant they were all about to put in some serious overtime.

Everything was in place for making the One line a reality—*almost* everything. She'd have to call her best friend and business partner, Sydney Crane, and let her know that the sketches were finalized. But first, one important question still remained to be answered.

What's my tagline? She tapped the end of her graphite pencil against her chin, turning ideas over in her mind. She needed something catchy, but not cheesy or cliché. Something that would express the purpose behind her designs in just a few succinct words. She sat up, scooting her back against her white couch, listening to the whir of the ceiling fan.

The ringing of her smartphone snapped her out of her thoughts. Twisting around, she grabbed it from the couch cushion. Seeing Maxwell's name on the screen, she answered it. "Hey, bro."

"Honestly, Alexis. I've been calling you for the past two days. And so has Mom. What in the hell is going on with you?"

"I was working." She balanced the phone between her ear and her shoulder as she climbed up from the floor. Her back muscles immediately contracted, cursing her for spending so much time on the carpet. She settled onto the couch.

"Good grief. So you mean you were on another one of your 'art benders'? Where you're so busy being creative that you can't even bother to take calls from your family?" His tone held a mixture of mockery and annoyance.

She shook her head. Her brother had a penchant for dramatics. "Maxie, I'm fine. This is how I work."

"The way you work is weird."

"I'm an artist. I'm allowed my eccentricities."

"Eccentrics do things like wear paisley with polka dots, or talk to their potted plants. You're just an oddball."

"Shut up, Maxie." She teased him right back, calling him the nickname he hated. He thought "Maxie" was too feminine for him. He was four years older and had been teasing her for as long as she could remember. "Besides, you're kind of an artist. Don't you ever get wrapped up in a project, to the exclusion of everything else?"

He feigned offense. "'Kind of an artist.' Lex, please. I *am* the artist. I'm responsible for some of the most breathtaking buildings in this country."

The Devers children were an artsy bunch, alright. All were NCCU alumni, having attended the college where their parents had met and fallen in love. Alexis was a fashion designer, Maxwell owned an architectural firm, and… she stopped herself, not wanting to think about something that would ruin her celebratory mood. "Arrogant, much? Now you see why I didn't answer the phone when you called yesterday."

"Not arrogant. Confident. There's a big difference, but that's beside the point."

"Then what is the point?"

"Just answer my calls and we won't have a problem. Oh, and you should probably answer Mom's calls too, because if you don't, she'll assume you've been kidnapped, murdered, and decapitated."

On that, she could agree. Their mother, Delphine, professed nonstop worry about her children, all of whom were well into adulthood. At thirty, Alexis was the baby, and Delphine worried about her the most. "Mom does tend to go from zero to worst-case scenario in ten seconds."

"Yes, she does, so stop raising her blood pressure."

Alexis ran a hand through her short-cropped curls. "Fair enough. Why were you trying so hard to reach me, anyway? Is something wrong?" She paused, as a terrible thought entered her mind. "Did something happen with Kelsey?"

"No, Kelsey's fine. I mean, considering the situation." He coughed. "Everything is fine. I was just trying to invite you to something."

"Invite me to what?" She stretched out her legs in front of her and leaned forward, releasing tension in the angry muscles of her lower back.

"There's a step show tomorrow at Central. It's a TDT thing, but you know your girls from Alpha Delta Rho will be there too, since that's our sister sorority."

Her mood brightened at the thought of returning to her alma mater. "Oh my gosh. I forgot about that. Teresa texted me about that, like, two weeks ago. It's tomorrow, for real?"

"You do realize that time is still passing while you're locked in your little creative bubble, don't you, Lex?"

She rolled her eyes. "Yes, I do."

"Just thought I'd ask. So are you going or not?"

"Yeah. I'm finished with my project. What time does it start, and where?"

"Two o'clock, at the gym building."

It had been ages since she'd seen her sorority sisters, and it was high time she rectified that. Based on Theresa's text, at least a few of her girls would be turning out to watch the Brothers of TDT rep their organization at the step show. "I've got a lunch meeting, so I might be late. But I'm definitely coming."

"Good. It's time for you to get out of the house and rejoin the living."

"When I see you, I'm gonna give you a smack right upside your head, Max."

He laughed. "Whatever. I'm like twice your size."

"Then I'm just the right height to punch you in the stomach," she retorted playfully.

"I'll see you at the step show. I *dare* you to leave your sketch pad at home this time, Lex." Without waiting for her response, he hung up.

She set her phone aside, shaking her head. *Max and his stupid dares…*

A squeal of delight passed her lips as the perfect tagline came to mind. "Dare to Be Demure!" she shouted into her empty condo. As much as she detested Maxwell's tendency to "dare" her, she was glad he had today. The tagline was succinct, evocative, and not at all cheesy.

Jumping up from the couch, she jogged down the hallway to her master bedroom. After several days trapped in the house, a shower would be the first order of business. Then she'd have the pleasure of calling Sydney and telling her they were ready to roll.

———

Bryan strolled into the gym at Central, his eyes scanning the space. The bleachers on either side of the polished basketball court were already partially filled with spectators. It was just before two o'clock, and people continued to stream in around him. He moved farther in, searching the bleachers for Xavier and Maxwell.

He spotted them in the center section on the western side of the gym, toward the top. Jogging over to the bleachers, he slowed to climb the steep stairs. When he reached his boys, he gave them both a brief handshake. "Did I miss anything?"

"Nah," Maxwell said, keeping his eyes on the preparations happening down on the gym floor. He wore a Theta Delta Theta T and a pair of khakis. "The kids are still lining up to do their routine." He leaned back, letting his elbows rest on the rung behind him.

"They did practice a few steps, but it hasn't really kicked off yet." Xavier loosened his tie. Now that he served on the city council, the man was rarely seen in public in street clothes.

"Where's Tyrone and Orion?" Bryan asked.

"Tyrone's working late on a deposition or something," came Xavier's absentminded reply as he kept his eyes on the floor.

"Orion's on tour with Young-N-Wild. You know

those kids need a chaperone everywhere they go." Maxwell stifled a yawn. "He'll be back in a couple of weeks, I think."

Bryan eased into an empty spot on the end of the row next to Xavier. Xavier glanced at his watch. "Looks like they're going to start late. Apparently, our little brothers aren't as organized as we were back in the day."

Maxwell elbowed him. "Xavier, come out of that tie and sport coat. It's obviously making you uptight."

Shrugging out of the sport coat, Xavier removed the tie and tucked it into an inner pocket. He draped the coat over the bleachers and clapped his hands together. "That's better. But they're still running late."

"Come on, X. Don't you remember the step show we did during junior year?" Bryan tapped his shoulder. "That one didn't start on time, either."

"Oh yeah. The one where Maxwell got caught in the broom closet with one of the girls from Alpha Delta Rho." Xavier swiveled around to look in his direction.

"I don't know what y'all are talking about." Maxwell's eyes twinkled.

As the marching band filed into the gym, Bryan and his boys turned their attention back to the floor. The drum major stepped forward, and the drumline began to play a complex, catchy rhythm. Soon the entire Eagles Marching Sound Machine was playing in all its glory. The rousing music cued the entrance of the young brothers of Theta Delta Theta, proudly wearing the fraternity colors, complete with faces painted half silver, half green.

As was customary, the senior member of the younger set took the mic and called out for all Elite Alumni of TDT to "represent." All around the gym, whole sections of the bleachers rose to their feet, cheering and pumping their fists. Bryan, Maxwell, and Xavier joined in, standing and raising their hands and voices in celebration of their fraternity's proud legacy.

After they returned to their seats and the show kicked off in earnest, Bryan watched the complex formations the little brothers made as they stepped to the music. Putting in extra effort, strictly for visual appeal, was part of the TDT tradition. "Look at those young brothers. They are killing it."

"I gotta admit, I'm impressed. That ain't easy." Maxwell nodded in the direction of the gym floor.

"Whew!" That came from Xavier as one of the young brothers executed a perfect backflip. "He nailed it."

"Hey, X. How's married life treating you, man?" Bryan leaned back against the rung behind him.

A goofy grin spread across Xavier's face. "It's beautiful, man. Waking up to Imani every day is way better than I could have imagined. We always make sure to eat breakfast together before we go in to work, and—"

Maxwell's dramatic gagging effectively interrupted Xavier's sentence. "Please, dude. You're killing me."

Xavier punched him in the shoulder. "What are you, twelve? If you knew like I know, you'd be looking for a good woman yourself."

"Whatever." Maxwell sat up a bit and appeared to be looking around. "Where is she? She's gonna miss the whole damn show."

"She who?" Bryan asked.

"My sister Alexis. She said she was coming today." Maxwell stood, peering down toward the entrance. "Never mind. I see her."

Bryan followed his gaze. A group of Alpha Delta Rho women was entering at that moment, decked out in the sorority colors of purple and blue—or "lavender and lapis" as ADR ladies referred to them.

The young brothers on the floor ended their routine, and everyone applauded, including the sisters holding court by the door. As the applause began to die down, Maxwell cupped his hands around his mouth. "Lex!"

As Maxwell's shout rang out, one woman in the group turned her head, frowning as she searched the crowd.

Bryan's eyes were glued to her as she started walking toward the bleachers. *That's Maxwell's baby sister?*

Gone was the cute little teen who'd visited Maxwell on campus. The woman currently coming their way oozed femininity from every pore. She was tall—at least five eight—and she walked with confidence. Her lithe, curvaceous frame was draped in a fitted lavender top bearing her sorority letters, and a knee-length denim skirt that revealed the tempting bronze length of her legs. Short brown ringlets of hair framed a heart-shaped face that could only be described as elegant, and her hazel eyes were fixed on Maxwell.

"Damn." The word fell out of Bryan's mouth before he could stop it.

Maxwell cut him a look. "Damn, what?"

As Alexis came abreast of them, Bryan blurted, "I can't believe you're Maxwell's baby sister."

One of her perfectly arched brows hitched, her rose-tinted lips thinning. "Who are you?"

About the Author

Like any good Southern belle, Kianna Alexander wears many hats: loving wife, doting mama, advice-dispensing sister, and gabbing girlfriend. Kianna discovered romance as a teenager, when she read Beverly Jenkins's *Night Song* and was first bitten by the writing bug. She's a voracious reader, history nerd, and craft fanatic. Kianna lives in North Carolina with her husband, two kids, and a collection of well-loved vintage '80s Barbie dolls. Writing has been a salve unlike any other, and Kianna hopes her writing can create a respite for her readers.